To the man grown, the long crowded mile of his boyhood becomes less than the throw of a stone.

WILLIAM FAULKNER, *Absalom, Absalom!*

Adults are children that have gone off.

LITTLE GIRL, *on a bus.*

CONTENTS

PART IV

PART V

PART VI

PART VII

PART VIII

PART IX

THE DESCENT

The siren came from beneath their feet, rumbling through the earth, a low and melodic growl. It infiltrated living rooms, punctured windscreens, swept up and over steering wheels, past helmets and spectacles, hunting for a way inside. A number of people, several million perhaps, tried to pinpoint its origin, but for those brief moments, it seemed that every object in human earshot resonated with the eerie, aberrant thrum. To Giles, it wasn't a siren, but a thousand drunken trumpeters, clumsily announcing some grand arrival, far away. Then the sky brightened, and with little to no ceremony, the entire human race shrank to one-tenth of its previous height.

It was not an easy transition, the kind accompanied by twinkling auras and a cascade of chimes. Instead, the Descent of July Second was the kind of event it would be polite and advisable to look away from. Strictly speaking, this was not the first transformation of its kind – two hundred million years earlier, something very similar occurred. Though, in that instance, once it got started, the shrinkage took about fifty million years to run its course. It happened so slowly that no one even noticed. Our own metamorphosis was far less gradual and, unless you were asleep at the time, impossible to ignore.

The previous victims were the theropod family, who counted tyrannosaurs and raptors among their number. These creatures underwent twelve substantial decreases in size, shedding ninety-nine per cent of their body mass, to become archaeopteryx – earth's first birds. Humankind's rebirth, done all at once, was the cause of immeasurable suffering. Yet, considering the cycles of life and death needed to fuel fifty million years of theropod evolution, one might argue the ordeal was comparatively painless.

Afterwards, July Second went by many names – from the French *Jour Vomissures* to the Hawaiian *La o ka Hookolokolo*, both of which translate roughly as *The Day of Disgorge*. Whatever the name, all who survived agreed it was a day they'd much rather forget. Across the British Isles, July Second became known as *The Descent* – the day we were sent scrabbling from our thrones down to the bottom of the food chain.

For many, the siren signalled the end. Countless souls disappeared into the odious pools that sprung up around their dwindling bodies, unable to fully escape the expunged excess matter. More still succumbed to inorganic material, foreign objects inside the body – paperclips, contact lenses, cavity fillings and the like – that slowly ran out of space, as stomachs, mouths and eyelids contracted about them. Some survived all this, only to be snared by the wheel of a loaded trolly, sealed beneath a wardrobe mid-transit, or caught by piles of books, playfully balanced on heads at precisely the wrong moment.

A sad place to dwell, so let us hurry on to the one in nine who lived. To those whose bodies shrivelled down to one tenth of their previous height, roughly the span of their own hand, and by a series of unlikely little miracles, survived. Bespectacled folk who left their cavities unfilled, who took small bites and did not swallow paperclips.

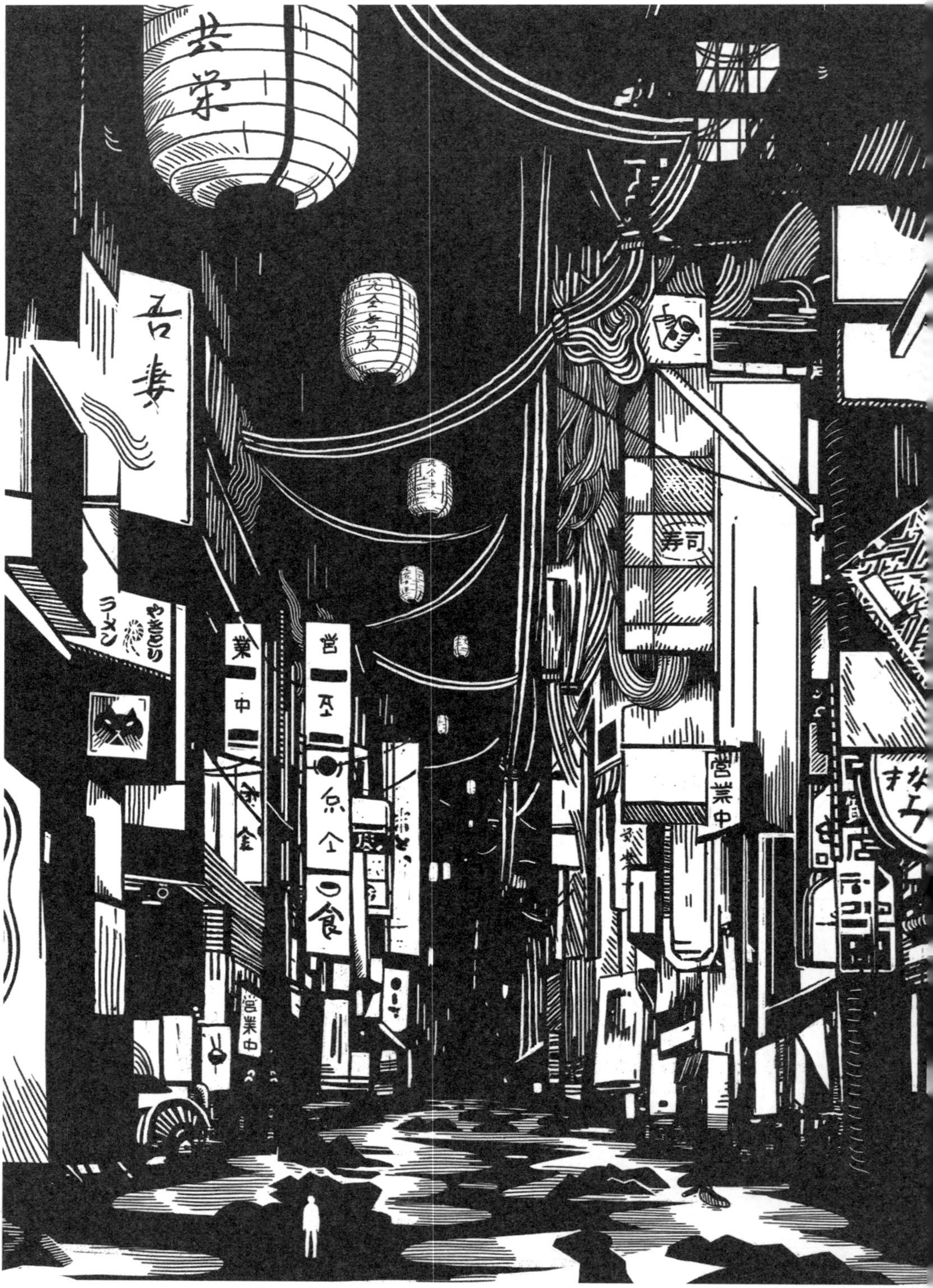
やきとり
ラーメン
寿司
営業中
営業中

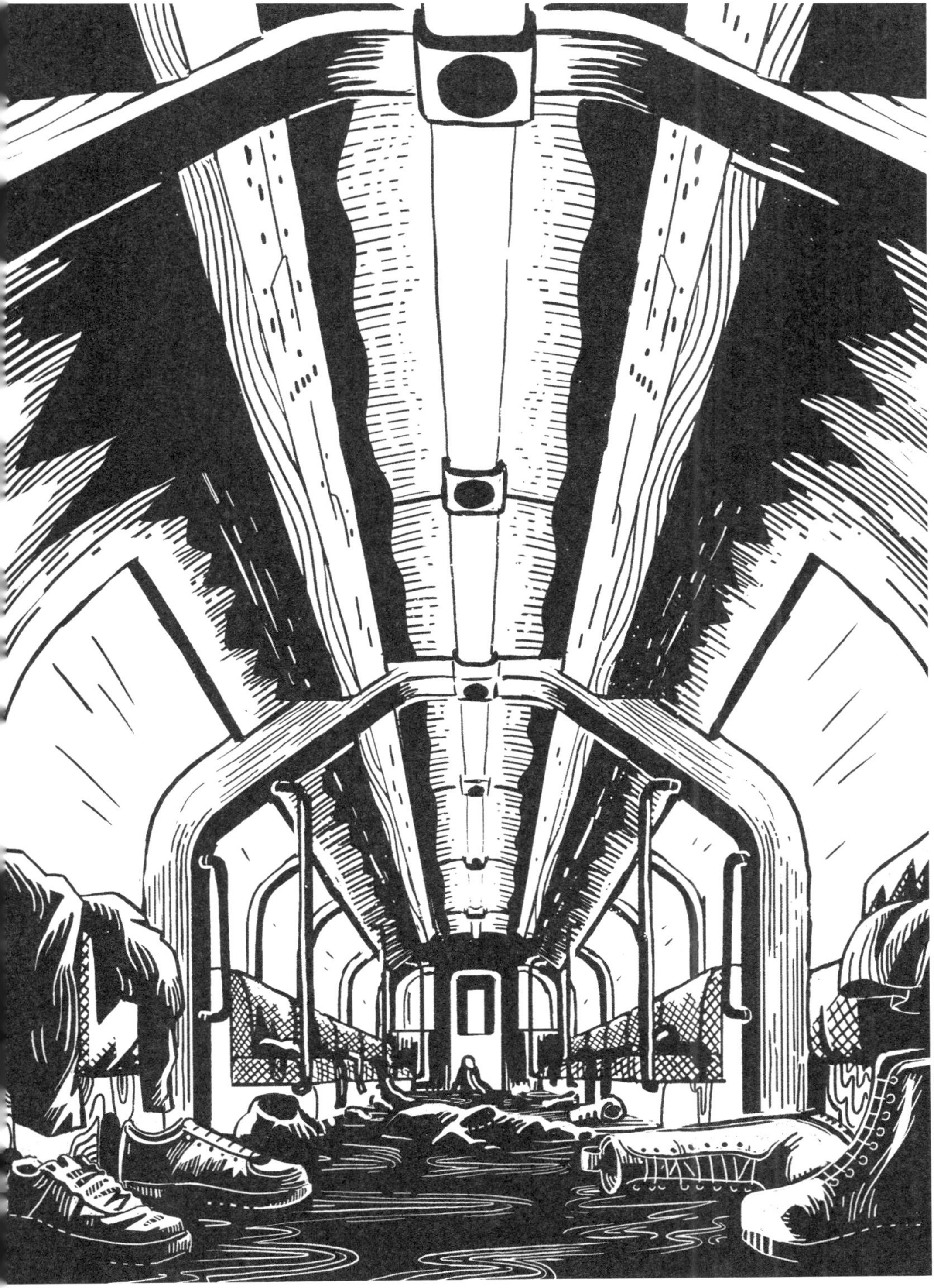

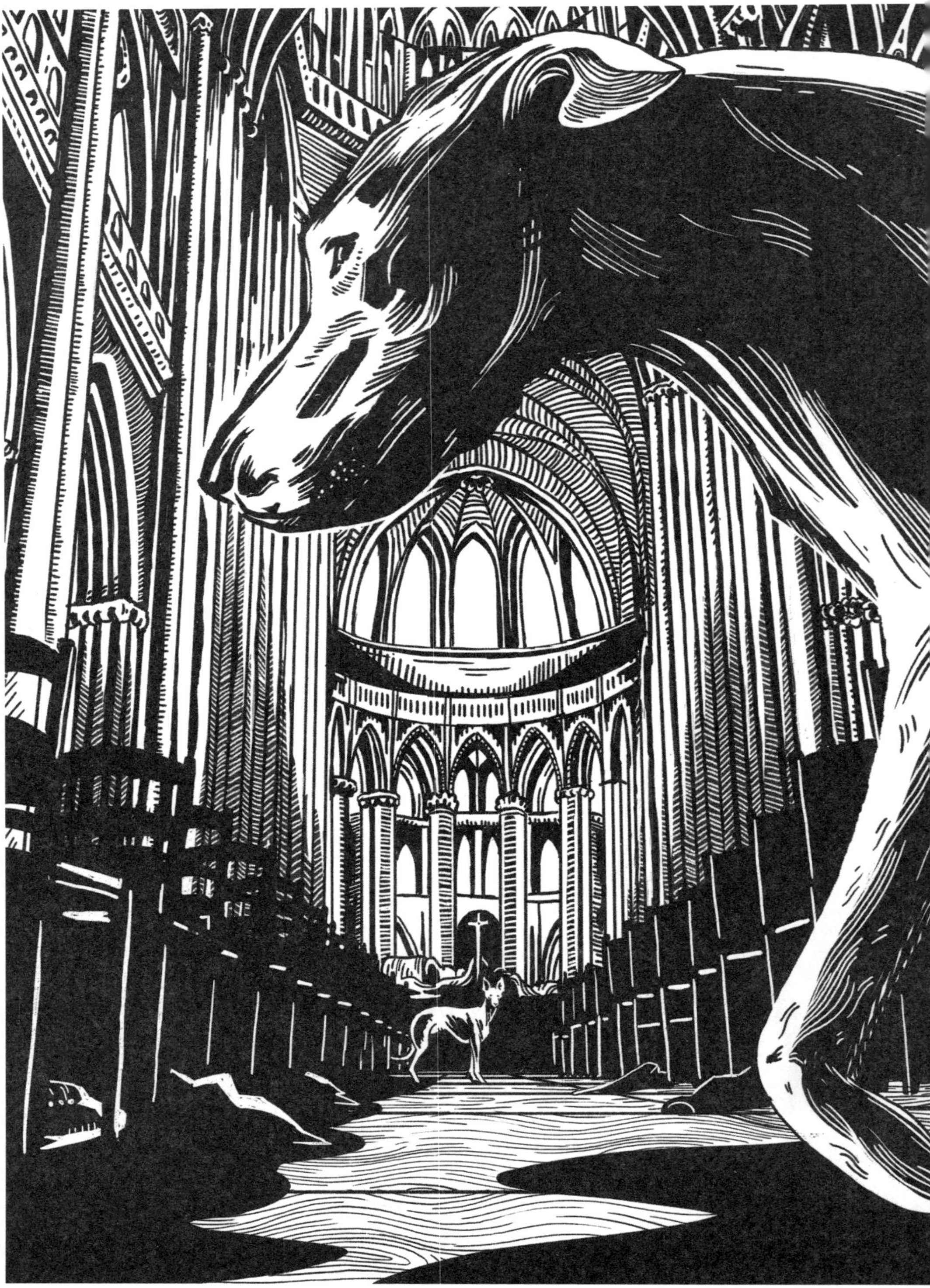

PART I

CHAPTER 1

ELIZABETH GOODWIN

The Professor hurried across the cobbled courtyard, or at least, she hobbled energetically. The grey evening was beginning to spit at her when, several yards ahead, a light flickered on inside the abbey illuminating a stained-glass window, wriggling with snakes of rainwater, coiling their way through saints. Elizabeth Goodwin's gaze continued up the building, coming to rest on a series of angels ascending a ladder. The uppermost statue posed smiling, looking back over its shoulder.

'You've nothing to smile about,' croaked Goodwin and added, as if in insult, '*stone* person.' Above the angel, a slack-jawed gargoyle straddled twin pillars. Like Buster Keaton, she thought, atop two horses. She was chuckling at the comparison when the gargoyle screamed. Startled, Goodwin slipped on the wet cobbles and might have landed splayed in the gutter were it

9

not for a lucky catch of her cane, which wedged between paving stones, leaving her wobbling but upright, an awkward human tripod. Blood pounding in her ears, she watched as the white wings and thin yellow bill of a seagull stretched out from the gargoyle's mouth. The gull squawked, then settled back into its nest. Goodwin glanced behind her, ready to scowl at any onlooker who might be amused by her misfortune. Instead, finding herself alone, she turned to the gull and bared her teeth, hissing like a cat.

Above the gargoyle were fringed arches carved with florets of holly and hawthorn. And crowning the whole wedding cake of a building was what would have been the architectural marvel of the age: a towering spire, an antenna to God. To Goodwin's amusement, the base of the spire had been buttressed with scaffolding and clad in yellow tarp, giving the abbey the appearance of wearing a gigantic neon witch's hat. The way the material rose and fell with the wind, one would be forgiven for thinking the building was breathing.

She leaned on her cane and shuffled closer to touch the ornate arch doorway, tracing a bony finger along the path of a figure falling through the nine levels of hell, wrapped in tentacle and flame, to be torn apart by devils at the base. The carvings were monstrous – ridiculous even – and to no one in particular, she muttered, 'silly little nightmares'.

Inside the abbey, a choir began to sing a low, singular note. One by one, layers of harmony stacked until the building hummed with a symphony that, for some reason, jangled Goodwin's spine. In time, she would recognise the chant as the Benedictine Solfeggio Scale – an eleventh-century hymn believed to open a channel of communication with the Divine. A secret chant, written with a complexity designed to befuddle the layfolk. It was a song that would haunt Goodwin until her dying day. But for now, she simply shuddered and shuffled on.

'Mrs Goodwin?'

Elizabeth looked up. Emerging from a side door at the corner of the abbey stood a short, slender man wearing an immaculate green suede suit. He had a salesman's face, silver hair, a ruler-line fringe and cheeks that curved perfectly into a sharp little chin. His whole head, so smooth and oval, suggested an inverted droplet. Goodwin pulled the strings on her hood, bunching her face into a knot.

'Professor,' she corrected, and the man grinned, exposing rows of neat little teeth.

'*Professor* Goodwin, from the complex in the forest?'

'The same.'

'Forgive my approaching you like this. It's just, well, you're quite the celebrity around here.' His eyes twinkled with mischief as he stepped forward and popped a turquoise umbrella.

Goodwin straightened and smoothed the zip on her jacket, then quipped, 'I'm afraid you've mistaken infamy for celebrity.' The man laughed politely, rummaged in his pocket and produced a folded pamphlet – *Historical Sights of Lyndhurst*.

'I recognised you by the … what would you call that?' He gestured to a sepia portrait printed between pictures of the abbey and another of a stone circle. The image appeared to be a poorly rendered bust of Goodwin, strong boned, hair slicked back, staring majestically into the middle distance.

'I'd call that my mother,' said Goodwin, coughing into her sleeve, embarrassment mingling with irritation. 'Bit of a show-pony.'

'Oh! It's a striking resemblance. And you've taken up the family business?'

'In a sense.' Goodwin sidestepped the man and continued across the courtyard. Undaunted, he swung about to walk beside her, raising the umbrella to keep them both beneath it.

'The pastor was telling us all about your work. Fascinating. *The lake beneath the dome of—*'

'Oh, yes,' Goodwin interrupted, 'It's quite the theme park.'

'*Wonderful,*' he enthused, oblivious to her sarcasm. 'We – my choir and I – would be delighted to visit. If you'd permit it?' Goodwin stopped dead.

'Absolutely not.'

'Just the seven of us – *The Silver Ring*. We're touring the south for little over a month. Our own forty days in the desert! I spied you listening to our rehearsal and thought, oh, I must say hello.' He turned to admire the abbey.

'Magnificent, isn't it?'

'No, it isn't,' grumbled Goodwin.

The man seemed not to hear, since he replied dreamily, 'Yes, yes. Quite lovely.' Goodwin swatted the umbrella away, resumed her shuffling and this time, the stranger stayed put, calling after her through the rain, 'It need only be a *short* visit.'

'Out of the question,' she replied, not turning.

'Another time then, perhaps. I – I just wanted to say, I have the *greatest* admiration for you.' At this, Goodwin turned to study the man, searching for some sign of mockery, ready to bite. But he seemed genuine, and added with utmost earnestness, 'Well, people *like* you – making the world a brighter place. The conservation of all God's creatures is so vital, now more than ever.'

'Is *that* what I'm doing?'

'Absolutely! The real concert's tonight. I hope you can make it, Professor. Just ask for me, Leonard Leaf.' Misinterpreting a brief, rude hand gesture for a wave, Leaf waved back enthusiastically, calling, 'I'll save you a seat!'

As Goodwin hobbled up the hill, away from the music and back towards her lake, a stone-faced figure in an identical suit came to stand beside Leonard.

'Well, I thought that went *very* well.' Leaf patted his companion's back, 'Let's – let's ready the choir for a lovely afternoon out.'

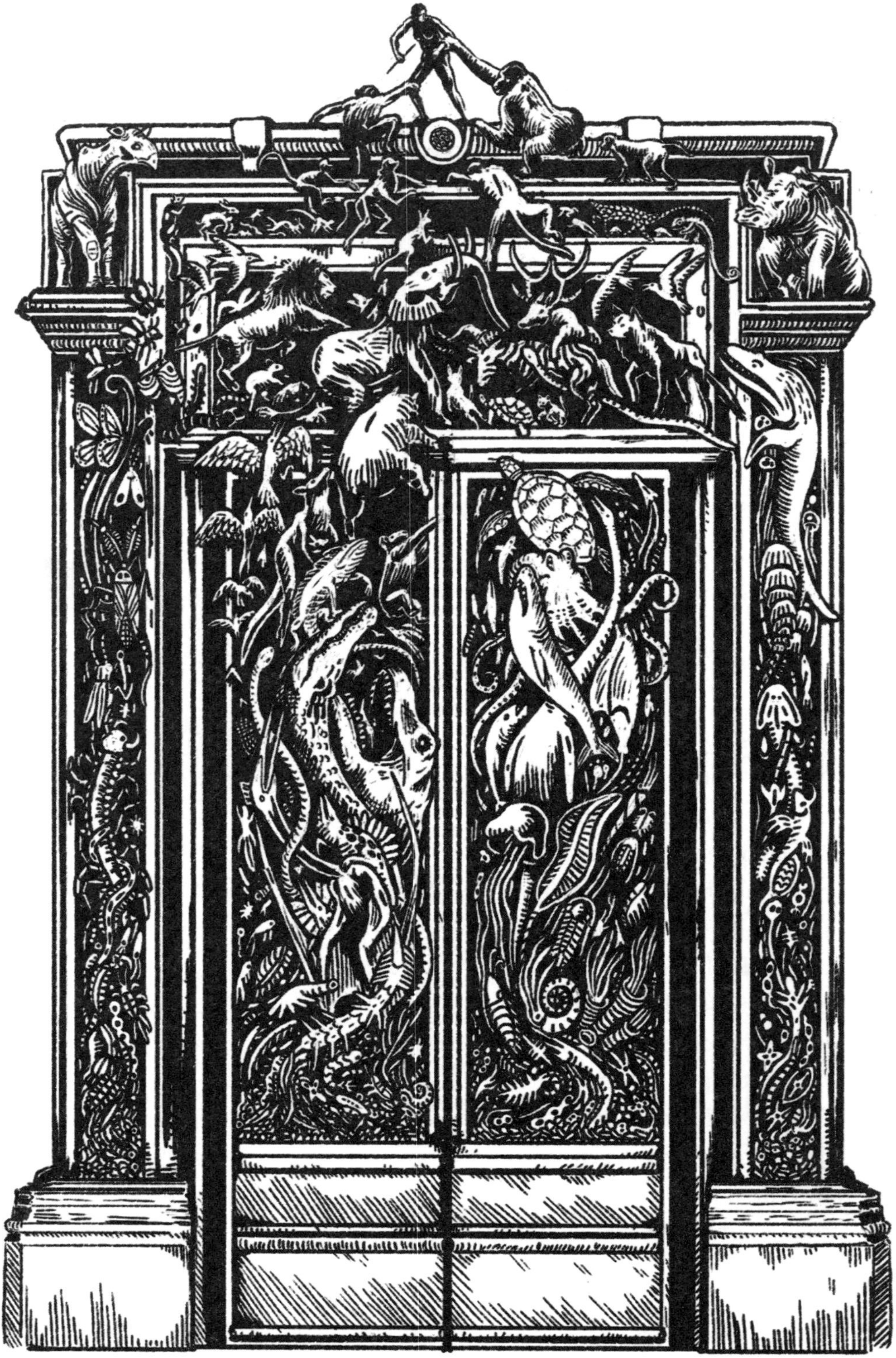

CHAPTER 2

GILES AND THE COCOON

Giles awoke naked, lying on his side, blowing bubbles in liquid so thick that it would have been easier to suffocate in it than drown. Growing pains, an affliction he hadn't felt in decades, ran through his body in dull, aching waves. As he rolled onto his back, blood sloshed around what felt like a half-empty skull. Beneath the swells, his brain, a tiny, pickled walnut – it must have been – collided with a wall of bone. He winced, then, without lifting his head, pressed his hands against an uncomfortably close ceiling.

He was cocooned within what seemed to be a large, wet, loosely folded carpet. Ahead, a thin slit of light denoted an exit, and Giles crawled towards it, easing through congealed fluid, trying to ignore the tingling sensation spreading though his limbs. Fogged by pain and an unholy stench, he tried to recall the string of events that might have led to this unpleasant moment. Had he been drinking? Perhaps he'd lost his way returning to the cabin, and fallen into a fouled rivulet? Shielding his eyes from the piercing light, Giles pushed his face through the thin fabric fold and took in a welcome lungful of cold, clean air.

Shade by shade, blinding light gave way to blurred patches of green, blue and white, which focused into fields and sky and strips of jagged cliff face. He was not at the mouth of a wastewater ravine, or in the woods beside his cabin, but on a wide, boulder-strewn path, closed on both sides by an unfamiliar species of tall and slender fern. Half hanging out of the incongruous cocoon, Giles gathered his breath and examined his hands, finding them wrinkled and prune-like, with the buttery translucence of having been in the bath for too long. His nails, usually cut close, were splayed at the ends, breaking into rough and splintered shards. Holding a hand to the light, he turned it over, appalled by the growing realisation that the cocoon had *poisoned* him. Somehow, Giles was melting. Seized by the sudden urge to escape, he gripped a nearby frond and pulled until his body mass shifted enough for gravity to take over and deliver him onto the dirt. As he fell, an afterbirth of unnaturally long hair followed, slithering through the cocoon's mouth and collapsing on top of him. It couldn't be his *own* hair, and yet a sharp pull confirmed the sinuous threads stemmed from his scalp. Gathering the wet mass into his arms, he attempted to stand, misjudged the strength in his legs and sent a knee to collide with his chin. A fresh, sharp pain shot through his sinuses, strobing the landscape. Giles lurched forward, straining to remain upright. He clawed uselessly at the fabric mound, caught a toe on a jutting rock, tangled his feet in his own hair, and toppled like a felled tree into the dirt.

Where his knees hit rock, the skin didn't break. Instead, it smudged. Hoping to settle his strobing heart, Giles clawed at his

16

chest and, to his horror, watched the tips of fingers disappear to the first joint. He gasped, making a noise between laughter and disbelief, as trembling hands scraped across his ribs, peeling away the skin in soft, powdery scoops. Manically, Giles excavated, flinging pale clods left and right, half expecting to find that he was fudge all the way through, certain he could dig a hole in his middle until light poked out from the other side. With relief, he hit hard skin.

His eyes flitted from his chest to the slender fern, now seeing the plant for what it was – vastly oversized marram grass. There, in the space between one moment turning into the next, Giles understood. The world had swollen. It had been magnified through a magnificent lens. Pores on clover stalks, fur flecks on mud boulders and a network of hexagons all fell into focus. Desperate, he searched for an anchor to the old world of moments before, something familiar, reassuring, untransformed in scale and volume. Sinking into the nest of hair, on the cusp of losing consciousness, Giles found the sky – and took slow, deep breaths of it. As vast, flat and without scale as last he'd seen it, the sky settled over him.

Giles opened his eyes. Hours or days might have passed. Close by, half submerged in bracken, were his clothes – the cocoon from earlier, he now realised – piled in a heap beside what might have been a crumpled leather tent. Eagerly, he scrambled forward, unhooked the worn leather straps of his outsized backpack, and hoisted open the heavy flap. A twist of a flask lid later, and a torrent of cool water washed over him. He drank greedily, letting the liquid run through his hair, beard and newly thickened eyebrows, clearing away dirt and the putty-like skin that had begun to solidify and crack in the heat.

*

Resting against the leather, Giles traced wrinkles in his exfoliated palm. The furrows spread up his arms, fanned out and criss-crossed his torso. It was as though his body had ballooned, then been drawn taut, casting the random folds into hard, jagged fault-lines. With great reluctance, Giles moved to explore his face. Three perfectly straight crevices wrapped about his skull and intersected on his left cheek. His face, like his body, had been shattered and crudely reassembled. His head swam and, feeling suddenly cold, Giles wrapped his knee-length hair about him like a cloak. Above, a lone bird broke the clear sky, hovering up, then down, at once far away and very close. Lost in space and scale, Giles couldn't tell if the creature was coasting on an air current or being held aloft by the strength of his breath. How funny, just a bird. Then he remembered where he was and who he had been with.

'Dad!' Giles pushed off from the pack and immediately re-gretted it, feeling his brain ricochet from cranium to mandible. Steadying head in hand, he stumbled onto a footpath, scanning its length for the pile of clothes that might belong to his father. High in the leaves of a nearby buckthorn shrub, a map flapped feebly. Giles fumbled towards it, over rocks, and into the thick tangle of grass.

He thrashed forward, arms and legs carving a path through the swardy forest, the splitting of brittle trunks of grass underscored by a drum-rattle drone of insects. Then Giles saw it, wedged into hawthorn and looming above the canopy like a lost Inca temple – his father's hawk-head walking stick and, sure enough, on the ground before him, a mound of clothes and a familiar odour.

'It's me!' Giles approached the pile, pressing the back of his wrist against his nose. 'You'll be all right. Just, don't fidget.'

Lifting the neck of a jacket, Giles squinted into darkness and held himself against the sudden squall of fetid air. Then, with the zip in hand, he ran down the jacket's length and flung one half open to expose a wet, floral shirt. He crawled towards the neck, popping buttons and peeling fabric back like theatre curtains. Three buttons from the top, Giles stopped. Ahead lay a distinct bulge, a little less crumpled than the rest, where the cyan flowers of the ornate pattern were blooming red.

'Don't worry, Dad.' Giles spoke more softly now. 'You'll never believe it, but I think I saw a red kite earlier. Another one off the list.' He held his breath and pulled at the cloth.

For a while, he didn't look down and, instead, held the blurry image in his peripheral vision, letting his focus enjoy the details of the jungle. A dragonfly, turquoise and blue, came to perch atop a hiking boot, twisting its head and flickering wings.

Giles threw a pebble. 'Go on! Get on! Get!' As the dragonfly flew away, he forced air through his nostrils and turned to look at Morris. Scale aside, his father was almost unchanged. If anything, the transformation had done him some good – the wrinkles that now stretched back over his bones had taken years off. He had a full head of hair. The only unsightly element was the way in which his lips pulled tight, baring teeth. Giles rested a trembling hand under the chin and gently closed Morris's mouth.

The blood came from a wound in the back of his head, where a thick, grey cable wove behind his ear to a small, manilla disk about the size of a ten pence piece – the cochlear implant. Giles furrowed his brow in anger and then, as if his puppet strings had been cut, slumped beside the body and allowed his face to crumple. He remembered Morris in his study, crouching on the floor among files and blueprints, his father passing from left to right as Giles spun in an office chair. The feeling of being carried across a leafy footbridge high on his father's shoulders. Rough wool against his face as Morris wrangled him into his jumper in time for school. A callused palm, stroking his back. He saw Morris doing a hundred things. Throwing keys to his first car. Hammering tent pegs in the rain. Carving a turkey. Cleaning a window. Fixing a puncture. Ironing a shirt. Giles kept his eyes shut tight for as long as he could.

Despite the circumstance, Giles was determined to bury Morris with a sense of ceremony and, if possible, a sea view. With the largest, softest leaf he could find, he wrapped his father's body and hoisted the slight weight into his arms. Heading towards the sound of waves, Giles pushed through a wall of greenery and then staggered back, suddenly bathed in brilliant uplight. Somehow, the sun had flipped its orientation. At the cliff edge, staring from what felt like the boundary of the world, he shielded his eyes and squinted at the sea. Like him, the ocean had transformed. No longer the murky green-grey synonymous with the British coast, instead, the water was opaque, pale as milk, and a perfect mirror to the sun.

Waves of grief resurfaced. Giles blinked at the bone-white sea, then looked away, overwhelmed. This was too much. It was unreasonable. He would ignore it. Giles lowered his father's body, cocooned by the velveteen leaf, into a small cliff-face enclave, then covered it with soil. Returning, dragging the hawk-head tip of his father's stick, he sealed the tomb, twisting the beak to point at the horizon.

Feeling that any meaningful speech would be undermined by his diminished physique, trail of unruly hair and his newborn nakedness, Giles opted for silence. He might have slept there, on the hillock of rocks, were it not for the mounting cold and hunger. So, with a shuddering breath, Giles stood, kissed the hawk-head's beak, sighed at his broken reflection and murmured simply, 'Thank you, Morris.'

Sat on the edge of his long-dead phone, Giles feverishly devoured several chocolate-coated seeds from a bag of trail mix, then returned his attention to the chasm of his backpack. Inside was one last item of actual use – a bright orange snap-blade scalpel. Extending the arm-length razor, stained green from the many sapling stems it had severed, he sliced at the air, as if the tool were a samurai sword. Then, retracting the blade to the tip, he went to work on his hair and beard, losing anything that fell below the shoulders. Next, he cut a double-layered poncho from a cotton shirt and fastened it about the waist with a shoelace from his father's boots. Finally he bandaged each foot with a strip of gum tape. The front of a bum bag, with holes punched for arms, made for a crude backpack stuffed with trail mix, matches and extra cloth. Each task set to with the same pragmatism he had harnessed to bury his father – thought and emotion blinkered, disbelief suspended.

Giles held his breath, then plunged into the jeans pocket to retrieve the sodden mattress that was once his wallet. From beneath a plastic window, he pulled out a photograph of himself with two scruffy young girls, each nestled under his arms like rabbits in the roots of a tree. Sadie, the elder of the two, stared back at him, her arms crossed below a scowl of defiance that had only deepened in the years since this was taken.

'Well, this wasn't *my* fault, poppet.' The photo remained unimpressed. Giles looked to the younger girl, Ava, whose broad grin cradled a thin transparent tube that ran along her upper lip and forked into her nostrils. 'Yes, I think you'd find this rather amusing.'

Over a year had passed since Ava had been free from the cannula that supported her weakened heart. Still, the memory of cyanosis, her fingertips purpling from a lack of oxygenated blood, made his stomach knot. Yet, despite the sadness in the photo, Giles could not help smiling. The change in scale had altered the picture's nature. The swell from pocket-sized to poster had rendered it more colourful, comic even, transforming its subjects into caricatures, exaggerated versions of themselves, radiating joy.

Though as ever with his family, this was not the whole picture. Slowly, he folded forward the photo's hidden third to reveal the image of a woman, one arm around his waist. Years of facing into leather had aged her. Still, she smiled up at him with long, tangled blonde hair. Giles refolded the photo, and was tucking it carefully into his pack when he froze. He felt light-headed. A second later, the photo was in front of him again. His finger trembled as he traced the line of the tube along Ava's lip.

This may have been an isolated incident, a dream, or a hallucination. Perhaps he had died, and this coast with its eerie ivory sea was some kind of afterlife. For all he knew, beyond the next hill, the world carried on, unaltered. But there was the alternative – that he was alive and awake, and the wider world – *his daughters* – were diminished as he was. He thought of the implant behind Morris's ear and then of the valve that had saved his daughter's life: a small plastic disk no bigger than a button, deep inside Ava's heart.

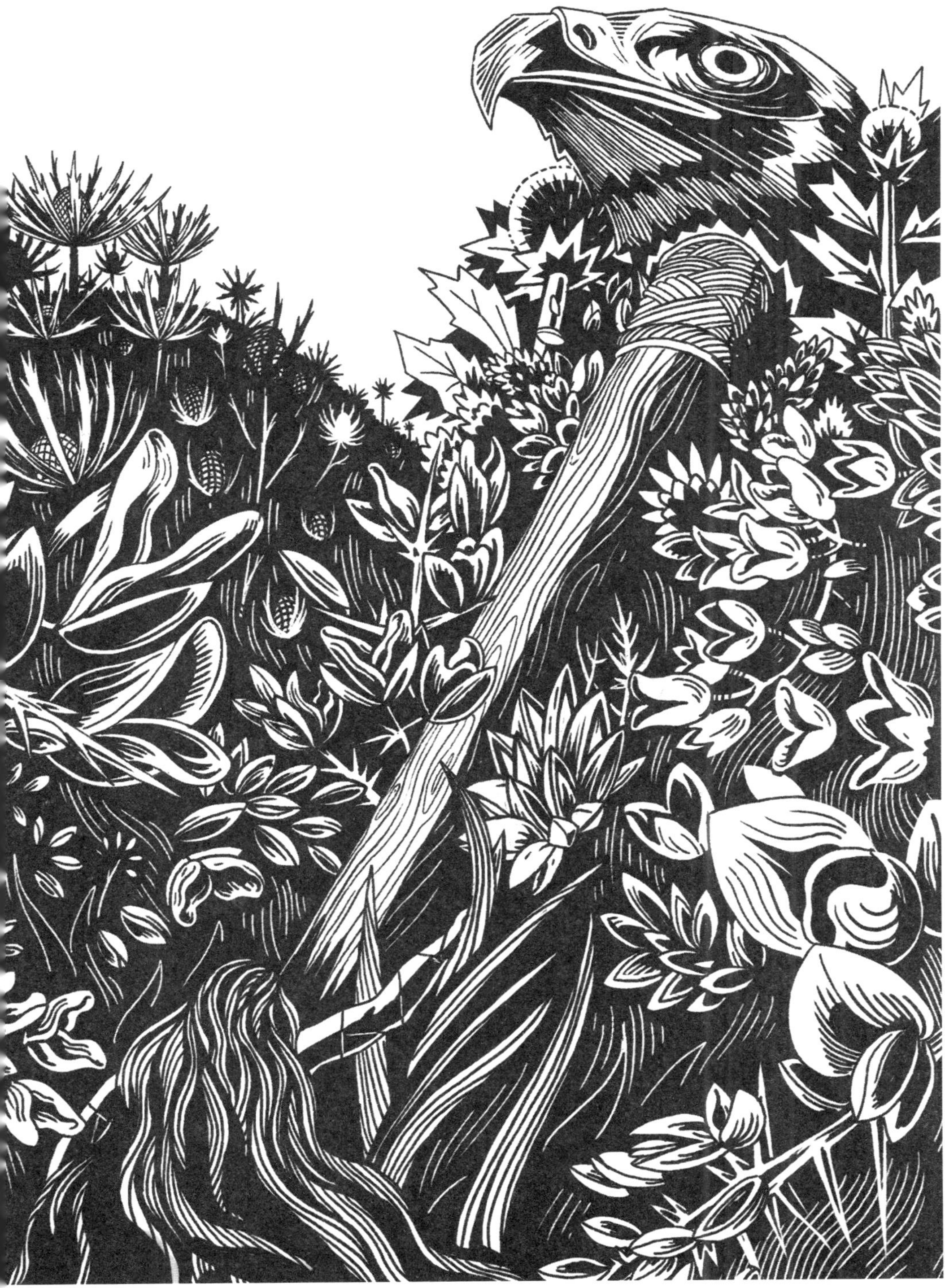

CHAPTER 3

JACOB'S LADDER

Goodwin stared at the plastic cube stuck to the end of her thumb, then peeled it away to reveal three faded letters – ESC. Carefully, she replaced the key into the keyboard and continued to pummel it up and down, her face scrunched into a meaty ball of concentration. The table shook, and the old PC erupted a puff of dust from its vents. It was a relic, and it had frozen for the umpteenth time, and she'd be damned if she was going to retype the day's transcription. There should be other people here to do that sort of thing. She owned the company, didn't she? She was a multi-millionaire, wasn't she? She didn't, and she wasn't. She had been at one point, and somehow the mentality of having money had been a lot more resilient than the money itself.

'It's frozen, again,' Goodwin spat into a microphone by her desk. She paused for a response but was met with silence. She was about to repeat herself when she realised she hadn't opened the channel. Her arms shot up in protest. 'Release me,' she beseeched the empty room, then pressed a red button on the mic stand, sending a screeching howl through the wall-mounted speakers. The intercom that linked this archive booth to the pool on the other side of the facility crackled into life.

'I swear to God, Laslett, you can redo the inputs this time. The damned thing's frozen again and my fingers are bleeding at the tips.' Static fizzed, then a young man's voice, calm and slow, as if speaking to a child in tantrum, replied, 'Have you tried pressing alt, shift and escape, together?'

Goodwin made a rude gesture, swore, and turned her glare to the bulging beige monitor. She tried the key combination. The cursor unstuck itself from a line of code and shot rapidly around the screen, making up for lost time. Green and blue columns of text shuffled to align themselves beside simple, white geometric shapes, like students partnering at a dance class.

'Never mind, it's working now anyway,' Goodwin grumbled. 'Let me know when the grids are ready for a test run.' Goodwin closed the intercom and slumped back in her chair. She hated that her career had come to this, having to accept help from someone like Laslett – a man half her age with absolutely no sense of deference. The boy was only in this for reflected glory, but his name would be nowhere near that soon-to-be-hers Nobel. After all, this was Goodwin's idea, *her* brainchild for the past decade. Sure, he had secured the grants, buying the extra time to complete the project. But the discovery had been hers alone, and she would be the one to carry the torch across the line.

There were just the two of them now, in the whole of Catalant. Her and Laslett. The other employees – down to the last, wheezing security guard – had stopped coming in to work as soon as the coffers dried up and the company became consumed by lawyers, fair-weather shareholders and pending bailiffs. She hated them all. She hated many things, but today they could all be dismissed as mere irritants. Today she would bulldozer them into obscurity beneath a layer of quantifiable success. Goodwin stared at the convex screen. What they were doing here was more important than the success of a single company, more important than her own life, possibly the most crucial conscious effort in all human history. Today they were going to speak to God.

A decade or so ago, Catalant, a three-hundred-acre estate in the New Forest Reserve, had been the flagship research facility for Iplan Hawkes International, one of Europe's most prestigious pharmaceutical companies. To the surprise of both the board and Elizabeth herself, she had inherited the position of CEO, after the passing of her mother, Miriam Goodwin. Prior to their resignation and removal, the board frequently debated exactly which aspect of the appointment was most concerning – Goodwin's lack of relevant qualifications, her vocal disdain for the very nature of the business, or her open dislike of her mother and her mother's morals, or, as Goodwin would point out, complete and utter lack of them.

Throughout her teenage years, Goodwin had made a point of leaving any room her mother entered, convinced and repulsed by tabloid tales of exploitation and malpractice conducted under her leadership. When Elizabeth later pursued a career in conservation, Miriam presumed it to be a phase, a lingering expression of her daughter's youthful rebellion. That may well have been true to begin with, but soon Goodwin was bitten by genuine conviction. The very centre of her being was forged upon a desire to protect the biosphere and undo the harm humanity had wrought. Gaining a PhD in marine microbiology, she made a name for herself by developing sporing techniques which saved the blue-tailed nudibranch – a rare breed of algae-eating sea slug – from the brink of extinction, thus revitalising much of the North Atlantic's barren coral reefs.

'The species of earth are a house of cards,' she would tell her students, 'One wrong move could topple the lot!'

Her mother, keeping a watchful eye on her future heir, was less interested in the breeding habits of sea slugs than she was in Elizabeth's Svalbard subterranean drilling project. While investigating the possible exploitation of sub-mantle prokaryotic bacteria as a renewable energy source, Goodwin had, inadvertently, perfected natural gas extraction from shale. The fossil fuel industry had been steadily failing – beset by a lack of viable sites, mounting costs, lawsuits and loss of reputation – when her chance discovery helped prolong it by a further half century. So much for the *Keep oil in the soil and coal in the hole* sticker on her bike helmet. Elizabeth had single-handedly pushed the earth into a downward belly slide. The backlash from the conservation community had been instant and brutal.

Friendless, jobless and out of options, Goodwin accepted a charitable point zero, zero five per cent profit share. Overnight she found herself worth upwards of eight figures, in the pocket of an oil baron and watching her life's work burn into the atmosphere through concrete turrets. She was lost, alone and revoltingly rich. Years later, she realised that had she simply held onto the patent, stuffed the thing under her mattress or burned it in her barbecue, she would have rendered the process commercially useless.

Her mother saw her apparent failure in a wholly different light. Goodwin had taken the path of an outsider, one of non-conformist ideals and whimsy, and found a way to turn it into a mainstream

27

thoroughfare of commerce. She had circumvented convention and found success. Elizabeth Goodwin was the Steve Jobs of gas extraction, and Miriam scolded herself for not recognising her daughter's unorthodoxy for the canny business sense it truly was. And like many children when met with the unjustified approval of their parents, Goodwin had failed to correct her. So it was with her dying wish that Miriam Goodwin passed control of Iplan Hawkes on to her daughter. She became CEO at the peak of the company's market domination and, without losing a beat, began to scheme and plan how she could steer the weight of this juggernaut to bring about the earth's redemption, and her own.

Scraping forward in her chair, Goodwin traced her finger down the long list of symbols and letters as the last of them clicked into place with a satisfying electronic bleep. She leaned into the microphone.

'We're all set this end.'

'Good news. I'll start dialling in,' replied Laslett.

'On my way.' What might have been a silver tea coaster ejected from the side of the PC. The affectionately named Rosetta Disk was made of polyvinyl, graphene and glass, the latest in analogue data storage – attractive as vinyl with a shelf life of centuries. Goodwin, appreciating the poetry and practicality of the design, grinned at her own reflection. Ten years ago she might have skipped out of the room. Instead, she pulled the stand of her IV drip to her hip and double-tapped the base on the hardwood floor with a satisfying *click-click*. Tonight, at last, all would be redeemed.

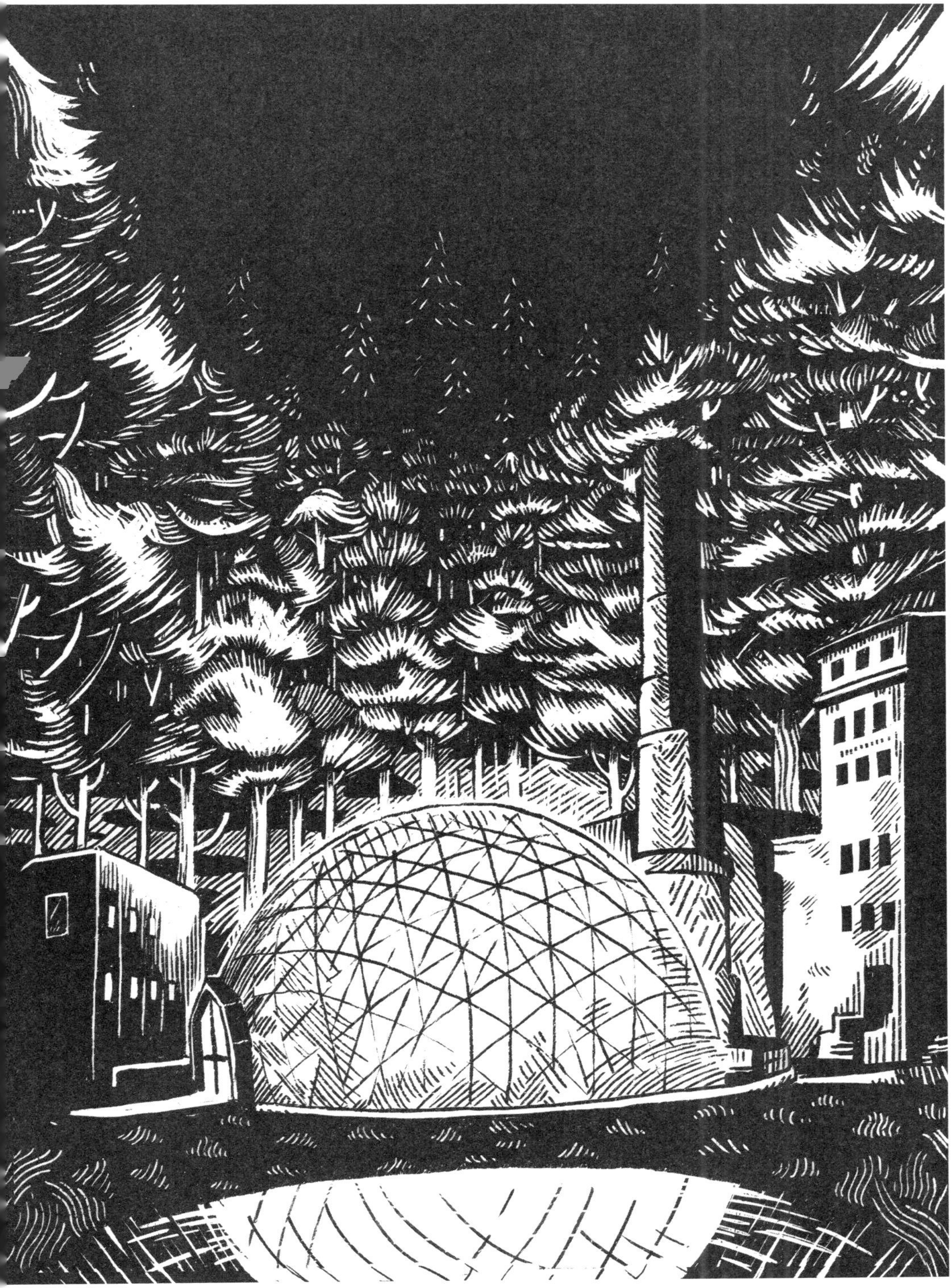

CHAPTER 4

THE CANVAS CITY

Giles surrendered to the pull of profound fatigue, and slept that first night inside his pack, cushioned by the sleeve of his jumper. There he dreamed of a mountain rising from a desert and woke a day later to relive the horror of his transformation all over again. Achingly hungry and cold, his skin raised in a thousand tiny bumps, Giles severed the woollen sleeve with the snap-blade, pulled it over his shoulders and plunged back into the bag of trail mix. Warm, nourished, rested and safe from collapsing yet again, his focus narrowed on the task of Ava and Sadie and how best to find them. Though his phone was dead, there was a chance, albeit slim, that given power it might still work. And so, hefting the lifeless device onto a sleigh of sheet plastic, he set off towards the nearest refuge of civilisation, the caravan campsite.

*

The journey had been slow and arduous, but filled too with revelry at the sight of the enlarged landscape, his low perspective lending majesty to lichen-covered rocks and forests of underbrush. Though his head rattled with questions, he knew one thing – that this affliction had beset others, beyond the coastal towpath. It was the quiet, the absence of screams or sirens, that told him. The silence said that he and Morris were *not* alone. As the sun lowered behind hills ahead, revealing a field speckled with domed tents, cars and long white mobile homes, Giles knew for certain. The site was too still. None of the comings and goings of campers, the frisbee-throwing, the water-pistol-toting mayhem he had left days earlier. Instead, just discernible through the gloaming, Giles saw small piles of clothes peppering the grass, sitting clumped on folding chairs and picnic blankets, marking the exact spot where two dozen more miserable miracles had taken place.

In the dwindling light of dusk, Giles scrambled beneath a turnstile and entered the campsite. Above him, ferns unfurled like palm trees from a fever dream. Passing empty, sodden pile upon pile he wondered if this was a global event, and if he might be the sole survivor and what that might mean. The life of a wanderer. Lone, hard survival and scavenging. Hard, yes, but with it, a freedom from responsibility. Freedom from judgement. He shook the creep of those darkling ideas away and waded into knee-deep grass, marvelling up at the mishmash of anchor lines, pylon cables and canvas domes – the once pedestrian tents, now a shanty town of neon cathedrals. Like the photograph, it seemed that the same thing but bigger was not the same thing, at all.

A jolt of nervous energy rocked his stomach as a faint cry broke the silence. Seeking its source, the dark gave way to a single dot, a light flickering inside a red dome tent on the far edge of the field.

Giles ran towards it, elation at the sound of another living soul mixing with trepidation. The survivor inside might be unchanged. To them, Giles would be a monstrosity. Then, an ugly hope simmered, that if they *were* in trouble, injured perhaps, he could help. He would be of practical use. Approaching the tent door, he felt a pang of guilt, disgusted at the idea that a shared suffering would somehow be a good thing. Nervous, Giles pressed his ear to the canvas and listened to the murmur of not one, but several distant and indistinct voices. Steadying himself against the fear of what he might be about to discover, he stepped through the zip.

Inside, the tent was dim but homely, furnished with an airbed, throw cushions and piles of blankets. Two suitcases fringed a fur rug, above which a low-hanging lantern swung lazily. Huddled about a burning gas camp stove were several mounds of cloth which, by their movement, gradually revealed themselves to be other people, strange and shrunken, like him.

He must have made a noise, a gasp or a groan since one of the bodies turned quickly, partially exposing a cracked face beneath crumpled linen. Lantern light illuminated lines that crept up from the chin, and disappeared beneath tufts of thick, wiry hair. For a moment, Giles thought he was looking at a troll, a stone-faced creature from another time. And then they blinked, human again, and he saw the figure was a boy, young, Sadie's age perhaps. The face regarded Giles passively, then turned back to the warmth of the stove.

More figures emerged from the dimness, a dozen or so souls, and all of them children. Yet this was no holiday tent; it was a war-zone garrison, a refugee camp for survivors displaced by scale. And all so young. Were the adults elsewhere, foraging? Looking for help? Food piled in corners, and makeshift beds of appropriate

32

size came into focus. No, these children were not abandoned. The tent was organised, someone was already caring for these people and, moving further in, Giles saw who. Hunched atop the airbed sat a scrawny, half-naked, wild-haired young man, singing softly to a girl nested in fabric. She let out a cry, more bestial than human, then lunged at the man, scratching at his face. In a deft manoeuvre, he avoided the claw and pulled the fabric, a sock perhaps, up to the girl's shoulders, pinning her flailing arms. Then he leaned forward and continued to sing quietly, stroking her head, hugging her and settling her back down.

Feeling a sudden sense of intrusion, Giles turned. He should withdraw, leave these people to themselves. There was nothing he could offer here. Plus, he didn't need their problems. He had his own. All Giles needed was a battery pack, something to jumpstart the dead phone, and find out where his daughters were. Perhaps he'd find a charger in one of the caravans, or he could root through the other tents or – Giles had one leg back through the zip door when a woman's voice, low and rasping, commanded, 'Hold these.'

Giles ducked as thick metal rods swung from a gap between two outsized crisp packets. Reflexively, he caught them. The voice instructed, 'Clamp those tight and give them a pull.' Whoever this was, she was confident that Giles would do precisely as he was told, and caught in the spell, he obliged. He pulled the metal levers until they jammed, and the voice called again. 'Tug it like you mean it this time.' Giles yanked, harder, then fell backwards as a barrel tumbled from between the packets and came rolling to rest at his feet. He pieced the scene together – the rods were handles of a tin-opener, levering this drum – a can of processed pasta. Giles looked up as the woman came to rest her elbows on the tin's side.

Her face, like Giles's, was divided by thin straight channels, making a mosaic of her skin. There was grace too amid the disfigurement, by way of her eyes. The pigments of her iris must have been compressed during her transformation, squeezed into two vivid green dots of piercing intensity – a once light olive, crushed to a deep parakeet. She stepped around the barrel and pulled Giles to standing.

'Sorry. I thought you were Ash.' She gestured to the man on the airbed, disentangling himself from the girl in the sock. The woman smiled. 'Gosh, you're tall. Well, obviously not, but comparatively. I'd ask you what the weather was like, but I guess that's annoying and,' she paused to think, then added brightly, 'doesn't apply anymore.'

'Don't think it ever did,' agreed Giles, suddenly conscious of his loosely latched toga. Her clothes, like his, were makeshift – a red jumpsuit of torn wool bound with cord about the legs and waist. Thick, black tufts of hair covered her head, a bad haircut that seemed to have befallen most of the tent dwellers.

'I'm Isabel. Izzy.'

Giles stared at the outstretched palm. Seeing the others from across the room in the fading light had been unnerving. A mirror to his own metamorphosis. But this person, so close, talking and behaving as if the world had not upended, was downright absurd. Frustrating even. He shook her hand, and his irritation turned to sympathy and a little relief. Her fingers were rough like his, and trembling. Like Giles, she was in shock, dealing with the unimaginable by adopting a brisk demeanour. By the time their hands parted, the world seemed a fraction more familiar.

'Giles.'

'Are you hurt?'

Giles patted himself down, wincing as his hand moved across a cut beneath his chin.

'Only everywhere. Might have fallen or kneed myself in the face. Can't quite remember.'

'Here,' Isabel motioned for Giles to take the other end of the pasta tin, 'let's move this.' Together, they lifted it onto an enamel plate. Unsure where to begin in his questions, he said simply,

'I'm looking for a phone charger.'

Isabel appeared not to hear, leaning her shoulder into the ring pull until it snapped and the lid peeled forward. She rolled the tin, and a tide of orange tomato sauce spilled onto the plate, carrying with it several anaemic pillows of ravioli.

Isabel beckoned to the children beside the stove and, one by one, they emerged from their blankets and crept forward, gathering about the circumference of the plate.

'They get so hungry. This is the third dinner. Need to think up names for all these new meals. Do you have any medical experience?'

Giles looked about the tent. Apparently, no one was injured, not badly, at least. Aside from the six children tearing into the pasta with fingers and broken matchsticks for cutlery, the tent felt calm.

'I've done basic first aid, long time ago.'

Isabel turned to Giles and smiled.

'That's good. Good. Take one of these.' She hoisted a miniature bottle of cognac from beside the crisp packets and rolled a second towards Giles.

He followed her outside, towards a small, green ridge tent a few minutes walk away. Light spilled out as she pushed aside the canvas door, revealing two figures huddled around a tea light.

'Giles, meet Maya and Evelyn, the oldest of our ... team. Besides Ash, myself and now you of course.' Giles nodded, guessing the girls were teenagers – fifteen, sixteen perhaps.

'Any changes?' whispered Isabel.

'They're all still sleeping. Though number three has been making strange noises. Can – can we go back to the big tent?' asked Maya, casting a nervous glance behind her.

'Yes, thanks for keeping watch. I'll come and get you in a little while, OK? Well done, you two.' The girls hurried off, notably relieved. Isabel stepped around the mosquito net. Giles followed, then faltered.

'It's not that we're trying to hide them, you understand,' said Isabel, rubbing her neck, 'it's just that the younger ones finally stopped crying once we moved them here. It's more sterile and . . .'

The sparse furnishings were arranged about a central lantern, as the previous tent had been, except here, raised on upturned Tupperware tubs, were a dozen dark, twisted forms. Bodies, Giles realised, as he took in the extent of the wounds, their coarse detail on display through clear plastic. Isabel added the contents of her bottle to a large bowl effusing the unmistakable smell of alcohol. As Giles followed suit, she scooped up a capful, like a bucket from a well, and carried it to the side of a young man lying beneath a sheet of torn shopping bag. He let out a sharp cry as Isabel peeled the plastic away from a purpling, strangely angular bulge in his stomach, lacerated on one side where the skin had split.

'Ash found him in one of the caravans. We don't know *what* that is.' Isabel said grimly, pointing to the protrusion. She soaked a strip of cloth in the alcohol and laid it over the wound. The man folded, groaning.

'Ssh,' soothed Isabel, trying to calm him, but his cry woke the others. With an urgent look of instruction from Isabel, Giles held the man's arms down as she rearranged a loose bandage and settled the sheet. The man fell limp. Isabel took another strip of fabric, dipped it in a second bowl, then squeezed the water over his lips.

'Do you know him?' Giles whispered.

'No. None of them.' She took a fresh cap of cocktail and repeated the procedure on an older woman with a rupture in her side. 'I tried to stitch this one. Found a sewing needle, but it was so thick, like a knitting pin.' Beside the entrance, an older man stirred and looked up, drowsily revealing solid black eyes.

'You gonna baptise me, missy?'

'This is Alwyn,' said Isabel, resting a hand on his shoulder, easing him back down. 'One of our chattier patients. Used to be in the army, apparently. Alwyn, meet Giles.'

'Another grown-up. Hmm.'

'Hello, Alwyn.' Giles turned back to Isabel. 'Do you have any glue?'

'Glue?'

'Superglue, for the wounds.'

'Aye, glue me up, ye bastard. Why not throw me in a ditch while you're at it? Keeping an old man away in a tent like this. Should be *me* making the decisions, ye know? I'm an *officer*. You're a bunch of effin—'

'Hey. We can't keep you in there. Not with *your* potty mouth. Besides, it's cleaner here.'

Alwyn shrugged, then nodded, a little confused. 'I was quite sweary, wasn't I?' Isabel sniffed the air, then frowned.

'Have you been drinking from the gin bowl?'

The older man grinned at Giles. Isabel dabbed at a tear over his ribs, and Alwyn let out a pained wheeze. Watching her wipe the tub, wring the cloth and straighten the sheets, Giles recognised a part of himself. The need to keep busy, to focus on a task, even a futile one. Like him, she was a spinning top, held upright by sheer momentum.

37

'Ash – the guy on the airbed – he'll have glue. He seems to have everything. Maybe your charger, too.'

Ashraf was in his late twenties and Giles later learned he'd been here on a weekend break with his partner when the world inverted. Giles didn't need to ask where she was, understanding the inflexion in Ash's voice that rose like a question mark when he'd said her name. He'd found Ash round the back of the tent, kicking hell into a tea strainer. Spotting Giles, he had frozen, foot hung on the backswing. Then his face had realigned, all the rage and grief suddenly replaced by coy embarrassment. He shrugged at the twisted net of metal between his feet.

'Bloody tea strainers. I mean, what sort of person brings one of *these* camping? That's what tea *bags* are for. Ain't they? Daft, these strainers. They're a smite in the eye of good, honest progress. I'm Ash. What can I do for you?' He had a soft Geordie accent, a square jaw and a crooked nose that complemented the jaunt of a crudely cut fringe. A wide smile revealed several missing teeth, and the lack of bleeding suggested they had been absent for some time. Giles explained about the glue and the charger. Ash clapped delightedly, leaped over the strainer remains and set off at a pace, scooping up a tall stick as he went. The makeshift staff had a small plastic bulb taped to the tip and with a squeeze of an exposed wire, it lit up, lending Ashraf the air of a wayward wizard.

'Old Wendy – my campervan – she'll have everything we need. It's unlocked, of course, though I've not been able to pop the door. But between my ingenuity and your comparatively generous altitude, I reckon we'll figure it out.'

*

In the shade of a gnarled old oak sat the VW camper, a rusty orange relic, its bumpers tattooed with stickers and windows adorned with garlands of plastic flowers. The two of them stared up at the driver's door handle, impossibly out of reach, a four-storey climb away.

'We could lean a branch against the side and climb up?' suggested Giles.

'True. But that's a big branch, and even if we got up there without it falling sideways, and somehow manage to pop the handle, the door's not gonna swing out on its own. She'll need a push or a pull. That's giant business. Plus, you'll scratch the paintwork. How about, hear me out, we go in through the roof?'

Giles looked to the top of the VW. Its roof had been raised to make space for the bed inside, revealing an easily accessible fabric window. With a swelling sense of dread, he imagined scaling the van, from bumper to spare wheel, climbing the grill up onto the windshield and using the wipers to reach the roof.

'I don't know ...'

'Not that way, Jesus,' said Ash, following Giles's eyeline. He pointed to the oak tree, tracing his finger up the knotted bark to a thick branch overhanging Old Wendy.

'You're kidding?'

Ashraf beamed, and slowly shook his head.

With pegs and guy rope pilfered from a nearby tent, the two of them set to climbing the oak, working their way around the weathered wrinkles, kicking away loose flakes of bark.

'Hard not to look down,' admitted Giles, fixing his eyes on the branch that would serve as the bridge to the campervan.

'Don't worry *too* much about falling. We're smaller *anchors* now.'

'What's that?' asked Giles, sinking his fingers into another gnarled rivet.

'Anchors. Since we got smaller, there's less to stop us drifting off into space.'

'Uh huh,' said Giles, not quite following.

'Less meat for gravity to sink its teeth into. Also, we have less volume compared to surface area. Point is, we can fall further, and not get hurt. Our body is like its own parachute.' Giles, distracted by this idea, rested his weight on a flake of bark which snapped, sprinkling Ashraf with splinters. Ashraf shook off the dirt. 'Best not to test that theory too far, ay? Course, downside to the volume-surface-ratio thing is we also lose more heat. We're metabolising quicker to make up for it. It's why everyone's so blummin' cold and hungry.'

'That so?' said Giles through a clenched jaw, as a centipede as thick as a snake entwined itself around his arm.

'Yep! That, or our bodies are trying to bulk up again. Not sure. I reckon if you compare the—'

Giles gave a frenzied spasm, shaking off the creepy-crawly with its rippling legs.

'Let's – let's just get to the branch.'

The drop to the van's roof was further than it appeared from the ground, at least three times Giles's own height, and staring over the void he felt the lightheadedness of his awakening return.

'I'll lower you down,' said Giles, coiling the guy rope about a protruding knot, 'Then, you latch one end around that rack rail, and lower me next.' Ashraf nodded, wrapped the other end about his waist and gave a salute of approval. Slowly, careful not to let too much rope slide at once, Giles eased Ash down until his feet hit the soft tin roof with a clang. Moving quickly, Ash secured his end about the roof rack bar, and signalled to Giles who eased himself over the other side of the branch. As soon as the line took his weight, the wooden knot gave way. Ashraf screamed, cord zipping through his fingers. Seized by panic, Giles tried to grip bark, slipped and fell. Turning in mid-air, spun by the rope about his waist, Giles reached desperately for a handhold as leathery leaves swept past and hard metal accelerated upwards. Moments from hitting the roof, his fingers found a leaf, puncturing the green flesh. He tore down its centre, the resistance slowing his descent just enough that he came to a dangling stop gripping the leaf's tip. There he swung, toes brushing metal. Heart pounding and slightly embarrassed, he stepped onto the roof, as the branch bounced softly above him, and the oak leaves flapped in mocking applause.

Ashraf smiled. 'I think falling would have been fine.'

Inside the van, the pair slid down easily over mattresses and blankets, and as Ash heaved the driver's door open, Giles made quick work gathering supplies. He was noisily pulling a cigar-shaped battery pack over the foot well when suddenly Ash hushed him and pulled the door to, leaving a gap just wide enough to peer through.

'What is it?' Giles asked, shuffling up beside him.

'Oh, nothing. Just, I think a mammoth and a T-Rex had a baby. That, or in that field over there, there's a dog.'

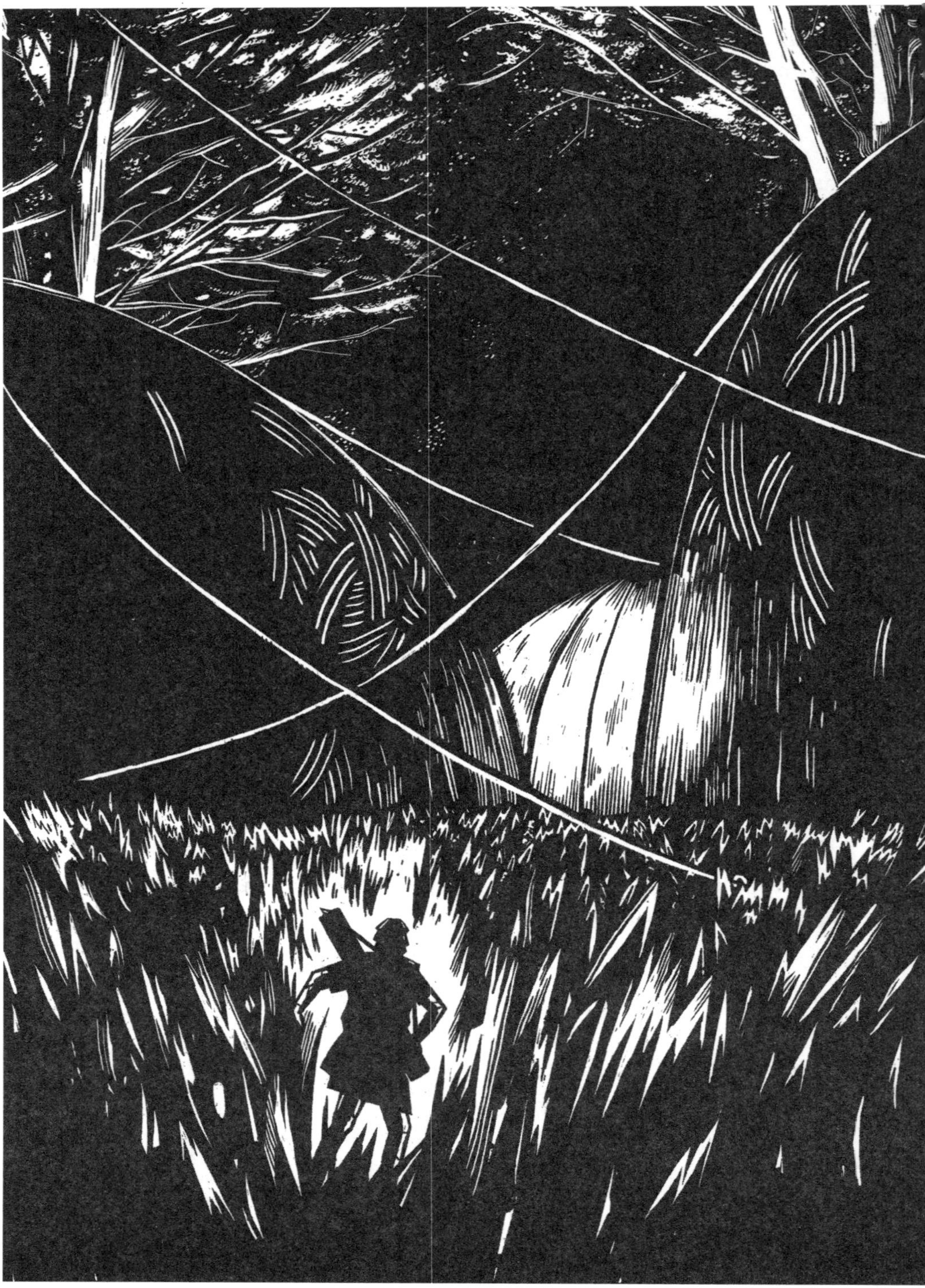

CHAPTER 5

ELSEWHERE,

SHENZHOU STATION

At the moment of transformation, there were eight people in space, distributed evenly between four spacecraft, travelling in low earth orbit, approximately two thousand kilometres above the earth's surface. Alas, they were still too close.

Suited up, outside the craft, the Finnish were first to perish. They thrashed and kicked at the insides of their suits, desperate to press hands over ears and unhear the song, as fluid drained from their bodies. Visors caught the spray, as did boots and gloves until the hollow space suits sloshed with noxious soup and shrivelled spandex unitards. Implants and imperfect shrinkage claimed the

Russian and American spacewalkers. Only on Shenzhou Station was a single soul spared.

Jiao Huan awoke alone and confused among lengths of black rope that splayed out in every direction. The cords swayed like a seaweed forest and seemed to follow and respond to her movements, rippling as she turned in the air. She twisted to be free of them, searching desperately for their origin, before realising that *she* was the centre of the thicket, sprouting from her head. Panic took Jiao, and she squirmed and scrambled on the spot, pulling at the ropes so that they wound into a knot, forming a cocoon that choked her throat and constricted her chest. On the brink of losing consciousness, she stopped struggling and allowed herself to float, holding that last breath long enough for the cocoon to loosen, letting her chest expand and draw air in shuddering gulps. With slow and delicate manoeuvring, she slipped free from her tangled knot and, length by length, pushed the hair behind her into a loose ponytail.

Beyond the final veil of hair was the vast central cabin of the service module, where spheres of foul-smelling liquid danced about the chamber like nightmare jellyfish. Pushing off from a hatch door, she floated naked and tiny through the ship's central corridor, a coarse black tail trailing behind. Below her, half-spheres of fluid undulated atop consoles and monitors like sea anemones on a coral reef. Mesmerised by their softly swaying bodies, Jiao was caught off guard by a globule, as big as a whale, stretching and squeezing towards her, absorbing particles into its surface tension. Jiao kicked and, in a deft manoeuvre that would have made her gymnastics coach proud, she pirouetted backwards, narrowly avoiding consumption into the whale's bilious belly. As the liquid vessel slunk past, two hazy silhouettes emerged from

44

deep below its surface – her crewmates, suspended like flies in a horrible amber.

Transfixed by her reflection and the theatrics of the cabin, it was another hour before she looked out the porthole. At first, she mistook the strange state of the earth for cloud cover. Then she doubted her eyes. Why should her eyes remain faithful when the rest of her body had betrayed her so cruelly? It wasn't until she coerced a monitor into playing back the camera feeds that she accepted the porthole view as truth. Beyond that window was an ivory, alien planet. The pale blue dot had grown several shades paler. She replayed the feed, over and over, watching the milky swell from Europe bloom outward in all directions, past Norway, sweeping the Atlantic in a slick of white oil. A fungal bloom in timelapse. She wasn't sure why, but Jiao was crying and then she was smiling.

She resealed the airlock. In what might have been a scene from an elaborate heist, Jiao wound cables around dials to redistribute the weight, pulling, leaping and releasing the line at the crucial moment. She amazed even herself. *Shenzhou*, meaning *the divine vessel*, was comprised of three sections – orbit, service and re-entry modules, and under normal circumstances, Aerospace City in Beijing would have triggered the re-entry module's release. Still, such was her determination that she managed to perform a manual override by reconfiguring several circuit boards, a challenge somewhat aided by her newly miniaturised fingers. As she climbed through her suit's visor and fastened herself into the chin strap, the thought returned. It was the only thought she'd had since looking through the port window, and still, it turned over and over like a song or incantation. *Someone needs to see this. Someone needs to see this*. If her life amounted to nothing more, so be it. So long as she could share what she'd seen.

The capsule release went to plan. The ablative heatshield maintained integrity. Once inside earth's atmosphere, a thousand kilometres above sea level, a trio of parachutes deployed. Suspecting that a sea-retrieval was unlikely, she had aimed for land, and floated dangerously close between two tower blocks. Braking rockets fired, and Jiao landed safe, if a little bumpily, on the edge of a city park. It took her another day to reacclimatise to gravity and when the hatch finally cranked high enough for her to squeeze through, she slid down the smooth metal side onto the São Paulo soil and wept. She drank in the air and laughed at the sun, cradling in her arms a key stick. On the stick was a video of the milky earth in its moment of rebirth, and she hugged it tight to her chest.

Then a cat ate her. It ate her the way cats eat mice, slow and cruel, with a sense of gleeful play. Through the grill of a nearby drain, tiny human eyes watched, unable to help. Jiao sought them out, and with her dying cries, she told them to save the stick. The *stick* is important. They needed to see what had happened to them all. They needed to see the way she had seen from up there. Then they would understand. They would understand *everything*. The earth reborn as the heavenly river. Jiao was fluent in Portuguese, but alas, in her final moments of pain and regret, she cast her words in Mandarin. Upset and confused, the Brazilian children slid back into the drain, and the stick sank deep into soil.

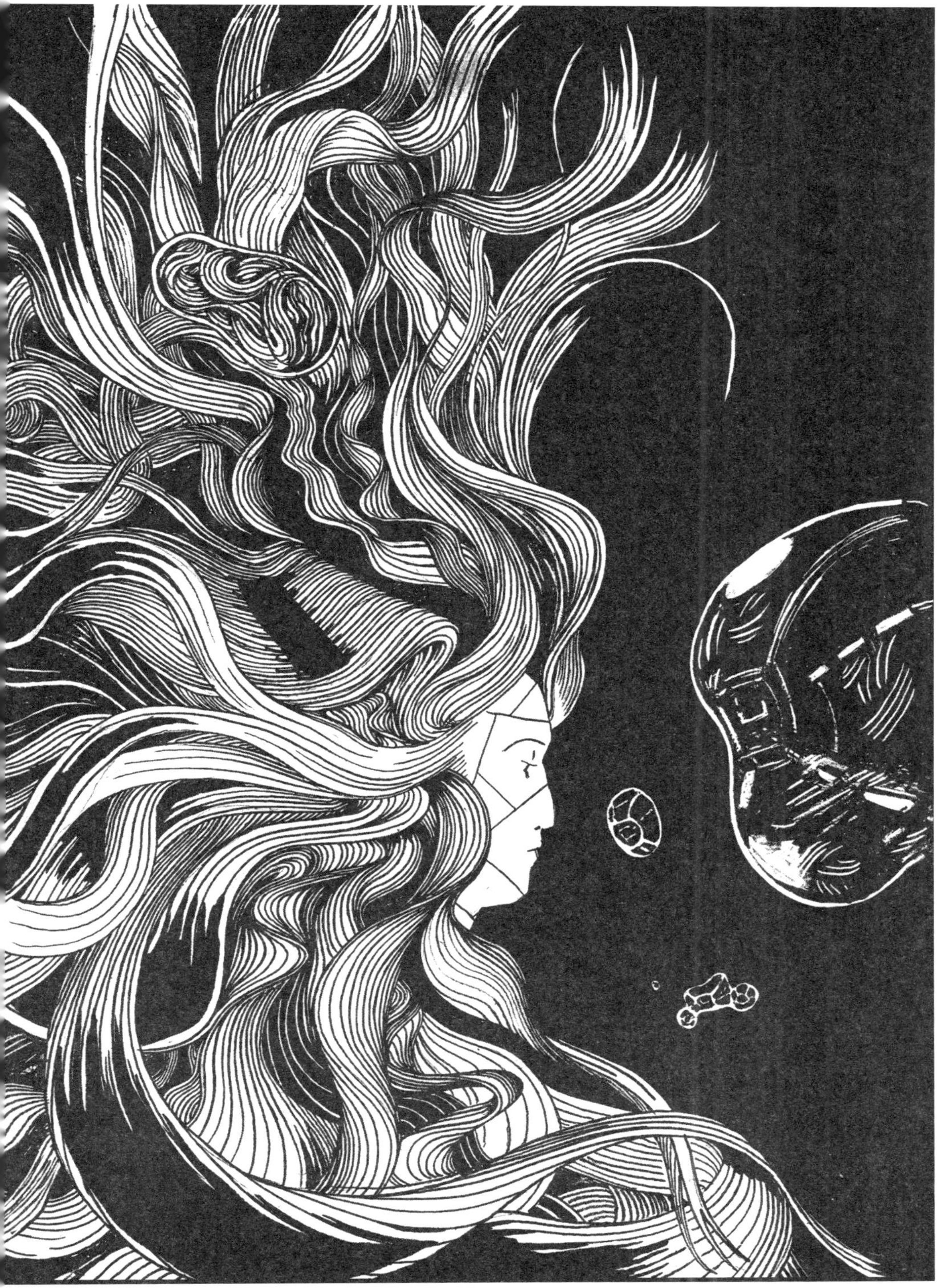

PART II

CHAPTER 6

COCCOLITHOPHORE

During her early years at the helm of Iplan Hawkes, Goodwin kept herself busy in the research department, reacquainting herself with her first love, marine microbiology. There, she focused in on one of the world's mightiest and most miniature creatures, the coccolithophore. Individually easy to overlook, as a collective this phytoplankton made up the largest biomass on earth. Stacked on a scale, they weighed in at about a billion tons. Hundreds of thousands could be contained in a single teaspoon of seawater, and their swarms were sometimes visible from space – coiling about the Cape of Good Hope, meandering through the English Channel.

An average coccolithophore shell comprised of three dozen chalk disks that lay flat against its spherical body, rendering the phytoplankton chalky white. Upon death, these scales turned ninety degrees outward, opening like a Venetian blind to let the light through. The cell flooded with water, and the creature would die and all but disappear. Coccolithophore were white in life, transparent in death and a decade-long obsession for Professor Elizabeth Goodwin.

Interns and researchers fresh from college would all, at some point, fall victim to Goodwin's *dirty milk trick*. This involved switching the milk in the lab canteen for a white, highly concentrated coccolithophore solution. When the intended victim poured the creatures into boiling black coffee, their milk would magically disappear, often prompting the drinker to take a curious sip. The resulting spitting and shrieks of disgust would send ripples of laughter through the canteen and, on occasion, even elicit a smile from the professor herself.

Good times, thought Goodwin, as she passed through the empty canteen on her way to meet Laslett on the other side of the facility. Like much of Catalant, these rooms were hibernating, quietly gathering dust, limbs on a failing body shut down to preserve the essential organs. Only the archive booth and membrane pool remained in active use now, both hooked up to generators since the mains power was cut. Rain tapped the windows like the fingers of credit agents. Outside, a solitary amber security light cast prison-bar shadows through the industrial grilles. One might have expected her mood to be gloomy in such austere conditions. Yet Goodwin's footsteps had evolved into a three-step jazz rhythm – the sharp metallic click of her IV stand followed by two softer shuffles, and she couldn't help but hum a cheery melody along to the beat as it echoed down the empty halls. The hum became a mantra – *rum-rum-ting, rum-rum-ting*, as she passed rows upon rows of empty cubicles and labs, striding forward with ever-increasing purpose.

From her station in Svalbard a decade earlier, Goodwin had been convinced that the entire Arctic continent would melt into the sea before the century was out. In the face of this cataclysm, she had found a task the scale of which might somehow redeem her previous affronts to planet earth. Without the atmospheric cooling effects of the vast Arctic white reflecting sunlight into space, it was reasonable to predict that earth was on a catastrophic upwards bake. Yet, despite all the facts, the actual temperature increase had been comparably moderate.

While we were pumping twenty-two billion tons of carbon dioxide into the atmosphere each year, only half of that was accounted for. Upon request, NASA had allowed her access to satellite imagery, showing that in direct correlation to the decrease of Arctic landmass, the milky white swirls on the fringes of the East Asian coast and the centre of the Adriatic Ocean were swelling. As the ice caps melted, the coccolithophore biomass inexplicably increased.

Goodwin tried to join the dots. Carbon dioxide was being sucked out of the air to form the chalky carbonate shell of the coccolithophore. Not only were they releasing oxygen as a by-product, but the resulting whitening of the ocean's surface was reflecting sunlight, making up for lost Arctic landmass. It seemed too much, too unlikely that this overlooked amoebic organism, considered little more than whale food, was single-handedly altering the atmosphere, independently turning back the tide of human wantonness. Goodwin was determined to understand them, help them, cultivate and perhaps even, one day, control them.

A hundred acres of Catalant were cleared. Diggers rolled in, and ton for gallon, the soil was replaced by water. Atop of this new salt pool, so large it may well have been classified as a lake, Goodwin built a geodesic dome. *To keep out the pigeons*, she said to the Lyndhurst locals who thought little of this blot on their landscape. To them, Goodwin was the Wicked Witch of the West, and her employees a band of flying monkeys. To the wider ecological community, they were far worse – washed up and irrelevant traitors. But with the world and her redemption at stake, Goodwin couldn't care less.

She rarely left the pool, sleeping instead on a sofa bed in her office. Increasingly she retreated from her company duties and channelled her resources towards an enterprise in which her shareholders and board members failed to see commercial benefit.

But if Goodwin's behaviour was strange upon inspection, it was nothing compared to what the plankton were up to. Inside the dome, the coccolithophores proved highly sensitive to atmospheric changes – dying if they were too cold or warm or the alkali levels skirted too far from their optimum. Yet within minutes of any one change, the plankton would react in a way to re-establish their preferred conditions. If it got too warm, they would breed and reflect light until the temperature cooled, and the formation of their new shells would lower the acidity of the water. The moment it got too cold, whole swaths would flip their shells open and die, reversing the effect. Regardless of the individual's desire to sustain life and procreate, it seemed that millions of these creatures would put the needs of their environment ahead of their own lives.

In effect, these plankton were a mindless, self-regulating community, a feedback system that stretched across the entire globe. Darwin's close collaborator Alfred Wallace first speculated about a mysterious organic device, a regulator to keep the biosphere in check. Could her coccolithophore be the key, wondered Goodwin, the planetary thermostat that biologists had been hunting for decades, centuries?

In junior school, Goodwin had been taught that earth sits within our solar system's Goldilocks zone, the only spot that was *just right*. Not the scorched sands of Venus or frozen wastes of Mars, but the one place where liquid water was possible. And at the advent of life, some three point eight billion years ago, that had been true. Since then, earth's spiralling orbit has pushed us further and further away from the sun, and if our atmosphere were to disappear today, our planet would freeze. Fortunately, as we drifted, we kept our warm winter coat, our biosphere, and the question both Wallace and Goodwin obsessed over was – who or *what* has been keeping our coat so beautifully waxed?

Contrary to every other known form of life on the planet, coccolithophores – in a manner of speaking – cared more for their surroundings than their own proliferation. Goodwin knew there must be a reason. Nothing in this world was selfless, or it would have been crushed out of the evolutionary race long ago. There was a survival advantage to their altruism, and Goodwin was determined to find it and use it.

Three years after the last digger drove out from the facility gates and two years before the first creditor came calling, Goodwin made her breakthrough. She had increased the water temperature by two degrees, and as usual, one-third of the coccolithophores turned transparent, sacrificing themselves to cool the water. On a typical day, Goodwin would have left the sample to grow back before collecting the data, allowing time for parent cells to split into daughter cells until the bloom replenished. But on that particular day Goodwin was waiting for some results of a more personal kind, concerning her troubling health, and so in need of distraction, she stayed to observe the white chalk spheres divide and shift.

Through her compound microscope, as if from a balcony above a crowded patio party, she watched in astonishment. The cells were moving in formation. She repeated the test, filmed it, overlaid the footage, and sure enough, their regrowth was not arbitrary but patterned, as if each cell had found a special place within the swarm, and was hurrying to get back to it. Three and half million pounds later, and Goodwin had engineered a network of grids and microfluidic capillary tubes which allowed her to record their movements en masse. Through the newly built membrane system, she saw, to her utter bewilderment, that the patterns of death and life in the coccolithophores were not random and chaotic – they were decisive, complex and repeating themselves perfectly. Far from a mindless mechanical device, the coccolithophores were behaving with a single intent.

Goodwin stretched out a hand and stroked the photographs lining the walls of the corridor – NASA's satellite images of white swirls spreading their fingers between the Indian and Pacific Oceans, engulfing the Isle of Wight, skirting the coast of Greenland, connecting the entire world in their web. She hummed along to the tapping of her stand, *Rum-rum-ting. Rum-rum-ting.* The ocean was alive, and Goodwin was about to say hello.

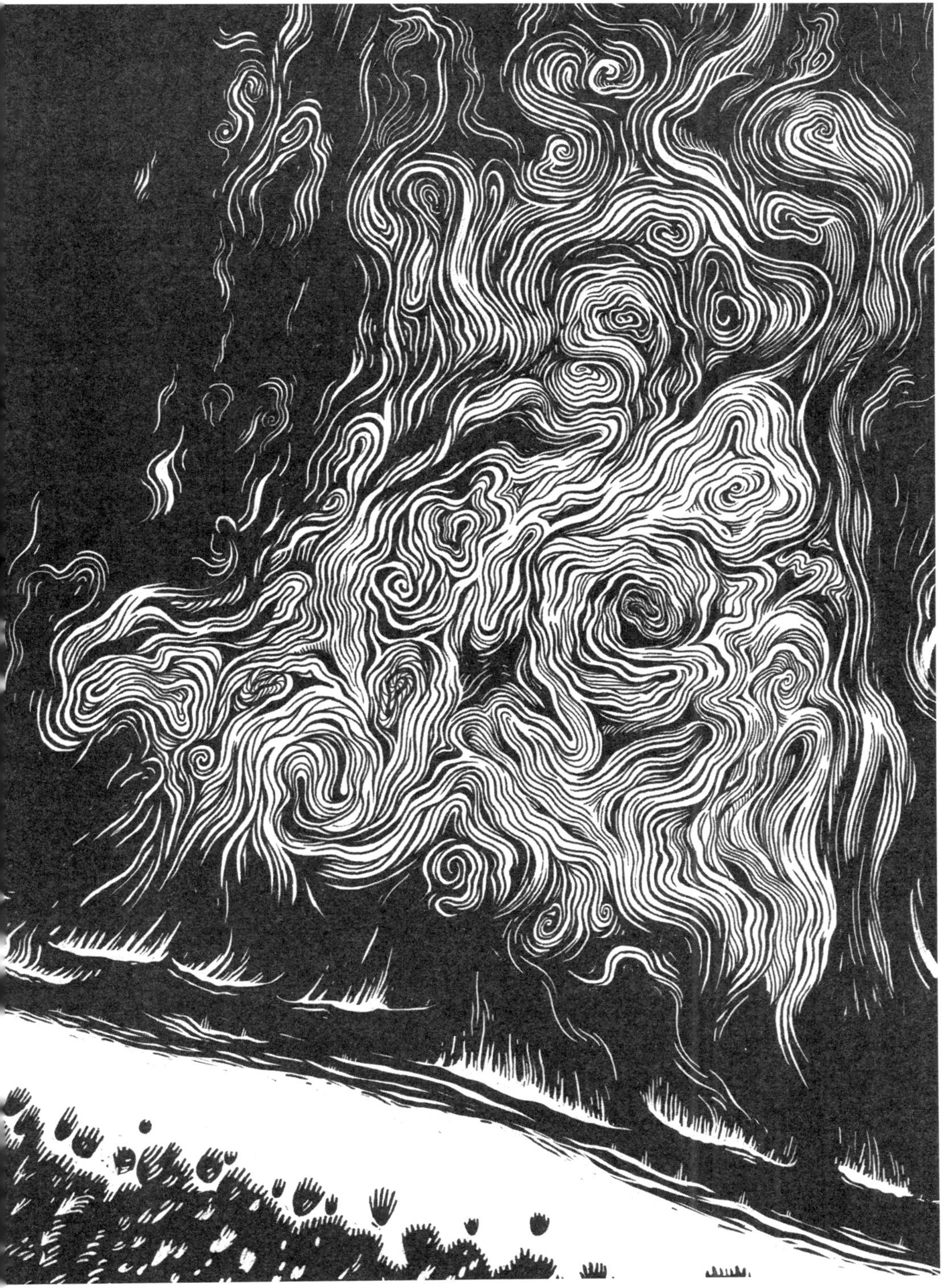

CHAPTER 7

HELL HOUND

They ran. Ash was first to reach the tent, tumbling headfirst through the zip. Giles fell in close behind, dragging the battery pack and superglue with him. Behind them, in the dark, the animal barked – a rasping, rumbling sound like the revving of an engine. Isabel ran over and the three crouched at the entrance, scanning the distant glow that implied a horizon, searching for movement. A heavy crunch sounded close by, and the three of them edged away as a cry of human terror rose in the night air and something surged in their direction, through the grass.

Giles unslung his snap-blade scalpel from over his shoulder and extended the blade with a ratcheting *click-click-click* as he saw a human figure barrelling straight for the tent. A naked older man, rust red from head to toe, burst out from the grass, stumbled in through the zip and sprawled onto the fur rug. He rolled over, spluttered, croaked something inaudible, then leaped at Giles as if trying to climb his shoulders. Giles dropped the scalpel and pushed him back and the others were quickly on him, restraining the feral figure to the ground. He writhed, eyes darting wildly from Giles to Ashraf to Isabel, then into the dark obscurity that loomed behind them. His fist, pinned at the wrist below Ashraf's knee, raised, and a shaking finger extended towards the door. Then, with surprising composure and eloquence, he whispered, 'You might want to close that door. The hounds are upon us.'

Giles had chosen Cadland View for the weekend away with his father for three reasons. Firstly, it was a short drive to Deadman's Cove, a quiet, secluded beach he had frequented as a child. Back then, they'd go fossil hunting in the loose shingle below the cliff, build rafts from driftwood and twine, and throw pebbles at precariously stacked piles of other pebbles. Secondly, the site had walks that boasted a bounty of rare birds – Dartford warblers, red kites and a colony of wild ring-necked parakeets to the west. Birds his father had studied through journals, but never seen in real life.

For Giles, the greatest draw had been the castle. He loved the ancient, absurdist, romantic relics, and jutting out on a peninsula just four fields to the west was Calshot Castle, replete with turrets, arrow slits, cannon holds, moat and drawbridge. At the back, facing into the forest, sat a small church boasting tombs of actual knights. Yet he had been disappointed by Saturday's visit. The cannons and turrets he'd loved as a boy felt unsavoury as an adult, reminding him of violence and privilege. His enjoyment had been further dented by the signposts fringing the forest, warning ramblers to stick to the coastal paths, with strictly no access during hunting season. A not-so-subtle reminder of the castle's patrician ancestry.

Hunting season was a long way off, but Giles reasoned that dogs trained to hunt and kill continued to exist outside of the winter months, and quickly he turned to help Isabel lower the jammed tent zip. They saw it then – a juggernaut on four legs, moving unnaturally fast for an animal so large. Giles liked dogs, but the creature bounding towards them was something else. Nearing the tent, torchlight peeled up its snout, revealing oily fur spiked like pine needles. Sleek, muscular and silvery grey, scale had transformed the dog into an alien thing – prehistoric, ferocious and utterly uncanny.

The zip tore open, and the elephantine creature thrust its head deep inside. Giles and Isabel fell back, and in the moment the dog adjusted to the light, contracting its dinnerplate pupils, the stranger darted forward and pinned the lower zip up beneath its neck. Teeth and jaws pulled wide to reveal a cavern that, judging from the stench, stretched towards hell. Giles scrambled sideways as the dog bit at the ground, and a gigantic wet nose connected with his torso, flinging him onto the rug. His snap-blade skittered across the canvas and Ash lunged to grab it but retreated as the head swung towards him. With his back to the tent door, the older man, stronger than he looked, pushed the zip further until it began pinching at the dog's throat. Shadows danced drunkenly, the lantern swayed on its string and the room felt as though it was tilting. Isabel made a fumbled dive for the blade, caught it by the handle and collided with Giles who had scrambled to the door. With a violent thrust, the dog butted the newcomer away from the entrance, and the opening tore wider as a wet, muddy paw burst into the tent. Giles caught the lower zip pull, halting its descent, trapping the leg behind the knee, shaking under the strain until his spine felt like it might crumple. Pressure mounted. Giles's knees gave way, but as the leg forced through, the zip pull twisted sideways, jammed, and Isabel brought the butt of the blade handle down on the animal's nose. The dog barked, a horrible ear-splitting sound, and lurched back out of the tent. The room shook, the lantern crashed into the stove, and the light went out.

Giles slumped against the wall, ears ringing. Something about this moment felt familiar. Not the setting, the absurd circumstance, but the feeling, the intense humility of being vulnerable and cowering in the darkness, trying not to make a sound while a behemoth stalked the earth nearby. It felt ancient. It felt, somehow, correct, grounded in nature and myth in a way Giles had not experienced since childhood. It had done for him what the castle could not. He was eight years old again, muddy and barefooted, building dens in the woods, years before adult concerns had stamped away magic. This had been the life of his ancestors, long before the insulations of modernity. Here, cowering against nature's wrath beyond the cave wall, he felt a kinship with those early people, cradling the sharpest, heaviest implement they could find – in his case, the handle of a tin-opener.

As the dog paced outside, searching for another way in, Giles felt each impact of paw meeting soil with a jolt of morbid thrill. He looked back into the tent, half expecting to be met with nods of gratitude from the survivors, thankful for their rescue from the beast. Instead, he saw the dozen or so children had condensed about Ashraf, their faces turned into him as he cooed quietly, bringing as many as he could into the circle of his arms. The tent rattled and a series of loud, quick snorts caused the inhabitants to shuffle closer together. Giles pictured the dog, fast and muscular, several times his height. Even if man and dinosaur had overlapped in their occupancy of earth, he doubted whether humankind would ever have faced a creature so menacing.

The footsteps receded, stopped, and Giles released his breath. A tiny snort and a rustle of canvas sounded nearby.

'The other tent!' hissed Isabel.

As if in response to her words, a rip broke the silence, followed by an awful shriek, a frenzy of tearing, scrambling and short, soft snaps. Giles found his feet and rummaged in the dark, throwing boxes and plastic cutlery aside. Tucking a thick black handle beneath an arm, he staggered back and withdrew a shiny, serrated bread knife, the blade as long as he was tall. Ashraf blocked his path.

'Come on, don't be daft.'

But Giles was already pushing past and out into the night.

The smaller tent pitched as the animal inside twisted and leaped, the entrance flaps billowing. Giles was thankful for the darkness, allowing only a glimpse of the horrors within. Strangled shrieks grew fainter and sparser as the dog tugged at something caught, not letting go. Then, with a soft snap, its rear legs staggered out of the tent, tail thrashing. Giles inched closer, balancing the knife blade above him, wondering where to strike – the hide, the ankle? His vision blurred, head swimming at the horror of such violence. The animal turned.

At first, only its eyes were visible. Then, the dog's magnificent head slid forward into the full glow of moonlight. A crumpled plastic sheet hung from its lower teeth and, wrapped inside it, a small figure writhed. The dog lowered its head, pinned the plastic to the ground with one paw, adjusted its bite and pulled. Huge neck muscles flexed. The trapped body stretched and gave a quiet chiropractic click. Then the sheet and its contents tore in two.

Giles found himself running forwards, the knife leaning back into a dangerous tilt. A roaring in his ears and rumbling in his stomach met midway to form a cry in his throat. He sprang, swinging the blade. Momentarily startled, the dog took a half-step back into the tent, easily avoiding the knife, which wedged harmlessly into mud. Still, it was enough. Giles caught the zip cord and dragged it down with all his force over the dog's bloodied snout, trapping it inside. He staggered forward, heart racing, and levered a tent peg loose with the knife's blunt edge, allowing a guy rope to spring free. The central pole swayed back and forth. Then, with a violent final thrash, the tent collapsed.

Giles inched towards the writhing fabric mountain, two steps forward in hope of finding survivors, one step back for fear of teeth ripping through canvas. The dog bucked and snarled, and Giles heard a muffled human cry from beneath the sheet. Images of Morris lying beneath the flower-patterned shirt stirred in his mind's eye and within three strides, he was atop the collapsed tent, knife raised. But there it hung, his arms unwilling to follow through and bring the knife down. Then the older man was beside him, his red hands pressed over Giles's own, pushing down, plunging the blade through fabric, deep into something soft, then solid, catching like a spade striking stone. The mound rocked back, a wild mare refusing to be tamed. Giles tumbled to the ground as the newcomer, still caked in crimson, gasped, gripped the handle and braced. The howl took Giles by surprise. Not a monster's roar, but the sad and pleading cry of a dying animal. As the writhing settled into spasms, the man withdrew the blade and plunged again. On the third thrust, the mound stopped resisting. Black spread through the fabric from the knife hilt. Giles emptied his stomach and slumped against the side of the collapsed tent, feeling the rise and fall of breath slow until still.

Isabel scaled the mound, heading for the older man, and Maya joined Giles beside the tent's entrance, brandishing a pencil as if it were a weapon. Behind her, several smaller children peered from shadows, their startled faces trying to glimpse grisly details from the scene. Ash stepped out between them and, swiping his illuminated staff like a shepherd's crook, herded the pack back into the red dome tent.

'Should we look inside?' asked Maya, nervously twisting her pencil. Giles looked at her. She was so much like Sadie, he saw now – the black straight hair, her hunched, imp-like posture. Like Sadie, Maya seemed vulnerable, not cut out for the brutality of this world. The pencil wasn't even sharpened. Maya hooked the zip handle with its blunt point and eased it upwards.

'Don't,' said Giles, turning her back towards the tent to join the others. 'I'll do that. In a minute. Something I need to see to first.'

Moments later, crouching in the quiet porch of a nearby box tent, Giles's phone flickered into life, bathing him in green light. A flat line denoted a lack of signal, but amid the small stack of day-old notifications lay a something wonderful – a message from his eldest daughter.

'Giles . . . it's Sadie.'

Static amplified her distress, and though small and far away, she sounded very much alive. Poor reception cut holes through her sentences and Giles pressed his ear deep into the headset, not daring to breathe.

'*Something's happened. I wan ... to ... et you, but I don't know how.*'

The phone shook in Giles's hands, and tears warbled his vision as he stared at the holes in the earpiece, as if hoping to catch a glimpse of his daughter.

'*Mum's ... ibble ... but we're fine, Ava's OK.*'

Giles shuddered a breath.

'*Mu ... igured it out ... miracle, really. We're at ... ver ... need you.*'

A long silence followed.

'*I'm sorry about th ... ope you didn't think that meant I don't ... if you can – if you're not – if you make it, we're at ... with t ... ot to go. I'll try the cabin line, and leave a message there, too. Righ ... well, Bye.*'

Giles played the recording again, again. He wanted more. Where were they? He needed to get to them. That's what they wanted. Sadie had said so. She needed him. If he came back for them now, it wouldn't matter that he'd had to leave. That he had let them down. That Ava had nearly died because he couldn't afford her treatment. That he'd had to go begging to Roland, of all people. He pressed the phone again, noted the screen smeared with blood, then looked to his hands.

The rumble of crashing waves interrupted his thoughts. There, through a gap in the shrub, lay the ocean, white even in the darkness. He was not alone in his transformation. Now he knew his daughters were safe, the idea of a ubiquitous change didn't seem so terrible. In this remade world, if that's what it was, there were no bailiffs, landlords or creditors. No fines, legal fees, regulations, or standards of practice. No red tape,

65

forms or terms and conditions. No liability. No litigation. No undeserved authority.

The world had been made as primitive as he had always felt. A place where getting ahead had nothing to do with posturing and presentation, saying the right thing and reading the small print. The slippery currency of that old world had been replaced with something tangible. What mattered now was what you could build, what you could make with your hands. In this new currency, Giles felt wealthy for the first time in his life. Bureaucracy had died with his phone, but this was not the end, it was the beginning of an age of abundance.

He pushed his palms into the head of a dandelion flower, letting the settling dew absorb the blood. Then he stood, turned, and ran back towards the sound of voices.

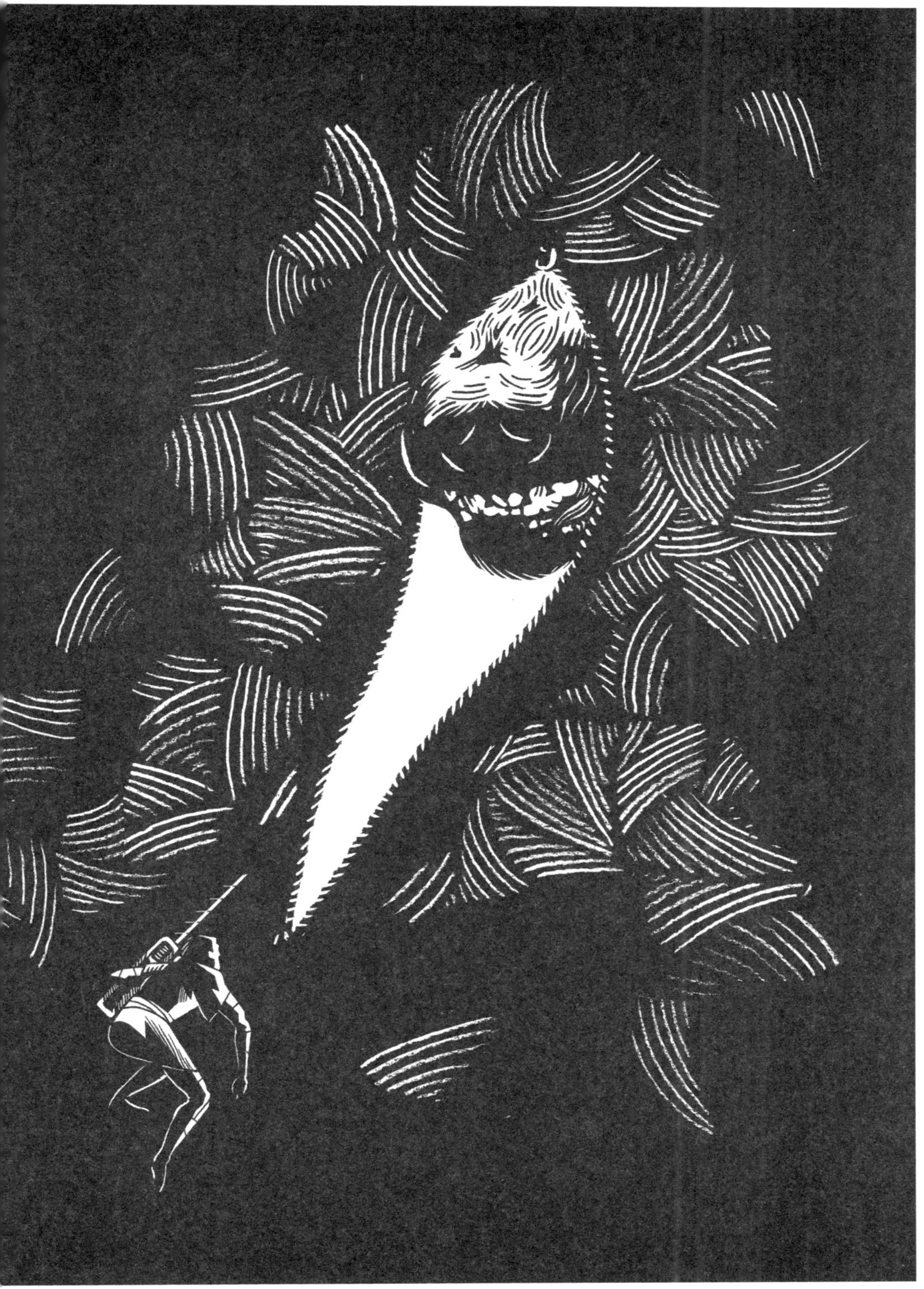

CHAPTER 8

ROSETTA DISK

Goodwin's face glowed blue as she nestled the IV stand into her armpit and shoved open the double door to the membrane pool. The gesture might have been triumphant had the doors not caught the base of the stand on the backswing and pulled her into a tangle of tubes and her own feet. Fractal patterns played across the underside of a glass dome high above – liquid blue twists of light, reflections from the myriad mass of pipes that snaked through the salt water below. Laslett was in a panelled glass booth on the other side of the pool, with his back to Goodwin, screwing hard-drive cables into sockets on a deck of computer consoles. He was a gangly mess of limbs topped with a mop of blond hair. His jacket hung lop-sided over narrow shoulders, a garish green leather that clashed with every other item he had on. All his clothes clashed. He was a walking crescendo of mismatching items. Even the blue of his shirt turned the hue of his skin several shades more pallid. Yet somehow, despite himself, Laslett looked well put together, a stack of odd numbers coming out even, and tonight Goodwin was unusually well-disposed towards the young man who had helped her get this far.

Shuffling about the pool's edge, mindful of how easily one might lose their footing, Goodwin caught her reflection wobbling in the water and sighed. The past few years had seen her scalp infiltrate her hairline and her cheeks had been set free to run away down her face. In part, it was the medication, but she knew the bulk of the blame lay with her work. She could see it in Laslett, too. The boy she met at the symposium now seemed middle-aged, though only a handful of years had passed.

'And how is my connectome looking, lad?'

Laslett startled at her voice, then beamed up at Goodwin from behind a bastard of cables. He stood to his full height, habitually stooping despite the ample headroom, and pushed a curtain of hair from his face.

'A thing of wonder. We're all set here. You have the disk?' The boy was keen and competent and had proven himself a hundred times over. Still, Goodwin had been distrustful and dismissive of Laslett's contributions to the project. *You're a miserable old hag*, Goodwin told herself. *Worse: you're turning into your mother.*

'Of course, my friend. Here she is.' Goodwin patted him on the shoulder, rested her hip against a desk, and slowly withdrew the small circle of silver from her pocket with delicate hands. Yes. A handful of years. That's all it was. And look how far they'd come.

'Good evening, Mrs Goodwin. How are we feeling? Pumped for the big show?' The man with the mohawk ahead of her jumped

69

the stairs two at a time as Goodwin clutched the handrail, hugging the concrete wall as camerapeople and sound technicians ferried equipment to and from the stage.

'It's *Professor* Goodwin.'

The shiny-faced man, sporting a polo shirt and radio earpiece, craned his head back and chirped, 'What was that?'

'Oh, nothing,'

'Great – we are just so psyched to have you come down. The EC tells me it was touch and go there for a minute.'

Indeed, it had been. The invitation to talk at the symposium had been anything but inviting to Goodwin. She loathed the idea of distilling decades of research into a pamphlet-sized presentation with neat little answers and witty quips. She wouldn't have even entertained the possibility under normal circumstances, but the coffers were near empty, and the National Academy of Science had an audience – a broad, respectable audience. Young too, dotted with valley tycoons who might have a recreational interest in this kind of work – the type with little to no commercial application but heaps of kudos. So, here she was.

Words like *God* and *Gaia* and *prokaryotic-micro-bacterial-super-consciousness* had been carefully deleted from her presentation. As she climbed the stairs, running through the talk in her head, she was glad of it. She felt ridiculous enough as it was, partly thanks to the advice of this preppy-punk liaison, to swap out her brogues for trainers. The flimsy shoes offset her *unyielding* demeanour, apparently.

'Just to loosen up the formality of it all,' she'd been told. 'It's all about breaking down this impenetrable science speak into something bite-size. Heck, if you can present your thesis in three words, then all the better. Am I right?'

No, you're not bloody right, Goodwin thought as she left the steps and emerged side stage into the curtain folds of the auditorium. *To every complex question, there's a simple answer that is wrong.* Ahead of them, in a spotlight, a young man wildly gesticulated as infographics exploded into pictograms behind him. *Oohs* and *ahhs* of delight rose from the crowd with each rainbow eruption of data. He was flanked on either side by illuminated plastic vac-formed models of brains and household tools – spanners and handsaws, the relevance of which Goodwin failed to comprehend. This was going to be awful. A crude butchery of her work. How could she communicate the majesty of her findings in twelve minutes, with a few slides and no notes? She stepped back into the curtain folds as a technician fitted a microphone to her shirt.

'Remember, we want to engage people. This isn't the King's speech! This is a *conversation*. If you want to do any back and forth – *when you say H, I say 2-O*, sort of thing, go for it. Haha! The look on your face! No, I'm kidding. But seriously, they love that. Yeah, go for laughs. We calculated that the amplitude of laughter directly correlates to the online hit rate. Isn't that fascin—'

And then Goodwin was blinking into the lights, unsure how she got centre stage, the rows of seats curving before her like a tidal wave, while her tongue scavenged for saliva.

'Binary code.' Her voice was sandpaper. 'Cold, hard ones and zeros. Familiar? Good. We can apply many a friendly metaphor to this elegant mathematical language.' She coughed, 'Soften it up a bit. The ones and the zeros could be ... truth and lies. Yeses and no's – all very nice. To me, binary is best expressed in terms of life and death. Imagine an organic, living machine – it breeds its ones and kills its zeros. Who can tell me why this language wouldn't work, hmm? You say hey, I say ho – sort of thing?' The liaison winked and gave the thumbs up. The room was quiet. Goodwin blinked down at the scrawled ink on her palm, bullet points blurring with sweat. Then, from the auditorium, came a quiet voice.

'Life would try to outweigh death, or death would build up over time. The numbers would go out of balance, one way or the other.' Goodwin seized upon it.

'Precisely! Yes. Death accumulates, and life proliferates. Spencer's old epithet, *survival of the fittest*, rings frustratingly true. True to all species, with one exception.' Goodwin clicked her first slide into place, a black and white sphere comprising several overlapping white discs. 'The coccolithophore – a selfless, self-regulating phytoplankton that might just be our planet's best chance at climate control.' Spectacles, beards and hard-line fringes bobbed in the darkness and, feeling encouraged, Goodwin unfurled her findings. The biosphere thermostat. The repeated patterns. Order where there should have been chaos. They cover thirty-five per cent of the ocean floor, in some places, the sheets are kilometres thick – *oohs*. The most long-lasting species on earth – over two hundred and eighty million years old and still going strong – *ahhs*. This was going well.

'As the cells regenerate, the patterns repeat in blocks of eight. Let's continue our binary metaphor and, borrowing a computer term, we'll call those blocks bytes. When we examined the phytoplankton on mass, we saw the emergence of a set of bytes – two hundred and fifty-six distinct variations, distinct patterns of life and death. Two hundred and fifty-six characters of what I propose to be *an alphabet*.'

Still riding the high of her presentation so far, Goodwin nearly missed the snort of laughter, quickly muffled. There was an uncomfortable ruffle of shifting seats. Somewhere at the back of the auditorium, a door creaked. She had reached the edge of normal science, and now she would have to tread carefully. Goodwin fumbled for her slide remote and sent it clattering across the wooden stage. Stooping to fetch it, her toe caught through the hoop of a shoelace, and only the cradling embrace of a giant plastic spanner stopped her from falling face-first into the parapet.

'Stupid goddamn shoe,' she spat, and her voice boomed about the room. She kicked it loose, sending the shoe spiralling across the stage towards the cringing liaison.

'They made me wear these blasted things,' Goodwin was fumbling with the microphone cable, about to fling that too, when from somewhere in the crowd came a – '*Woo!*' Then a – '*Yeah! Screw the trainers!*' followed by a smattering of applause. The crowd were with her again. Goodwin rubbed the last inky bullet points onto her trousers and walked lopsidedly back to centre stage.

'I didn't want to do this talk. There's nothing neat about what I'm doing, not yet. This is still very new to me. To all of us. However, if I am sure of one thing, it is that this is an alphabet – a new grammar of understanding in biology. And by degrees, that means there must be a language. And there is no language without thought. Some would argue that the same is true vice versa.' To hell with it. She was going to let it all out. Tell them everything. Her fear of being plagiarised, or worse, of being mocked, had vanished.

'These little things are acting with purpose, in unison. They *are* bio-binary. Computer language rendered in organic matter. Data. Records. Patterns passed from body to body. They may as well be electric currents through neurones. Yes. This ancient network, I believe, is *intelligent*.' Groans from the crowd now, people muttering among themselves. Goodwin pushed through, speaking louder, faster. 'The ocean is alive with thought. A body of water imbued with a unifying consciousness. All around us. Omnipresent. And if that's not something holy, then I don't know what is.'

Her voice melted into nothing. Unable to face the silence that fell upon the auditorium at the 'H' word. She turned her back and skipped through the remaining half of her slides, disgusted with herself. She had been preaching, coming across as some biological numerologist. Satellite images of blue-white plankton blooms, cross-cuts of ocean beds and pages full of eight-pronged linguistic symbols flickered in front of her. The last slide locked in place. A large black tombstone, chipped at the top left corner and engraved in Latin, Greek and hieroglyphics.

'Of course, I am not so lucky as those eighteenth-century explorers who uncovered the Rosetta Stone, unlocking the lost language of Egypt. I have no key from which to apply meaning to my alphabet.'

She turned to face the audience, the spotlight obscuring the details of their faces. Goodwin wiped sweat from her brow, smearing three ink-black streaks above her left eyebrow, and continued.

'With the correct stimuli, I can arrange the cells. Effectively, I can write with their letters. But alas, without translation, everything I say ...' Her head felt suddenly very heavy, and she let it droop. 'Everything I say is utter gibberish. Erm. Thank you.'

Goodwin pushed her way through the foyer, through the crowd of attendees. She kept her head down, not because people might be staring, the opposite – she worried she was being avoided. The revolving doors spat her onto the street. Wheeling her case up to the taxi stand, Goodwin heard her name and turned to see a young man in a dark yellow raincoat, hunched over with an arm outstretched towards her, catching his breath. His socks were opal, and his shoes were orange, completely mismatched yet held together by some strange cohesion of fashion. Wheezing for breath, the man straightened and extended his arm.

'Professor Goodwin? Astonishing presentation, simply – I can't quite put it into words. I was hoping I might catch you. Trying to sneak away?' Relief spread through Goodwin. Someone wanted to talk to her. Over the man's shoulder, she caught sight of more people looking in her direction, a dozen peppered throughout the crowd. Quickly, they turned away.

'Thank you, that's kind. I'm afraid I've a train to—'

'Time for a cup of tea? Cake? My treat. My name's William Laslett.'

'Well . . .' Goodwin glanced from the taxi stand, then back to Laslett, who added cheerily, 'I have a proposal for you.'

In the greasy spoon across from the NAS conference centre, Laslett talked, and Goodwin sat and listened. He had loved the presentation.

'The most enlightening four minutes of my adult life.' He wanted to help Goodwin. Perhaps they could help each other. Laslett claimed himself to be a leader in the field of connectomics, a new branch on the ever-growing tree of neuroscience. He studied, in almost impossible detail, the wiring of the brain. Connectomes were the pathways of neurones. A map of connections within a brain. Like a dot-to-dot picture, but without the picture. His team were mere months away from mapping the first entire human connectome and decades ahead of their nearest rivals.

'Everyone else has been going stem by stem, re-building these complex trees in 3D, trying to connect a forest by looping strings between each individual branch. So, a worm brain has three hundred neurons and seventy thousand connections. A human? Something like one hundred trillion connections. You see why it's taking a while. My team's advantage is that we're not looking at just *one* brain. We're looking at several at once, comparing them and averaging the pathways. Looking for similar types of trees, if you like. What we found, like you, is that these trees, these webs of connections, are not infinitely variable. They repeat in very particular shapes. And all these different trees – we call them clusters – they fit together. You see, all brains have similar clusters. Like a palette of colours. Now, something in your talk nearly sent my heart into palpitations – can you guess how many distinct clusters we've found?'

Goodwin looked up from her treacle sponge tart, eyebrows raised. 'Two hundred and fifty-six?'

Laslett grinned mischievously.

'Well, no, actually – Two hundred and fifty-one. But that's close enough, right? There must be a link. Two hundred and fifty-ish of whatever they are – characters in an alphabet, patterns in a brain. I think your "bytes" and our "clusters" are one and the same – a new biological grammar. The language of thought.'

Laslett beamed, perhaps expecting Goodwin to fall backwards out of her seat or start applauding. Instead, she scraped away at the tart, took a sip of coffee, then dribbled it back into her mug, spluttering apologetically, 'Oh. It's cold.'

Laslett stared at her, confused. He started to explain his findings a second time. Clearly, she hadn't understood. Goodwin gave a sad, maternal smile. 'It's incredible, what you describe, I'll give you that. Well done, indeed. But in the end, I can only offer my deepest sympathies. You're in no better position than I am. You still don't understand your – what was it? *Clusters*. You know your letters, but like me, you cannot spell. You don't know what these symbols *mean*.' Goodwin scooped up the last spoonful of pudding. 'It was very interesting meeting you, Mr Laslett. Really, I wish you all the best. Now, my train.' She stood, pulling her jacket about her shoulders.

'There you have me. It's true I'm far from figuring it all out. I can't help you find meaning, a translation for your alphabet. But these are common platforms, bio-binary as you put it, with the same sets of rules. They must be relatable, transferable even, like Greek to Latin.'

Goodwin wove between the floor-mounted tables, crammed with teenagers and office workers on their lunch break. She had one hand on the swing-door handle when Laslett called across the cafe.

'I may not be your Rosetta Stone, Professor Goodwin, but I can help you write your mind in plankton.' Goodwin paused, and the waitress nearly dropped a plate of fried eggs. 'Plus,' he pushed his hair back from his face, flashing that mischievous grin, 'I'm very well-funded.'

Beneath the shimmering ceiling of the geodesic dome, Goodwin eyed her wobbly reflection in the back of the silver disk and then handed it to Laslett. The Rosetta Disk, complete with the two sets of grammar, two hundred and fifty-six characters. Neurone and plankton perfectly aligned – the missing five clusters having surfaced in the months following that first meeting.

'Now,' Laslett lifted a clear lid on the stack of consoles and slipped the disk onto a turntable-like stage, 'are you ready to see your mind made of plankton?' Four small tanks sat on either side of the console – one side full, the other empty. The disk spun. Needles lowered. The soft thump of a pump filled the room.

Goodwin watched the fluid filter up through a capillary network of tubes from the full tanks on the left and disappear into the console below the disk. There, membranes filtered groups of cells, and via acid and heat, forced them into new formations. Minutes later, the first drips spiralled slowly into the tanks on the right, invisibly transformed.

By the time the transcription had run its course, the day had come and gone. Laslett nudged Goodwin awake and the two of them marvelled at the copies of her mind, the four glass jars alive with silver-white swirls. Only then did Goodwin wonder how the ocean would receive her connectome. When they merged their data, combined the contents of one of these jars with the consciousness in the pool, would they hear her as a disembodied voice? A schizophrenic episode, a dream or a foreign memory? A headache, perhaps? It saddened Goodwin to think that, for the time being, they were unlikely to know. Tonight was a one-way conversation. A whisper in the ear of God. Not the dialogue she had hoped for, but hell, at least now she'd be heard.

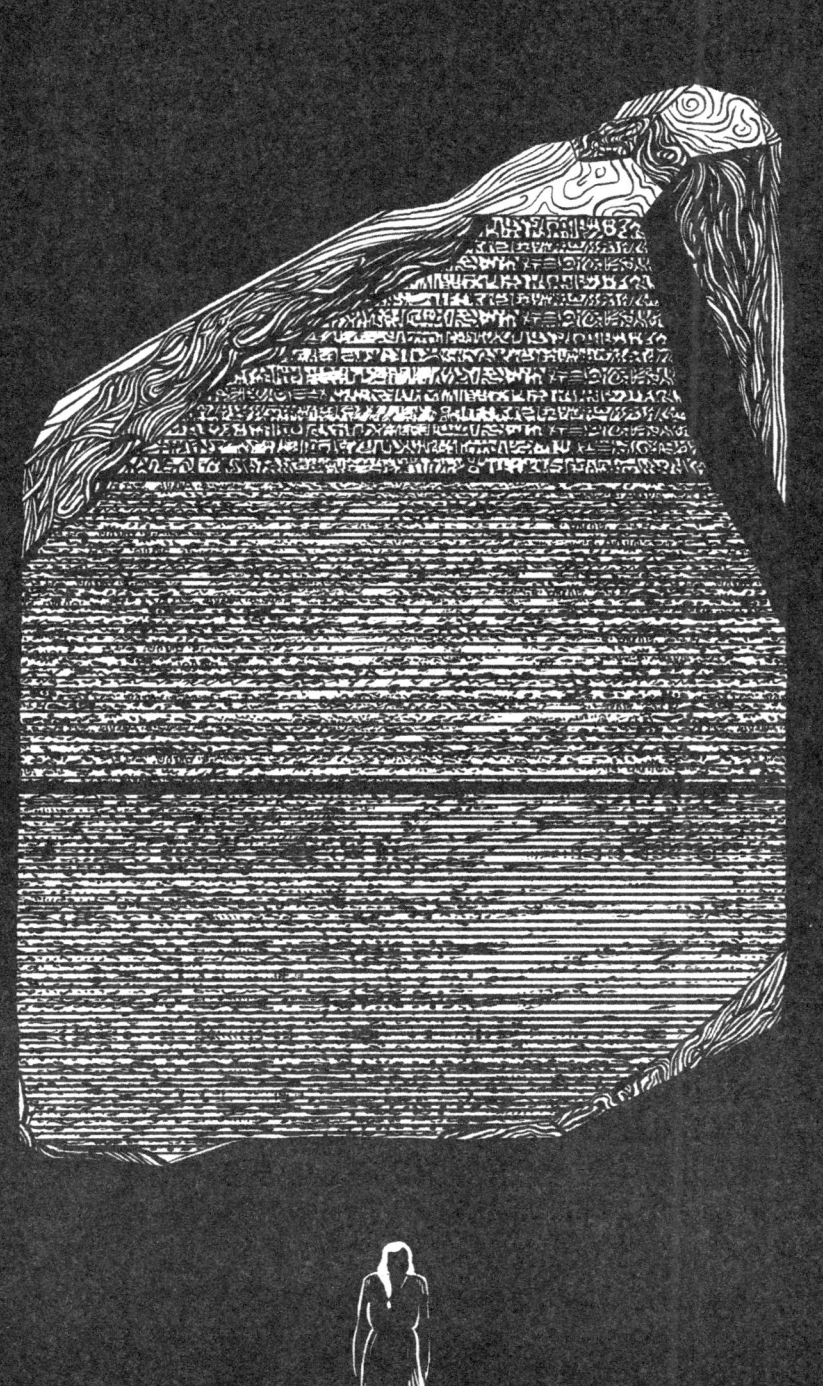

CHAPTER 9

A FUNERAL OF SORTS

A single survivor from the infirmary tent, the Welsh man named Alwyn, had been prised from inside a plastic tub, cursing and panting. The rest had not been so lucky. Unsure what to do with their bodies, Giles, Isabel and Ashraf solemnly wrapped them in strips of canvas and laid them beside the collapsed tent. Nearby, the newcomer, Richard, hunched over a saucer of water, made futile attempts to wipe away the crimson stains on his skin.

'How many of those hunting dogs were there?' Ashraf asked in a hushed whisper.

'Two,' Richard replied, accepting a bottle cap of ravioli from Evelyn.

'So there's another one still lurking out there.' For a moment, Ashraf looked anxious, a weight pulling behind his eyes. Then he quickly, visibly, pulled himself back from whatever darkness was calling. 'Well, we could . . . perhaps we could tame it?'

'If it comes, we'll bait it, trap it and alas we must kill it. As before,' Richard replied in a solemn tone, tearing a handful of pasta from the makeshift bowl.

'Or that. Yes.' Ashraf reluctantly agreed.

'But for the time being, let us be thankful we're alive – in no small part due to the actions of this man. A veritable Thor!' Richard turned from Ashraf and offered the bowl to Giles.

'I'm good, thanks,' said Giles. The older man's flippancy irritated him. But then Richard hadn't seen the bodies.

'Giles, is it? I'd say you're in a position of quite some significance.' He looked Giles up and down. 'You must have been, what – a good seven feet tall, before? Lucky you.'

But Giles had never felt lucky. Granted, he hadn't needed a walking stick, and people didn't stop him in the street for photographs the way he'd once seen a sufferer of true gigantism accosted. For most of his life, his stature had worked against him. He wasn't a giant, medically speaking. Though at fifteen, when Giles shot up a foot above his father's height, Morris had taken him to have his pituitary gland tested for signs of the tumours that cause gigantism. When the tests revealed perfectly normal glands, Morris reasoned it was a blessing. Some people were just lucky.

Still, the extra head of height was enough to make a difference. Years of hunching through doorways and lowering his head to join the conversation had rounded his shoulders. Not to mention the small beds, low ceilings, short trousers, awkward hugs and the repeated joke about how the weather was up there. The last place his size had worked in his favour was in the face of a playground bully three decades earlier. The adult world had made no allowances for his stature. If anything, the difference had counted against Giles. His size went in hand with mistrust and threat. Assumptions were made. Typecasts were set.

Giles straightened his back and felt his shoulder blades click. Now the world had been levelled to fit him.

'Six-eleven,' Giles replied, shifting uncomfortably.

Richard clapped his hands, pleased. 'Well, we're most fortunate to have you on the team.'

'It's a team, is it?' said Ashraf, mumbling. 'So far, you've contributed a dog.'

Richard ignored him, turned and made his way to the inner tent. Giles found himself following. Richard had not asked, yet the request to follow had been implied. There was an air of authority about him. He reminded Giles of someone he couldn't quite place, his father perhaps. Richard stopped, surveying the dome, and Giles came to stand beside him.

All twelve children – *the Pack*, as Ashraf had begun calling them, were awake. Though it had only been a couple of days, a loose hierarchy was beginning to form, with Evelyn and Maya at the head, self-appointed guardians and distributers of supplies. Below them, a pair of slightly younger boys who took small delight in bossing about and entertaining the group's most junior members. Some gathered in pairs, tending to wounds. Others sat alone inspecting themselves, still exploring the cruel yet-to-be-observed nuances of their transformation. The tender scalp. The hardened palms. The cracked teeth. A trio of kids, no older than six, amused themselves by making small displays of strength for one another, lifting a bar of soap above their heads and quietly giggling when it slipped between their hands. Another pair quietly held each other, the elder cooing in the other's ear.

Isabel sat on the edge of a board-game box, the snap-blade

scalpel laid across her lap, looking past Giles and Richard out into the field. Clouds parted, and the moon rendered the campsite in peaceful hues of blues and dark purples. Giles guessed there might have been two dozen tents in the field. From them, seventeen survivors had emerged, huddled now beneath a single temporary shelter. Were the other bodies still out there? Richard sat beside Isabel and motioned to Giles. 'Please, please, have a seat,' and as if in response to Giles's thoughts, he asked, 'You've checked the tents?' Isabel nodded.

'We found about forty-odd piles of clothes, me and Ash. The rest must have been out when it happened.' Isabel sank her palms into her cheeks and let her fingers run up through coarse, dark hair. And perhaps thinking of the lives lost in the infirmary tent, she added in a whisper, 'What was the point?' Giles imagined the piles of fleece and jeans and wellingtons speckling the countryside, shrines to the people who once wore them.

'The other bodies, they're still in the tents?' asked Giles. Isabel looked offended, perhaps taking this as a slight on their efforts.

'To get everyone together, with the wounded and the—'

Giles was about to interrupt, tell her he meant no criticism, when Richard beat him to it.

'I don't know how you've managed it, bringing us all together like this. Well done. Still, seventeen out of forty . . .' he sighed and looked lost in thought. 'Doesn't bode well. When you factor in the children, I think elsewhere we're looking at rather harsh odds.'

'Meaning?' asked Ashraf.

'Well, look at them. The little ones seem to be more or less all intact. A lack of fillings and false hips, I suspect. With this being a family hot spot, the density of youth is naturally higher. If one-in-three survives in an Eden like this, I'd expect the rest of the populous is, well . . .' his forehead furrowed, thick broom-like eyebrows swamping his eyes as he crunched the morbid calculation. 'I'm sorry to say, one in ten seems generous. Even if they make it through the transformation, the others won't have a Norse god between them and the wrath of nature,' he added, resting a hand on Giles's shoulder, casting him a kind, worldly smile.

Isabel rolled her eyes and stood, brushing off her red woollen smock. 'We can't stay here.' Her gaze, those two intense spots of green, turned on each of the three adults. 'It's not safe. We need to find help. Find others.'

'I agree with Isabel,' said Richard, 'there's strength in numbers. Might I suggest, since the two of you are clearly the most responsible—'

'Oi!' said Ashraf, mumbling through a mouthful of pasta, 'I'm very responsible.'

'Apologies, of course.'

'Apology accepted,' grinned Ashraf, squeezing in beside him on the box.

'Might I suggest then that the four of us craft a plan to move on? If not to return the young ones to their homes or an authority, a plan to take them somewhere safe?' There was a murmur of agreement from Ashraf and Isabel, but Giles remained silent. This was not what he had in mind. He thought of the message. His daughters. The dog. A caveman with a kill across his shoulders. Where were his girls?

'I . . .' Giles rubbed his eyes. His head still swam. The dog again, its jaws peeling wide open. A silver hawk-head. His hastily buried father. The whimper. He stammered, 'I don't . . .' Isabel gripped Giles by the wrist.

'We have to move. One heavy rain and what's difficult now will become impossible. We could *all* die here, Giles. All of us. We need to leave. Find a house. Find help.' Giles shook his head. 'Anything's better than sitting here,' she pressed.

'You don't understand. I'm agreeing with you,' said Giles. 'Those are good ideas. I think you should do that. I think *you* ...' he let the word linger, 'you should do that.' He felt her eyes burning into the side of his head and heard a small gasp of disbelief.

'You're leaving us?'

'I think ...' Giles kicked the dirt, 'I think I'm going to bury that dog.'

Giles had set out to do precisely that but instead found himself wandering the field. There, he'd come across a set of clothes strung haphazardly over several guy ropes, beneath which stood a tall boot, one waxed trouser leg still tucked into the top, a horrific series of events spelled out in the arrangement of the wreckage. The victim had hung on to the ropes as the transformation did its work. Expunged bodily fluid had then funnelled through the waterproof trouser leg, carrying the shrunken person into the abyssal boot. Giles heaved the wader onto its side, spilling pungent liquid and an emaciated body onto the grass.

After that, Giles had gone from tent to tent, gently gathering the sad forms that were once people onto a tarp and carrying them to be with the others lining the perimeter of the verdant canvas, fanning out around the body of the dead dog. Ashraf, Isabel and Alwyn – who had complained less of his wounds since his close encounter with the animal – joined Giles on the mournful collection.

Now he squatted in front of the canvas pyre with a matchbox clamped between his knees, preparing to strike. Burying the dog might have been optimistic, but a cremation was still a ceremony, of sorts. Once the rows of wrapped bodies were soaked in spirits and covered with dry grass, others joined him. A few people laid flowers about the edge – buttercups, daisies, wild cowslip. Most of the younger children had been on a Scout trip and, so far as they knew, had only suffered the loss of their clan leader. A handful of others – Maya, Evelyn, Jayden – had lost people much closer. They seemed to instinctively gather around Ashraf, who sat with them, ruffling hair and pulling them into hugs, whispering words of comfort. Cradled in Ashraf's lap was a Hello Kitty pin badge – a keepsake, Giles assumed, a reminder of his girlfriend, who now lay with the others. Only he and Isabel, who had been travelling alone, seemed free from personal attachment to the bodies on the pyre. And then there was Richard.

'Might I say a few words?' asked the older man, who had been standing silently behind them. When no one answered, he leaned close to Giles and whispered, 'Ever had a dog?'

'More of a cat person,' Giles grunted in reply, still poised with the match.

'Ah yes, me too. Divine creatures, some say.' Patches of olive and a darker green, almost black, mottled the canvas mound around the three small tears at its peak, the points at which Richard had plunged the knife. Or had it been Richard, Giles wondered? Giles had certainly held the knife, felt it bite on bone. He gripped the match and leaned in to strike. 'I like dogs too, of course.' Richard added, 'Even though it chased me for a day and a night.' Giles took the man in. Sixty, perhaps, athletic, and capable too if it were true that he'd evaded the animal for so long. 'Just a few short words,' repeated Richard, assuring the group, 'I'll be brief.'

Alwyn promised a few short, four-letter words in return. He

had taken a dislike to the newcomer and the way Richard had assumed a quasi-leadership role. Alwyn was an ex-army officer after all, with a lot of experience in being in charge. With general nods of assent, Richard cleared his throat and stepped forward.

'Well, let me see,' he kneeled and picked up a loose canvas edge, rubbing it between forefinger and thumb. 'It's been a rather strange couple of days, has it not? We've all lost something – a few feet and several stone.' Richard widened his eyes and grinned expectantly at the crowd, who remained silent. He continued, eyes closed, suddenly very solemn. 'And yet we've gained something too . . . new *friends*.' Alwyn hooted in delight at how badly his few short words were being received. Undeterred, Richard continued, louder, 'A great trauma has rocked us, and from what we know, we're not alone in our suffering. How and *if* the scales will reset remains to be seen. We are less and the poorer, but one thing is for certain, we can be strong so long as we are together. Strangers though we might be, we are joined by our common humanity, never more acutely felt than today.'

The crowd settled, turning their heads to listen. 'We send these souls to rest in peace. As they were beloved to us in life, so shall they remain dear to us in memory.' Giles was about to strike the match when Richard turned to him directly.

'I know you feel bad for what you had to do to the dog. But there is no need for regret.' Giles, sensing attention turning to him, felt the sudden urge to drop the matches and back away, but Richard's gaze held him to the spot. 'Death comes to all things. To feel sad for the inevitable would be like mourning the sun when it sets. It serves no purpose. Instead, turn the energy of your sorrow to the uncertainty ahead, to the lives that might or might not persist. Those are the ones worth your worry – the living. Because only to them can your regret and learning make a difference.' Richard turned back to address the group, 'So, knowing this, we send the beast to rest in peace. It was terror from afar, but like Death, when unmasked, she showed us a friendly face.'

Richard crossed himself, then turned and whispered, 'Please, go ahead, Giles.' Shaken, he nodded, struck the match and carried it like a torch to the tent's edge. The small flame took. Amber melted into greens and blues as the tent caught light, and a halo of fire encircled the mound, crackling at dry grass. Black butterflies of soot trembled upwards, and Giles followed their path down to the flames, which fizzed like television static.

'That was pretty good, actually,' he said quietly.

'Well, yes. Thank you,' said Richard, brushing char from his cloak. 'It should be. I'm a priest. It's sort of my job.' Giles looked down at the man, who remained transfixed by the blaze. He tried to imagine Richard in his previous life, and it made sense, thinking of him in a collar, on a podium, instructing a crowd.

'That so?'

Richard nodded.

'Though I must admit, it took me a while to remember, with all that's happened.'

'In that, you're not alone.' Giles patted his shoulder, and Richard gave a weary smile.

'We're not really meant to include dogs in funerals, but I consider this a special circumstance.'

The flame caught a pocket of something flammable, and a blue-white wave swept over the pile, melting the fabric away to reveal the fur beneath. As Giles watched, spellbound, he saw it was not a dog under the canvas after all. There lay his father, Morris, small and curled atop a Viking funeral raft. He let his knees give way and sat cross-legged, his body relaxing, the tension he hadn't even known was there, evaporating with the heat.

'You have to wonder,' Richard slurred, cradling a capful of dark, golden liquid, 'You have to wonder – why us? Why not the birdies, the beeses and all the wee beasties, hmm? Far from accidental. Four words: *In – His – Own – Image.*' Giles nodded politely, and Richard continued, 'I'm telling you – we are sinners, and now we're being punished.' Richard necked the rest of the cap and jealously eyed the bottle beside Giles.

'What you said about trying to fix the things that haven't happened yet. That made sense to me,' said Giles. From his pack, he unfolded the photograph of the girls tucked beneath his arms like two snared rabbits, and showed it to Richard.

'That's Sadie, and the little one's Ava. Fifteen and nine.'

'Delightful. Are you going to drink that?'

'All yours.' Richard heaved the miniature spirit bottle onto the ground between them, sloppily refilling his cap. Perhaps because he knew Richard wasn't listening, Giles began to talk.

'It made sense because, well, I let them down a few years ago. It turned out OK, but after that, I sort of took a step back. Better off without me, I thought. Truthfully, I've always been a bit out of sync, you know? Not sure I was born in the right century. Probably better off swinging a club. But the way the world is now, if this is how it'll stay, I think I can find my place. Be of some use. I think I can help them again.' Giles gave Richard a hopeful smile, but the priest was fast asleep.

He stayed to watch the fire die down to its embers and was kneeling to stand when, through the last twists of smoke and sparks that spluttered into the early dawn, Giles saw a woman. She

89

clung to a branch, high in a tree on the edge of the campsite, her black hair nearly twice the length of her body, wiry and peppered with dirt. She was naked and brick red from head to toe. Her skin, like cracked clay, obscured her age, and perhaps it was a reflection or a trick of the light, but her eyes appeared to be on fire. Then Isabel was by his side, and when he looked back, the woman in the tree was gone.

'Come on, it's not safe out here, just the two of you.' Isabel clamped a hand across her nose and mouth, 'Plus, it smells terrible.' Richard stirred and slurred.

'You missed a beautiful ceremony.'

'Oh, I was there,' Isabel assured, scooping Richard under one arm as Giles held the other.

'I did well, didn't I? *Convincing.* Just like the real thing.' Together, they carried Richard through the waist-high grass towards the tent.

'You thought any more about what I said?' asked Isabel as they laid Richard into a fold of the fur rug. Giles looked up at the rows of sleeping socks. To his left, slumped and snoring against a suitcase, sat Ashraf, cat pin on his lap.

'If I can find them, I can help them,' mumbled Giles. He thought of Sadie's message, *I'll try the cabin line, too.*

'Help who?' said Isabel, not following. Across the field, the first rays of sunlight caught of the rims of a dozen vehicles and a brightness filled Giles that he hadn't felt in years.

'I'll stay with the Pack. And like the old man said, we'll take them somewhere safe.'

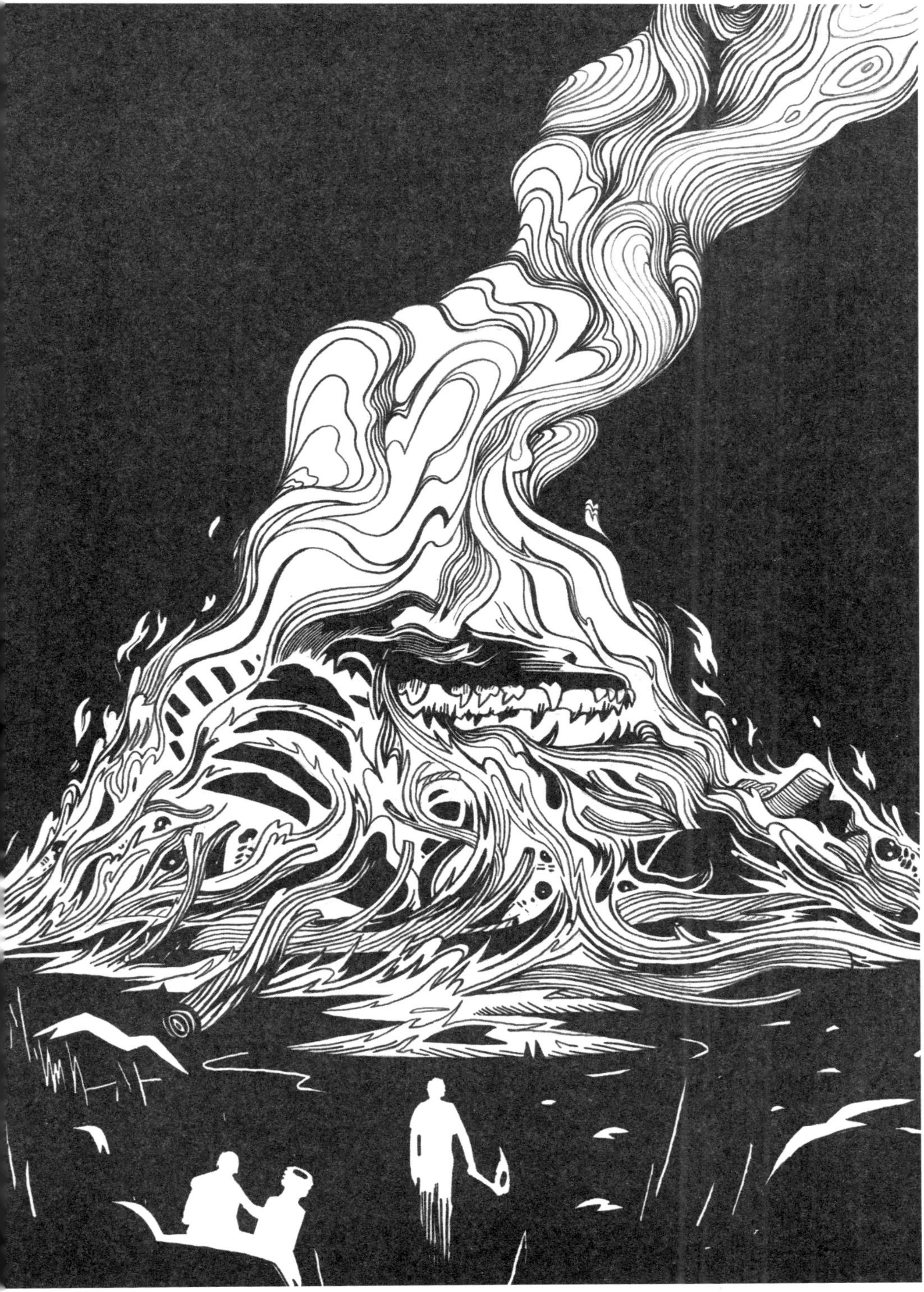

CHAPTER 10

ELSEWHERE,
A WAVE OF CHANGE

Contrary to popular belief, the Descent was not a single event.
While it's true that the major incident, the one that began at
eleven minutes past twelve on July Second outstripped the others
in terms of scale and drama, it was neither the first nor last. Seven
waves brought about our transformation, and they occurred over
the span of two years.

Another misconception is that the major event of July Second
happened in a flash. Certainly, for those near the Point of Origin,
matters progressed quickly – the process of exocytotic reduction began within seconds and took less than a minute to run
its course. By the time thirty minutes had passed, the radius of
change, expanding roughly at the speed of sound, had just broken

ground in Paris. Within five hours, the horizon line of white bloom rising from deep within the ocean had crept across the globe to reach the Americas. While to the east, in New Zealand, Britain's most distant neighbours had a whole fourteen hours to watch the tide roll closer.

So it was, on that miraculously integrated planet, there was plenty of time to panic. Among the first to do so were the sports fans. Across the globe, late-night bars and crowded living rooms were filled with shocked screams, stunned silences and the nervous laughter of disbelief as live feed from the Stade de France showed twenty-two international football stars slowly reduced into piles of soft, indistinguishable matter. Around them, eighty thousand spectators followed suit, shrivelling down into raisins, juiced like a barrel of grapes to make a hideous wine.

The rumour mill churned. Eyewitness reports lit up newsrooms. People buried themselves in basements, hid in nuclear bunkers and hijacked flights to the Arctic in vain attempts to flee the inevitable. Brave men and women in military jets flew towards the light and never returned. A handful of remotely accessed operational drones transmitted grainy footage from far-away silent shores. Foreign traffic cameras were hacked by government agencies and by teenagers in their bedrooms, trawling the internet for an escape raft from this rapidly sinking ship.

And then they found it, a single transmission laying everything out from beginning to end. An older lady, dressed in stripes, explained what had happened and why, who had done it and how to survive it. For those who saw her message, it made every difference – doors were opened, supplies prepared, fillings removed. But for the masses, the instruction never came. By the time the people in charge had got out of bed, put on their suits, made it to the office to peer at the footage and clamp their hands over their mouths in horror, the song was already creeping through the shutters. It did not happen in a flash, but a handful of hours is no time at all in the lives of busy people.

By the time those few hundred stadium survivors crawled out of their cocoons and onto seats, having slept off the hangover of their lives, there was no one left for them to warn. They never got the chance to say what it felt like, share their new perspectives, and offer words of advice or comfort for what was to come. In that general sense, the misconception is true. It happened in a flash. We were there one moment and changed the next.

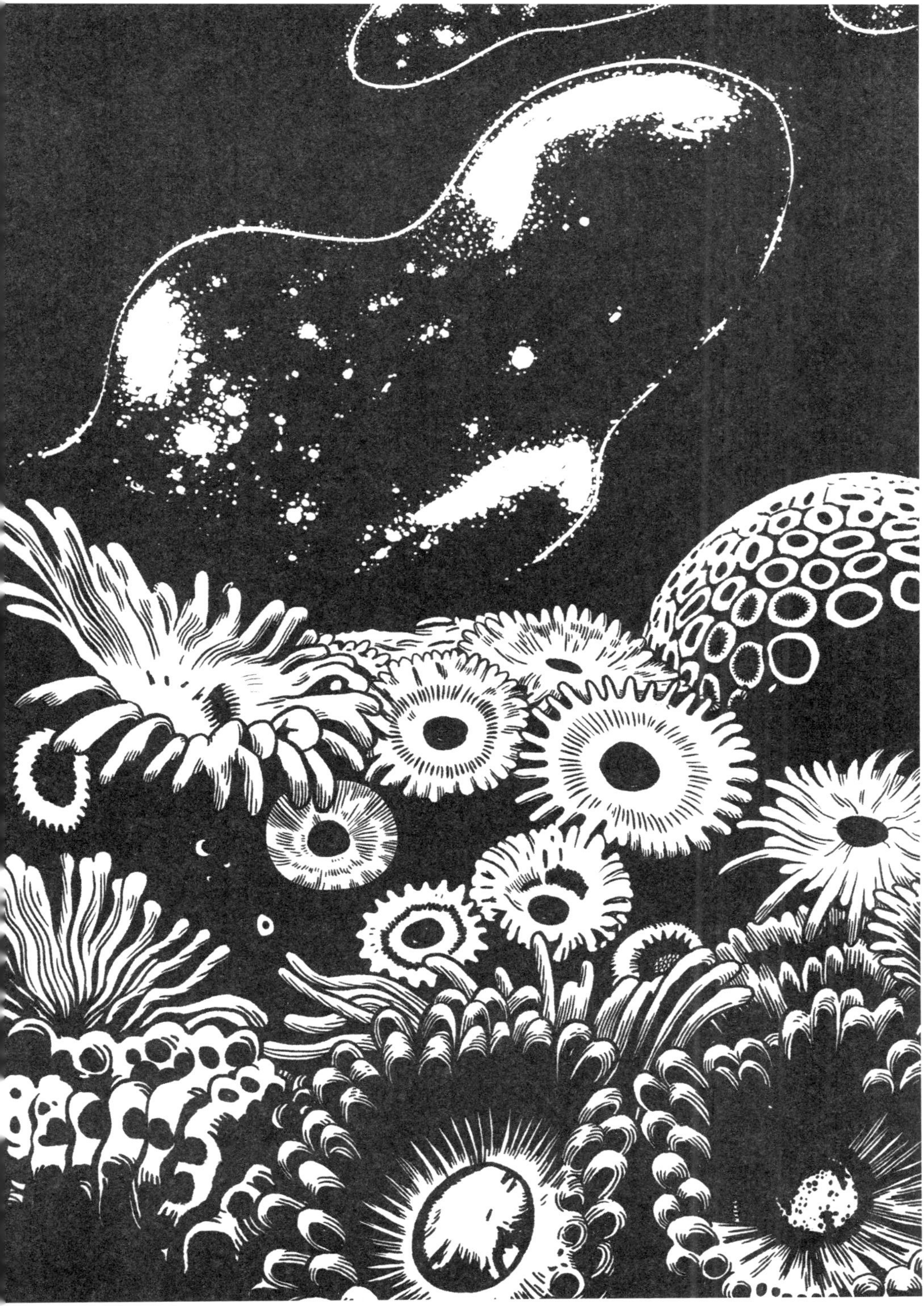

PART III

CHAPTER 11

THE SILVER CIRCLE

'This'll show the bastards, right William?' Goodwin and Laslett cheered each other – Goodwin with a lab beaker of whisky, Laslett with his flask of mead – then turned back to study the monitor, a dense 3D web of twisting white lines. Though it bore no resemblance to an actual brain, Goodwin was certain she could recognise her own connectome.

'You know what I was thinking about during the scan? I was thinking, if there were one thing I could say to Ms Coco-loco-phore – I'd tell her ... Well, first I'd issue some sort of grovelling apology for all the mess. *Then* I'd tell her that *we*, people, that is, can work it out. Patch things up. All we need to do, really, is breathe in. Slow down. Find a way to live in line with her, instead of—' Goodwin looked over to see Laslett was ignoring her entirely, fiddling instead with a knot of intestine-like tubes spilling from a cupboard. She clinked her beaker against the glass of the booth, stood as straight as was possible and cleared her throat. 'I owe you a great deal, William. I appreciate everything you've done here.'

Laslett raised his head, his face a mingling of surprise and suspicion. Then he smiled and continued connecting the capillary tubes from the pool to the stack of computer consoles beside three white tanks. The glass vessels, each not much larger than a bottle of wine, swirled with white clouds – a concentrated plankton solution arranged in the language of the Rosetta Disk, which spun gently atop a nearby terminal. Laslett had kept his promise, he'd transcribed her mind in bio-binary.

'I mean it. Your work here is, well – it's unparalleled.' Goodwin stood and added, with meaningful emphasis, 'The point is, I'm privileged to have you as a collaborator. Here's to you, Sage of the Circuit Board.' She raised her beaker, fixing the back of Laslett's head with a stern stare. 'Excuse me. I'm making a speech.' Laslett looked up, grinning.

'Are you going to cry again?'

'No, I'm bloody not. Shut up and drink up.'

Lowering their glasses, they both stared as the last white drop snaked through the tubes. Beside them, the small silver disk stopped spinning. 'There you have it – as promised.'

'It's strange how the colour changes, so much whiter.' Goodwin stroked the nearest tank. 'But frankly, I'm a little insulted the whole thing fits into such a small volume.'

'I shouldn't worry too much. Your mind may be contained, but your ego is forever unbound. Here, give me a hand connecting these up.' They sat midway between the pool and Goodwin's brain in a jar, and twisted together bundles of tubes, tying knots that would soon connect her connectome to the pool.

*

They were down to the last handful when they heard the music. Voices, singing in harmony, grew louder from the corridor on the other side of the pool. The double doors swung open, and the dome's acoustics came alive. Several figures stood in the doorway, led by a small man in a green velvet suit. They swayed as their voices resonated together into a frequency that made Goodwin's stomach shudder.

With more than a little flourish, the man in green caught an invisible fly between his finger and thumb and sliced the air with it, signalling the others to stop. Goodwin pulled herself up on the IV stand and strode towards them, face reddening.

'What in the seven bloody hells are you doing here? Get out. Private property!' she bellowed.

Leonard Leaf wandered in, with a casual ease and air of authority that Goodwin recognised immediately from decades of dealing with men who felt they had a natural claim to her work, to her building.

'I'm sorry,' he said. 'The door was unlocked. And I can never resist a little theatricality, given the opportunity. You didn't come to my concert, Dr Goodwin. Thought I'd show you what you missed.'

Goodwin stopped and squinted at the man, with his upturned droplet head and annoyingly neat haircut, as he kneeled and peered into the pool. 'You're Mr Leaf, from the choir.'

'Absolutely. Nice to see you again.'

'I told you, no site tours.'

Leaf, ignoring the remark, reached into his jacket pocket, withdrew a small disposable camera and wound on the film. He craned his neck, pointing the device up at the ceiling, which was writhing with eclectic blue snakes of light.

'Magnificent. The harmonics here are terribly interesting. I think the water rather deadens many of the high frequencies, but the dome adds some wonderful reverberations, bounces the sound all over the place, wouldn't you agree?' – *click* – he wound the camera. 'Fantastic construction. Worth every penny.' Leaf edged further about the side of the pool, pointed the camera at the glass booth and clicked again.

'Stop that. We are in the middle of a very complex procedure.' Goodwin blocked the narrow path beside the pool as the eight silver-haired choir members edged in behind Leaf. She could tell something was wrong by their body language, the way they spread out, moving as if in practised formation. Goodwin turned to face Leaf and prodded him hard in his ribs. 'What are you? Luddites? Crusaders? Here to smash things up? Burn the blasphemers, is that it?' Goodwin was shaking now, her IV stand rattling against the porcelain tiles.

'Please, Professor Goodwin, calm down.' Leaf's sharp little chin softened into a smile. Goodwin watched the choir filter around the room, as an over-cheery Mr Leaf sidestepped her like a crab and extended his arm to Laslett.

'William. How *are* you?'

Goodwin turned to see Laslett, a little sheepishly, take Leaf's hand, as Leaf, in the practised embrace of presidents, doubled down on his grip and turned back to smile at Goodwin.

'Laslett? What is this?' asked Goodwin, letting the IV stand take her weight.

'Elizabeth,' said Laslett, not raising his eyes to meet hers, 'I'd like you to meet Leonard Leaf, our generous benefactor.'

Leaf smiled. 'And I see it's all been put to excellent use. Worth *every* penny, truly.'

'What? What about the Oliver grant? I – I saw the paperwork.' Laslett looked up, and to Goodwin's horror, his expression was one of sympathy.

'Four years straight? Come on, Elizabeth. You knew about this. There was a reason you never questioned it.' Leaf approached Goodwin with his palms up.

'My dear Elizabeth – may I call you Elizabeth? We – myself, my friends here, Mr Laslett included, represent a group of individuals who have a great interest in your work – your *specialism*, shall we say.'

'And what interest is that?' spat Goodwin.

'Why, speaking to God, of course.'

Around a plastic fold-up table at the end of the pool, eleven people sat on upturned boxes and deckchairs in stubborn silence. Leaf sipped from a plastic cup.

'Umm, this is *lovely* stuff.'

'It's dog piss,' mumbled Goodwin. 'You're sitting on a crate of it. From Cash and Carry. *Cheaper* than dog's piss.' Goodwin refolded her arms and continued to glare at Laslett. 'Another of *his* choices.'

'I see.' Leaf dribbled his mouthful back into the cup and placed it on the floor. 'Elizabeth, the truth is, we've lost. Our current set-up is obsolete. The tank's empty, and we're running on fumes.' Leaf beamed jovially at an unresponsive Goodwin, then continued, quite serious. 'We can no longer plausibly dispute scientific reason. Our own narrative is full of too many contradictions, plot holes and leaps of, well, *faith*. It's simply not sustainable. Those unquestioning few are either stubborn or misinformed, and that just won't do, not in the long run. Truth will out, so they say.'

Goodwin's frown became the slightest smile as she began to enjoy the speech. Leaf continued.

'Though our story might be faltering, our continued role in

the organisation, and *unification* of humanity must continue. It's time we reinvented ourselves and scaled down our expectations of God. At least what our ancestors used to think He might be. Get the best of us back on board. It's time we stopped thinking about Him as some deity from an alternate dimension. People don't want *ghosts*, Elizabeth. They want something real. That's all they've ever wanted – a parent, something bigger than themselves to defer responsibility to. They want a cradling hand, a listening ear. And that is exactly what your work can offer.'

Goodwin stopped playing with her cup and asked, 'So you work for the church? Which one?' Leaf chuckled politely.

'Our organisation, the Silver Circle, supports the scientific pursuit of the divine. Alas, scientists of credential, such as yourself, are often hostile to our mission. Hence the clandestine nature of all this. I do apologise. Though I was straight about the name though, wasn't I? If it's any consolation, in the new arrangement, once we come out with your findings, I think you'd make a fabulous archbishop.'

At this, Goodwin laughed. Leaf and Laslett smiled too, feeling the tension ease a little.

'We've funded all sorts of projects over the years. Got it wrong plenty of times. We've had sentient nebulas, voices in hypersonic frequencies. Intelligent design theory, that was one of ours. We've had people looking for passages of the Bible spelled out in junk DNA. We all got very excited when the Genome Project announced DNA obeyed the same rules as human language. We pounced, as you can imagine. *The Genome Project*, you don't get much more legitimate than that. Of course, with a billion potential letter combinations, you can write "*God is the light*", but you can also write "*Zippy went to Toyland*". So that was that. Until we happened upon connectomes.'

Leaf looked to Laslett, whose gaze remained locked on his drink. 'Our greatest venture yet. If there were shadows in man's understanding, they lay within the folds of the mind – the eighty per cent of brain seemingly unused; surely those complex, shadowy webs were the perfect recess for the divine? Alas, what a letdown that turned out to be, hey William?'

Laslett's head dipped a little lower. Leaf placed a supportive hand on his shoulder and whispered a word in his ear. Laslett nodded, murmured thanks, and Leaf continued.

'Yes, a little disappointing. But then there I was, at your talk. We all were. With a little nudge, yours and William's paths converged, and now here we are, at the moment of truth! I'm absolutely tickled to bits.'

Goodwin drained her glass, shaking her head in disbelief.

'You people. Christ. First off, whatever you think you've contributed over the last four years is nothing compared to what I've sacrificed – *nothing*. You think you own this? You don't.' She stood, wrapped a shaky hand about her IV stand and set off in the direction of the glass-panelled booth.

'But, if you want to stay and watch, fine. I suppose you've earned that much. The data is data – however you want to spin it, that's up to you. People will see what they want to see. I always knew that. I don't care. But sit over *there* – on the other side – and no bloody singing. You sound terrible, by the way. I'm not sure what you're expecting either. We're just saying hello. We're not getting a hello back. This is simply making *Her* aware we're in the room – first contact. William, I'll need your help.' Laslett stood and followed obediently. Behind him, Leaf stood up.

'Fantastic. It was so important to me that you appreciated what we were trying to achieve. Now, yes – this first contact. You two carry on, just as you were, only, we'd like to suggest a slight change.'

Goodwin was already halfway about the pool, nearing the tanks, when a baritone with bulging eyes beat her to it.

'I told you to watch from over *there*, you blithering idiot,' spat Goodwin.

Leaf continued, shouting from across the pool. 'Yes, we'd like to change the *messenger*. We were thinking of someone with slightly better people skills, don't you agree? If this is *the* higher being, the wet nurse at the cradle of life, the shepherd who steered us from amoebas to anthropoids, don't you think a more *humble* servant should be the first voice they hear? And if there's no objection, I'd like to nominate—' Leaf irradiated the onlookers with his beaming smile then placed both hands on his chest, '—*me*.'

Goodwin turned to see him striding cheerily towards her along the pool's edge. *No*, thought Goodwin, *surely he wouldn't*. He would. Leaf did a little jump and clicked his heels.

'Over my dead body.' Goodwin growled.

Suddenly Laslett was standing between them.

'Leonard, this *is* just a test. It doesn't make a difference whose connectome we use. We're simply observing how the two languages interact, how they line up against each other.'

Goodwin turned on him. 'It makes every difference. We're saying hello to a higher intelligence. Of course it matters who's bloody talking.'

'I'm afraid I agree with Elizabeth here,' replied Leaf, 'there is a proper way to conduct moments like these, of great importance. Ceremonial, if you will.'

Shaking her head, Goodwin screwed up her nose. 'To hell with that. Not in my lab, you won't.' Goodwin patted a grey wisp of frizz back towards her scalp. 'I will make a perfectly serviceable ambassador.' Leaf smiled sympathetically as two choir members edged closer to Goodwin. She reddened. 'You arrogant little twerp. At least I know my place – *our* place. Whereas you? You think we're above it all. You don't want to *commune*, you want to suck up. You want to place us even further outside of nature. Well, I've got some perspective. We're not above it. We're a part of it, and so is She, so is my connectome. We use my connectome or no one's. God knows what sort of ideas she'd get from *you*.'

Laslett held his breath, watching the stand-off, and when Leaf chose not to provoke her any further, he risked an intervention.

'Come on now, Leonard. We're so close. It'll take months to map your own connectome. And then we'd have to transcribe it to plankton. We've been prepping Goodwin's since October. It's—'

'It's quite all right, William. We've made the preparations. The connectome scans are taken care of.' Leaf motioned to a choir member carrying a small, grey case. 'And the transcription – a matter of hours if I'm not mistaken?'

Laslett looked from Goodwin back to Leaf and conceded, 'A half-day's work.'

'Wonderful. So, let's get started.'

As Leaf turned, Goodwin saw her moment. She swung the IV stand at the baritone, knocking him back just enough to allow her to push past him into the booth. Several loose tubes spilled from the cupboard, and she began frantically plugging them into the console below the white vessels of plankton. Two tubes remaining, then one, and then – a cloth pulled over her face, the sweet smell of solvents filled her nostrils, stung her eyes, and a moment later the room went black.

A song swelled in the darkness – six ascending levels of harmony, layered one by one, building to a pitch that drew Goodwin back to consciousness. She screamed for it to stop but, lungs weak and tongue numb, only a low groan escaped her mouth. At last, a voice, thin and sharp as paper, cut through the melody, silencing the din.

'The pool, it's salt water?'

'Yes. Filtered of extraneous material.'

'And sealed off from the sea?'

'That's right. It's a test sample – the tubes lining the edge will map how Emiliania reacts.'

'Emiliania – that's the pool?'

'Oh, yes. There are many sub-species of coccolithophore. We believe each of them forms a part of the mind, serving a specialised function. Emiliania Huxleyi is the most common species. Hence the name.'

'So, the pool here, it's composed entirely of this *Emiliania Huxleyi* variant?'

'That's right. She's the best performer in lab conditions, the most stable.'

'William, when we converse – you and I – do you segment your mind?'

'Pardon?'

'Do you separate your memories from your ability to reason, your visual cortex from your primal reflexes?'

'Well, no. I see where you're going, but—'

'I don't talk to severed limbs, William. I talk to *people* in their entirety. In our case, that would be the Ocean, would it not?'

'Mr Leaf, sir, the *pool* is how we monitor results. Here, we can measure the response, keep it on record. We might be able to translate it, one day. After all, that's what . . .' Laslett lowered his voice to a whisper, 'That's what *the other team* are working towards, isn't it?'

'You're completely right, William. But this moment – it's not about monitoring and measuring. You've been around *that* woman for too long. Don't you see? It's about the *connection* itself.'

As her eyes grew accustomed to the light, Goodwin saw that she was still inside the glass booth, sat in a thick office chair, and to her left, a heavy looking steel crate had been wedged against the door. Through the glass, she saw Leaf gesture to the ceiling and around the room, a gesture that took in the broken table, the spilled bottle of mead, lichens crawling up the outer walls.

'None of this is right. We need to do this *our* way, somewhere a little more fitting.' He tapped his foot and started to hum. From across the pool, the choir members harmonised with him. Goodwin gave a muffled yell of discomfort and slapped feebly against the glass.

'The harmonics in here really are fantastic. William, the coach is parked outside. Show the chaps what we need for the transcription, just the essentials.'

Drowsily, Goodwin watched as, piece by piece, the choir members dismantled her lab and ferried it from the room. She must have drifted off again as she woke to find Laslett gone and Leaf facing her through the glass.

'Elizabeth, you must forgive us. You'll be cosy enough in there, I hope. The cushions should be comfortable to sleep on, and we've stocked the crate with plenty of food and water to keep you going until tomorrow. I'll send someone back when we're ready to carry on and then, dear colleague, you can run all the little tests you like.'

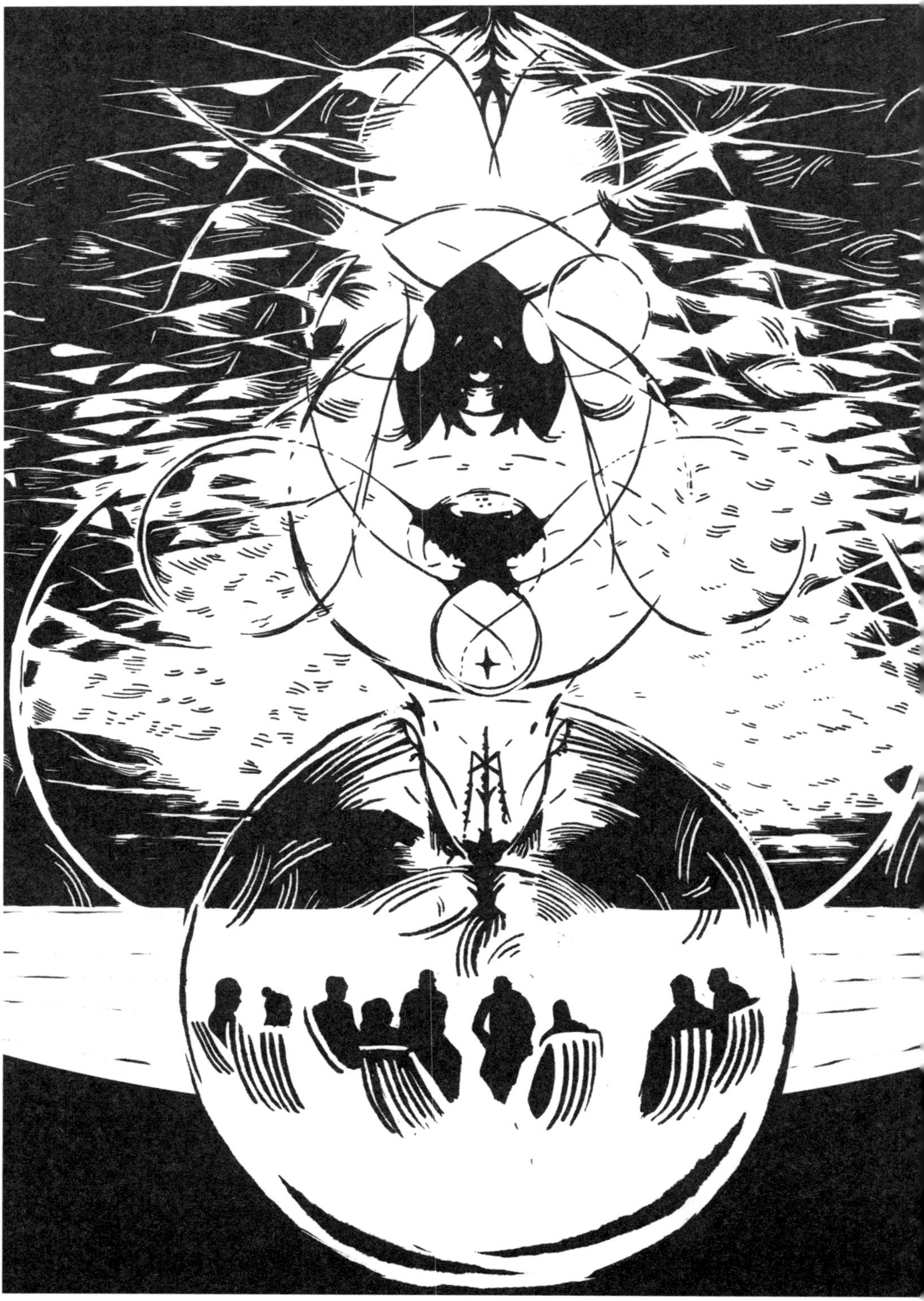

CHAPTER 12

GALLEON

On the face of it, the plan seemed impossible. The image of his old family car – a weathered red square-box sedan – being piloted by a team of six, had raised more than an eyebrow from Ashraf. But as the two of them discussed the details, the less they laughed and, by the time the fifth design had been scrapped, it was a question of *how* and not *if*.

Giles rolled finger and thumb around a dewdrop caught between forking blades, pressed his lips to the meniscus, and drank.

'How's that?' asked Ashraf, flattening the grass beside him with a wheel of black electrical tape.

'Best dew I ever had,' said Giles.

'I'd murder a coffee. Laced with hard liquor. Or psilocybin.

Or – you know, Isabel just caught me eating instant granules. Disgusting, to be fair. Have you noticed how everything tastes disgusting now? Well, not disgusting exactly, just *intense*? Like it used to, but more so. Bigger molecules for the tastebuds, maybe?'

'Why didn't you add water? To the coffee.'

'Yeah, 'swhat she said. Let's try this then.'

Ashraf bent and slurped a freshwater droplet. 'Ech! Even the water tastes like soup ... So!' He clapped his hands, making Giles jump, 'You definitely wanna use that grandaddy car of yours?'

Giles shrugged apologetically.

'It's not too late, you know. We could still go with my camper van,' pressed Ashraf with an imploring grin. It was a broad and easy smile, pinched at the corners, infectious, even with half the teeth missing.

'Sorry, Ash. The sedan's automatic. We don't have enough people for a manual.'

'What are you talking about, man! There's a bloody army of children back there!'

'They're *children*,' said Giles. Ashraf frowned.

'Would children do *this*?' he pushed back a length of hair re-vealing crude, offensive biro drawings down one side of his neck.

'Yes. Though that one does seem rather ... mature.'

'OK. But come on. Van's cool as crap. Fold-out tables. Pop-roof. New stereo.'

Giles hesitated, pretending to weigh it up as an option. There was a brief stand-off of wincing grins, and then Ashraf broke.

'Yeah, fine, OK *captain*.'

'Think about it this way,' said Giles, 'whichever vessel we choose, something tells me it's not long for this world.'

*

The two of them set off towards the row of cars on the other side of the field. It might have been easy to get lost in the tall grass were it not for several saplings and their protective mesh tubes that towered above the canopy like Victorian gasometers. Giles lugged a large battery pack, keeping pace with Ashraf, who was easy to spot thanks to his whistling and flamboyance of costume, refreshed this morning with strips of fluorescent fabric tied about the torso below a yoghurt pot lid sombrero. On the side of the outfit hung the Hello Kitty pin badge. Not for the first time that morning, Ashraf slowed, quieted, and stroked the enamel. He stood stock still, and Giles stopped behind him, knowing exactly where his mind had wandered. The buzz of an insect brought Ashraf back, and suddenly brightening, reanimated, he fixed Giles with a lopsided grin and resumed his whistling.

By mid-morning, they had made good headway. Screws had been drilled about the circumference of the steering wheel, serving as handholds on what now resembled the helm of a ship. Unlike a ship, *two* helmsmen were needed to work either side of the wheel, pushing up when the other pulled down. Giles shuffled the battery over to Ashraf, who heaved it into the base of the drill. Then, after much huffing and kicking of feet, Ashraf hugged the handle. A jolt ran through them, the drill clicked into life and the screw sank another inch into the pillar of wood they had levered up against the base of the driver's seat.

'A platform to stand on! Solid as a rock. Sort of.'

It had taken two long hours to build the platform, screwed directly into the plastic below the wheel, and two seconds for it to collapse the moment they stood on it. After some bickering, they arrived at a second solution – a short deckchair plank, one end resting on the glove box, the other held tight by squeezing it into the cushion of the driver's seat. Simple, effective and, 'Not to toast my own crumpet ...' entirely the result of Ashraf's engineering acumen.

Driving the car would require six people – two to run the floor pedals, one for the gears and handbrake, and two more to steer the wheel. All that remained was to cut an indent into one of the headrests for the final team member – the navigator, perched high enough to see through the windscreen, whose job would be to co-ordinate these disparate people into one body.

'So, there's you, me, Isabel, Richard and Alwyn. We're still short by one.'

Ashraf smirked, 'Looks like you're giving up the captain seat to a wee one, after all.'

With Isabel's help, the car was soon packed and ready to go. Giles squirrelled away his building materials in the footwell, cramming the space with tools and batteries. The customisation of the car had been a welcome distraction, a purposeful pleasure, and he wondered how else he might put his hands to use.

They climbed the makeshift network of steps into the back of the vehicle, where the seats were folded down to form a large open area padded with sleeping bags, pillows and plenty of socks.

'It's weirdly nice in here,' observed Isabel, pushing a barrel of curried beans up the gangplank and letting it roll into the space behind the driver's seat, already packed out with food and water.

'At least there's no danger of starving. This should last us months,' noted Giles.

'So long as you don't like your food fresh,' said Ashraf, then added brightly, 'which I don't.'

*

With the sedan made ready for its maiden voyage, Giles and Ashraf joined Alwyn and Isabel inside the domed tent, huddling in beside an A to Z atlas of Britain. Outside, the gleeful laughter and raucous shouts of the Pack came through the canvas like a broadcast from the old world. To close your eyes and listen, it was as though nothing had changed. These twelve children, as newly minted as their adult counterparts, continued to adjust to their unfamiliar state at a pace Giles found disconcerting. With all they'd been through, how could they be running, laughing, playing? Evelyn poked her head through the tent zip, panting, her dark skin flushed red. A smaller child clinging to her shoulders cast a shy look through coils of hair at the assembled adults, then shuffled back from view.

'Anyone seen the matches?'

'What for?' asked Ash.

'Arson,' Evelyn shot back, then rolled her eyes. 'A *campfire*. Going to toast some mallows, if it's *OK* with you?' Isabel rummaged in a wall pocket, and passed a small box to Evelyn, who nodded thanks and hurried from the tent.

'How are they doing?' asked Ash.

'I've spoken to them. They understand we can't stay here,' said Isabel.

'Maya OK with that? She slept in her own tent last night. Want me to have a word?' asked Ashraf.

'She was all right once I said she could bring things with her, only what she can carry. Same for everyone. Said to meet back here in one hour.'

Ashraf eyed the field nervously. 'They shouldn't be out there.'

Isabel sighed.

'Richard's with them. They'll be fine'

Giles took the map and ran his finger down the index, coming to rest on page forty-six: the New Forest.

115

'So, what's the route?' he asked, flipping to the page.

'You're not going to like it,' said Isabel. She spun the map to face her. 'I know you wanted us to head towards that place – Waterhole?'

'*Waterlow*. Waterlow Manor,' said Giles, tapping a square of green in the lower corner of the page.

'Right, Waterlow. But we've got a bunch of them from Dorchester, another from Bath, two more from Newbury, Evelyn's from Woking, Maya the Isle of Wight, some villages I haven't even heard of, oh, and that little boy on Evelyn's shoulder, I think he's from Leeds.'

Giles pinched the bridge of his nose.

'Leeds? No. If we can get this car out of the field it'll be a miracle, let alone Southampton. *Leeds*?'

Isabel heaved the A to Z to the front page and showed Giles the route she and Alwyn had plotted, scrawled in pencil up and down the length of the British Isles. Giles held the corners of the poster-sized map, creasing it at the edge.

'I can't go this far. I've got to get *here*.' Giles tapped the page again. 'There's a message from one of my daughters here, on an answerphone. It'll tell me where they are.'

'I heard what you said, and I know what you meant,' Isabel interrupted. 'You'll help us as long as we go your way. I understand that. But – and don't take this wrong – but you need six people to operate the car. Ash and I, we're heading for London. Winchester, Waterlow, where you're heading, it's good for us. It's on the way. But these others—'

Giles pushed his wiry hair away from his face.

'How do we know that there'll be anything, *anyone*, waiting for them when we get there?'

'We can't kidnap a dozen children, Giles. They could still have family, people they know.'

'Sure, but this journey would take weeks, months maybe. If it's even possible. My youngest, she's—' Giles found a spot of empty canvas to focus on while he gathered himself. He turned back to Alwyn, Isabel and Ashraf. 'Let me find my girls. I – I don't know where they are, but if I can hear that message . . .' He circled the spot on the map and began scrawling a new line across the page. 'Waterlow Manor. That's a two-hour drive away, or at least it used to be. I'm guessing it'll take us a day at most. It's a safe haven – a good base. We'll do the school run from there. Even Leeds if we have to. OK? All of us.'

Isabel looked from Giles to the map and was about to reply when Alwyn leaned between them.

'All right. Time for my two pence. We don't know the first thing about diddly-squat out there. For all we know, the world is normal, and we'll be making a living as circus attractions for the rest of our lives. Or not. The whole place could be up a walloping turd-riddled creek. Then again, we might find something organised, proper like. Red Cross or my old regiment or what have you, to help us out. My point is, no sense in making plans and promises. Let's just get going, out of this field, and take it from there. All agreed?' Giles and Isabel looked ready to continue arguing, but Alwyn didn't give them a chance. 'Good. Now, how's about a nice cup of tea to settle the spirits, ay? Get the knots out your socks. Brew should be about ready.'

Alwyn shuffled behind a suitcase and re-emerged, holding a jar lid. Balanced on top was a colourful assortment of bottle caps, sloppily filled with brown liquid. Ashraf took a tentative sniff, then a sip.

'Not too shabby. Got any biscuits?'

Alwyn's ancient face crunched and reformed into a wrinkled smile. He shuffled off again, waggling an excited finger in the air. A moment later, a wheel of digestive rolled over and settled between them. Giles sipped the tea, feeling his insides warm, and for the briefest moments they were just four people sharing tea. He exchanged a look of bemusement with Isabel as Ashraf leaned forward and, with a cry, karate chopped the biscuit in two.

A few tents away, near the edge of the tall grass, a ring of stones surrounded the charred remnants of a long-extinguished fire. Atop the rocks sat the Pack. Some cradled their neighbours in protective embraces, muffling quiet sobs, while others idly kicked their dangling feet, lost in thought. At the circle's centre stood Richard, ankle-deep in ash, speaking in soft, earnest tones. The stones, arranged as they were, had become a henge, casting the priest in the role of a druid or shaman. As Giles approached, Richard clapped his hands, wrapping up his sermon.

'For now, let's be thankful we have each other. So, who still has items they'd like to take with them?' Two boys, slightly younger than Evelyn and Maya, raised their hands. Richard sighed, then smiled wearily.

'Of course. Alex, Jayden, let's go then. Giles, would you mind watching the rest while I serve as escort.' Giles looked uncomfortable, but before he could protest, Richard was ushering the boys away, despite their insistence that they were old enough to go by themselves.

Giles startled as a young girl with wild black hair and cruelly cracked skin scrambled up a rock behind him. In her arms was a pink toy troll, topped with a shock of bright purple hair, its prominent choke-hazard warning laughably obsolete. In other ways, the inflation in scale had improved the toy, making the once fine detail appear rough and loose, like folk art. Again, the same thing but bigger, was not the same thing.

The restless children were a sad sight, reminding Giles of wartime refugees about to board a train to the countryside. If Ashraf were here, he'd walk between them, rustle their hair and lend the moment some levity.

'Stop,' shouted Giles at two girls wandering into the long grass in the car's direction. They turned sheepishly. 'Don't want you getting lost in there. Easy to do so. We'll all go together.'

Giles ushered them back to the group, noting that they were shy of him, avoiding eye contact. That wouldn't do. He was nothing to be scared of, though admittedly, so far all they'd seen him do was help kill a giant dog. He waded into the ashes, to the spot where Richard had stood.

'Hello everybody, can I ...' his voice squeaked. Giles cleared his throat and called louder. 'Oi!' Heads turned. 'Hello. *Hello*. Yep, over here. Now, I know haven't had a chance to get to know you all yet, but I'm looking forward to that.' He pressed a hand into his chest and beamed at the circle of blank little faces. 'My name's Giles. In a minute, we'll set off for the car. There are no seatbelts – none we can use at least – so we've tried to make it as soft as possible in there, because you're probably going to get thrown about a bit when we're on the road and we don't want to be scraping any of you off the ceiling – ha ha.' The few children actually listening stared at Giles with absolute terror.

'That – that was a joke. Nothing's going to happen. You're quite safe.' This wasn't going well. Giles wondered how Richard had handled them. Said something profound, probably. He adopted a more serious tone.

'It's been a strange and sorry couple of days. We're all scared. We're all lonely. And now, more than ever, we all have to look out for one another. If you see a friend without a smile, give them one of yours.'

He was starting to feel like he was on a roll when the girl with the troll sat up and asked, 'Where are we going?'

It was a good question and with it, the children shuffled, giving him their full attention.

'The plan is to take you all home. The problem, well. The problem is you live in different places, around the country. So first, we'll go somewhere safe – a base, if you like. Then, we'll look for people who might help us, like the police or the army.'

'Grown-ups?' asked a boy wearing what Giles could only guess to be a goalie glove. The extra fingers gave him the appearance of having four legs.

'Well,' said Giles, slightly offended. '*I'm* a grown-up. But yes, *more* grown-ups. And if we don't find any, we'll set about taking you home ourselves. That sound like a deal?' The girl with the troll scrunched her forehead in hard concentration and then extended a tiny hand.

'It's a deal.'

Giles heard the tall grass rustling and turned to see the two boys, Alex and Jaden, approaching the edge of the stone circle, dragging a T-shirt bulging with toys, snacks and some sort of digital tablet.

'Where's Richard?' asked Giles.

'Oh, he said to carry on. He'll catch up. Something about attending to nature.' Alex, the larger of the two, chuckled, scratching at his downy blond moustache. Giles walked over to the grass. There was a rough track, but really he should cut a proper path, a perfect job for the snap-blade scalpel, back at the tent.

'Right. Wait here,' he said to the children. 'I'll be one minute.'

*

As Giles approached the tent, he noticed an unusual hush. Stepping across the threshold, his skin prickled with the feeling that something was out of place. Isabel kneeled at the nearest edge of the rug with her back to the door, gently stroking a figure nestled in fur. Moving closer, Giles saw thin, outstretched legs and then Alwyn, laid prone, his eyes fixed on the ceiling, glassy and lifeless. Beside him lay the snap-blade, shimmering crimson in the matted wool, wet from the blood pooling beneath a cut, deep in his neck. Giles let out a cry and stumbled back.

Isabel startled and spun, her green eyes stark against her pale face. 'Giles?' He steadied, then raised his arms as if approaching a wild animal.

'What – what happened?'

'I – I don't know. I found him, just now. He's dead.' As if noticing the knife for the first time, she shoved it away. Giles picked the scalpel up, retracted the blade and tossed it towards the door, as far away from them as possible. Isabel repeated, '*He's dead*,' her voice muffled through hands cradling her face.

The blade had sliced through Alwyn's clothes and, judging by the stains on his hands and the trail on the rug, he had clawed the wound and staggered through the tent before falling. Could the injury have been an accident? Had Alwyn been playing with the knife, perhaps trying to push the handle down, and slipped? He took in his pallid face, Alwyn's mouth a shocked black hole, and a sting of recollection hit Giles – a floral shirt where the flowers bloomed red. Not wanting to look at the body, he turned to help Isabel pull Alwyn's broken robes back in place, feeling a tremble as she rested her weight on him. Giles brushed a hand against the older man's head. Still warm. An accident, it must have been. And yet, there, conspicuous as the slice on his neck, sprouting from between Alwyn's hooked fingers, were several strands of dark brown hair confirming the truth. Alwyn had been killed.

'Anyone here when you came in?' asked Giles. Isabel, swaying slightly, shook her head, her eyes still fixed on the body. Giles took in the rest of the tent, trying to pinpoint what exactly had felt so out of place upon entering. There on the far side of the space, between airbed and suitcase, he saw a vertical line of light, a door where there shouldn't have been one. A shadow flickered across the gash in the canvas and Giles called out – *'Hey!'* He ran forward, leaped over Alwyn's body, squeezed past the airbed and tumbled out through the gap. 'Hello?' he called again, but besides soft wind stirring the hip-high grass, the field appeared empty. Still scouring for movement, Giles called back to Isabel. 'Better get everyone together, to the car, out of this—' The words caught in his throat as he turned around. A figure stood behind Isabel. At first he thought it might be an animal, a rat, its silhouette a rough oval of matted hair. Except as it moved into the tent, it did so on two feet, stepping so quietly Isabel hadn't noticed.

'Hey!' Giles squeezed back past the airbed. Isabel looked up, confused. The figure took no notice and instead, it stooped and quickly rose up again brandishing the discarded knife. Giles stopped and, following his eyeline, Isabel turned, screamed and scrambled away from the stranger in the doorway.

'Who?' stammered Isabel.

Giles knew. It was the same woman he had glimpsed through the fire. He'd dismissed the memory as delirium, a product of exhaustion from the encounter with the dog. But here, closer, in the light of day, she was a tangible certainty. Giles put her somewhere in her late sixties, though the cracked skin that afflicted them all made age hard to judge. Though slight and sinewy, he could tell from the way she moved, bouncing silently from heel to heel, that she was agile and strong. Her colouration, a rich rusty red, appeared to be a thin layer of clay which caked her from head to toe, contrasting against her near-black hair, busy with small sticks and leaves. Her only concession to clothing was an ornately patterned metal tube worn on one forearm, like a plaster cast.

The woman turned the knife curiously in her hands and extended the blade with a familiar, ratcheting *click-click-click*. Giles glanced from Alwyn's body to the knife, to the torn doorway behind them.

'Let's go, very slowly,' he whispered, pulling Isabel by the hand. But she refused to budge.

'You. *You* did this?' she was shaking with anger, and Giles felt her strain against his arm, as she readied to launch herself at the woman. At that moment, Richard strolled breezily into the tent.

'Shall we try and get a couple more—'

Startled, the woman spun, swinging the scalpel in an arc. Richard fell back, crying out and clutching his chest. As he fell into the grass, Isabel dashed forwards, barrelling into the woman, knocking her off balance. Giles was quick behind her, and the three figures pitched through the tent door. For someone so small, the woman was surprisingly sturdy, and the red matter covering her skin made her slippery and evasive. They tumbled in the grass, struggling for the upper hand. At last, Giles had her by a grip around one wrist and was hoisting her to stand when he felt the sting – a slice so sharp it took a moment to register the pain. Then a hot spill covered his hand and Giles let go, staggering backwards and clutching his shoulder.

She was feral, animalistic, a creature masquerading as a person – Giles was sure of it now. She dropped the scalpel and hissed, exposing a smashed piano smile. Giles could see Isabel creeping up through the grass behind her and, too late, he realised he had given away her position. As Isabel lunged, the wild woman was already turning, her arm held up, and seconds later the metal armour landed against the side of Isabel's head with a painful clank. Isabel fell away, clutching her temple, and as Giles stumbled forward, the woman dropped to all fours and raced away into the shimmering grass.

They waded into the field. Isabel and Giles carrying the limp forms of Alwyn and Richard, the latter slung over Giles's good shoulder, moaning softly. Across the other, the string handle of the snap-blade rubbed against the fresh laceration. The children, still strewn about the firepit stones, quickly sensed something was wrong and turned to gasp at the sight of the wounded quartet.

'Let's go!' shouted Giles, gesturing with the outstretched blade, 'To the car!' Ash emerged from the grass nearby and stepped in beside Giles, helping take Alwyn's weight.

'What happened?'

'She . . . she killed Alwyn,' said Isabel.

'What? Why? Who?' stammered Ashraf. He cursed and wiped a hand over his face, his brow scrunched. He punched the leathery leaf of a nearby plant. Then again. 'He was just a lovely old bugger. Made tea and . . . *hell*.'

Giles shook his head in agreement. He couldn't believe what he'd just seen, what was happening – the cold immediacy of Alwyn's death, the uncanny spectre of the red woman.

With Isabel and Ash leading from the front, the Pack hurried into the grass forming a kind of convoy, snaking through a field that felt increasingly like a forest – the seeding yellow grass trunks stretching higher above their heads the deeper they went. They were past the first of the three sapling towers, the red-box sedan just visible above the canopy, when a voice ahead cried out, shrill and indistinguishable. Giles strained to listen. It called again and Giles made out Maya's voice, and the word 'dog'.

Forty metres ahead and lumbering closer – a twin of the canine Giles had helped kill. A twin, he thought, or perhaps a ghost. A hush fell over the party and instinctively they crouched, nestling down into ankle-high roots. He couldn't imagine a rougher, more tangled terrain through which to escape at pace. They had done well not to panic and run, if they had, they might have been caught in the undergrowth like flies in web. Ten metres out, the creature paused to sniff the air, and as its head turned, Giles quietly gestured the nearest trembling children to make their way slowly towards the far sapling tower. As they set off, a twig snapped underfoot and the dog's head swung towards them, brushing the grass overhead, carrying with it a gust of earthy, salty air. Giles lowered Richard to the ground and readied the blade, ineffectual against a creature of such size, but perhaps it would buy them valuable seconds. Towering less than a tail's length away, the dog snorted. Twin blasts of hot wet breath suffused the grass. Then it relaxed, its mouth lolled wide, and it thudded away from them a few paces before it stopped and buried its head into Alex's abandoned T-shirt, with its bounty of biscuits and chocolate. They seized their moment and ran, their pace hastened by the sound of teeth grinding shortbread.

Giles was the last to reach the sapling tower, where he rested against its supporting wall of blue tubular mesh and let Richard slide to his feet. Ahead, the Pack, led by Isabel and Ash, nimbly hopped through the maze of roots and thick grass towards an open stretch that led to the car. The final run. They were going to make it. Giles was steadying Richard back over his shoulder, readying himself for this last dash, when a faint piercing tone cut through the air. Abruptly, the sound of frenzied canine consumption stopped. The dog raised its head, its powerful black snout contracting in and out. The note sounded again, closer this time, both shrill and barely perceptible. The animal agitated and, at the same time, movement flickered in Giles's peripheral vision. He turned to see, not three feet away, the red woman. She crouched in the grass, matted hair melting into the network of soil and roots. Cradled in her lap sat the metal cast. Staring unflinchingly back at Giles, she pressed her lips to the stubby silver tube and blew with all her might. The note rang out and behind Giles, the dog, biscuit crumbling from its mouth, turned to face them.

Giles felt the thud of paws reverberate along the ground. While the wild woman had disappeared into the grass, the others too had wasted no time. Exposed as they were on the open path, they had no choice but to run. Seeing the dog's attention drawn their way, Giles screamed, shouted, making as much noise as possible to draw the creature away from the convoy. As it altered its path again, and leaped closer, Giles tried to remember that this was just someone's pet. It had a name like Syrup or Strudel. With no hope of running, Giles turned and pushed Richard through a gap in the blue mesh, and then tumbled in after him, coming to rest against the sapling's trunk.

A moment later the dog's impact sent the sapling and its protective case lurching sideways. Jaws closed around the tube to the sound of groaning metal and splintering plastic. In that incongruous moment, an idea struck Giles and, resting Richard at the base, he quickly scaled the trunk as the dog let go and backed up, preparing for its second lunge. Elevated now, Giles breathed in and made himself as big as he could. He looked the animal in one eye and bellowed, 'SIT!'

To his surprise, the dog faltered, cocking its head to one side.

'G-good boy,' stammered Giles, and in as loud and commanding tone as he could muster, he tried again. '*Sit, boy, sit!*'

The dog panted and adopted a grin so absurd that Giles couldn't help but nervously return it. 'Yes, *yes*, that's it. Good boy, sit.' Giles coached, shaking with relief and exhaustion. Slowly, its hind legs lowered – then it leaped forward, toppling the mesh tower and sending Giles crashing into dry mud. He rolled and lay still, mouth filled with dirt and blood from a split lip. Nearby, Richard lay wheezing, clutching his chest. Behind them, the hound loomed. A growl like the rumble of a truck engine passed through him and the dog leaped again. Giles pulled Richard close and braced for pain. None came. Instead, an anguished animal yelp forced his eyes open. The dog was on the ground, frantically gnawing at the mesh tangled around its hind leg.

Giles seized Richard up again and, ignoring the strain of his entire body, ran for the clearing. Isabel and Ashraf hurried to meet them, and together they hauled the wounded priest up the plyboard gangplank and into the sedan.

The door swung to close behind Giles as the dog broke into the clearing. Feet from reaching the vehicle, a siren sounded, and the animal staggered. Startled, unable to stop, it crashed headlong into the side of the sedan, bouncing against the door as its snout reached around the frame. The animal winced and Giles stumbled forwards, intending to shoulder it free. His palm slipped sideways on the wet nose, landing deep in a nostril. Unable to dislodge his arm, Giles was sure he'd be pulled from the car with the retreating dog when three things happened in quick succession – the siren sounded, the dog sneezed and Giles was sent violently backwards, sprawling onto the seat.

Claws scratched on metal. Behind the car door, which might

have been the blast shield of a bunker, the huddled survivors held their breath and listened until, eventually, the creature padded away. Isabel lay Richard on his back, inspecting his chest wound. The cut didn't appear to be too deep. Still, he wailed as they lifted him over the handbrake and onto a folded backseat. Giles dug in the footwell for the first aid kit as, above him, Alex and Jaden punched the indicator handle, sounding the siren, recognisable now as the melodic car horn. As Giles climbed back onto the front seat, dabbing his own cuts with an antiseptic wipe, several small faces peered about the headrest, watching him.

'Got some admirers,' whispered Ashraf, nodding back at the line of children. The dark-haired girl with the troll, her once soft features cracked like glaze on old chinaware, gave a small wave. Giles returned an uncomfortable nod, then climbed up onto the dashboard and looked out over the campsite, searching for signs of the woman or the dog. Seeing only the gentle undulations of grass, Giles slipped down the dashboard and took up his position on the steering platform. He motioned to Maya and Evelyn, 'You two, on the pedals.'

'No time for a test drive?' asked Ashraf.

'I guess not,' said Giles. Lying flat on his belly, he pushed his shoulder against the key, twisting it until the engine juddered into life. Lights flickered along the dashboard, and the vibrations scattered the line of children into the back of the car. Giles jumped down, shuffled the gear stick into drive, and then lowered the handbrake.

'Isabel,' Ashraf shouted back into the car, 'wanna be captain?' Wiping her bloodied hands on her jumpsuit, Isabel scrambled up the side of the driver's seat, wedged herself into the headrest and fastened a twine seatbelt about her waist.

'Who *was* that woman?' asked Ashraf as Giles joined him on

128

the platform and gripped the opposite rungs of the wheel. 'Why would she do ... *that*, to Alwyn?'

Giles craned his head to peer through the window, again. Nobody had any answers.

'I guess not everyone's as well adjusted as us lot.'

He looked up to Isabel, still silent and staring out over the campsite from her high seat in the headrest. Giles followed her gaze to the smouldering ashes, the clothes strewn between guy ropes and, in the far distance, the shimmer of an unnaturally white ocean.

'Isabel. Where to?' asked Giles. Without looking down, she answered.

'Anywhere. Anywhere away from this God-damned field.'

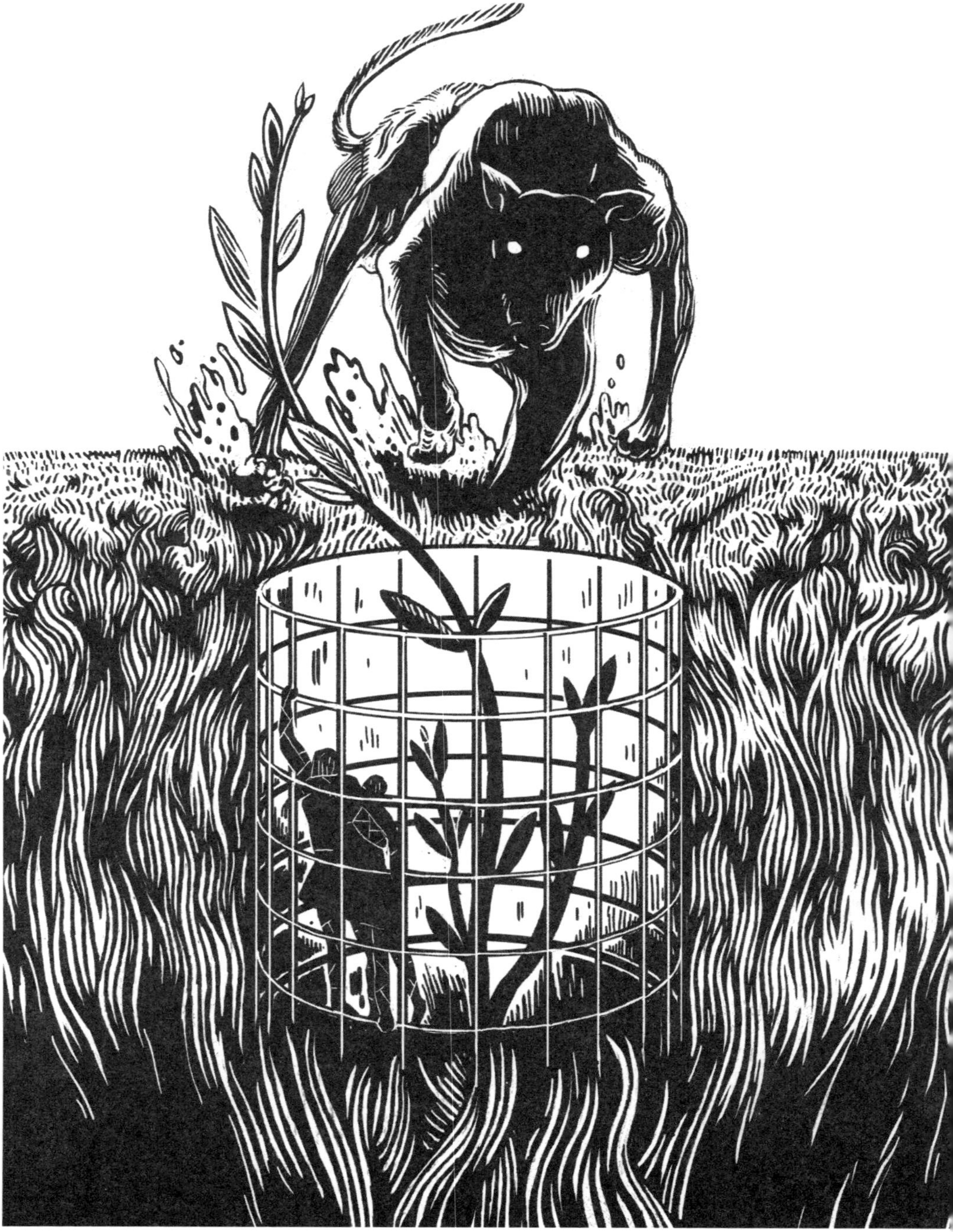

CHAPTER 13

A GLASS BOX

Goodwin pressed her palms against the door of the booth and heaved. Many hours had passed since Laslett and the choir had sealed her there, since they ferried her equipment away to perform their pointless ceremony. The metal cabinet on the other side of the door showed no sign of shifting, and Goodwin fell back, defeated. She would have shouted, called for help, rattled through her ample range of profanities, but her voice was already hoarse from doing exactly that. Besides, there was no one left in the facility to hear her.

Slumping back into the office chair, she bit a fig roll in two and chewed angrily, scowling at her reflection in the glass. Those psychotic evangelists had taken her equipment, her dignity and her only friend. But the thing that stirred rage in her veins was that they were going to talk to God without her. And what's more, they'd take all the bloody credit. This had been Laslett's plan all along. She could see it now – the snake.

To add to her humiliation, she had been imprisoned in a free-standing box made of glass. *Glass.* Ten years younger and she might have had the strength to topple the cabinet blocking her exit or swing her IV stand through one of the panels. Not now. A lobbed stapler had bounced off one of the windows and narrowly missed her head. More behaviour of that sort would likely land herself an injury. She looked to the supplies left by Leaf's cronies – a crate spilling water bottles and protein bars, and a bucket that didn't need much explaining – and sighed. The safest bet was to do as she was told and wait for their return. Mr Leaf would open the door, all false smiles and apologies. She could picture the group, Laslett included, laughing quietly. Perhaps, just to spite them, she'd die. The thought gave Goodwin a jolt of sardonic pleasure, imaging Leaf and his crusaders, their smug little smiles dropping when they opened the door to find her dead. That would put a dent in their Holy Quest.

To hell with it. Goodwin shuffled to the far corner of the booth, unhooked the IV bag from the stand, slipped it into her jacket pocket, and hobbled at speed towards the door. Her shoulder crunched hard above the handle, and for a moment the door shifted forward, just an inch. Then the weight of the cabinet on the other side pushed back, sending her tumbling over the crate, onto the floor, her elbow cracking a console along the way. She lay there, sprawled out amid the toppled bucket and scattered plastic wrappers, staring defeated up at the ceiling. Then she saw it. A way out – a loose ceiling tile revealing a widely spaced beam. An awkward shuffle later, Goodwin was climbing up onto the seat. She stabbed at the ceiling with the butt of the IV stand, cracking the tile in two, releasing a waterfall of tiny white balls.

After half an hour, surrounded by a snowdrift of polystyrene and fibreglass, Goodwin gingerly climbed a jaunty staircase of stacked crates, chairs and folders leading from the console, up through a sizeable hole in the roof. Untangling herself from a web of cables, and brushing her clothes, she emerged on top of the booth, triumphant and free at last. There was just the small matter of how she'd get down. She was toying with the idea of sliding along the length of the cabinet wedged against the door, when the decision was made for her. There was a crack. The rim of the booth, not designed to take weight and softened from years of exposure to moist pool air, gave way. Goodwin yelped, tumbled backwards over the edge of the roof and disappeared into the pool.

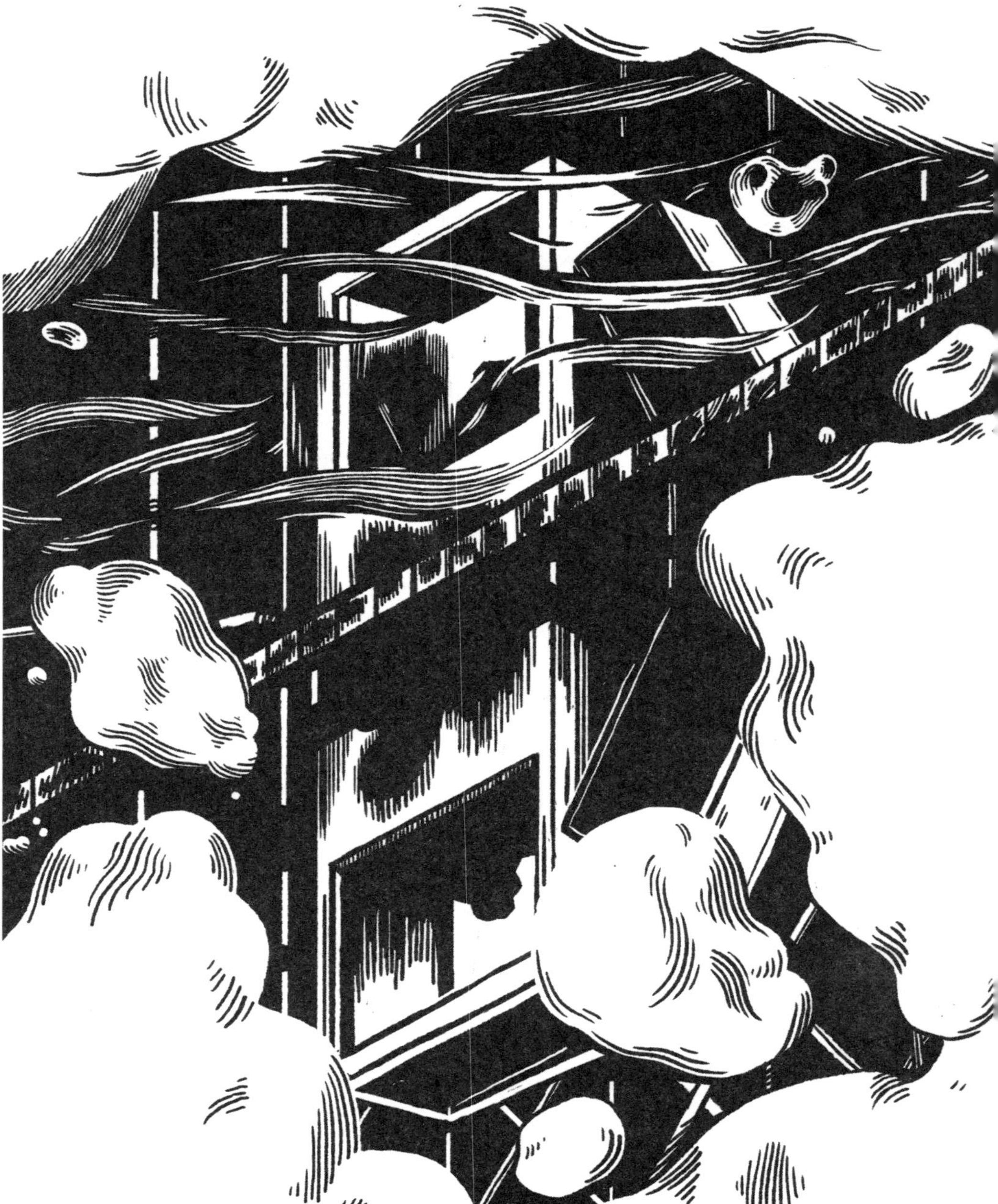

CHAPTER 14

TROLL

It came as a genuine surprise to Giles that coordinating several shrunken strangers to operate a single vehicle was *not* straightforward.

'Delusion is the engine of achievement,' proclaimed Richard as the passengers climbed back into their seats, having been thrown forwards from another violent lurch.

The car had been in motion for less than a minute when, under instruction from Isabel to '*proceed cautiously*', Evelyn had punched the accelerator flat, and the car had ploughed into Giles's flower-patterned box-tent, buckling it in two. Giles's groan was joined by a discordant chorus of children's screams as Isabel, clinging onto the headrest and bracing for further impact, cried, 'Brake! *Brake!*'

'You, down there. What are your names, again?' called Giles, his arms wrapped about the steering wheel for support.

'Who, us?' asked Maya, the imp-like girl who had reminded Giles so much of Sadie. She drummed her feet nervously against the brake pad.

'Of course he means us,' said Evelyn, sat beside her, feet either side of the accelerator.

'I know that. It's Maya. I was just—'

'Never mind,' interrupted Giles, 'from now on, your names are Stop and Go. Maya, you're *Stop*. You. You're *Go*. Got it?'

'Fine. Whatever,' answered Evelyn, scowling up at Giles.

'OK, you – Jayden.' The stocky boy peered around the gear-stick. 'How about we put this guy in reverse.'

Several awkward manoeuvres later, the vehicle passed through the gates at a steady snail's pace. Giles and Ashraf got the hang of the wheel, careful not to overexert from one end, feeling the pace from the other side, pushing the handholds up one by one. Cautiously, the vehicle wove through the tents, narrowly missing a large pothole as they pulled out onto a track.

Isabel called directions, instructions, trying to find the right tone of encouragement and authority. 'Right – right. OK, go. It's so hard to make spatial sense of it all – everything feels so bloody close. Left. It's like driving a house.'

The caravan canteen by the campsite's entrance looked deserted, apart from two piles of clothes slumped over a picnic table. The bodies had long since been replaced by a pair of squawking sea-gulls, who pecked happily at an abandoned box of chips.

Ben, the little boy who had been clambering on Evelyn's shoulders back at the tent, dressed now in a customised knitted mitten, craned his head out from the side of the driver's seat and asked, 'Do you think birds will want to eat *us*, too?' Giles looked up at the swarm of gulls dogfighting against a sky of overcast clouds.

'Not you, I'm afraid. You're far too scrawny,' smiled Giles. Ben smiled back, and Giles continued, matter-of-factly. 'Polecats and badgers, on the other hand, they'll eat just about anything. They can squeeze through the tiniest of gaps and—'

'What's a polecat?'

'A weasel, but wild, bigger. Like a wolf to a dog. They like to keep their dinner alive by piercing the skull with a long tooth, then—'

'Ahh, don't worry, Ben,' interrupted Ashraf, 'we don't have things like that in boring old England.'

The boy was gawping at Giles in absolute horror.

'Oh, polecats are quite common these days,' Giles continued. 'Reintroduced to the New Forest a decade ago. Actually, there's been an amazing rejuvenation of wild animals in Europe. There are bison on the back of Poland. Wolves forty miles from Paris. Otters in Devon.' Ashraf shot Giles a concerned look. 'Right, sorry. But we're safe in the car. Nothing to worry about.'

'Ben,' said Ashraf, 'what did I say about being in the foot space while we're moving? Birds and polecats will be the least of your worries when that bag of marshmallows smothers you to death. Go on, take one for the group and get back up there – ye scally-wag.' Little Ben scrambled back, tugging a pillowcase of puffed sugar behind him.

'You know all their names?' asked Giles, heaving upwards on the wheel.

'Oh, you know. Pretty much. I've done a whole load of children's workshops and stuff. The really young ones are the best. It's like hanging out with drunk people. You have to hold them up. They bump into things. They cry, laugh, wet themselves.'

'Just like the real thing,' noted Giles.

'Exactly. So don't worry, I'm well-seasoned to deal with this lot, but I guess you are too. You have kids, two girls, that right?' Giles nodded and glanced at the back seat. Little Ben bounded onto a cushion and began tearing sticky chunks from the marshmallow and handing it out.

'We should make a register or something,' Giles suggested, then looked up to see Isabel watching him.

'Eyes on the road, Isabel.'

'Right,' she replied. Ashraf pushed up, and brambles scraped the wing mirror. 'No, no, I mean, *correct*. Ha. OK, left a bit.'

Exploiting his comparative advantage in height, Giles peered over the dashboard. The road from the campsite was quiet, no sign of life. Nothing suggested that the world had changed, at least for some of its creatures. A field flanked them on one side, its hedgerows well-trimmed, home to a single horse, grazing and oblivious. Further along, neat blue fences led past saplings that gradually thickened into forest. Moving on, the road hugged the hillside, a thin winding country track squeezed between steep drops on one side and tall conifer trees on the other. It was only when the roadside brambles condensed into a low wall of green that Giles noticed the first hole, a break in the vegetation flanked on one side by a tree whose bark had been deeply gouged. The vehicle that had caused the damage was nowhere to be seen, lost somewhere in the valley below. There were no tyre marks in the road, and Giles noted, with some solemnity, that whoever had careened off that edge hadn't even applied the brakes.

The driving was difficult, and the team kept alert, listening and responding to each other's commands and observations. Perhaps it was a blessing that the road twisted in the way it did. Had other vehicles come to a stop, their path would have been blocked. On

138

a sharp corner, where the road turned into a gully, they saw their first crash up close, a burned-out metallic husk that blackened half an oak tree.

'Should we stop and look?' Isabel asked, without conviction and when no one answered, they moved on. Breaking the crest of the hill, silver birch and beech trees peeled away from the road to form a clearing, and the landscape was laid bare before them. The hills rose and fell, like the earth breathing in and out. Here, a barn house. There, a field with cattle.

'Stop, stop a second,' said Isabel, pulling herself up straight and squinting through the glass. 'There.'

The road sloped down to a T-junction where several cars scattered the left-hand fork. One car pointed up from a ditch, its wheels dangling in mid-air. Two others embraced head-to-head, the result of a collision, while two more were wedged snugly into the hedgerow.

'Another crash. Want to look for survivors?' asked Giles.

'No. Well, yes, sure – but look.' Giles squinted through the glass, following Isabel's outstretched finger.

'You see somebody?'

'Police tape,' said Isabel, her frown breaking into a smile, '*Police*.'

They approached slowly, and an excited murmur filtered back through the car.

'You're sure about this?' asked Ashraf.

'Yep. Right now, I'd be thrilled to get arrested. A nice warm bed, my very own cell to keep out the beasts. Go, edge the car forward, slowly,' said Isabel as the bonnet broke the police tape like the chest of a marathon runner through ribbon. The children pressed their noses up against the windows in the back of the car, searching the scene for morbid details that did not reveal themselves. The drivers had lost control, and like the others, there were no tyre marks on the road. They had collided at full speed, the car's front halves an indistinguishable knot of machine parts and frayed metal. Attempts had been made to wrap the wrecks in plastic sheeting, but the weather or something else had torn the material into strips that hung limply on the ground.

Ashraf squinted through the glass. 'What's with the sheets?' Giles shrugged.

'Trying to seal something in, perhaps?'

'These look a few days old, at least. Let's keep weaving through. Left – left – right,' instructed Isabel.

'The accident could have been from before,' suggested Giles. 'You know, before we changed. This could just be a regular crash.'

'Five at once? No, look,' said Isabel, pointing through a tear in the sheets to an open car door. A pile of stained clothes strewed the driver's seat. 'What happened to us, happened to them. It's the same thing'. Two diversion signs stood guard at the other end of the crash site, and Ashraf added, hopefully, 'The police *were* here.'

The car pressed forwards and nosed through more tape that fell unceremoniously beneath the wheel.

'If there are regular people out there, unchanged by whatever happened to us, then we'll find them,' Giles assured, but as he said it, he felt his stomach twitch in disappointment. Shamefully, he had hoped that their transformation *was* universal. A new world in which there was if not the promise, then at least the possibility, that he might finally be of use. He thought of his daughters. The message from Sadie. They were safe. They were small. And he would help them. Indeed, in this new world, only he *could* help them.

'Let's carry on,' Isabel called down from her seat, 'This road should take us all the way up to Southampton.'

'How far off are we?' asked Giles. Outside, the light was fading fast, swept from the landscape by a broom of long shadows. Isabel eyed the dimming hills.

'We won't get there before dark, and I don't like the idea of arriving in a city at night.'

Giles, thinking it best not to argue, replied, 'Let's – let's just get as far as we can, then find a place to pull in.'

'Ah, Southampton,' mused Ashraf, with an air of worldly wisdom, 'if the best roads lead to the worst places, let's hope the opposite is also true.'

They could have stopped in the middle of the road for the lack of traffic, but habit corralled the group to pull up onto a gravel patch beside a wooden gate. Giles sat on a flattened headrest, looking over the mounds of cushions and pillows, illuminated by the dim ceiling light. Most of the children had settled down to sleep, and Ashraf moved between the clusters, tucking them into socks, pulling the hem of a T-shirt up over a huddle of three, all the while softly singing a wordless tune.

At Giles's feet, Richard slumped against the side of the headrest in a crumple of cloth, still visibly drained by his injury, a manilla plaster wrapping his chest illuminated by a small thumb torch. He looked up at Giles.

'Such a difference it makes,' he said, pulling the makeshift bedding further up his lap, 'the fabric not being soaked in excrement. Greatly improves one's sleep, I think.'

'Good to see you're feeling better.' Giles smiled, then instinctively pushed the slung knife further behind his back. Richard had been lucky, luckier than Alwyn, whose body he and Isabel had just finished burying behind the gate. Giles wiped muddy fingers on his robe, its floral pattern duller by several shades since it was cut. 'This blade. An inch closer and … You should count your blessings.'

'Oh, I do,' replied Richard earnestly, 'so should we all.' There was a brief silence, then Richard added, 'You know, I never asked if you'd like to talk about your father.' Giles was startled by the statement and began picking invisible pieces of fluff from the headrest.

'Oh, don't worry,' Giles smiled unconvincingly. 'You should rest.'

'Consider it my pastoral duty. Now,' Richard straightened up, assuming a more dignified posture, 'was there anything you would have liked to have said to him, given a chance?' Giles shifted uncomfortably.

'Did you bring that from your tent?'

'Pardon?' Richard looked up, confused.

'Your torch,' said Giles, pointing at the little light in Richard's hands.

'No, no. I found it in the back here. Must belong to one of the children. I wasn't camping. However, I have camped there once or twice with nephews. Lovely place. No, I live at Calshot Castle. Now, your father—' Giles's eyes widened.

'Is that where you were? At the castle? When you woke up?'

'Hmm? No, I – I was at my parish. The church at the back, which isn't far off, actually. The dogs, they belonged to one of my parishioners. Horrible things. Never got on with them. Hunting breeds. Chased me for hours. I must have travelled a mile, at least. Every time I fell into a ditch, hid in dirt or crossed a stream, somehow, they'd find me again.' Richard itched at the plaster.

'Perhaps they could smell the, well – I assumed it was blood you were covered in when you first came running over that field?'

'Oh, this?' Richard examined the cracks running up his arm. While the lines in Giles's skin were a darker shade of his natural pigmentation, those criss-crossing Richard glowed with the redness that had once covered his whole body.

'Not blood. I – embarrassing really – I must have fallen into a shopping bag.' Richard gave a feeble laugh. 'Woke up covered in spices, as if it could get any more ridiculous. I was going to make a roast veg stew for the parishioners. Stung like the devil, I tell you. But there was so much else going on it hardly mattered.' With a nod of assent, Giles took Richard's thin bony wrist and turned it in his hand, examining the red stains.

'If anything, the – paprika, is it? The spice would have muffled your human scent. Where I work, I sometimes scatter that kind of thing – chilli powder, citrus, mothballs even, about the chicken coops. Keeps the foxes away. Might just have given you a head start.' Richard mused on this a moment, then clapped with delight.

'Is that so?! I tell you, Giles, my blessings are multiplied manifold upon themselves.' He smiled and gave Giles's shoulder a gentle squeeze.

'How far are you planning on coming with us? Don't you want to find somewhere closer to your parish? Closer to your church? You know we're heading towards Winchester.'

Richard sighed, patted Giles's hand and then looked away.

'Oh, well, who knows what we'll find out there. And besides,' his voice fell flat, 'there is nothing on this earth that could take me back to that place. What I saw, when … I was the *only one* who …' His voice trailed off, then he turned to Giles, smiling again. 'I am more than happy to tag along wherever it is you're going. I'm – I'm far more content with a flock to help shepherd.

143

Now, I'd ask again about your father,' he winced, holding his side as he shifted about in his fabric fold, 'but you're off the hook. I believe Ash is trying to get your attention.'

From behind a side seat, Ashraf waved his arm, gesturing for Giles to come over.

Tucked up to their necks in wool, a gabble of small faces looked up to Giles as he rounded a mountain of sleeping bag.

'Right, you lot – Giles, meet the seven dwarfs. Dwarfs, meet Giles, the Big Friendly Giant.'

'We met already,' said a well-spoken young boy with a pronounced fissure that ran down the middle of his face, 'and there's only five of us and I resent being called a dwarf.'

'And I resent being called friendly,' said Giles, frowning at Ashraf. 'You can call me the B.U.G. – the Big Ugly Grouch.' Giles pulled a playful scowl and there was a smattering of actual laughter.

'Well, *Grouch* here will give me a hand making sure you all have a restful night, ay? He's going to keep watch, keep us safe.' Reading Ash's cue, Giles planted his fists into his hips and pushed himself up to full height, causing his back to click. The gabble stared, wide-eyed and Giles held their gaze.

Ash grinned and whispered, 'Nice one. Got this from here.' He turned back to the children. 'I'm so bloody proud of you lot. You've been dead brave. We'll be on our way in the morning. So, to sleep now.' And with that, he began his quiet song, and Giles, sensing his moment had passed, wandered away.

Half an hour later, Ash joined Giles, who had set to walking the length of the vehicle, weaving through the sleeping bundles, in what felt like a night-watch patrol. With barely contained excitement, he waggled a piece of paper at the taller man.

'I present you with … a register!' On it, a dozen or so crudely rendered portraits jostled for space beside a list of names. Giles smiled.

'Very … efficient.'

'Ah, well. Never do a job half done. Or something. Chilly in here, ay?'

'It is,' agreed Giles, stepping between two pillows. 'Might be our metabolism, or …' He put his hand against the glass then licked his palm and waved it about him, like a mime exploring the inside of an invisible box. 'Can you feel that?' he asked, 'It's a breeze.' Giles crouched on all fours, shuffled among the blankets, and then, leaning forward as if into a dive, he let the fabric swallow him up.

'Giles, where'd you go, mate?'

Moments later, Giles emerged from the folds at the back of the car. 'Ash, come and see this.' Ashraf followed, sliding down behind the pillows to find Giles hunched on the floor, reaching into the dark. The breeze was subtle but distinct.

'It's coming from here. The boot, it's open.'

'No. Boot was shut. We checked it, I—'

'I know. I checked it too. It's been popped since we parked up. We would have heard the alarm if it was open on the move. Here, help me with this.' Giles and Ashraf gripped the boot door, let it rise above their heads, and then yanked it down until they heard a click. Giles found Ashraf's face in the dim light, a grim look spreading across his lopsided features. 'The boot, it was opened from the outside.'

Moments later, Giles was in the footwell, snap-blade scalpel slung about his back, throwing aside packets of firelighters and paracetamol and tossing several cumbersome torches up onto the pillows, where Maya and the older children gathered them up. Ashraf leaned over the edge. 'I checked the register. We're missing Elfie.'

'Who?'

'Aelfrieda. A little one, about six or seven. Black hair. Carried a goblin doll. You seen her?'

Giles shook his head and scrambled up footholds cut into the folded seat.

'Turn on the headlights. Point the torches out of the windows.' Spotlights lit up the road ahead, and one by one, fingers of light stretched sideways and combed the ground around the car. Two children manoeuvred each torch, weaving the lights about the field gate and hedgerows, across the tarmac and into tall conifer trees that skirted the forest's edge. Giles, Isabel, Ashraf and Richard hurried between the passengers, pressing themselves up against the glass, searching. Shifting in the breeze, the verdant landscape became a Rorschach test, every mossy rock and twisting branch suggesting a human form.

'There, starboard side,' called Isabel.

'What side?' asked Giles, bounding over the pillows in strides that sent him careering into the rear windshield.

'On the left, see, by the embankment.'

Giles saw her. In the darkness, the child was near indistinguishable from the other organic forms that rustled and swayed with the wind, but there she was. Her long black hair obscured most of her back, but her troll, a small purple sprig of it, stuck out over one shoulder. Giles went for the passenger door, and Isabel slid down beside him.

'Stay,' said Giles, 'In case. They'll need you more than me. Just keep the lights pointed my way.' Isabel nodded.

'Take this,' said Richard, throwing Giles the thumb lantern.

146

Isabel kicked at the door handle, and Giles dropped to the gravel outside.

The girl was over the embankment, staggering through grass towards the woods. As well as the troll, she had another object in her arms, and Giles skirted sideways to get a better view. *Christ, I've forgotten her name*, he thought, crossing the road and reaching the embankment edge.

'Hey!' he cried, 'Little girl,' but the wind had either blown away his words or she had chosen not to hear them. Strange sounds came from the blackness ahead, and Giles's imagination gave colour to the noises, adding legs and claws and teeth. Blurred human shadows entangled with brambles. He shuddered, trying to shake away the feeling of being watched.

From atop the embankment, the shadows clarified into sticks, grass and stones. Giles relaxed a little. Perhaps the car boot hadn't been firmly shut after all. The girl might have slipped out by herself. But another thought had wormed its way to the surface of Giles's mind and sat there, squirming for his attention. The wild woman. In this gloaming, he'd never see her coming. The way she moved, so powerful and fearless, conjured feelings of terror in Giles and of awe too. Were they all destined to become like her – feral, untamed, and recluse? Had their transformation not simply been a reduction in size, but a descent into savagery? Then again, maybe the woman wasn't even here. Hadn't he watched her dissolve into the grass roots back at the campsite, disappear in stark daylight? The idea that she had emerged and clung to the sedan as they drove away was highly improbable. Ridiculous, even. He allowed these thoughts to comfort him, enabling him to tread with confidence. Then he saw what the girl was carrying.

Wrapped in both arms, resting on top of the toy troll, was a stubby silver tube. With the tiniest of jumps, the girl hopped off the embankment's edge, into the forest and out of sight.

'Shite,' whispered Giles as he slid down after her and away from the light of the car.

His thumb lantern, tucked beneath one arm, was dwarfed by the enormity of darkness, a white drop in a black ocean. Brambles with knife-like thorns coiled above him like pythons, meeting in knots to form what might have been a series of ornate, demonic gates. As Giles shuffled through, a scattering of tiny legs ran over his foot, and he redoubled his grip on the snap-blade scalpel.

'Hey,' he hissed, 'little girl.'

If there was ground in front of him, Giles couldn't see it. Each step was a small leap of faith that ended with his feet sinking into mud, soaking his shoelace sandals. Perhaps he'd be better off losing the lantern, let his eyes adjust to the dark, but as convincing as the logic might be, his hunger for light was stronger. Insects clicked. An owl hooted. Vast tree trunks barrelled above him, and Giles followed a network of roots up to a hard mossy bank. He felt his way around the bark, following the sound of tiny snaps ahead until he reached a wall of dry grass.

Pushing the papery curtain aside, Giles whispered, 'Little girl?' Two green orbs, as large as dinner plates and an arm's length apart, descended upon him. He screamed and fell backwards through a carpet of leaves that cracked and split. The orbs retreated. He heard a crunch of feet, and then the creature advanced again. There was a green flash, and Giles swept the extended snap-blade upwards, hitting the beast straight between the eyes. The predator fell away, folding into the darkness. Giles stood shakily and thrust his lantern over the ground, revealing the beast to be nothing more than a moth's mottled wing twitching among the leaves. Cursing himself, Giles stumbled forwards.

'Hey, little girl!' he called louder as he scrambled back through the grass curtain. Behind it, illuminated by a clearing in the canopy above, were two large fallen logs, moss draped across them in sheets that hung like wet hair. Beneath them stood the girl, looking left to right as if lost in a supermarket.

'Hey there, my friend with the troll,' whispered Giles, and was almost at her back when she turned. She looked up, her cracked glaze face startling.

'She left it behind,' explained the girl, showing Giles the silver tube.

'I – I know. You can't be out here, sweetie. Come on. I wasn't kidding about the polecats, you know. What's your name?'

'Aelfrieda.'

'That's right, Elfie.'

Giles had the girl by the hand and was leading her back towards the car, when something skittered through the low branches above them. Without hesitating, he scooped Elfie up in both arms. The troll fell from her grip; the silver tube followed. As she protested for him to stop, wriggling to get free, she kicked the lantern from Giles's hand, sending it to tumble beside the other items.

Giles was all set to ignore the lost possessions, ready to run with Elfie through the pitch black, when an inscription on the illuminated tube caught his eye. As he leaned closer, in his peripheral vision, a mass of matted hair descended slowly onto the moss-laden logs. An animal? Or perhaps – Giles darted back, knocking the wood pile and causing a shower of woodlice, each the size of a bread loaf, to scuttle out from the folds of wet bark, their sharp little feet tapping staccato across his shoulders, back, chest. The figure, most certainly human, leaped from atop the logs and landed out of sight. Shuddering, wriggling to be free of the crawling creatures, Giles scrambled, slipped his free arm through the open end of the silver tube, and with Elfie cradled in the other, he ran. The figure pursued them, bounding on all fours.

Wearing the metal tube over his right arm, Giles swept the brambles aside as he stumbled back towards the headlights that dappled the trees ahead. He hurled Elfie up onto the soft embankment, then crawled after her, turning at the top to see the figure behind them rise onto two legs and dart into the undergrowth. A moment later, the person emerged through nearby branches, straight into the beam of a torch, shining from the car. The light dispelled any remaining doubt – the red woman had followed them. She was here, in these woods. She shielded her eyes from the torch, then shrank back in alarm like a sea anemone prodded by a finger.

With Elfie safely in his grip, Giles ran for the car. The door creaked open, and to his immense relief, there was Ashraf reaching down. With Elfie safely back in the sedan, Isabel helped pull Giles onto the seat where he lay sprawled, shaking, catching his breath. Something scrambled on the gravel outside and Ashraf pulled the door shut with a slam. Giles collapsed, panting and brushing dirt and the memory of woodlice from his robe. Isabel climbed up from the footwell, brandishing a strand of purple hair. 'This was trapped in the door,' she explained.

Opening the door a fraction, they pulled Elfie's toy free, caught between the door and the frame. 'I think she was trying to give it back.'

A half dozen small faces peered down at Giles from around the seats. He turned to Maya and Evelyn, who were straddling the steering column, sharing the weight of a small torch. 'How about we use that central locking?' With a squeeze of the starter key, the five doors about the vehicle gave a satisfying electronic click.

'Nice armour,' noted Ashraf. Giles unslung the snap-blade, slipped the metal tube off his arm and rolled it onto his lap.

'It's *hers*.'

'Then what you doing bringing it back here? Let her have it. Jesus, Giles.'

'Look. Look at the tube,' insisted Giles, rolling it under the light.

As the tube turned, Giles showed the others what he had seen beneath the logs, caught in the lantern's light. Intricate engravings of men on horseback, a pack of hounds, a fox. Giles smiled at Ashraf, Isabel and Richard.

'It's a dog whistle.'

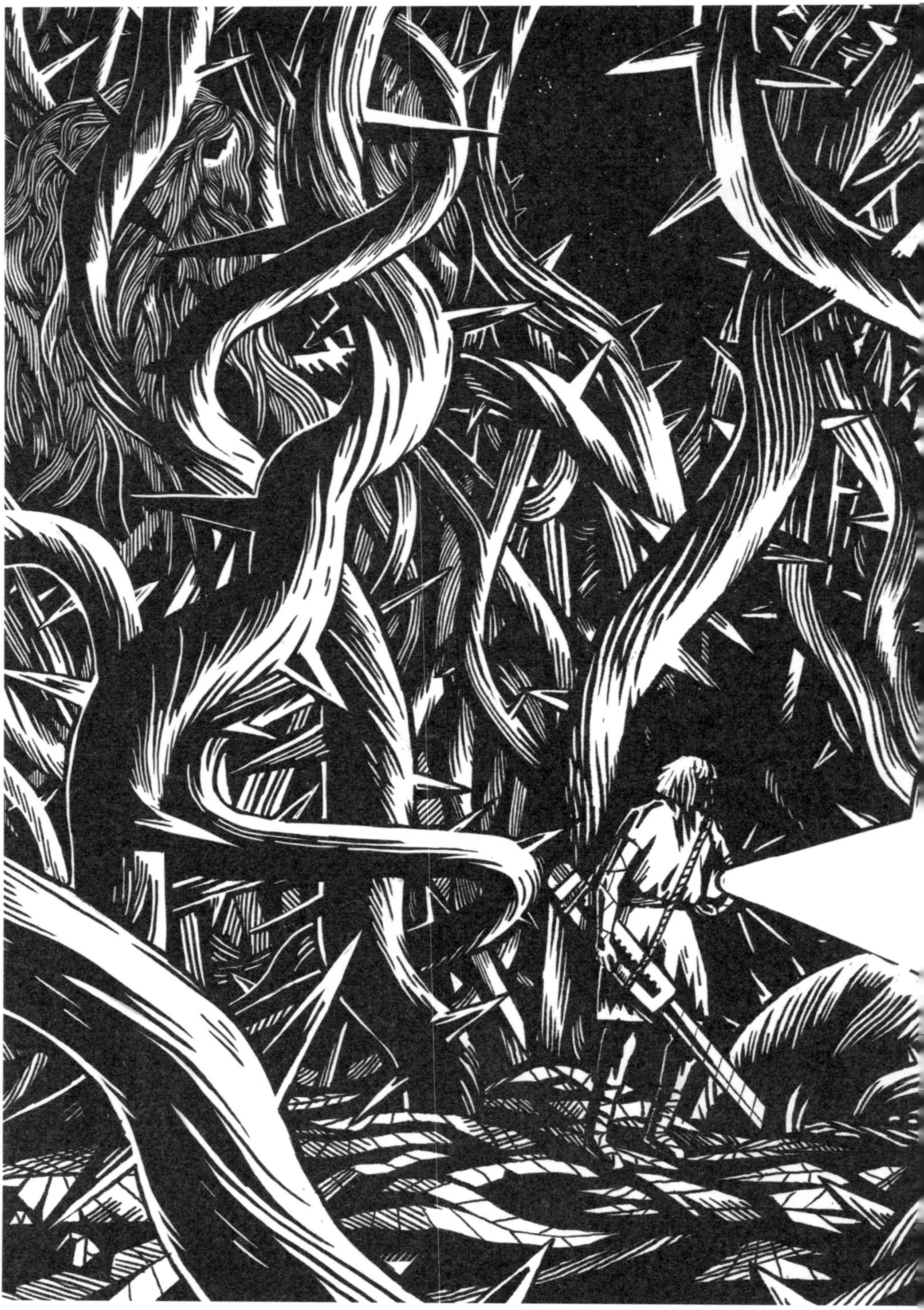

CHAPTER 15

ELSEWHERE, THE
LEGEND of SIMA QIAN

Many of those who knew what was coming tried to run away from the sea. The furthest you can run on earth is 2,645 km before you start to run back towards the sea again. To get this far, escapees would have had to be running through a Chinese desert near the Kazakhstan border, towards the Eurasian pole of inaccessibility, the furthest point from the ocean on earth. Nobody made it, but if they had, they would have met Sima Qian. He would not have had much to say to them, even if they did speak Mongolian, because, due to his long-standing battle with leprosy, Sima Qian had no tongue.

On the morning of July fifth, year one, three days after the Descent, Sima rose at dawn to go and see his nearest neighbours,

153

the settlers of Suluk, eleven kilometres due east, blissfully unaware that the world had irrevocably altered. He made this trip once a month, carrying baskets atop his head woven from the colourful shrubs that grew near his shack. At Suluk, he would trade these baskets for dried meat and fish and other such good things. Sima was thankful that his hands had remained strong over the years while so much of him had waned.

The significance of the shack's location was not lost on Sima. The spot had been marked out twenty years earlier by two British explorers who had cycled from Bangladesh, up through Tibet and ceremoniously buried a letter in the dismal ditch. The remote nature of the spot, the location of that letter, was the very reason Sima had built his shack there. It was both a point of pride and a reminder of his shame, that he had been banished, figuratively speaking, to the centre of the earth.

Sima was at home in the landscape – his cracked, brown skin was a beautiful extension of the water-starved ground beneath his feet. He walked in all weathers, monsoon, heatwave and dust storm but was thankful that this morning the conditions were favourable.

The baskets balanced on his head shaded his eyes from a cool sun, a breeze was behind him, and his spirits were light. He arrived at Suluk by mid-morning, and though donkeys brayed in the backyards and linen blew between the mud-brick houses, the town was otherwise silent.

He was about to look up when a stone hit him in the head. Smiling, Sima kept his eyes downcast, for he did not want to frighten the children with his face. How could he be angry with them? Had he not played similar games as a boy? Besides, he was used to this kind of treatment. Though his visits were tolerated, they were not warmly received. '*Sima the Leper who smells very*

154

bad,' was the usual cry from these local children on his approach to town. The only surprise now was the size of the stone. It was little more than a pebble. Sima's heart sank. Had they lost interest in his visits? The ridicule had at least been acknowledgement. Far more terrible to be ignored.

As he rounded the corner to the market square, he stopped in his tracks and his baskets tumbled from his head, into the dust. Hard-baked mounds of clothes littered the ground. And they were crawling with creatures. At first, he thought they were rats, then one of them stood up. They were clambering over the piles, pulling items from pockets and rolling pieces of fruit towards the alleyways. At last, he recognised them. The town had been taken over by dozens upon dozens of Ta'ai.

Sima pressed a free finger and thumb into his eyes, trying to rub away what was surly a heat stroke induced delusion or, at last, his illness addling his mind. His grandmother had told him tales of the Ta'ai, the small people. The shrunken devils who lived beyond the prying eyes of ordinary folk. Now here they were, for real. *The Ta'ai!* They had taken over. Sima gurgled a cry. The cursed beasts had slaughtered the village and were feasting on their remains, just as it had been told in the old stories. He was about to flee when, as though in answer to his sob, a howl rung out from the far side of the square.

There, emerging from the tannery door, was a black Kunming wolfdog. Like Sima, these wild dogs had been a problem for the village. They were shot, and eaten sometimes, and Sima might have felt an affinity with them had they not, on several occasions, chased and bitten him on his walk home. The dog too must have heard his grandmother's stories, thought Sima, as from the shaded doorway, it snarled and barked at the tiny devils scavenging their spoils of war.

The Ta'ai scattered as the dog leaped, snapping and tearing at them as they tried to escape. Yes. This was the thing to do. Both he and the wolfdog had been rejected and unloved, but together they would avenge the fallen villagers. Sima clapped his strong hands, brandished a rusty spade and ran into the square. Ta'ai dived beneath mounds as Sima and the wolfdog met at the centre. The dog circled then pounced beside him, pinning a Ta'ai against an upturned table with both paws. Another small rock hit Sima in the back of the head. Sima swung the spade about in a half-circle, but before it came to meet its target, he shuddered to a stop. Looking up at him from beneath a shard of broken pot was a small boy. Not a Ta'ai. Not a devil, but a boy. They had not killed the villagers. The Ta'ai *were* the villagers. They were the little people, their skin now cracked and broken like Sima's own. He swung the spade in another half circle, and with a single blow, the wolfdog fell dead.

So it was that Sima lived out the rest of his life in the highest seat of honour among the shrunken settlers of Suluk. His strong hands rebuilt their town to fit them. He repaired the burst riverbanks after the flash floods came. He shepherded and tended the field. With a wave of his giant hand, disputes were settled. They loved him, and he loved them back. Children soon forgot Sima the Leper. For now, he was Sima the Earth Giant, since it was told he had been carved out of the rock he so closely resembled. And when Sima's time finally came, he was mourned and celebrated, his image carved into the side of the largest building, revered and remembered for generations to come.

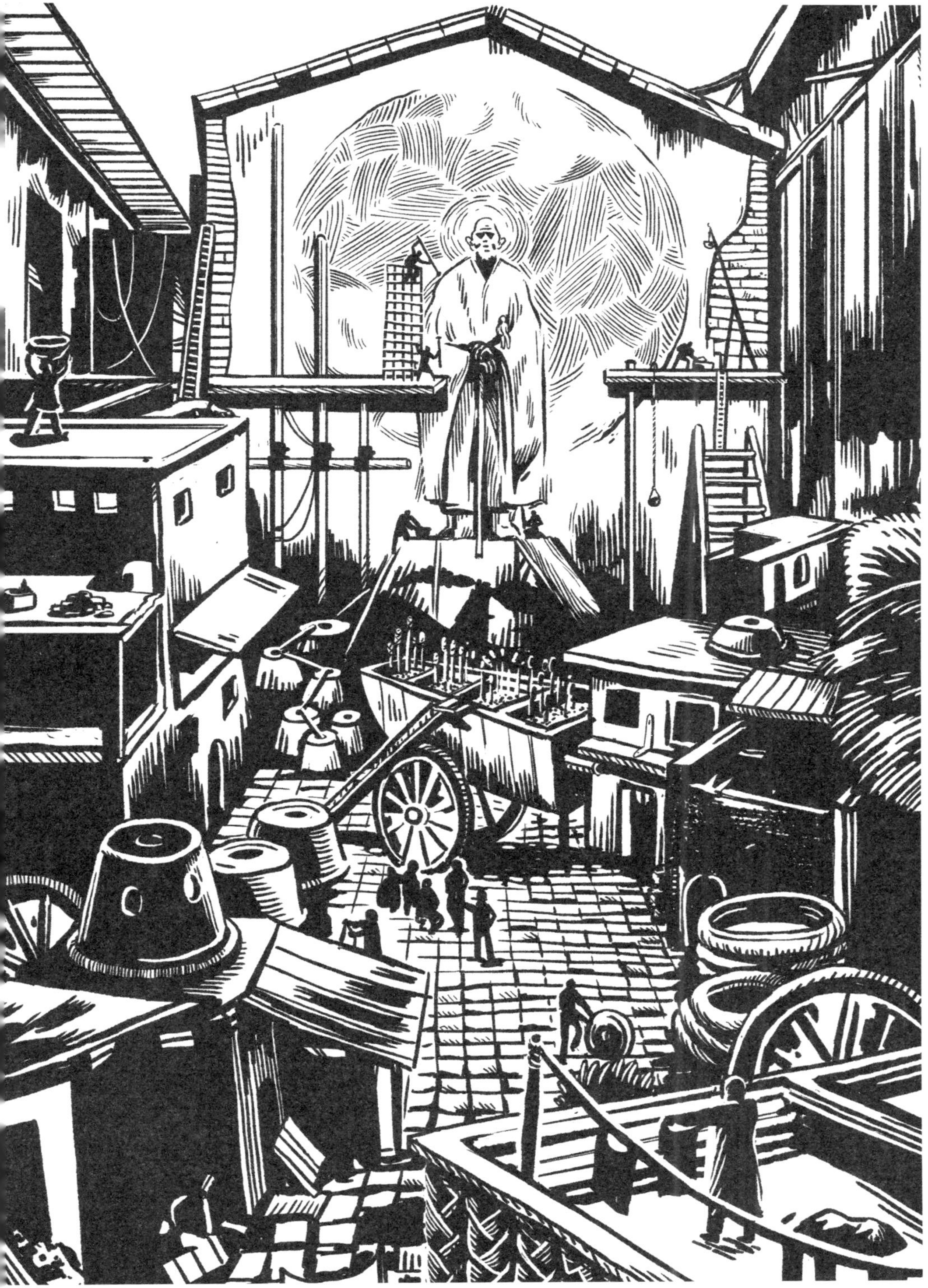

PART IV

CHAPTER 16

THE DIRTY MILK TRICK

The only noise was the diminishing gurgle of bubbles breaking on the water's surface. Then a splash, a scream and, soaked through and panting from effort, Goodwin heaved herself up over the rim, crawled across the tiles and rested her back against the poolside wall. Pulling at the tube that stemmed from the needle in her arm, Goodwin dragged her IV bag along the wet floor like a bloated fish on a reel and slipped it back into her jacket pocket.

The consoles were gone. So too were the tanks, along with Goodwin's connectome – the copy of her mind written in bio-binary. The pool itself was untouched. The tubes still wound about the edge, casting their poor man's aurora borealis across the ceiling. Even if she had her connectome, with no equipment to record the results, fusing it with the pool would be pointless. The phone was still there. She lifted the receiver and considered calling the police, but what would she say? However much she hated it, she still needed Mr Leaf's money. Perhaps she would sue. But then, who *were* those people? How clandestine was their organisation? Dodgy enough to have access to chloroform of some sort. Was Leonard Leaf even his real name? It didn't seem likely. The best thing she could do, for now, was wait.

She slumped into a deckchair beside the plastic fold-out table and let her head sink into her hands. Then, reaching into the box that had served as Leaf's seat a few hours earlier, she withdrew a bottle of Cash and Carry's finest economy mead. The golden liquid glowed green under the blue ceiling light and disappeared quickly down Goodwin's throat.

The second and third bottles vanished just as fast. But as she went to knock back her fourth, something in the liquid's complexion gave her pause. The bottle was the same shape and size as the others, but the liquid inside was white, not amber. As with all economy products, the labels were plain, the sparse design serving as a friendly reminder – and a signal to others – of the purchaser's limited means. Scrawled across the ample blank paper, Goodwin recognised Laslett's handwriting:

Elizabeth,
    Forgive me. Managed to save these three. We'll carry on, as we were, when I get back. Try not to drink it all!
    Best,
    William.

There were two more white bottles beside the first. *My connectomes*, she thought. *Laslett, you bastard.* Goodwin laughed, then

162

spat angrily onto the tiles. She unscrewed the cap of the connectome and, with a bottle of mead in the other hand, stood at the pool's edge and raised a toast.

'To this historic moment, a meeting of two great minds.' From her left hand, she took a swig of mead. 'One for me,' and with her right, she emptied her liquid mind into the pool of a billion coccolithophores, 'one for Emiliania.'

She held her breath. Where she had expected to see the white coccolithophores bloom beneath the surface, there was nothing, just clear water mixing with clear water. Goodwin had just enough time to say, 'Very good – the dirty milk trick,' before the pool turned white and the room began to hum with a frequency that rattled her spine and shook her sober. She dropped the bottle, pressed her hands tight over her ears and tried her best to scream.

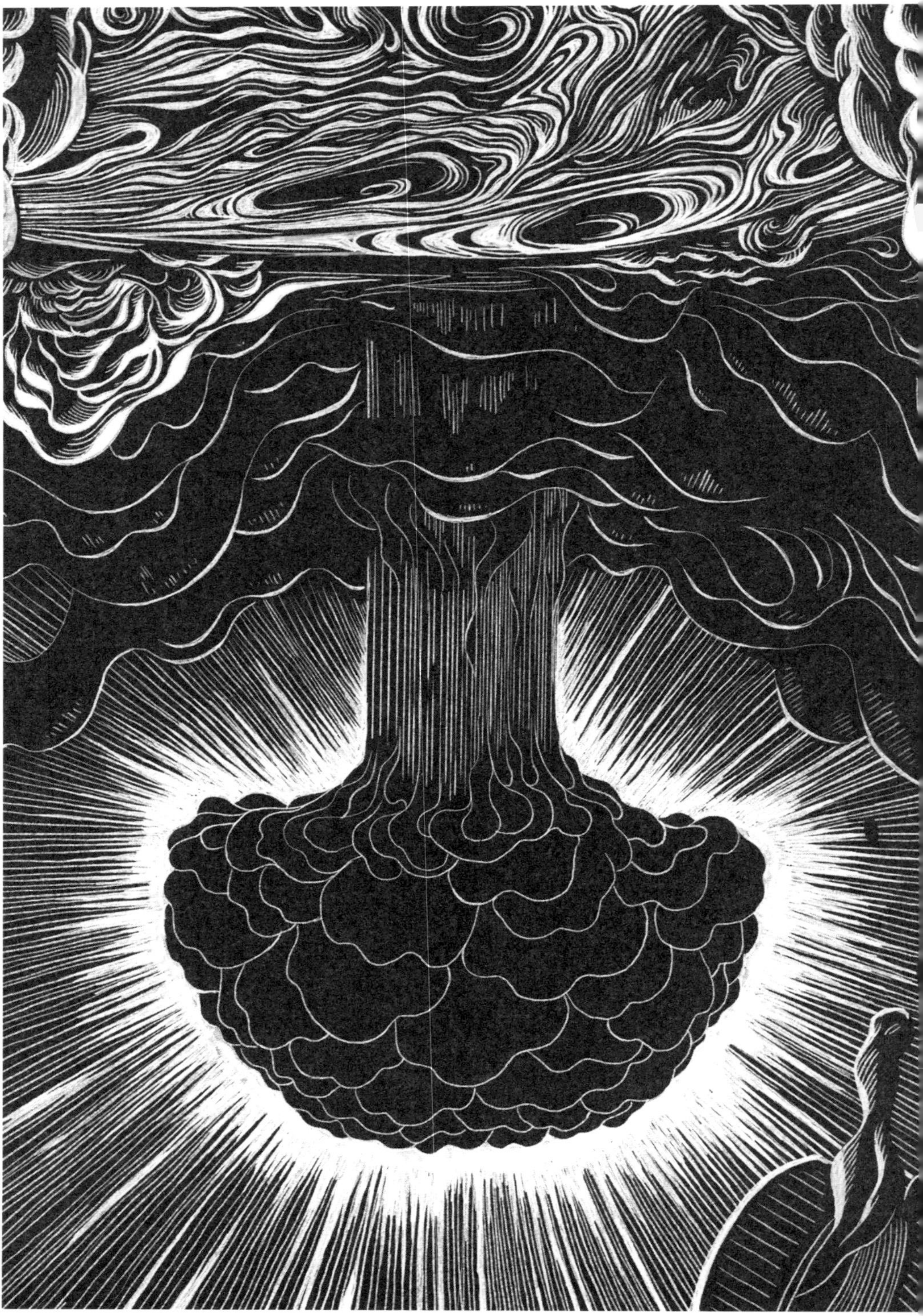

CHAPTER 17

EVERYONE woke up TINY

The sign for the New Forest Wildlife Park boasted lynx, giant otters, bison, wolves and fun for all the family. 'We're skirting a *wolf* enclosure?' asked Ashraf, eyeing the friendly painting of a woodland menagerie with considerable unease. 'Badgers – *they'll* eat anything. Once, a badger attacked my friend Amer's toes sticking out of a tent because it thought they were a row of little eggs.'

From up on her perch, Isabel laughed. Giles grinned across the wheel at Ashraf and assured, 'We'll be past it soon.' He squeezed the button on the fob below his platform, knowing that the sound of electronic locks would settle an anxious mood. Below them, Alex and Jayden, having taken over pedal duties, visibly relaxed. Behind the team of drivers, scattered across the back half of the car, the Pack had organised themselves into a miniature workforce. Maya and Evelyn passed strips of leather, harvested from the seats, to a cluster of three younger boys who sewed and glued them into makeshift shoes. Ben and Elfie worked opposite ends of a pair of scissors, cutting cloth to make shoulder-slung satchels. Manoeuvring a world ill-designed to fit them had forced cooperation and coordination onto the children. Others fussed with adjustments to their bright and colourful garments, loose hanging robes knotted about the waists like Arabic thawbs. A pair of twins had customised black leather gloves that fitted like catsuits and they entertained themselves by striking dramatic poses in the window's reflection.

Despite the trauma not so far behind them and the uncertainty that lay ahead, the Pack seemed well-adjusted, on the surface, at least. They were clean and fed, and while he wouldn't go so far as to say they looked happy, they were coping. Perhaps suffering the shock as a collective had made it easier than if they had suffered it alone. Though Giles liked to think he too had played some small part in their recovery, he knew that the vast majority of credit lay with Ashraf, and his ability to connect on their level. By contrast, Giles realised, all he had done was run, hit, carry and kill things.

They had set off at first light and the driving that morning had been slow. The closer they got to the edge of the New Forest, the more difficult the roads became. Twice, they navigated their way around burned-out pile-ups that blocked both lanes, forcing the car up onto grassy banks, risking running aground in ditches and soft earth.

'No sign of police tape,' observed Ashraf, downhearted.

'That doesn't mean there's no one out there,' said Isabel. At the end of Deerleap Lane, where thankfully no deer had leaped, they pulled onto a dual carriageway, beside which ran a stretch of terraced houses. The sedan crawled alongside this uncanny row of skyscraper-like cottages.

This is worse than the wilderness, thought Giles. Natural organisms grow and therefore exist on a variable scale. The colossal plants were feasible since they might have swelled to that size in a tropical climate. Immersed in the wild, it was possible to fool yourself, for a moment's relief, into believing it was not you but the occasional artificial object – the giant car or the colossal field gate – that was out of place. Here, as they drove into the suburb of Claybourne, human-made structures crowded every view. Fencepost monoliths, doorframes of biblical proportion and rows of palatial front gates dispelled any uncertainty. They, the small figures staring up at the buildings from inside the car, were the pieces of the picture that did not fit.

As they drove down the road's central grass strip, all lay still and quiet. Beside a bus stop, piles of clothes denoted the passengers who once waited in line. A little further up, Giles saw the double-decker bus toppled onto its side, having careered up the curved wall of a concrete tunnel.

'Probably people in those houses,' Ashraf observed.

'Well, at least they're home. If we see anyone, we'll stop,' said Giles. Ashraf nodded and heaved up on the wheel as Isabel thundered directions like a rowboat coxswain.

'It's just so *quiet*,' Ashraf mumbled, still scanning the houses for life. 'You'd think we'd have seen *someone* by now.'

The terraces made way to warehouses, and across the bridge overlooking Southampton, tower blocks came into view. Among the red-roofed suburbs were pillars of smoke – black streaks that cut across the otherwise blue sky in diagonal parallel lines. Far away, a low rumble sounded as an unseen structure succumbed to gravity's pull. It felt as though the city was restless, shifting uncomfortably – like them – settling into its new skin.

'Need to find a way around that,' Giles said, peering over the dashboard at the tumble of cars blocking the road. He hopped down onto the driver's seat as the vehicle came to a stop and heaved up the handbrake. Isabel slid off the headrest to meet him and unfolded the map.

'The most direct route is across this bridge, then onto the motorway.'

Ashraf was on the dashboard, pacing up and down its length, craning his head, trying to see a clear path. 'I don't know – no wiggle space up there – two lanes, high walls either side. We get stuck – well, I'd love to see us reverse out of that jumble. Reckon there's people in there too?' Giles climbed back up the steering column and surveyed the wreckages strewn across the bridge. Among the crumpled and burned-out were several vehicles still intact.

'Unless we want to double back half a day, which we don't – it's the only way forward. I'll scout ahead, see if anyone's there while I'm at it.' Pulling the snap-blade from beneath the platform, he slung it over his shoulder and jumped the small gap to the door handle.

Outside, the air was cool and a welcome contrast to the close confines of sixteen people. Giles ran to a low concrete wall, the lane divider that stretched the length of the bridge's central reservation, and climbed a tendril of ivy, pulling himself rung by rung up the well-spaced petiole. Atop the thin strip of stone, he was thankful for his new steady leather shoes – two flaps, glued like a slipper and bound about the ankle with a loop of lace. Ahead, the length of the bridge was a tangle of collisions: heavy goods vehicles zigzagged at awkward angles, coiling with and ploughing over unfortunate cars that had got in their way.

In the old metric of measuring distance, the bridge stretched a couple of hundred metres, but to a human a handspan in height, the length was a mile at least. Giles breathed deep and set off at a pace down the promenade wall, confident he could hit the end and get back in twenty minutes, plotting a course as he went, from the partition's higher vantage point. As he ran, he called out for survivors and, hearing no response, Giles hopped down from the wall and ascended a railing, a twisted strip of metal which ran closer to a line of cars. Craning his neck to peer inside a nearby van, Giles found, to his frustration, the window covered by a thin layer of fog, a wet film riddled with swash lines and fractal forks. Window after window presented the same strange membrane barrier through which only the blurry outline of clothes could be seen strewn over seats and steering wheels. Again, Giles felt a sense of crushing guilt. He had been enjoying himself, taking pleasure in the ways in which the group were adapting, exploring. But that pleasure had been bought by a cruel enormity of suffering. These metal husks, a hundred of them, were coffins, each a cathedral to the tiny body laid to rest somewhere in its centre. Perhaps the condensation was a kindness, a veil of dignity there to obscure the occupants.

The route from end to end would be tight, but if they took it slow, the sedan could just about squeeze through. Walking back along the central reservation wall, some of the thrill knocked out of him, Giles sought their car through the thicket of tyres and felt a growing affection for the vehicle. It was an ark in a forsaken sea. Then his eyes caught movement. At first he thought it was just a miasma, some heat shimmering off the tarmac. But when a breeze calmed the distortion, he saw them. A mob. A crowd of shrunken humans, advancing towards their car. Giles doubled his walking pace, then fell into a run, and soon he was sprinting along the wall. A handful of minutes later, he tumbled down ivy and onto the grass verge beside their car. The side door creaked open and several hands hoisted him up.

'Have you seen them?' panted Giles, catching his breath.

'Seen who?' asked Richard. Before Giles could answer, a squeal rang out from the back seat. The pattering sound might have been rain, but wasn't. They were everywhere – on the tarmac, scrambling up onto car bonnets, climbing high into roadside shrubbery. Suddenly, dozens of grubby little faces pressed up against the glass, and Giles saw that they were children, tens on tens of them, their average age perhaps twelve years old. A few of the gleeful younger ones ran naked, wild, with matted lengths of uncut hair dragging behind them like a squirrel's tail. Most wore strips of torn cloth, tied in makeshift tunics about the waist; a few brandished sticks and cutlery. The twelve lost children in the back of the car stared at their dirty counterparts on the other side of the glass. Though their time apart from adults differed by only a handful of days, the contrast was startling.

'Jesus Christ,' said Isabel, 'They were hiding from us.'

'It's the Lord of the bleeding Flies,' said Ashraf. Suddenly, the faces squinting through the glass turned as one, shifting their attention to the road behind them. Giles looked in the wing mirror to see a leonine long-haired ginger cat. The tribe outside scrambled to gather behind the car, becoming a single mass of bodies. They were small, but together their volume was greater than the animal they faced. Still, the cat stalked towards them from the shadows, its body crouched low to the ground.

A hand shot up from the front of the group, and, as one, the children screamed, shaking fists and sticks and hurling gravel.

The cat hissed and arched its back as the group shuffled forwards, roaring and peppering the cat with small stones. Giles marvelled at this powerful display of strength in numbers. The cat bolted and Richard's voice boomed from an open window above him.

'Bravo!' The group turned to look at Richard and, shooting a cautious glance back in the cat's direction, made their way towards him. 'You are a fierce-looking lot,' he said, leaning out the window, beaming manically. A little girl wearing a hooped diamond earring about her neck snarled and spat on the floor.

'Excellent work. Well, you're all local, are you?'

'Who wants to know?' came a voice from below the car. The group parted like a murmuration of starlings in the wake of a hawk, and Giles saw a solitary figure standing centre, clad in armour moulded from tin foil. The man was older than the rest. By how much, it was hard to tell since his badly cracked skin obscured the usual indicators of age. He was skinny, but Giles placed him somewhere between fifteen and forty from his size and voice. Around his waist hung a gold metal wrestler's belt that, at second glance, Giles recognised as a Casio watch. Beside it hung a pair of craft scissors, slung by a finger hole over one shoulder, the blades stained dark red. The intention was clearly to denote authority, but to Giles it looked pompous and uncomfortable.

'How are you driving the car?' He spoke the way a mouse steals – quick, quiet and full of suspicion. The group sat in vigil behind him, not making a sound.

'We converted it so that it might be driven by a few of us as a crew,' replied Richard, delighted by the ripple of excitement that filtered through the crowd.

A thick-set boy with rosy cheeks saluted, clicked his heels together and cried up, 'Permission to climb abo—' then fell silent as a tall girl wearing the head of a Barbie doll smacked him about

171

one ear. Two holes sat where the doll's eyes had been, and again, Giles got the impression the mask was meant to be intimidating. Instead, the makeshift helmet looked awkward and impractical.

'Where are you going?' continued the man with the scissors, placating Richard with the thinnest of smiles.

'We're heading to Winchester. Why don't you join us?' At this, Isabel pulled Richard inside as the children below huddled and whispered.

'What are you doing?' hissed Isabel, 'we don't know anything about these people.'

'We are *all* strangers, relatively speaking. Isabel, look at them. These are lost souls,' said Richard.

'Sure lost something,' agreed Ashraf. Richard frowned and placed his hands on their shoulders, drawing Ashraf and Isabel fractionally closer. Giles stepped in, completing the circle of four. Richard continued.

'They're children. We were all children once, every one of us. Everyone woke up tiny, alone and crying for help. For us to be standing here, alive, all these years later, there must have been someone there to answer that cry. Someone to pick us up, give us food and shelter, a sense of identity. Is it not our duty to do the same when someone calls on us?'

'They're not exactly calling,' observed Giles, watching one of the children throw an exploratory punch at the car's tyres, 'and they're not all children. By the looks of it, I'd say they want to steal the car and feed us to the cat. Plus, they've got plenty of food and shelter back there.'

'Yes, well, there's a difference between physical and emotional wealth, Giles. You can be well catered in one department, yet starving in the other. I suspect these youngsters require some of the latter sustenance. Shouldn't we offer help if they'd have it?'

Giles looked down at the vagrant group on the ground. It was true. They were lost. Something had happened to them – an animal attack, or worse. Giles wondered where the other adults were. He could see fear, perhaps grief, in the way their heads flicked nervously from shadow to shadow, how their hands clasped and unclasped their implements, how they crammed close, but not too close to the man dressed in tin, as if there were a goldilocks radius of protection around him. The wilderness was trying to reclaim them the way it had reclaimed the red woman, yet so far, it was just biting at the edge.

The driver's door creaked open, and Isabel looked down at the assembled crowd of smiling, grubby faces.

'OK. One at a time. No knives or sticks or whatever *that* is.' Isabel lifted the strip of packing crate that served as a gangplank. It was barely over the doorframe when hands shot up from under the rim. For a moment, their smiles held. Giles bit his lip, hoping his suspicions were unfounded. Then the serenity and pretence dropped. Isabel was shoved to one side as the chaos descended. A wave of bodies scrambled past her onto the seat. Giles and Ashraf caught pairs of the invaders in their arms, like a rugby scrum against a tide of rodents, pushing back the advancing swarm.

'Goodness, they're enthusiastic!' said Richard, nervously.

'That's not what this is,' said Giles, in panic, as he watched the tin-clad man climb the steering wheel, run his hands over the screw-grips and inspect the platform.

'How about *we* drive from now on, eh?' He didn't look down from the platform. It wasn't a question.

'Get down from there,' said Giles as the two ferret-like children under his arms kicked and scratched.

'Come on, mate, we just want to drive the car,' he repeated.

173

Giles deposited the two children back onto the gangplank, and edged it off the doorframe with his foot, sending it thumping to the ground.

'Thing is, Winchester's full of dickheads. We're gonna go somewhere much better. Aren't we?' he shouted out of the window and the crowd on the grass below whooped and cheered.

'OK then, mate,' said Ashraf, 'so, we're not going the same way. We'll help you convert a car of your own. Ay? How about that?'

'Sure, we *could* do that. Or we could just take this one. Looks like you've done a proper good job.' Giles climbed up to the wheel, the long blade purposely visible on his back, and the tinman raised his arms in defeat.

'All right – all right. Fair enough. You lot,' he addressed his troops, 'back off. The nasty adults don't want to help us.' He shuffled around Giles, tin foil crinkling with each step. Shoulders slumped, the man swung his legs over the platform's edge, and with a wave of his hand, the horde ceased their efforts to re-erect the gangplank, letting it fall. Giles, feeling a sting of shame for using the knife as a threat, was about to offer some kind of entente when the man fixed him with a grin. Confused, Giles stepped closer, and to his alarm, he saw the stranger's hand resting on the key in the ignition. With surprising speed, the man pivoted and dropped from the platform, twisting the key and pulling it free as he fell. A moment later, he hurled it through the open door and into the crowd.

'No!' cried Isabel, springing from the seat and landing on the tarmac. A naked, scrawny boy with a thicket of knee-length ginger hair emerged from the back of the mass of children and sprinted towards the houses, the key tucked beneath one arm. Urgently pursuing the boy, Isabel pushed herself through the mob, then broke into a run.

In three quick jumps, Giles hit the gangplank. Already ahead of him stood the tinman, raising his scissors and pointing them towards Isabel's back as if leading a charge. Stumbling forward, Giles tackled the man about the waist, and the two of them fell, then rolled. Beneath them, the foil suit crumpled and tore, and as Giles found his feet, he looked back to see the thin metal had knotted into lumps, fused about the elbows and knees. Giles continued running as the children set about the prostrate tinman, cautiously untangling him like plover birds cleaning a crocodile's teeth.

High grass whipped at Giles's face as he scrambled over roots and rubble, trying to keep Isabel in sight. Emerging into a clearing strewn with cigarette butts and sweet wrappers, Giles saw the boy with the key halfway up a wall that skirted the berm ahead. He was moving furiously fast. The boy looked back, gave Isabel the finger, and then hopped gleefully out of sight.

'Come here, you stinky little Ewok,' cried Isabel, who cursed her lack of shoes. Already her feet were covered in a mesh of cuts from the short run over the kerb, laced with tiny glass shavings that had not bothered the boy. Giles caught up with Isabel and gave her a bunk onto the wall. Ahead, the boy slid down a dry dirt slope towards rows of terraced houses that melted into suburbia. Beside the houses were a string of back gardens. Lakes fringed with monolithic gnomes and sheds like temples poked out above the canopy of blackberry brambles.

'If he gets in there, we're screwed. We'll never find him,' said Isabel. Ahead, the boy slalomed between dry tufts into the thick grass at the bottom of the slope. Giles slid down after him, as Isabel tore a gum foil in two and plastered each half to her feet.

Head and shoulders above the grass, Giles spotted the boy

emerging beside a tall wooden slatted fence skirting the nearest garden. He scurried back and forth along the edge like a mouse desperate for an exit. Failing to find a crack worthy of squeezing through, the boy ran back towards the terracotta buildings.

Past the fence, Giles and Isabel rounded a corner into an alleyway pinned on all sides by high brick walls. Two wheelie bins spilled over with rubbish, the only objects betraying their scale in the otherwise featureless brickwork box. A scuffling sound drew their attention to the wall at the far end, just in time to see a small grubby foot disappear inside the end of a drainpipe. Giles leaped forward, cramming into the mouth after him. Above, at an undignified angle, he saw the naked boy, hands and feet wedged against both sides, the hoop of the keyring hung about his neck.

'Hey – hey there, buddy,' said Giles, and the boy froze, fixing him with a stony stare, a thief caught in the beam of a torch. 'How about we work something out?' Giles gave his best smile, hands outstretched in a gesture of peace. The boy looked back, his face tensed up as if about to cry. 'It's OK,' whispered Giles. The boy nodded, relaxed a little, and then emptied his bladder.

Shrieks of laughter echoed up the drainpipe as Giles staggered back, shaking off the amber stream. '*Right!* You little—' he leaned in again as the boy clambered out of sight. He slipped, twisted and squeezed his body against the rim of the tube, but it was no good. For the first time in days, Giles felt oversized. He wiggled out and looked up the length of the pipe. 'Isabel, give me a hand.' Hoisting up onto the first bracket that fixed the pipe to the wall, Giles wrapped his arms around the warm black plastic and climbed. He made quick progress, hugging the pipe like the trunk of a palm tree, the way he'd seen people climb for coconuts. He pressed his ear against the pipe as he rose, listening for the boy. Overtaking him, Giles stopped, wedged against the wall and kicked. The pipe rattled, and somewhere inside, to Giles's sardonic pleasure, the boy shrieked. Far below, Isabel looked anxious. She steadied her feet, ready to catch whatever came out from the curved black shoot.

Nothing. The pipe was silent, and Giles shook it again. Then, with a trickle of laughter, he heard the soft patter of hands and feet continue their ascent above him. Giles scrambled after the noise. He was halfway up the wall when he saw the rest of the children spilling over the embankment and running towards them, hooting and screaming.

'Isabel!' called Giles, but she had heard them too and, armed with a plastic fork from the bins, turned to face them. Giles reached the guttering that ran along the roof's edge, clawed at the plastic, and tried to heave himself over the rim. Dry, weathered flakes of paint fell away under his fingers. The makeshift leather sandals fell away too as Giles kicked his heels, allowing his toes to gain grip on the tubes edge. Desperate, he thought of his two girls, lost and alone in the ruins, then of his friends trapped in the car, and then of this boy who had stolen the key – the literal key – to saving them all. Far below, Isabel was trying to defend herself. She swung the fork in wide arcs as the mob of wildlings tightened around her.

Body shaking with exhaustion, Giles heaved himself over into the black guttering and plunged shin-deep into soft green sediment lining its length. In a daze, he pulled a loose shard of roof tile and lumbered towards the top of the drain. Giles heaved the jagged red clay onto his knee, then raised it high over his head, up over the dark hole as the boy's grubby face emerged into the light. His tiny eyes fixed on the boulder in Giles's hands. The child was small, no more than eight or nine years old, and terrified.

'I – I was only mucking about,' stammered the boy. Giles

blinked, as if emerging from a dream, and let the shard thud into the sediment beside him, splattering flecks of green against the side of the drain. His stomach lurched. For a moment, just a moment, the dark cloud that had been gathering inside him had risen to the surface. He'd felt it stir on the cliffside towpath. Known its lure as he'd straddled the tent-trapped dog. Seen it reflected in the savagery of the red woman.

'I – I'm sorry. Give me your hand,' Giles said quietly, reaching down to the trembling boy as he took the key and then the lad out onto the sediment. Then, far below them, Isabel cried out. Giles turned to look over the edge, shocked to see how high they had climbed. Several children were throwing missiles. Two grappled with Isabel, trying to disarm her. Advancing on them all came the foil-clad man and with him the girl wearing the doll's head.

'Looks like we've got us a misbehaver!' said the man, unhooking the scissors from his shoulders.

'Isabel, I've got the key. Get up here!' called Giles. Needing no more encouragement, Isabel threw the fork at the mob and leaped at the drainpipe. Giles turned back to the boy, just in time to see him slip. He fell, scrambling, backwards towards the maw of the down pipe. Giles dropped onto his belly, catching the boy by his elbow. But, like a fish that didn't want to be caught, the child slid through his fingers. Giles watched in horror as the boy's face was enveloped by the darkness, leaving only the sound of his body as it bounced through the pipe, plummeting towards the ground.

The mob fell silent. Giles craned his head over the rim of the gutter, wiping green slime from his face and chest. Isabel too had stopped midway up the pipe to inspect the scene below. There, sprawled out on the concrete at the mouth of the pipe, surrounded by a circle of tiny figures, was the boy, shaking and broken. Giles clamped a hand across his mouth to stifle a cry as, from between the huddle of heads, a pair of scissors raised and pointed right at him.

Ashraf pressed down on the plastic button, confirming the door was still firmly locked for the fifth time that hour. In the fading light outside, a few of the children were still visible, watching them. There had been plenty of chatter about how best to defend the vehicle – windscreen wipers, soapy water jets, and projectiles from the sunroof. There had even been talk of using the petrol reserves in the water bottles to make flaming arrows. Foolish ideas, quickly dispelled by Richard.

Ashraf too had mused on the subject. 'There's a load of other ways they might get in, air vents, through the engine. Just a matter of time.'

'Let's stay positive. The whole thing's madness. They're just children. The sooner the others get back, the sooner we can straighten this out.'

'And if they don't come back?' said Ashraf. He looked out at the ridge Giles and Isabel had disappeared over several hours earlier.

'Ash, please. They'll be back,' assured Richard, though, with each assertion, his conviction waned. Ashraf was moving onto the next lock when, over the rim of the embankment, came a procession of figures. The children were not frantic and scurrying as when they had last seen them. They walked with a slow determination. Leading the march was the tinman. Beside him, the girl with the doll head carried a limp figure in her arms, and several children at the back of the group were rolling a large object. They stopped at the edge of the grass, and the girl lay the small, grubby body onto the ground. He was stirring but wounded. The self-styled leader turned to face his troops and gestured from the boy to the car in fervent, angry motions.

'Do you think – do you think Isabel and Giles ...?' whispered Ashraf. Richard regarded the boy, then crossed himself.

'No,' said Richard, pressing his hands against the glass, 'but I don't think those children want to get in here anymore.'

'Well, there's good news,' said Ashraf, smiling slightly. Then suddenly, he frowned. 'Oh, wait, they're not going to let the tyres down, are they?'

The man was walking towards the car, dragging a matchstick behind him along the gravel. It sparked and then bloomed into flame as he raised it over his head. Behind him, Ashraf saw what the others had been rolling – a large plastic bottle of dark amber liquid.

'Good Lord,' gasped Richard, 'They're going to burn us alive.'

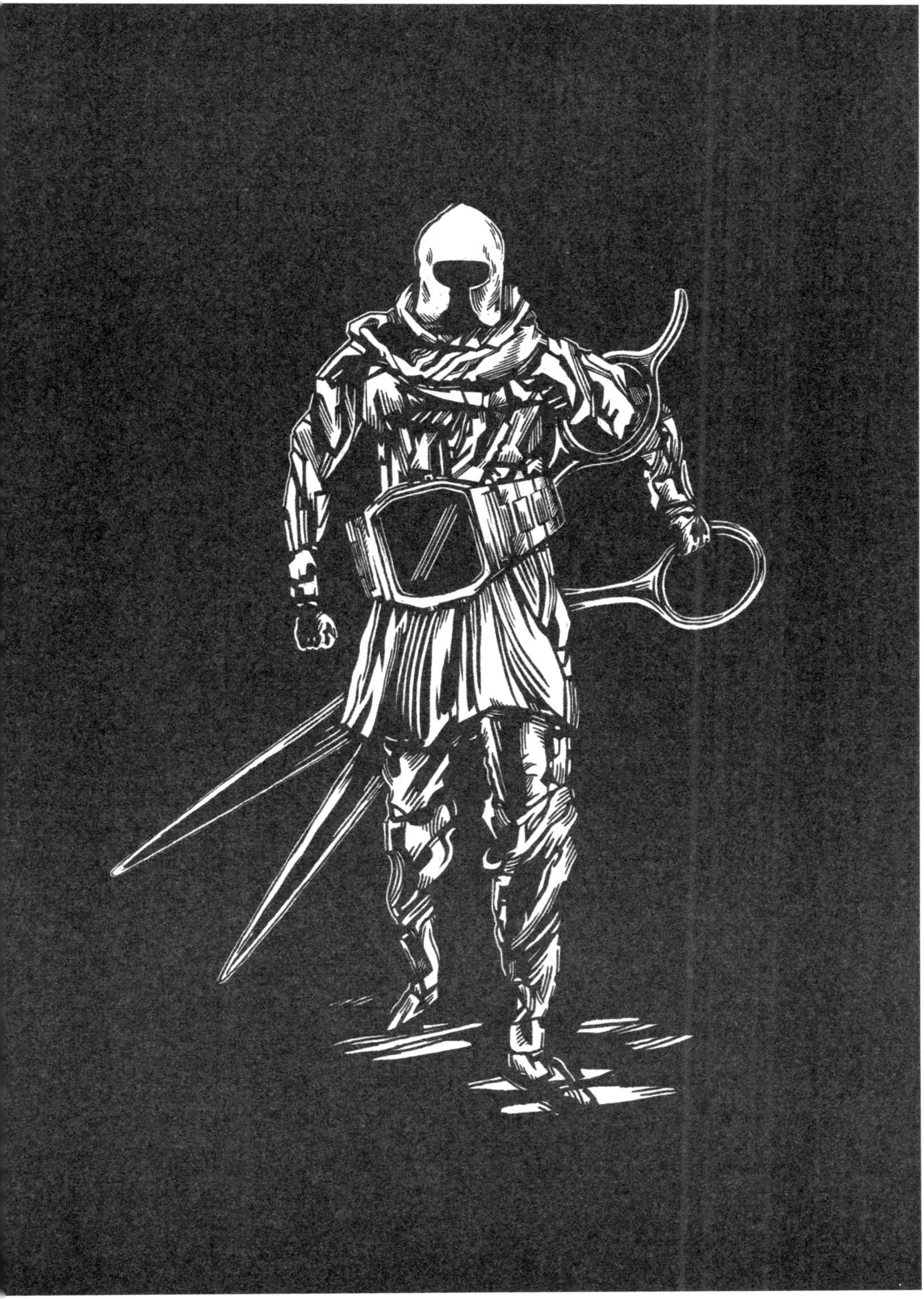

CHAPTER 18

THE GAIA MEDEA

Goodwin awoke to the stinging scent of ammonia and floundered through what felt and smelled like a shallow, eutrophic pond, struggling against hair that ensnared her like riverbed weeds. Her *own* hair, she realised. How had it grown to such lengths in a single night? Where was she? What had she done? And then she remembered the mead. Of course. The cheaper the stuff, the worse the repercussions.

Goodwin's head, a withered apricot in size and form, emerged from her shirt sleeve, gasping for air. Her brain struggled to orientate itself and locate the body that had, until now, been such a trustworthy vessel. But nothing made sense, God damn it. There was almost no correlation between the images her eyes were processing and her memory of how the world should look. Was there something else in those amber bottles? She wouldn't put it past the snakes who'd locked her in the booth. But no. They'd warned her this would happen one day, if she carried on abusing her body and mind the way she'd been doing for years. That day had finally come. The cart had been ripped from the rails. She'd tipped over the edge of sanity. She'd lost her mind. *Bugger*, she thought.

Goodwin clawed her way a few arm lengths further out of the sleeve. The crumpled fabric was surrounded by broken glass – curved, jagged shards that reached as high as her chest, thinly coated in something sticky and, from its smell, honey-sweet. Across the cathedral ceiling above, blue and white lines twisted and zigzagged, chasing each other's tails. At last, Goodwin recognised the room. Hours ago, the dome had been a grand spectacle, and now it was a national monument, a structure of unfathomable scale. She crawled forward again, freeing herself from the sleeve, and something tugged at her wrist. She looked down. A pencil-thick metal tube protruded from her arm, the skin about it pulled so tight that there was no sign of bleeding. Exploring inside the sleeve, she found the source of the resistance – a long transparent rope that led back within the folds of the tunnel.

Goodwin gathered the tube into her arms until it went taught. Then, as if bringing a rowboat to shore, she pulled her IV bag through the sleeve, slithering and landing it between her legs. Faced with such a clear comparison of scale, Goodwin saw the enormity of her transformation, and several things fell into place.

There was no time to lose. She stood, slipping on her heel, which smudged unnervingly against the tiles. Then, clearing aside the glass fragments so as not to puncture the IV, Goodwin put distance between herself and the pile of clothes.

Beside the pool, a hose dribbled happily into a drain. Goodwin went to it, laid flat on her belly and drank, letting the stream remove the soft outer layer of skin, while she took in great gulps of water. Ahead, through the glass, something flickered. She got to her feet and wiped away the condensation. Beyond the pine trees that fringed the facility grounds, Goodwin saw the shimmering, orange glow of fire that rose into the night sky to become a writhing pillar of smoke.

Quickly, she traced the cord from the wall and pulled it until a phone heaved over the high table's edge and came clattering to the floor beside her. She straddled the upturned receiver and pushed her full palm against three buttons. The operator answered.

'What is the nature of your emergency?'

Goodwin thought about this for a moment. She wasn't exactly sure. Then, in a flash, it came to her. She leaned in close to the mouthpiece and shouted, as loud as she possibly could, 'The earth is alive, and she hates us.'

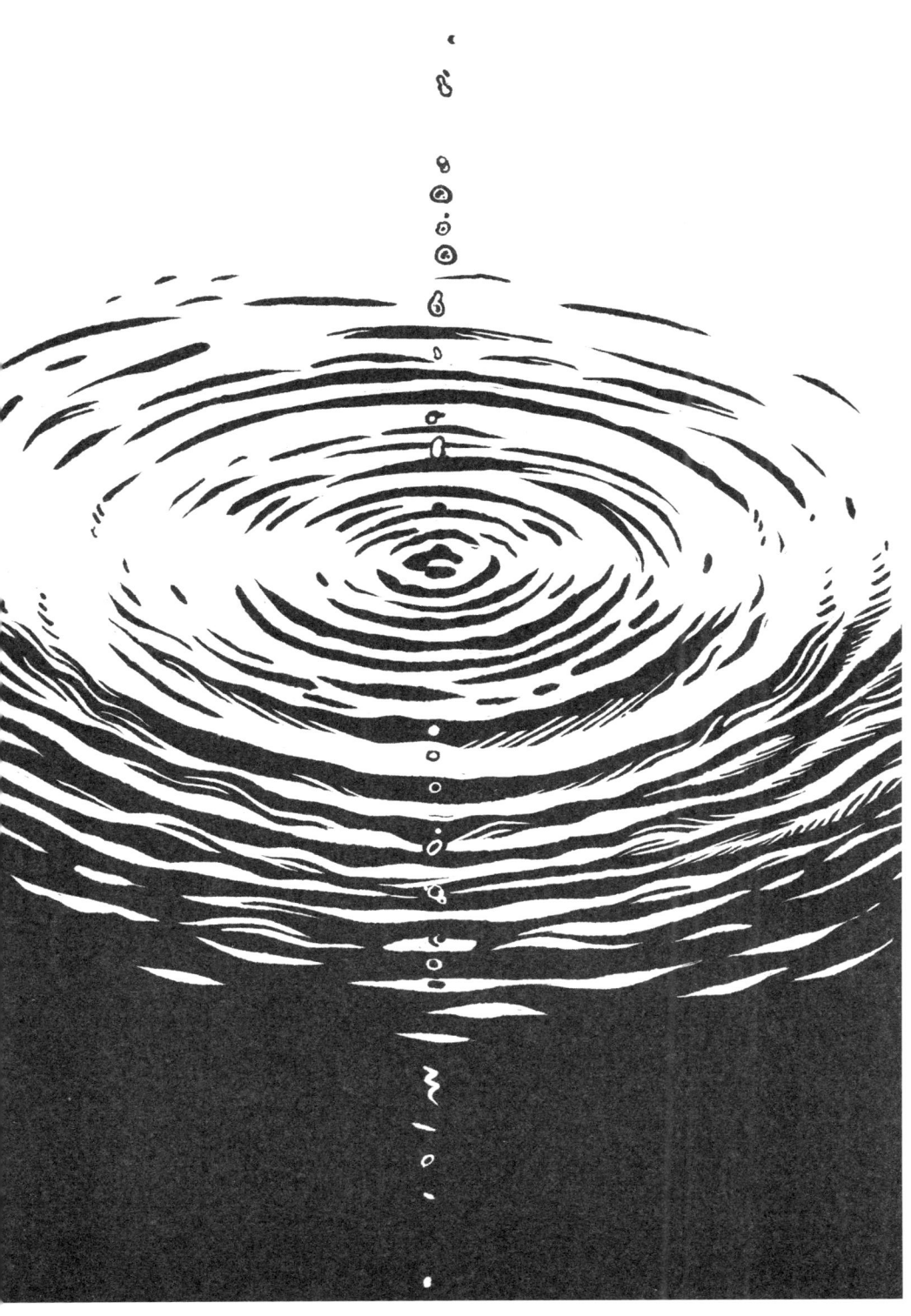

CHAPTER 19

TINMAN

Streaks of orange and lilac, like roughly torn strips of paper, collaged the sky into a brilliant sunset. Though the same elemental beauty did not extend to the street below, the houses themselves appeared to be making corrective efforts. Pristine, newly installed windows reflected the colourful sky, camouflaging themselves with exotic hues. Grey brick walls glowed amber in the evening light. The thin black rim of a red roof spilled over with green moss, a minor infiltration of wilderness, worn like jewellery. Crawling along the cracks of bitumen tiles were two small creatures, inconspicuous as beetles on bark. The shorter of the two slid down to the gutter lining the roof and leaned over the edge.

'Long way down. There, try and get that pigeon to give us a lift.'

'I'm out of breadcrumbs,' mused Giles, pausing a moment to look past the suburbs and over the woodland, 'I do like pigeons though. They get a bad rep, generally. Did you know they secrete milk for their young?'

'You can *milk* a pigeon?'

'Yes. Well, no. It comes out of their mouth. You wouldn't want to—'

'So, they suckle their young on *sick*? This has not greatly improved my opinion of pigeons.'

'Well, I *like* them. Nice to see birds in the city. Never enough birds. Too many cities.'

Isabel pushed away from the rim of the guttering and sank into an armchair of moss. Panting, she peeled off her gum-wrapper shoes and ushered Giles down to join her.

They had been lucky the children hadn't climbed the pipe, deterred perhaps by the wails of the injured boy. Still, it had taken them hours to work around the rooftops, keeping out of sight to lose the mob who had tracked and jeered at them from the ground. Tired from the exertion, Giles sank into the moss beside Isabel and closed his eyes. The boy's face was enveloped in darkness for the hundredth time, and he took another shuddering breath. Isabel squeezed his shoulder.

'It wasn't your fault.'

'I chased him. He slipped.'

'You were trying to pull him up.' Giles conceded a shrug. The car key lay in his lap, thick metal and plastic, like a glam-rock guitar.

'There was a moment, back there, when I was prepared to do anything, *anything* to get this back. All I could think of was my daughters and getting the key. It's terrifying, Isabel. For a moment, that little boy was nothing. All I felt was this awful, primitive urge.'

Isabel looked at him thoughtfully.

187

'These kids, it's been, what – three, four days? But to look at them, they might have been out here for months. To say they've suffered a dramatic upheaval hardly does it justice. They're in shock. We all are. We might not be curled up in balls, weeping, but I daresay at some point we'll have to face the horror, and the grief. Shock does strange things to people. One time, I fell out of a bunk bed and dislocated my knee. I went actual green. For about a week afterwards, I felt so fragile, paranoid. I imagined people were out to ambush me or that cars were going to swerve onto the pavement. I wasn't myself – more a puppet with something I couldn't see or name pulling the strings. And that was just a dislocated *knee*. This?' Isabel turned her impossibly small, wrinkled hands in front of her eyes, marvelling at them. 'Well, if you lot weren't here to back me up, I don't think I'd believe it.'

Giles thought of waking that morning on that coastal path, his father buried beneath the hawk headstone. Then of the red woman, scrambling like a rat through brambles and of how he'd watched in morbid fascination, feeling an urge to drop to all fours and scramble beside her. His thoughts turned to the message from Sadie, and how it had given him clarity of purpose, brought him back each time he remembered her voice. Isabel re-wrapped her makeshift sandals and tightened the belt on her red wool jumpsuit.

'I don't think I'd have fared well on my own. But I think you'd muddle through.' To his complete surprise, Isabel slung an arm around his side and squeezed. Giles was about to return the gesture when she let go, alarmed by something she'd seen over his shoulder.

Crouching into the moss, she whispered, 'Down, slowly. There, look.'

A little further up the road sat the red sedan, besieged by scores of rowdy children. A few metres away, a small fire burned with mounting intensity. The tinman walked over to it, lit a stick and with a furtive dash, tossed it under the back wheel. Without missing a beat, the window above it opened, and water poured out, quashing the flame.

'Jesus, they're trying to burn the car,' said Giles.

'They wouldn't do that. They're not psychopaths. They're children.'

'Same thing. Plus, they think I tried to kill their friend. And after all that's happened to them . . .'

'Well, doesn't look like he's having much luck.'

'Isabel, over there.' Giles pointed to a group of kids struggling to roll a large bottle filled with amber liquid over the embankment and onto the road.

'They'll never . . . they'll never get *that* to the car.' Isabel mumbled, uncertain.

'No, no. It's highly unlikely,' Giles nodded. But as he said it, he was on his feet, edging further along the gutter, his walk turning to a run.

A length of grey cable weaving through the brickwork proved to be the best of several bad options for descending the building. Halfway down, it passed through thick climbing ivy, giving valuable cover from a trio of children running from the embankment to the houses. As the small figures vanished beneath a gate, Giles and Isabel finished their abseil to the pavement and ran to hide in the shadow of a telecom box. The three boys quickly re-emerged, pulling behind them a bulbous mess of fluorescent tubes – a water pistol. With a jolt of horror, Giles understood the tinman's plan.

The children dragged the pistol down the bank, hoisting it onto a pile of clothes gathered at the edge of the roadside. With the antic coordination of circus clowns, they unscrewed a purple cap and began pouring petrol into the water tank. The tinman nodded a solemn approval, then, resting his shoulder against the handle, he heaved and angled the toy, repurposed now as artillery, to point directly towards the car.

Giles stepped towards the group, and Isabel pulled him back. 'Let them try. It's ridiculous,' she whispered, 'Let's get the key to the car and we can be gone before this starts.' And so, they ran, scurrying the long way, beneath a line of parked vehicles, going from wheel to wheel to avoid being seen. Behind them, the girl with the doll's head lit a sparkler and wedged it into the ground midway between the sedan and the pistol. A shower of sparks bloomed over her head with a phosphorus fizz, a beacon in the fading light. Below the pistol's nozzle, the tinman heaved back and forth, pushing and pulling the pump to build pressure, while the bantam faces of the children watched anxiously from the sidelines.

As Giles leaned around the last tyre in their line of cover, preparing for the final dash to the sedan, the key slipped from his arm, clattering on the ground. The tinman spun about and, digging in with both heels, twisted the pistol towards Giles and hissed, '*Do it.*'

A small girl tucked into the pistol's trigger guard kicked into the lever, and a jet of petrol shot in Giles's direction, going wide of both the sedan and sparkler. The wet trail splattered the ground behind Giles's feet. Relieved, he looked back to Isabel. She had not been so lucky and stood in a puddle of oily rainbows, her red jumpsuit soaked through. Giles turned to see the doll-headed girl light a second sparkler from the first and, to his horror, launch it towards them like a javelin. He and Isabel ducked and fell to one side as it clanged beneath the car. Tiny sparks ricocheted off gravel and with a sound like a small exhale of breath, the trail caught light. A wave of heat spread over Giles's back as snakes of fire rippled along the concrete and up the side of the nearest wheel. Isabel pulled him away from the flames, away from the deadly line of fire that now cut between them and their car.

Screaming faces pressed against the sedan's windows while the tinman pumped the gun, aiming it back at the captives. He barked a command and this time the jet shot true. Vapour perfectly clipped the top of the upright sparkler, igniting the petrol into a lance of flame that crashed into the back window before dissipating into a black cloud. From behind a soot smear that ran up the glass, came cries of terror. Fingers of flame dripped from the bumper onto the ground and spread beneath the tyres.

'We just need to get to the other side,' said Giles, taking Isabel's weight. She was shaking, dizzy from fumes so thick they warbled the air around her. The two of them had doubled back around the blaze to face a clear stretch of open space between them and the sedan, when they heard a fizz behind them.

The girl with the doll's head held her sparkler like a staff, creating an umbrella of sparks that bounced off the plastic mask, demonic in the flickering light, silhouetted against the wall of flame behind her. Tufts of hair fringed black holes where eyes should be, her dress singed and stained. She swiped at them with the light-crackling pole, leaving streaks of white that lingered on Giles's retina. He danced backwards, avoiding embers that bounced around his feet. It would take just one of those innocent little shooting stars to set them both alight.

'Stay back,' pleaded Isabel, 'this isn't a game.' She hopped away from a spark that skittered into nothing nearby, stumbling danger-ously close to the flames that snaked behind them.

The girl raised the sparkler like a spear, and Giles saw his moment. He lunged and knocked her off balance. As the sparkler fell beneath a tyre, the girl tottered on one foot, catching her mask on the wheel's rim. The plastic head came free and rolled into the fire, where the tufts of synthetic blonde hair melted into black, oily globules. She shrieked, then scrambled on all fours to retrieve it. By the fire's light, Giles saw she was young, fifteen perhaps, and seraphic were it not for the transformation lines that marked her face. She turned, revealing a second aberration – a split spanning her lip to her chin, in a spot where it would be easy to imagine a piercing once sat.

The girl retrieved the head from the flames, now a blackened husk, and pulled it abruptly over the wound. Slumping back against the tread of the wheel, her body curled inwards, huddling against the rim. Only the blank, expressionless head remained visible as Giles and Isabel edged a path ablaze on both sides, to-wards the sedan.

The tinman lowered the angle of the pistol and aimed at the car's underbelly. At his command, a flame lurched forwards, hit the sedan below the bumper and fanned out, forcing Giles and Isabel back. Blooms of orange rolled over metal machine parts before dissipating into lines of smoke that peeled either side of the car. Something stirred behind the exhaust pipe – a dark knot which fell onto the road. To Giles's surprise, it grew legs and at its centre, a small nucleus of red and a face like a skull appeared. The red woman scuttered over the concrete towards, then past him, making a path straight for the tinman. He signalled. The amber jet shot out, clipped the sparkler, and another jet of fire engulfed the back of the car. Lit up by the glow of the eruption, the feral creature bounded forward, swept around the base of the sparkler and pulled it away from the jet of petrol.

In three more strides, the red woman had reached the pistol, the dying sparkler raised high above her head, its length still glowing white. She crashed into the side of the weapon with a shriek. The tinman reached for his scissors, but she was already above him, feet on face. Then, with all her weight, she plunged the burning tip of the sparkler between his collarbone and neck, through the foil, down into the bulk of his body. Stars cascaded about him as the rod sank from view, extinguishing the sparkler with a cold hiss.

Next the woman swirled on the child curled in the trigger guard and shoved her tumbling into the clothes pile. The girl with the doll's head ran to the tinman, now slumped face down beside the pistol, and Giles was close behind. The red woman, startled, turned sharply, wielding the scissors, her arms wrapped through both finger holes, the blades pulled wide.

'Stop!' cried Giles, so loud the red woman froze. 'Stop,' Giles repeated, then added more softly, 'they're *kids*. Just kids.' She tilted her skull, inspecting the dirty faces, the pin-prick eyes peering from behind the embankment, through piles of leaves. 'Like … little animals.' For just a moment, her face softened, and Giles caught a flicker of the person she had once been. The scissors clattered to the ground. She stumbled around the fire, and disappeared behind the wall of smoke.

'You know she's still under there, under the car. Hanging on like an evil limpet,' said Ashraf, as he pulled Giles up onto the front seat.

'I know. Though, I think *evil* might be a bit strong. We don't know for certain that it was her who killed Alwyn.'

'Of – of course it was *her*. You caught her red-handed. She just kebab-skewered someone. She's a cold-blooded psycho.' Giles turned his face away from Ashraf. He couldn't say why, but for some reason, right then, he couldn't look him in the eye. He had grown very fond of Ashraf, his ingenuity, his playful spirit, how he tended to the emotional welfare of the Pack. Yet there was a feeling Giles couldn't shake. Twice he'd seen Ashraf lose his temper, the bottled-up grief erupting to the surface as rage. Giles had been the last person with the snap-blade, though it had been Isabel by Alwyn's side when the wound was fresh. Richard had been just around the corner, entering the tent moments after. But where had Ashraf been? If Giles was increasingly confident of one thing, it was that the woman with the red-stained skin had not killed Alwyn.

'I just don't think she's out to get us,' concluded Giles, pulling the door closed behind him. They climbed up onto their platforms either side of the steering wheel, slipped the key back in the ignition and coaxed the car to life. Through the side window, Giles watched the children outside huddle together by the firelight, backing away from the engine's rumble. He sighed, wearily rubbed his eyes, then kicked down on the key. The car came to a spluttering stop.

Obligingly, Richard wound down the window, and Giles leaned out into the night. 'OK. Anyone who wants to come with us can come. Drop your stuff, no weapons, no sticks or missiles, and don't try anything stupid again, all right?' He leaned back inside to an audience of shocked, tiny faces on the back seat and three understanding adults up front.

As Giles swung open the door, about half the children edged forward. 'Remember, we ride with the devil,' said Ash, gesturing to the car's underbelly. The girl with the charred doll's head looked up from beside the body of the tinman. Giles raised a shaky hand, and so did she. Then she flipped it and gave Giles the finger. With the help of several older children, she carried the tinman's body away, back towards the houses. The small boy Giles had chased up the drainpipe shuffled beside them.

Ashraf lowered the plank. This time the children were cautious, casting furtive glances left and right as if anticipating attack from every dark recess. One by one they gathered on the passenger seat, uncertain where to go next. Richard beckoned them into the back and, with his custom geniality, introduced the two clans of children, who regarded each other with resentment and suspicion.

Isabel climbed up to join him as Richard designated an area for each of the newcomers. 'Can we even do this? It's not like we're going to take them home – we're taking them *away*. Are we, what, building an ark?'

Giles thought a moment, then said, 'None of us have homes. Not anymore. Homes are places where we fit, where we're safe, where our people are. The buildings, all this, it's just leftovers.'

'So, the manor we're heading to – this Waterlow place – it's different, how?'

'It's hard to explain, but think of it like a base of operations, a little bastion of civilisation, while we figure things out.'

Isabel narrowed her eyes, then shrugged, placated. Giles had meant what he'd said, but it wasn't the whole truth. As she climbed back up to the headrest, leaving Giles alone on the driver's seat, he wondered if he'd done the right thing. They had grown from sixteen to a group of forty people, more or less. He had only needed six to drive the car, to get to the manor, hear the message Ava and Sadie had left for him there. Then he could find them. Help them. Make amends. Taking on passengers felt like the right thing, but it was also a distraction – an added responsibility. Though he was getting physically nearer to his daughters, it seemed to him that twenty more people were standing between them.

Giles reinstated himself on the steering column and Ashraf took up his spot on the opposite side of the wheel. He stretched to grip the handholds and looked back through the window. The remaining children had gathered on the embankment, scattered alone and in groups among the detritus. An object caught his eye – a remote-control truck, small and grey, sporting six thick wheels. A plastic figurine took up the cab, but the back was wide and flat, easily large enough for Giles to sit on. Nearby lay the controls. Perhaps the toy might be repurposed, he reasoned, to allow him to carry on his journey alone. A mad, guilty thought – quickly dismissed.

Behind him the passengers settled in, the original dozen making space for the newcomers. They *could* do this without him. Someone else could easily push this wheel. He'd give them directions, and drive beside them, even. Then if the sedan got stuck, if there was another jolt in their journey, he'd have the option of carrying on alone. He opened his mouth to float the idea aloud when Ashraf leaned across the wheel and said, 'Think you've got a fan club, mate.' Giles turned to see a row of grubby faces peering about the driver's seat as the girl with the troll, Aelfrieda, pointed to Giles, introducing him to a newcomer, and mouthed the letters – B, U, G.

Giles sighed, twisted the key, and the engine rumbled into life. Evelyn pressed the pedal, and the sedan edged a little further across the bridge.

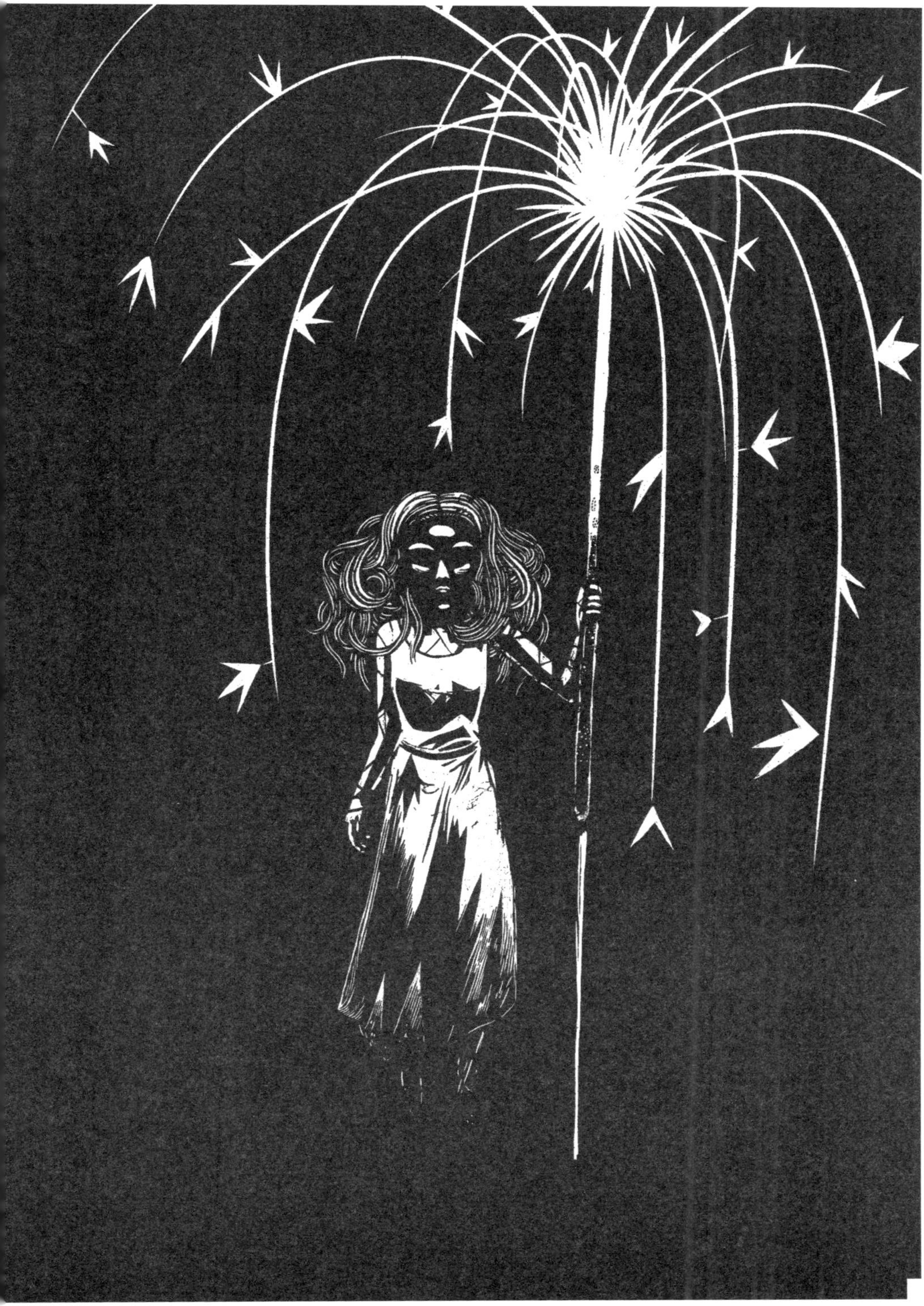

CHAPTER 20

ELSEWHERE,
CIRCLES of EMPATHY

People of the Palaeolithic period are generally considered to have had modestly sized circles of empathy, about the length and breadth of their cave. That is to say, their capacity for moral consideration extended to close kin and friends but oh, no further. It is an enlivening thought that in the hundred thousand years since then, our circles grew wider and wider, to the point that, on July Second, they had the potential to encase the entire planet. When earthquakes upset Tibet, the Americas rallied relief campaigns. When police overstepped in Detroit, protests were held in Paris. For all its faults and vices, the age of the internet would be remembered and lamented as a brief period, a fabled time, when all of humanity, in a sense, shared a single cave. And indeed, our hearts had never been bigger.

In the aftermath of the Descent, just how long the web held up depended greatly on where you were. On one end of the scale sat Pittsburgh, where it blinkered out in less than twenty-five minutes, due to a sensitive operation involving a uranium core at the very moment the wave broke ground. At the other end of the scale sat the Jutland province of Denmark where, thanks to a steady supply of wind power, the internet persisted for eighteen days, albeit in a dwindling capacity, as around the world servers and their back-ups dropped out one by one.

With the knowledge of its pending collapse (for surely how long could this daisy chain hold?) many rushed to elicit one last miracle from their obsidian mirrors. For most, the first port of call was to reach out to loved ones. Then came a gathering of information from this near-infinite library. News outlets from the western hemisphere, those who had watched the white wave spread across the ocean, made for the best sources. Of entertainment, there was plenty. User generated video platforms abounded with content – surveillance footage and reaction videos, compiled, edited and set to ominous scores. Some spoke, others sang together, shared experiences and survivalist advice. Cat videos took on a different meaning as foolhardy filmmakers tried to livestream reunions with their once feline friends. A surprisingly large percentage of users tried to safeguard their finances. Others attempted to back up the records of their bygone life, in the hope of preserving the people they once were. For in the years to come, no one would believe they had once been this big, this beautiful.

*

Perhaps the greatest agents in those early hours were those who sought to organise. Indeed, hundreds of newly formed settlements were credited to those first efforts, before the infrastructure fell, to designate meeting points, to head to areas of safety and plentiful resource. Countless thousands were set in motion on quests to reconnect with children, partners, parents and friends, heading for a point of rendezvous. Some took days, some took years. A handful spent the remainder of their lives making the journey across continents, across oceans, determined to reconnect, and fulfil the promises made.

The interconnectivity of humankind burned brightly in those last hours before it all fell silent. Of all the aspects of the old life, perhaps none were mourned so loudly, and so quickly forgotten, as the internet. When the users stepped away from their blank, lifeless screens, they found that, like the palaeolithic people of a hundred thousand years before, their circle of empathy had shrunken back, for the time being at least, to the modest span of their cave.

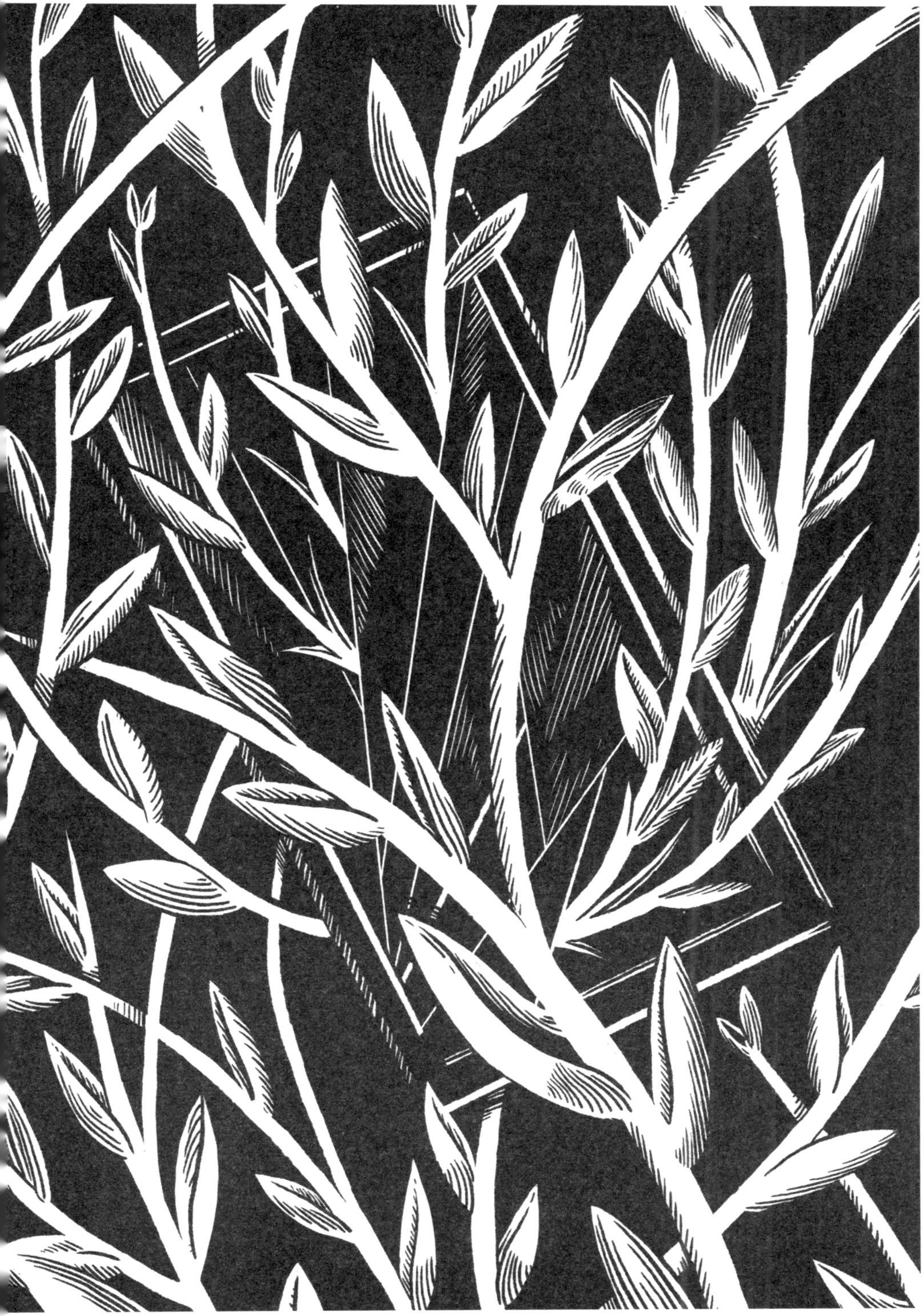

PART V

CHAPTER 21

MATILDA STROMHELL

The back-country roads were a mystery to Matilda. It didn't help that the signposts were either lost in darkness or swallowed by unkempt hedgerows, and now to top it all off, the sat-nav reception was in a perfect blind spot. Still, thanks to the inexplicable set of spotlights that lit up the pillar of smoke ahead of them, she had managed to find the crash site. 'Would you look at that?' said the officer beside her, lining up his phone and leaning into the windscreen to get a better view.

'I don't think you're allowed to take photos with that,' said Matilda, careful not to take her eyes from the road. 'You have to use the camera in the glove compartment.'

'Oh, this isn't for official purposes.'

'Then you're *definitely* not allowed. You can't take crash-site pictures for social media, Bob. You'd get in a load of trouble.'

'I wasn't going to *put* them anywhere. It's just interesting, you know – the patterns, how the smoke shifts under the light and—' Matilda pushed his phone down into his lap. Bob sighed and sat upright in his seat.

'Right, of course.'

They rounded the side of the hill, and the road ahead straightened. An elderly lady in a thick fur jacket waved them down from beside a parked car. Matilda could see the full extent of the crash site now. Two headlights from a hatchback stuck up at forty-five degrees where the vehicle had slid backwards into a ditch. A few metres ahead of it, the black blossom of smoke rose from a crumpled mess of metal. Matilda recognised the wreckage as a head-to-head collision. A little further up the road, wedged into hedges, they found another car and a van. She unhooked the receiver and squeezed the handset to her mouth.

'It looks like we have five vehicles involved. Four cars and one Transit van.'

'*OK SC Thirteen. Sending additional units,*' crackled the reply.

'There should be a fire engine and a couple of police cars already on the way,' offered the officer.

'I know, Bob.' Matilda smiled and scooped a stray strand of wiry blonde hair back into its bun. She stepped out of the ambulance. 'Until they get here, why don't you go and talk to that lady? That'd be really helpful.'

Where were those other units? It wasn't right that she was here on her own, babysitting Bob, a junior officer on what – his *third* night on call? It shouldn't be an officer at all. It should be another paramedic with her now, at a scene like this. If it weren't Saturday night, they'd told her, and we didn't need every medic on call in Southampton . . .

So here they were. The crash was as bizarre as anything she'd ever seen. Beyond the randomly stacked arrangement of cars and the lack of tyre marks, there was something amiss that she couldn't put her finger on. Hoisting the medi-kit to her shoulder, Matilda slammed the door and the sudden noise made clear what was missing. Aside from the creak of metal twisting inside the flames, the crash site was silent. Not a peep. In all her years driving the ambulance, she'd never come across a quiet accident. And yet here were five noiseless vehicles. She ran towards the hatchback sticking out of the ditch and rested her hand on the warm bonnet as she slid down beside it.

'Matilda?' Bob was calling to her from the ambulance, but the paramedic had a torch in her mouth and was trying to see inside, though the car windows were fogged-up from condensation and giving little away.

'Hello?' she called through her teeth, 'If you can hear me, it's OK. I'm going to get you out.'

'Erm, Matilda?' He sounded nervous. She felt bad about ignoring Bob, but he probably just wanted to know what kind of form the lady needed to fill in. Matilda kicked down the dry shrubbery wedged against the side of the door and heaved it open, taking its weight with one shoulder. The smell that hit her was horrendous. In the uncomfortably familiar way the most horrible smells are – distinctly human, rich personal odours that tell stories about the things our bodies do to stay alive. Blinking through the ammonia, she saw that the car was empty. Only a scattering of food packets and clothes. Fluid pooled in the footwells and ran down the length of the vehicle. She let the door fall shut.

'Did that lady see anyone leave here?' Matilda called back to Bob as she climbed out of the ditch, wiping her face against her sleeve.

'No, and she checked all the vehicles, even before this one caught alight.'

'And?' Matilda ran about the furnace that burned in the middle of the road, heading to the Transit van.

'And she says there's no one here. They're all empty.' Matilda stopped and turned to face Bob.

'And as far as I can tell,' added the older lady, wrapping her fur coat further up about her neck, 'they used their vehicles as a latrine before they went.'

Bob pressed his face against the window of the Transit van – a parcel delivery service – shielding his eyes from the heat.

'And it looks like they took their clothes off too. See? Uniforms over both seats.'

'Good detective work, Bob.' Matilda squinted and puffed out her cheeks, letting the air escape in a whistle as she jogged to the third car, wedged into the hedgerow. On the tangle of leaves behind the car, she saw the comforting pulse of blue lights. Finally, the back-up. The third car was the same as the others, fogged windows masking empty seats strewn with trousers, shirts and body fluid. The hatchback's headlights clicked off and, thinking that her colleagues might need some assistance without a beacon to guide them down these winding country roads, Matilda craned her head over the hedge, waving. She stopped suddenly, stared for a moment, and then called back to Bob.

'I thought we were first on the scene?'

'We are,' he assured, 'the others are having trouble finding us, but they're nearby, so they—'

'Then what, pray tell, is that?' interrupted Matilda, pulling back a branch in the hedge and pointing into the field. There, stationary between lines of barley, was another ambulance, facing the opposite way, its blue light bar still blinking. Tyre marks of flattened crops led back to the crash site and a disfigured section of hedgerow. Matilda stamped down the brambles, pushed herself past the leaves and ran through the field.

She recognised the ambulance cab number.

'Simian?' she called. She had seen him earlier at the depot. He was transferring a patient from Christchurch, a town on the other side of the New Forest. They should have been back in Southampton an hour ago, dealing with the Saturday night rabble. Panting, she reached the cab and rested an arm on the bonnet, feeling the rumble of the engine still running inside. Somehow, the ambulance had avoided collision and slowed to a stop on its own, just a few lengths of ivy trailing from the front grill, snagged as it had ploughed through the hedge. The windows to the cab were fogged, and this time, knowing what to expect, Matilda clamped a hand over her lower face and opened the door. A boot tumbled out into the barley and a ghost of foul-smelling steam escaped after it, evaporating into the night. A paramedic uniform, like hers, hung limply over one seat. She turned off the engine and, as she did so, heard a chorus of sirens coming over the hill, the actual advance of cavalry. Perhaps they would make sense of this and have some information that would reveal the obvious explanation she was missing.

Matilda refastened her hand across her mouth and opened the back of the ambulance, ready for another assault on her senses. Instead, the air was clear, bar the usual smell of disinfectant. She was about to close the door when she did a double take. On the gurney, beneath a blue cotton sheet, in the middle of this barley field, was a young woman.

The woman's pulse was regular, and according to her chart, she'd been given a heavy dose of pentobarbital at six thirty p.m. Anthea, the woman, had suffered a seizure, and the barbiturates were slowing the brain function down to reduce swelling until she could make surgery at Southampton. She was in a chemically induced coma. Matilda checked her watch. If Anthea didn't get another dose in less than forty minutes, she would wake up and die. Back in the driver's seat, Matilda held her breath, pushed the soiled uniform onto the floor, wound both windows down and started the engine.

Pushing up through the hedge, she saw that the cavalry had taken control of the scene. Two officers strung police tape across the road and set up diversion signs as firefighters tackled the blaze. Squad cars flanked either end, and ahead of her, Chief Constable Deverill, recognisable by her large helmet of red hair, was in heated conversation with Bob. Judging from his body language, the junior officer was not enjoying the chat.

'So, what, exactly, are you telling me?' the chief said as Matilda pulled up beside them, ivy still trailing from the bonnet. 'Am I to believe that six drivers simultaneously crashed their cars, soiled themselves, stripped off and then ran into the woods?'

'We're not sure, Chief. The lady here didn't see anybody leave the site, and she heard the impact. She was moments behind them,' explained Bob.

'Well, sod this. Wherever they are, I guess we'd better find them. What the hell is that?' said the chief, yanking free the ivy. Matilda wound down her window.

'Good evening, Chief Constable. This unit was down in the field. Simian – the driver – he's missing too, like the others, and there's a patient in the back.'

'Well, let's question her, God damn it. Get a statement.'

'I'm afraid she's in a coma.'

'Well then, wake her up.'

Matilda felt herself blushing, the way she always did for other people's mistakes.

'I'm not sure what she'd tell you. She was unconscious during the accident. I'm sorry, Chief, I have to take her back to Southampton.'

'Fine, but then get back here. We need every available hand combing these fields. And I want to know the moment that patient can talk.'

Matilda nodded, perplexed. The chief must have misunderstood the meaning of coma. But then, you didn't get to be chief for nothing. She probably knew something Matilda didn't.

She made it to Southampton Central in less than twenty minutes, driving with the sirens full blare, relishing the adrenaline of emergency, leaning into the corners like a bobsleigh rider. A nurse greeted her at A & E, and he helped her wheel the gurney up the slope towards the bright reception doors. Matilda pressed the patient's chart into his hands.

'Let me know how Anthea gets on. The chief constable wants an update as soon as she wakes up.' She smiled. He was a little young for her, but only just.

'Will do,' replied the nurse, and as Matilda squeezed past, she saw him gag.

She laughed self-consciously. 'It's the seats,' she turned to point at the ambulance, 'they're covered in—' but the doors had already closed behind him, 'crap.'

The lights of Southampton dimmed in the rearview mirror as she turned onto the B-roads leading into the New Forest. One of the other paramedics would drive this ambulance back. She'd make sure of it. She'd had quite enough of sitting in someone else's filth for one evening. Matilda nudged aside the uniform at her feet, moving it as far away as possible. Why hadn't she left it at the hospital? She almost considered throwing it out the side window, anything to breathe easier, when she saw something move among the fabric. Matilda screamed, slammed on the brakes and pulled into a lay-by, brushing up against a farm gate. Fumbling with the door handle, she tumbled out onto the gravel, grabbing a nearby fallen branch.

She held it like a lance and crept forward, edging its end under a crumpled shirt and lifting. As it untangled from the other wet garments in the footwell, Matilda saw long twists of ginger hair clung to the shirt like the slimy fibrous core of a pumpkin. They twisted around the branch as she pulled, until – with a slap – a small fleshy mass slid from the clothes and landed beside the pedals. Matilda leaned closer, prodding it with the stick. It was mammalian, underdeveloped, its skin peeling away beneath the slightest contact. Seeing that it wasn't a rat, as she'd first suspected, Matilda pushed aside the hair and saw, to her horror, a tiny human hand. She caught her breath as the hand flattened itself against the floor and pushed up a torso, dragging a head and a blanket of hair behind it.

'Simian?' Somehow, it couldn't be, but it was. His hair, long and light red, curled over his tiny, heaving chest. She must have made a noise because the head tilted back in her direction. Hair fell away, revealing his face, eyes still closed. She gasped. His features had changed, not just in size and texture, crumpled and semi-translucent, but also in structure. The proportions were all wrong, elongated, and hideous. There was something in his mouth, pushing his jaw a full jaw's length lower than it should be. Matilda leaned in closer still and saw, clamped behind his lower front teeth, a normal-sized tooth pushing up through the roof of his mouth, leading to a thin metal bar that pierced the soft flesh beside his nose.

She managed a second shaky, whispered 'Simian?' and just like that – his eyes flicked open. For a second, they looked at one another, person to person, and then Simian's face filled with a terror, only matched by Matilda's own. His few functioning jaw muscles must have clenched as the bar slid further up through the widening hole in his cheek. Tiny hands clawed at his tiny chest as the prosthetic porcelain tooth erupted between his eyes, splitting his face in two. Simian fell back, dead, and Matilda vomited onto the driver's seat.

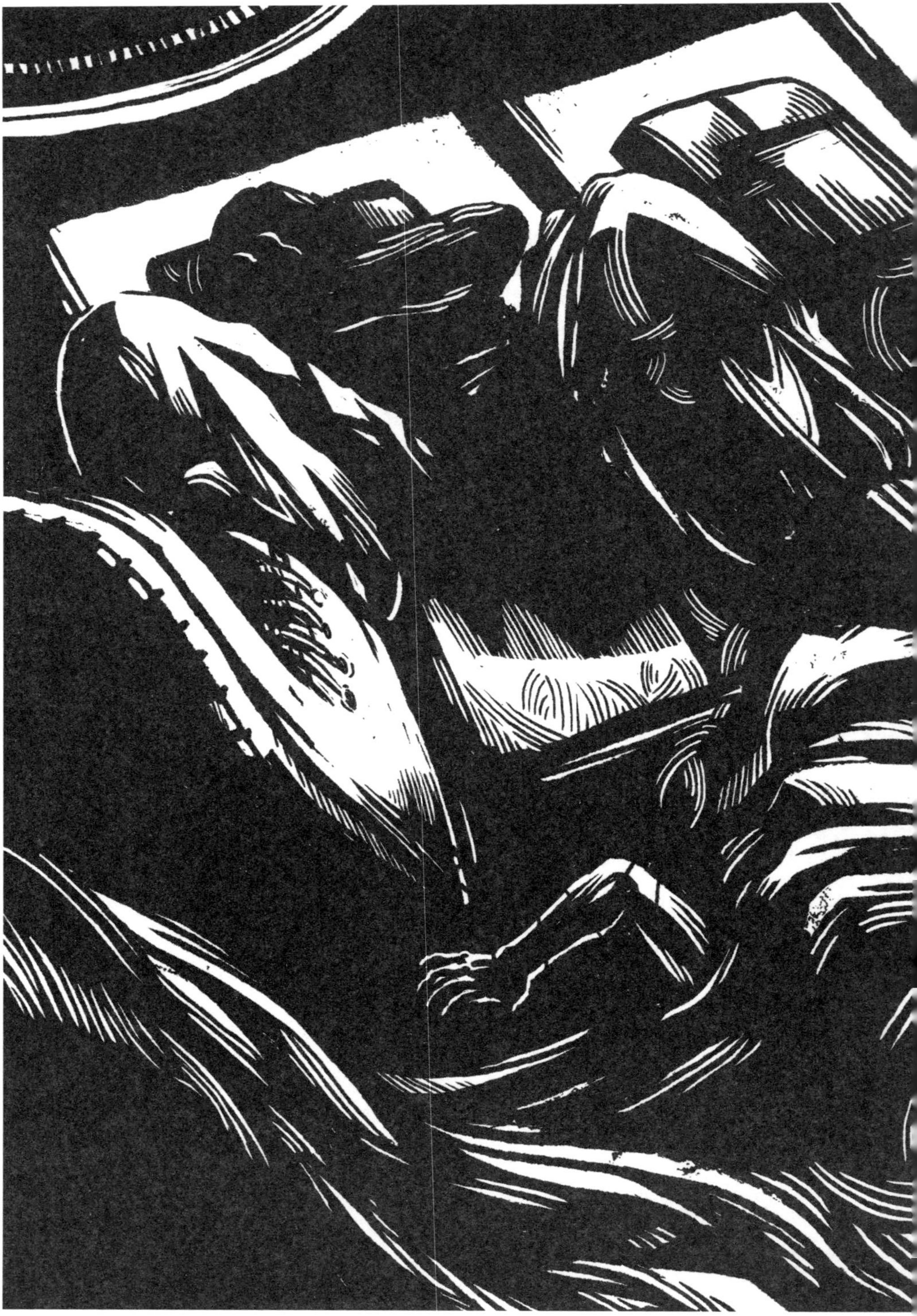

CHAPTER 22

AN ACTUAL CASTLE

The steering wheel lurched. Giles lifted off his feet, swung an arc into the air and flew like a ragdoll. Below him, the quiet order of the sedan collapsed into anarchy. Twine snapped. Planks upended. Ashraf tumbled into the glove compartment. Through the windscreen Giles watched the world turn on its side, concrete folding upwards as inertia met velocity and pushed his stomach into the underside of his lungs. A moment of weightlessness, then the inexorable pull of gravity began.

The sedan had traversed the bridge and around Southampton without incident, not counting the constant infighting that had at once erupted between the two tribes of children in the back seats. There had been complaints from the Pack that the new arrivals were not just unruly, they were feral, a different species.

215

'I saw that one eating a maggot,' Jayden complained.

'And I'm sure he'll share if you ask nicely,' comforted Ashraf, who continued to astound Giles with his consummate diplomacy, which was never more needed.

The traffic had been thankfully light around midday on Sunday July Second so that, taking to the wider roads, they had been able to pick up pace, allowing the car to cover more ground in one morning than the past three days combined. Giles attributed this, in part, to the improved rhythm of their collective driving. They were ever more in sync, as each operator learned to anticipate the other's movements. When he pushed up on one side of the wheel, Ashraf now exerted the exact counter-pull. Giles couldn't remember the last time he'd derived such joy from teamwork. It nourished him, and with each well-taken corner and successfully navigated pile-up, he felt the accumulating cloud within him recede.

From the confines of the car, the passengers watched the altered landscape unfold. Though the more populated areas remained at a distance, their route tying them to the motorways and A-roads, the scars left by the upheaval of the Descent – the clothes-pile cocoons, the vehicle wrecks, the thin tendrils of smoke – were well in evidence. Elsewhere, in a field, a game forsaken mid-flow. Elsewhere, a quiet and cluttered pub garden. Vacant at a glance, but if one looked closely, signs of life abounded. Doors hung slightly ajar. Branches lay like ladders. Airbricks peeled from walls. Small shelters constructed from street debris tottered in the breeze. Giles began to understand that life was not absent, but in hiding. The threat of the outside, the urban animals – cats, dogs and foxes – perhaps making survivors wary of wandering in the open. Here and there were the beginnings of adaptation. A tunnel of chicken wire ran atop a garden wall, creating a safe passageway to an open van, spilling with boxes. On a quiet terraced street below an overpass, Giles spotted a stretch of guttering shifted to create a bridge between two sills. Parked up on the second night, Giles counted dim flickering lights on a faraway tower block, concluding that Richard's morbid calculation of one in ten was not far off. On occasion they had seen people closer up, wandering the road, and the group agreed that the car would stop if heralded. The traveller would be allowed on board so long as they understood that mutiny would be met with a swift ejection and the route was non-negotiable.

In this way, they had taken on another eight passengers – children under the age of ten, four of whom had emerged en masse from a minibus. All had accepted the conditions in return for the sense of safety, purpose, and the promise of a better place. Many more had turned away, or watched with suspicion as the car, like a spectre from the old world, rolled past.

The new passengers brought the sedan's total to over fifty people. *Fifty.* Giles had only ever wanted to reclaim responsibility for two, his daughters, whose whereabouts were still unknown. Yet every manoeuvred obstacle brought him closer to the manor, to his desk, to the box beside the phone and the message that Sadie had said she'd leave him. It was a thin hope, magical thinking, and he knew it. Still, he had to believe the message was on that box, waiting. He pictured the girls in his mind's eye, himself beside them. Sadie had said they were safe. They had both survived the transformation. As soon as he knew where they were, he would find them. He would help them adapt, and not just survive, but thrive. Despite the broken scenery, to Giles the road seemed newly minted, and again he felt the thrill and the guilt that came with it. The path would end with Sadie and Ava, and the old world, along with his failure to provide and protect, would be forgotten.

It was this growing sense of urgency, and the excitement of entering the final stretch towards Waterlow Manor, less than a mile to go, that emboldened Giles to suggest pushing the accelerator. Taking advantage of an open stretch, the car had hit an exhilarating forty-five miles per hour. They might have been breaking the land speed record for all the delighted whoops and cries that came from the back seat. It was then the gangplank slid off the driver's seat and pinned Evelyn against the pedal. Maya leaned over and managed to free her friend, but by then it was too late. Ahead, a coach straddled both lanes. Ashraf and Giles had pulled the wheel in opposite directions. As the handholds slipped from Ashraf's grip, a screw in the side of the wheel clipped him under the chin, sending him toppling backwards. Giles kept hold a moment longer, and then the wheel had spun.

He thundered into the dashboard, skidding over the hot black plastic and becoming wedged in the ravine at the bottom of the windscreen. From there he watched in horror as the concrete beneath the glass turned to grass and they twisted over the edge of an embankment.

The car narrowly missed a tree's trunk and instead crunched through thinner branches that whipped at the windscreen. Giles waited, petrified, for the glass to smash, for the impact to crush him. But it did not come. Finally, the sedan slammed to a halt – her nose wedged between two forking branches. There, the car loitered at ninety degrees. People and objects piled on top of Giles. Children, cans of food, an atlas of Great Britain, all squeezing his skull against the glass. He stared at the dense foliage flattened to the windscreen, crushed by the car's weight, and was considering

218

their shared miserable fate when his centre of gravity shifted. The vehicle toppled over, pushed forward by its own momentum, breaking more branches and falling to rest on its roof. Released, Giles slid down the slope of the windscreen towards the ceiling, as the car sank to a stop in a cushion of brambles.

For a moment, all was quiet. Then the upturned vehicle filled, decibel by decibel, with the groans and cries of passengers dislodging themselves from debris. Giles rolled aside a packet of biscuits and helped Richard to his feet.

'Well, that could have been worse,' said the priest, as the two of them pulled Alex, Elfie and several others out from beneath a giant pillow. Still, they'd got away with sprains and bruises, not breaks.

It was then Giles smelled the petrol. Others had smelled it too, and they scrambled for the exits. Ashraf, emerging dazed from the glovebox above them, reached towards the handle and kicked, but the door held fast against the thick cushion of dense vegetation wedged outside, sealing them in. Panic rose in Giles; images of sparklers and snakes of flame filled his imagination.

'The window!' called Richard, and Ashraf turned his attention to the button beside the handle and kicked. The wall of glass raised like a castle gate, spilling thorns and broken branches into the car. A barrier of dagger like brambles pressed against the nervous crowd. Giles stretched his arms wide, trying to hold them at bay, and felt the sting of a thorn-tip in his lower back. It would take only one person to panic.

'Stop. Step away from the window.' Richard's voice was measured, catching the attention of the crowd. As they eased away, Giles found the scalpel, turned and with a practised flick, he began to prune them a path.

*

The convoy followed Giles and Richard through the tunnel of thorns and out into a meadow speckled with spider webs, each one a chandelier of morning dew. Beautiful, with palm-wide arachnids nestled at their heart. Shuddering, Giles turned back to the sedan, her four wheels still visible, a thin trail of smoke rising above the undergrowth. Behind the car lay a trail of destruction stretching back to a wide hole torn in the hedgerow, a now familiar roadside feature.

'That's everyone,' said Ashraf, as he and Isabel emerged from the corridor, Ash folding the register into his shoulder bag.

Giles nodded then announced, 'We'll go the rest of the way on foot,' causing whispers of discontent.

'I don't think we should stay out here,' murmured Isabel, who had caught him up, leaning close so only Giles could hear.

'What if a wolf attacks us?' asked Aelfrieda.

'Or a pack of pole-weasels?' squealed little Ben.

'Couldn't we try and convert another car?' asked Isabel. 'There's plenty up there on the road. Or just settle in one of the houses we already passed. Surely, they're as good as any, for the time being?'

'You have to trust me,' said Giles, 'where I'm taking us, it's not far now, and it's worth the walk.'

'Or an eagle?' asked Ben, thrusting himself between them, 'Or a hungry horse?' His arms were stained purple up to the elbow from a blackberry's mushy remains. Giles peeled off a seedpod and sucked the sweet purple jelly from it, shaking his head.

'I'm afraid I don't think a horse would be too interested in you. Even a hungry one. You don't need to worry.' Giles hoisted the boy onto one shoulder and pointed to a clump of trees. The rest of the group followed the line of his finger to a square of silver birch on a hill several fields away. 'You see that? Just beyond those trees is a place you'll be safe. At least until we can figure something better out.'

'Worthole Manor?' asked the boy.

'Almost,' said Giles, 'Waterlow Manor, just behind those trees. My home, and until we find some help, if you like, it can be yours too.'

The trek through the fields took the rest of the day, Giles walking ahead to clear away the webs and their arachnid architects. Richard stayed close, on edge, convinced that the red woman was following them through the grasses, biding her moment to finish him off. Rumours and paranoia wore at the already frayed nerves of the party so that by the time they reached the square of silver birch up on the hill, they were miserable and wretched and riddled with insect bites. Hence it was a great relief when Waterlow Manor revealed itself through the trees, and a palpable wave of excitement lifted the group, in all its factions. Maya startled Jayden by slinging an arm around his neck and pulling him into an affectionate headlock, and Giles was happy to see two of the Claybourne bridge children lift Alex onto a knot of roots to give him a better view.

A field of wildflowers, ringed by a stream and ancient oak woodland, led down to the old manor house. The property's boundary line was marked by a high dry-stone wall, fortifying the building itself, which was old and biscuit-box pretty. Ivy scaled ornate window frames the way Giles's beard overran his face – thick, uneven and probably crawling with insects. There were no cars in the driveway, no movement in the windows, no smoke issuing from any of the several stacks protruding between the red and black checkered roof tiles. Aside from its bucolic charm, the place would have passed almost without note had it not been for the Victorian botanical orangery at the back of the house, its majestic white wooden beams prominent against the rolling, verdant landscape.

'Beautiful, isn't it?' said Giles.

'Remind me again why we didn't stop somewhere closer?' asked Isabel, seeming less than impressed and nearly slipping on a wet rock as she clambered up to join him. 'Like a supermarket, or a petrol station?' Giles looked wounded.

'This is long term. For all we know, there's no help out there, no rescue or explanation for any of this. Here, if we need it, there's a future. We can grow tomatoes.'

'OK,' said Isabel suspiciously.

'And – and marrow, beans, courgettes, anything you like. It's a perfect little ecosystem, good all year round, and completely safe. Plus, there's freshwater nearby. Solar panels, though, those don't work so well. But there's a firewood central heating, a back-up generator. The house, well, it's more than large enough for this lot. The people who lived here—'

'Wait, you said this place was *your* home?' interrupted Isabel. Giles laughed.

'It is. But I don't *own* it. Jesus. What did you think? I'm a prince in rags? On a Roman holiday? Isabel, I'm the groundskeeper.'

'Oh,' Isabel smiled, 'right.'

'The family are on holiday in Madrid, and I took the week to go camping with my dad. I doubt they'll be coming back any time soon, though who knows? I suppose that'll be good news for all of us if they do.'

Giles and Isabel set off down the slope into tall grasses alive with the melodic hum of insects. A bumblebee, as plump and soft as a kitten, ambled between pompom dandelions. Wasps like small birds busied about the purple flowers above them, and when the children began throwing stones, Giles pointed out the creatures were in fact the wasp's fangless doppelgänger, the hoverfly.

'How long have you worked here?' asked Isabel, hoisting Ben, stained a delicious purple, onto Giles's shoulders.

'About two years. I moved down from London, the outskirts really, after my wife and I split up. This was nearer to the girls' school. So, you know, it made sense.'

'You worked in London?'

'I was a carpenter. Well, that's not true either. I ran a workshop for a few years, and when that went bust, I got a job making pagodas. Putting them together.' He lifted what looked like a daisy and crushed it between his palms. 'There. Can you smell that? Camomile. *Anthemis arvensis*,' said Giles.

'Stop showing off,' said Isabel, giving a half-smile as Giles lifted the crushed flower above his head for Ben to smell.

'The pagodas were made by Amish folk out in Ohio, without electric tools. We'd assemble them.'

'Sounds like fun work.'

'Ah, I dunno. It was a gimmick. For us, it was like putting Lego together. The Amish, they didn't use electricity, *but* they had hydraulic saws that were just as good, if not better. Cheating, really ...'

The light seemed to ebb a little from Giles's face and Isabel nudged his ribs with an elbow. 'But then you found *this* place?' Giles looked up.

'Sure. It's paradise, right? The family, they're good people. Kids are spoilt, but hard to blame them for that. Parents were into faultlines, dowsing and crystals. The dad was anyway.'

'There are worse perversions.'

'Agreed. Not my thing. You'll love the stone circle though, helped him install it. Just wait until I show you the garden.'

'Will there be animals in the garden?' asked Ben, leaning far over Giles's head to look him in the eye, perhaps to discern if his answer would be an honest one.

'Not big ones. The garden has a wall around it. In the woods, however, there are owls, foxes and badgers. But we're not going to see them now. They're nocturnal.'

'That means they only come out at night,' added Isabel.

'I'd keep your eye out for rabbits. No matter how many times I put them out, they always manage to find a way back in. If you catch one, I'll teach you how to ride it.' Ben's mouth hung open, and his eyes lit up with wonder. 'Oh, I'm kidding. You can't ride a rabbit,' said Giles bluntly. 'It'd bite your head off.'

Giles's fondest memories of Waterlow Manor were the school visit days. He'd listen to the students running up and down the steel staircase, in groups of ten or fifteen, filling out the botanical quiz while he worked the beds below. The others would splay out on the lawn or see how high they could climb the sycamore before the teacher shouted them down. The highlight was the garden walk when the children would follow their teachers through the small woodland, ticking off treasures Giles had hidden in bushes, behind small enclaves, and down overgrown paths. There was the giant bronze pear inside the burnt-tree hollow, the half-grown topiary woman erupting at the waist into wild flecks of vine, the fibreglass dragon salvaged from an old carousel and transformed into an object of higher status since the paint had faded and weeds had pushed through the seat. The algae-covered concrete sphinx submerged to its neck in the small pond, and many more.

Giles would have liked to have led those walks. He was planning to ask. There was no reason why not. He even had the DBS forms in a drawer at his cabin. But something had held him back. Perhaps fear that he wasn't good enough or that those young, insightful students would see through his role as tour guide to understand his position at the manor. That he had not really chosen it as a destination, he had just ended up there. In a sense, he had been banished, pushed here by a string of material failures that left him without any other option.

Now, as he ushered the convoy of dwarfed travellers through a drainage passage in the dry-stone boundary wall, his feelings were mixed. There was some elation at bringing these people here, excitement for their potential future, at having reached a milestone on the way to find his girls. Then there was something else, something sad. Isabel watched as Giles scrunched his face. Then, he burst out laughing.

'What's so funny?' she asked.

'Oh, it's nothing. It's just, for a moment I was getting melancholy because, well, I'm useless to this place now, more than ever.' He gestured to a cylindrical black steel framework in a clearing ahead, a hedgerow creeping up its side. 'That there was going to be a kind of standalone balcony to view the woodland and garden, been working on it for months. How'm I going to finish welding the platform now? Then I was thinking – how the hell am I going to prune back the beech trees in the autumn, or re-tile the patio? Paint the balustrades. I can't. Not anymore. And really, it doesn't matter.' Giles beamed at Isabel and spread his arms wide, encompassing the manor. 'Because there's so much *more* we can do. More we can build for us, as we are now. Made to fit. To them, this was a house. To us, it could be a whole town, the start of a new city.'

Isabel laughed. She leaned into the moss-lined passage, helping the last few stragglers through, then together with Giles, they rolled a large stone over the opening to the drain, sealing it shut.

'OK, Columbus. Don't get ahead of yourself. So, there's power here, and food, that's good. Perhaps we'll stay for a while. But let's take it a day at ...' she felt a nudge in her side and turned to see Giles nodding towards the manor's front door. Richard was clambering onto an upturned plant pot and calling the party together. He was doing well for someone so frail. With the greenhouse and turret-like chimneys behind him, she had to admit, the place looked magnificent, like something out of a fairy tale. Richard was stood up on the rim of the pot, holding on to a sunflower stalk and calling out over the assembled group – the dozen members of the Pack, the children from the Claybourne bridge, the eight others they had picked up on the road. There was something familiar about the unlikely assemblage of people, and it clicked. The four adults and forty odd children were almost exactly the configuration of one of those visiting school trips.

'I cannot speak for you all,' Richard began, 'but I feel as though I have arrived. Thank you, Giles. If I'm not mistaken, here, in this place, our luck may well be changing.'

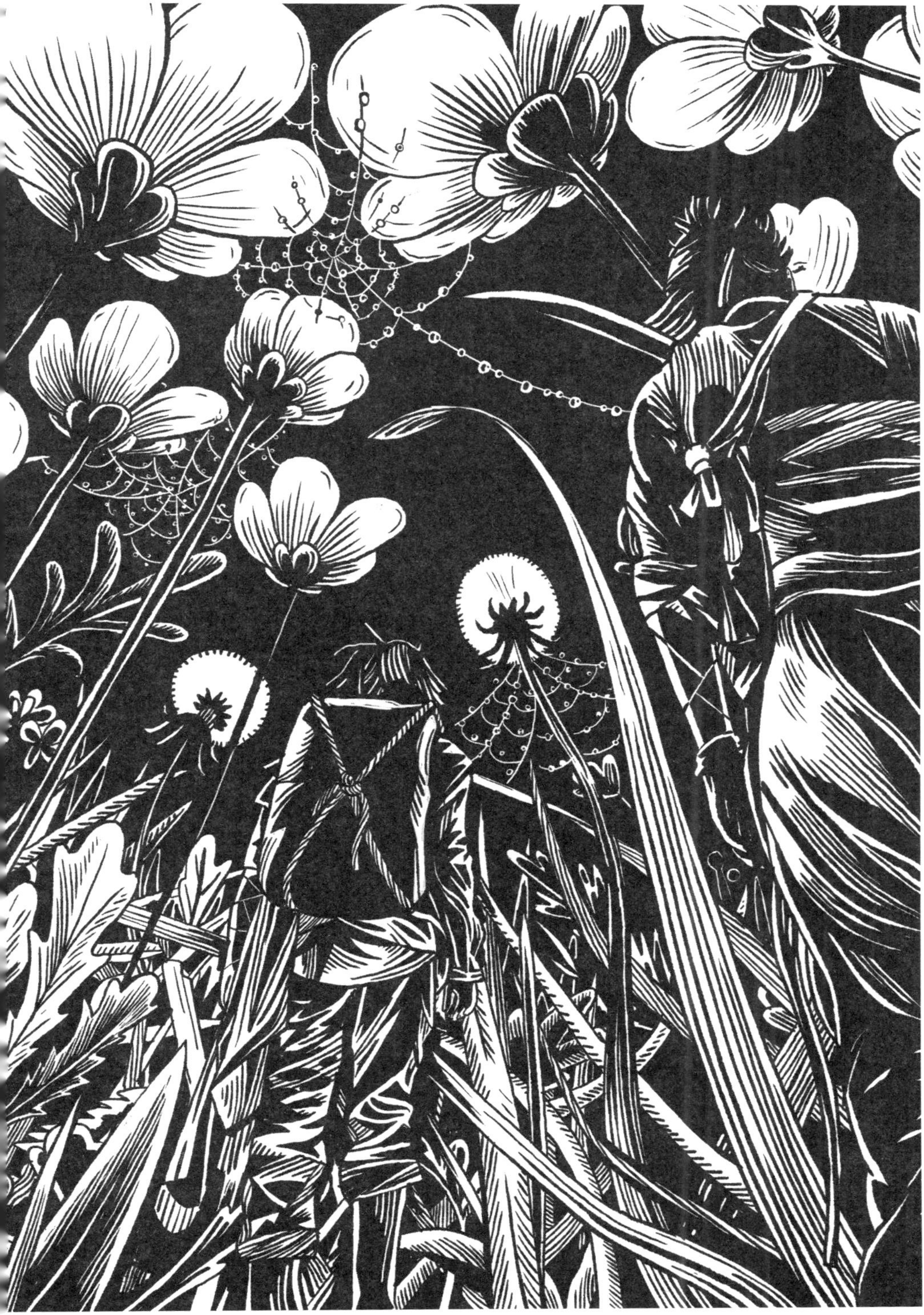

CHAPTER 23

THE IVORY POOL

'*M*atilda. *Matilda!*' It was Bob's voice, shaky and panicked over the radio. Matilda sat in the gravel beside the ambulance and looked wearily up at the receiver, which blinked red with the incoming transmission.

'*Matilda, pick up. You need to come back to the crash site. You ... you have to see this.*' Matilda stood and leaned on the doorframe, croaking into the handheld.

'Matilda here. On my way.'

'*OK. Be quick.*'

She replaced the receiver, gulped down half a bottle of water from the glove compartment, swilling and spitting the rest to clear her mouth, all the time careful not to look at what lay beside the accelerator pedal. Wiping what she could from the seat, she covered the stain with a blue sheet from the back, took a deep breath and looked down.

The tiny form was curled in a foetal position, hands still clawing at its chest, face still broken in two from the incisor wedged through its centre. She didn't want to touch the body. But she didn't want to step on it either. So, scooping it up in the paramedic's uniform, she folded Simian from view and placed him on the passenger seat.

Back at the crash site, the fire was out, leaving only a steaming knot of metal, neglected in the middle of the road. Bob, the chief constable, and several other uniformed men and women were crowded around the back of the ambulance Matilda and Bob had arrived in. Spotting her through the crowd, Bob hurried over.

'I've never seen anything like it. None of us have. It's ... it's impossible.'

Matilda knew what she would see long before she shouldered her way to the front of the crowd. Voices clattered about her.

It's a prank! Cut it open, see if it's real.

That's disgusting.

I could fit him in my pocket.

The small, shrivelled, lifeless form of a man, the height of a paperback novel, was laid out on a gurney, dwarfed by a surrounding sea of blue cloth. Fanning out from his head was a halo of thick black curls, and though his face was thankfully unpierced, his neck bulged unnaturally on one side. Matilda shuffled out of the pack and surveyed the crash site, taking in a deep lungful of air.

'They found it in the Transit van,' said Bob, wringing his hands beside her, shooting furtive looks back at the ambulance and looking mousier by the minute. 'What do you think it is?'

'I – I think it's a person, Bob. One of the couriers.'

'You think?'

'Yes,' replied Matilda, putting her head between her legs to get more air. Behind them, the chief was shouting.

'OK, that's enough. Everyone back.' The crowd shifted, revealing the woman with the helmet-cut of auburn hair. 'I'm calling in the biohazard response unit,' she declared dramatically. There was a groan from a corner of the group, and one of the firefighters raised her hand.

'Is that really necessary, Chief? It's just if you do that, we'll have to drive all the way back to Southampton and change our uniforms.' Two other firefighters nodded in agreement.

'Fine.' The chief shot them a scolding look and turned her attention back to the body. She laid a pound coin beside it for scale and took a picture on her phone.

'In that case, we'll section this off ourselves. I'll inform the super and see what they have to say about it.'

As the officers and fireman pulled tape and rolls of plastic sheeting from the car trunks, Matilda approached the chief.

'What is it?' she muttered, sensing Matilda loitering nearby.

'Were there any survivors in the other vehicles? Did you find anyone alive?'

'Alive?' asked the chief, without looking up at Matilda, still tapping a message into her phone.

'Alive and . . . like him?' said Matilda, motioning to the body in the back of the ambulance. The chief narrowed her eyes.

'The other cabs were empty, so far as we can tell. As for this . . . I'm not sure what it is, but it's certainly not *alive*. It couldn't be. Look at it.'

'I found another body,' Matilda said quietly, not wanting to seem insubordinate. 'I found Simian, the driver of that ambulance. He was alive. He – he woke up . . . briefly.' The chief's lips became tight and pursed.

'That seems rather unlikely, Miss Stromhell.'

'I can show you.' Matilda led the older woman to the other ambulance's passenger door, unfolded the uniform and stepped back. The chief shuddered then recoiled, her mouth agape.

'Good grief. This – this used to be a ...?' Matilda nodded, offering a sympathetic smile that reached out like a hand to support someone descending a crooked, unsteady staircase.

'Yes ... a *person*,' assured Matilda and touched the chief's shoulder. She jumped and, with a startled squeal, brushed the hand away as if it were a spider. Quickly regaining her composure, the chief turned sharply on Matilda.

'Right! All this needs to be sealed up. This specimen and anything it touched might be hazardous. Whatever did this to these people might be contagious.'

Matilda craned her head, looking past the chief to Simian laid out on the passenger seat.

'An outbreak is possible, I suppose, but ... look. Simian was alive when I found him, and I think the second victim ...' Matilda hurried past the chief to the other ambulance and rested a gloved finger on the side of the shrunken man's swollen neck. Then, pulling a cotton bud from a metal drawer, she gently prised the miniature man's mouth and probed at something solid inside. 'It appears that this victim choked. The transformation – if that's what it was – the transformation itself didn't kill these people. Other stuff got in the way – this crash, the impacts. Whatever happened, it must have been almost instantaneous.' The chief snapped her phone shut, cutting Matilda's sentence short, and braced her arms behind her back, looking like a teacher who'd just caught a student smoking on school grounds.

'Matilda, leave the police work to us. Do as I ask. Seal up the cars and that ambulance. And be thankful I'm not putting you all in quarantine.' Matilda looked from the shrunken body back to the chief.

'Thank you, Chief,' she mumbled, and pulled a plastic film roll from a shelf.

'Well,' said the chief, 'if I put *you* in quarantine, we'd all have to go. *Me* included. Thankfully I don't think that's necessary.' She smiled, then frowned. 'However, I would advise that you change your uniform. You smell utterly repugnant.'

Matilda changed and climbed back into her ambulance, her fresh, unspoiled ambulance, and looked out in dismay at the five cars entombed in plastic wrap. The two bodies, Simian and the man from the van, were in the boot of the chief's car, sealed in Tupperware and on their way to the station. Bob came to sit beside her, swiping images across his phone. The receiver blinked red.

'*SC Thirteen, this is dispatch. We'd had a call from a location near you. Are you available to respond? Over.*'

'This is SC Thirteen. We're leaving the current crash site on the B3055. Ready to attend. Over.'

'*Great, we're chock-a-block this evening. Updating your sat-nav now.*'

'We'll need manual direction, please dispatch. Reception here's useless.'

'*Copy that.*'

'What's the nature of the call?' Matilda winced, bracing for bad news.

'*Well. We're not exactly sure, SC Thirteen, still transcribing the conversation to text. She was in quite a fluster, but from what we could make out, get this, the fate of the world hangs in the balance.*'

*

The ambulance moved on. A hundred yards up the hill, the lights from the crash site were still visible in the rearview mirror. Matilda and Bob stopped beside a weathered and moss-laden sign reading *Catalant*. Bob climbed out and slid the rusted twelve-foot grill gate to one side.

'I've heard about this place,' he said, rebuckling his seatbelt. 'Read an article a while back. The locals hate it.'

The path descended into wilderness as three short industrial buildings emerged through the foliage, curved and crumbling, an antiquated vision of the future. Lights peppered the ground floor of the smallest building, the only sign that someone was or had recently been here.

'You're sure this is right?' Matilda asked, reaching for radio confirmation.

'Yes. This is it – look,' said Bob. Rounding the side of the building, they saw a small lake buttressed by pine forest. A geodesic dome, glowing phosphorescent blue, connected the lake to the shortest of the three curved buildings. Matilda brought the ambulance to rest in a weed-riddled car park, empty but for an odd looking single-seater vehicle – the offspring of a car and a mobility scooter.

An open door in the adjacent building led them down a wide hallway lined with framed photographs: satellite images of oceans filled with strange white currents that curled about continents like oil in puddles.

'These are fantastic,' said Bob, snapping a photo with his phone.

'Come on, Bob,' hissed Matilda, 'shine your torch over here.' Behind a set of double doors at the end of a long corridor refractions of water played blue waves across a high ceiling.

Moments later, they entered the geodesic dome. In its centre was a swimming pool filled with what appeared to be milk. A pile of clothes hung over the pool's edge at one corner. Broken glass bottles lay strewn on the floor. And beside a booth on the other side of the pool stood a tiny, naked older woman hobbling about with the help of a biro. She hadn't seen them enter, and she swore and cursed while trying to untangle her foot from a length of clear tubing. Bob steadied himself on the door handle.

'Hello,' Matilda said softly, as if waking a dozing child. Her voice echoed about the otherwise silent dome. The small woman startled, stumbled and, in doing so, succeeded in pulling her foot free.

She turned and surveyed the police officer and paramedic without any sense of awkwardness, surprise or – given their comparative size – fear.

'You must be the authorities? You were quick,' she said in a tiny but commanding voice, and began shuffling towards them. Matilda couldn't help but be disarmed by the small woman's display of confidence. Feeling it both appropriate and advisable – she'd be less likely to faint into the pool – Matilda got on all fours.

'That's right, and you are?' she asked, edging forwards, squinting, puffing out her cheeks, not quite believing the absurdity – the *simplicity* of the conversation.

'My name is Elizabeth Goodwin, and please, we don't have much time.'

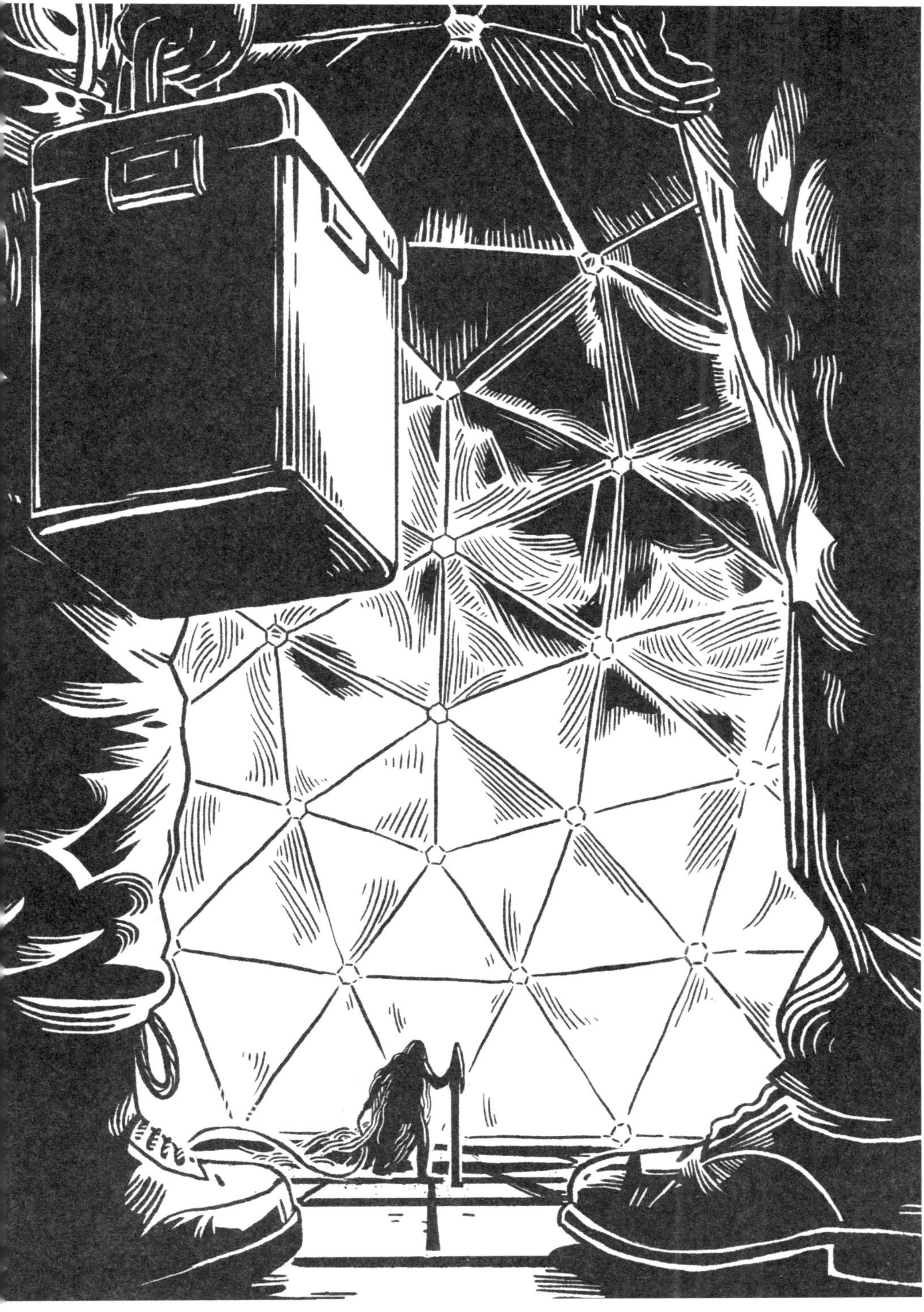

CHAPTER 24

AGE of ABUNDANCE

The dense cluster of poplar trees that surrounded the manor was no place to travel at night, certain to be crawling with raptor-like owls and foxes whose sole purpose was to catch small, furry, foul-smelling prey, such as himself, thought Giles. Dusk arrived and having been kept busy with teething issues – starting generators, opening doors – the opportunity to try the woodland crossing came and passed. He would have to investigate the cabin and retrieve the message from Sadie at first light, but for now, he'd enjoy the small victory of watching the group settle in.

He sat on a twist of broken branch and watched as two dozen children disappeared into the jungle of the orangery. He could no longer tell the groups apart. The Claybourne tribe had been cleaned up, their rags and crisp-packet ponchos swapped for fresher garb. Without the influence of the tinman and his lieutenant doll, they had calmed and settled, regaining some semblance of the people they had been before the Descent. Ashraf wandered between them, singing unabashedly.

Darkness thickened outside, still the orangery felt warm and humid. Water dribbled from a hose and evaporated off the slate tiles, keeping the plants from drying out. Giles felt a tickle of satisfaction at having had the apparent foresight, days ago, to twist the tap when he could still reach it. Tiny feet skidded across the wide walkway and explored the stone walls that skirted the leather-red soil beds. The great greenhouse divided into two levels. The ground floor housed exotic plants – ginger lilies, birds of paradise, angel trumpets and the like. Instinctively, the youngsters turned and struck poses in front of the gigantic alien blooms as if someone was waiting behind them to take a photo.

Edible plants were up a spiral of steel stairs – banks on banks of tatsoi, beetroot, peas, pak choi and radish. Directly above him hung a row of six blushing peaches. Elsewhere there were peppers, herbs, grapes and oranges, vines buckling under the weight of Brandywine tomatoes so large Giles could have hidden behind one. He was considering gathering a bounty of fresh crops for an inaugural feast when he noticed the fault in his plan. The metal grill walkway was as impassable to him as to the rodents it was designed to keep out. To reach the beds, he would have to tightrope walk along the thin metal grate without toppling through. Giles felt the panic rise, then subside – this was a surmountable obstacle. He would find planks, lay down a floor, just another thing to fix.

'Keep away from those,' Giles shouted to a small boy poking his head through a round hole in the side of a green plastic tub. 'Mouse poison.'

The boy ran away to join the others. Giles heard footsteps behind him, felt a hand on his shoulder.

'It makes sense.'

'What's that?' asked Giles, turning to see Isabel smiling at something high above them.

'Why you gave in so easily. Why you decided to help, back at the campsite.' She gestured to a corkboard beside a botanical illustration of tropical plants. Pinned to the board, between leaflets and a recipe for butterbean goulash, were photographs of Giles – throwing a branch into the fire pit, hoisting a plank onto the fork in the sycamore tree, leading the way into a dark corridor of woods, standing in front of a fountain cradling a net on a pole. In each of the photographs, scores of children speckled the scene. True, there might have been other adults in the pictures, but the way Giles towered made most people look like children by comparison. They were old pictures, but by being swollen to posters they showed Giles an aspect of himself he rather liked and hadn't before noticed.

'You're a big softy after all,' said Isabel, punctuating the point with a jab from her elbow.

'Ha,' said Giles, a toothy grin splitting his beard, 'Not really. I just needed you lot to drive the car.'

'No. I don't think so,' said Isabel as she ambled off into the fluorescent jungle.

Excitement faded with the light. The pattering of feet slowed, and by some unspoken consensus, the settlers migrated to the sitting room – a well-furnished, thickly carpeted space, all greens and oranges, the walls adorned with large, regal paintings. Beside a central wood-burning stove, Richard and Ash fumbled with a flick-lid Zippo lighter, trying and failing to start a fire. First nights in a new place were often uncomfortable, weary experiences, and though it was home for Giles, the same could not be said for the rest of the party. Small clusters and lone figures had taken up defensive positions, their backs against walls, wedged into corners, all with an eyeline to the exits. Now and then a creak or a bump would echo down through the house, and the general murmur that filled the room would quiet to a held breath. Giles knew the house would sigh and groan as a warm day gave way to a cool night. Still, he thought it might reassure the others if they knew he'd checked around and there was no reason to be concerned.

By the time Giles had dragged his body up and over the final wooden step and onto the landing, it felt as though someone had gone to work on his stomach with a meat tenderiser. Up here, night had turned the windows into perfect mirrors, and he startled as he glimpsed his own criss-crossed reflection. He looked back through the balustrades to the front foyer and imagined repurposing the family house into a bustling settlement. Adapting the staircase for people of his size. Each room split into multiple levels, and tables used as frameworks for new homes. Bookcases clad with facades, internally linked to create multi-storey structures. Grandfather clocks, wardrobes, cabinets, cupboards and chests of drawers – all pulled apart in his mind's eye and reassembled into new habitats. All of it built to last.

Somewhere off at the other end of the hallway he heard a scrape, then a thud, both out of place. Giles edged down the landing, stepping over cracks in the thick floorboards, his hand instinctively reaching round to the blade at his back. Hours earlier, several of them had jolted the basement generator into life so that, for the time being, at least, the house had power. Dim lamps flickered and warbled as Giles approached the half-open door to the master bedroom.

He pressed his shoulder against the wood, readying to shove through. Instead, it fell easily away, swinging inwards and sending him tumbling onto carpet.

Resting against the edge of the frame, looking down at him, stood Isabel. A large purse was slung like a handbag over one shoulder, and a thick black leather glove rested across the other. Back on the bridge, Isabel had replaced her petrol-soaked red wool jumpsuit with a sock-dress, tied about the waist with string, and the itchy, ill-fitting garment had been the subject of much complaint.

Eagerly pulling the snap-blade from under Giles's arm, she set to work on the glove, slicing free two of the fingers, removing the tips of the others and making a hole opposite the thumb. She disappeared behind the door, and re-emerged beaming, her rough, black tufts of hair fanning outwards as she spun on the spot in her newly tailored jumpsuit.

'Needs stitching, taking in here and here, but not bad.'

'What's in the purse?'

'Accessories, *darling*,' said Isabel, dropping a mock curtsey. 'Plus, things for the group. Jewellery bags will make good satchels, I think.'

She was straining against the clasp on the purse, trying to open it, when a scratching noise and a loud bang reverberated through the boards behind them, startling them both.

'Probably just one of the kids,' said Giles as they approached a panelled wood door, just ajar. Above them, a hazard-striped warning sign read, Enter at Own Risk. Together, they shoved it open.

They emerged into an ocean of clothes: a room that looked as though someone had detonated a laundry basket, scattering garments to the far corners. Clothes hung over the backs of chairs and gathered like weather fronts on the floor, and for a horrible moment, Giles thought the piles might be cocoons, soaked in a bodily fluid from which sinuous, shrunken figures would emerge. Isabel must have had the same thought as she kicked at a shirt sleeve, revealing it thankfully empty.

At the far end of the room, a small, gridded window swung open on its hinges, thudding into the wall, the latch scraping noisily against the sill.

'Just a window,' Isabel laughed, ruffled her hair and turned to leave. Giles gaped at the room, his mind a whir of excitement.

'I'll be out in a sec.'

Posters like billboards lined the walls, and monuments loomed from the discarded clothing – a skateboard, a half-strung guitar, an old desktop computer. Somewhere, hidden in this crumbling temple to adolescence, was a trove of great value. He found what he was looking for at the back of a cupboard – a cardboard box of toys, the like of which might be found in every twelve-year-old's room, artefacts the owner deemed too embarrassing to keep on display, yet were too beloved to discard.

Giles sliced at sticky tape with his scalpel. Cardboard doors parted and the box spilled a wave of matchbox cars, mutant action figures and a hundred other brightly moulded pieces of plastic. A suction-cup-dart gun, several Meccano sets and a Ken doll in a black tuxedo were all good, useful items. But what made Giles's stomach twitch was the remote control. He ran a palm over the smooth black plastic, jostled the joystick, pushed at a lever, and grinned with the satisfaction of this puzzle piece clicking into place.

Giles stuffed the bounty into a jumper, knotted the arms, dragged the haul onto the landing and sent it tumbling down the stairs. Isabel joined him, shoving a washbag stuffed with safety pins and thick thread.

'More tailoring?' he asked.

Isabel shook her head, and grinned, 'Grappling hooks.' She was handing the bag down to Giles over the upmost step when, at the far end of the hall, a figure emerged.

'Down, quickly,' he hissed, hurrying Isabel over the edge of the step. They peered back at the landing. Like a mouse furtively testing ground, the red woman crept into view. Reframed in this domestic setting, she appeared to him quite changed, moving in awkward, uncertain, skittering steps, no longer animalistic and threatening, but lost and elderly. Keeping to the walls, she shuffled towards a grill set into the skirting boards. Giles was readying to approach with his palms high in a gesture of peace, but before he could do so, she prised open the vent and slipped inside.

Minutes later, Giles and Isabel reached the bottom of the stairs and made for the sitting room, ushering some foyer loiterers ahead of them.

'So, she's in the walls. Richard's going to love that,' said Isabel as she and Giles heaved the door shut behind them. 'We should check these skirting boards for vents, block them up with books or furniture.'

'I guess,' said Giles, unconvinced and scanning the room. 'Speaking of Richard, where is he?'

'I think he said something about a welcome feast.'

Giles found Richard outside the orangery. Or more accurately, Richard found Giles, bounding out towards him at some pace, taking down a potted fern on his way.

'Giles, thank goodness.' Richard clasped his shoulder and

stooped for breath, looking back at the toppled plant. 'There's – there's something in *there*. Under the floorboards. Rats,' Richard leaned close and whispered, 'or worse.'

'No. No. I doubt that. No rats here. The odd mouse, maybe. Still, let's get you with the others.' As quick as he could, without appearing to run, Giles ushered Richard towards the sitting room. Nearing the open door, something moved in the crumpled coats to their right. A hand, rust red, reached around the cloth, pushing it aside to reveal a grinning skeletal head, baring broken teeth. It was *her*. Giles shoved Richard through the crack in the door, hoping he wouldn't see. But as he pulled the door closed behind them, Richard turned to help, and the red woman stepped into the diminishing slither of light.

The door clicked shut. Richard gurgled a scream and darted across the sitting room. Giles slumped with his back against wood and took in the room. Since he'd left it an hour earlier, the atmosphere had shifted, and now a warm glow filled the space. Where previously people had cowered in corners, they now gathered about the wood burner in a half circle. Beside the fire, like a showman at a stage, stood Ashraf, a long metal skewer balanced in the crook of one arm, turning thick chunks of meat over the flames. In the far corner of the room, behind a rack stuffed with magazines, Richard scuttled on all fours into the end of an upturned boot.

'Would you like a piece of charcoaled delight? Steak a-la-Ashraf?' Giles leaned around the boot's end, tore a chunk of meat in two and proffered one half towards the shadow.

'Oh. I – you found me. No. I'm hiding.'

Giles sighed, sat and rested his back against the boots rough curve, making himself as comfortable as possible.

'She's not a threat, you know. She's just lost, like the rest of us.'

Richard scoffed. 'She means to kill me. To kill us *all*. We – we should try and trap her.'

Giles shook his head.

'I think she's been *helping* us. Back at the bridge, she stopped the car being torched.'

'By *killing* a man.'

'That's ... that's a fair point. But if she hadn't, we'd have all gone up in flames. I'm not saying what she did was right, but ...' Giles leaned forwards and chose his words carefully. 'I think she's lost, forgotten how to be a person. She's like a field that's gone to seed. Wild, dangerous, maybe, but she's not out for our blood.'

'Then who killed Alwyn?' Richard persisted, unconvinced, 'Or perhaps he *tripped* on your knife?' Giles conceded the point. He scanned the room, his eyes resting on Isabel with a child on either knee, then on Ashraf, turning meat through the door of the wood burner. He returned his gaze to the priest cowering in the umbra of the shadow.

'I don't know, but I don't think *she* did it.'

'Well, I *do*, Giles. You see, the thing is, I *know* her. I know who she is. I told you the dogs belonged to someone from my parish, yes? Well, I wasn't sure until just now, but, when I saw her face by the door, I *knew*. Her name is Mary, and she's out to kill me.'

'OK,' said Giles, 'what makes you so sure she—'

'When I woke up, in my church, I thought I was the only one. I walked the aisles, going from pile to pile, those hideous tombs of cloth, looking for a sign of life and finding none. We were not the youngest congregation, granted, but I couldn't believe – I struggled to understand *why* no one was spared, but I.'

Richard shuffled forward and Giles saw tear lines running down his cheeks. He rested against the boot wall, took the strip of meat and turned it over, giving it careful consideration.

'Near the back of the congregation, there was movement. My heart leaped. Selfishly, I longed to find someone, not just for their sake, but to help dispel the growing notion that I had been cast into hell. I came closer. I called to the mound. The fabric moved, but it was not the body of a person that came forward – but that of a beast, the one *we* killed Giles, you and me. The *dog*!' Richard spat the last word. 'I ran, hiding beneath the pews which were too shallow for the hound to follow, and by some small miracle, I escaped the church. Thinking back, that first movement may well have been her – *Mary*. She was never quite right, you know? Yet somehow, she and I were the ones who lived. And I abandoned her. Her own priest. Perhaps she blames me for her suffering.'

'No one could blame you for running.'

'Not for running, for *causing* her suffering, for all of *this*.' Richard gestured to the room, milling with the refugees displaced by scale.

Giles ran a finger down a fault-line in his forearm, 'I don't mean to doubt your miraculous powers, Richard, but I think *you* causing all *this* is quite a stretch.'

'But who else *could* have done this, Giles, if not God, or one of his messengers?'

Richard sank his teeth into the steak, then continued, mouth full. 'Either way, I'm certain Mary came to that campsite for me, the leader who failed her, *summoning* her hell hounds with a whistle. I expect she mistook Alwyn for *me*. I could see how it's possible. He *was* terribly handsome.' Richard threw Giles a weak smile. They sat a moment eating in silence. Giles swallowed and turned to face the priest.

'OK, let's say that you're right, about Mary. I – I think we should still try to help her. I've had these moments, since it happened, where I've felt capable of doing things I would never have considered before. It's like a gathering black cloud. It's only being *here*, among this group, that's kept it at bay. What's happened to her, well, I can appreciate how someone could lose touch, left on their own.'

Richard seemed to consider this for a moment then replied, 'What bothers me most is – tell me, has it crossed your mind – have you ever questioned what else was squeezed out of us during the transformation? What we lost?'

'Apart from the contents of our bladders?' smiled Giles, and Richard chuckled politely.

'Apart from our bladders. Yes. We must have lost *something*, and I think – I worry – we lost a part of our humanity.' Richard gave a tiny croak of pain, and his voice lurched up an octave, 'And now all the humans are dead.' He hugged himself tight and half laughed, half sobbed, 'just when I was developing a bit of a soft spot for them.'

Giles looked away, wanting to give the man some privacy, feeling the discomfort of not knowing what to say by way of consolation.

'Well, we might look a bit funny,' he suggested, 'but here we are, walking, talking, driving cars and getting upset. There you go! Getting upset about *not* being human. If ever there was a catch twenty-two.' Giles got to his feet and offered Richard a hand as if that had settled the matter. Richard ignored it and continued to sniffle, staring into the opposite wall. Giles let his hand fall to drum the side of his knee. For someone usually so assured and upbeat, it was disconcerting to see Richard this vulnerable.

'OK, how about this.' Giles rustled his fingers through his beard, digging for an idea. 'We're what – twenty centimetres tall? About a tenth of what we were. As I understand it, we use or *used* about a tenth of our brain's capacity. The rest was surplus. What if all the junk was squeezed out, and now we've been left with just the good bits? Maybe now we use the full hundred per cent? Would you be happy that we're still human then?' Richard gave a sad smile and reached his hand out to Giles.

'I appreciate the effort, my boy, and I'd almost believe that.' Giles's helped him to his feet, 'Except, firstly, I'm almost certain the ten per cent brain thing isn't true. Secondly, we're a tenth of our previous height, which by the inverse cube law, makes us a hundredth of our previous volume.' Giles raised his eyebrows, and Richard winked. 'There's a surprising amount of maths in clerical training. I'm telling you, she's not human. I'm not sure any of us are. Perhaps we're more like tiny apes – confused and, in her case, full of rage. Ready to rip each other limb from limb, as chimps have been known to do.' Giles wanted to protest, but found he had nothing. Richard carried on. 'We've lost something. You know it. I know it, and I'm terrified to tears to find out what it is.' He sighed, then with a sudden shudder, seemed to shake away his sadness. 'Still, I mustn't complain. It's all part of the plan.'

'The plan?'

'*His* plan.' Richard smiled wearily, and patted Giles on the back. 'It might not feel that way, but I've never been more certain.'

After they'd eaten, Giles beckoned those still awake over to the fire, where he stood with the jumper full of the spoils from upstairs. One by one, the passengers came and rummaged. As well as doll's clothes, Giles had turned several soft toys inside out, leaving hollow jumpsuits that, with a tailored tuck here and there, would make fine fur-lined overalls. He had taken the Ken doll's tuxedo for himself. Though a little baggy, it felt good to be in something clean and civilised after all that talk of bestial devolution. In the corner of the room, Maya and Evelyn slowly turned the dial on a small radio, excited by the idea of connecting with other groups. Packs were being sewn, supplies divided up, and adaptations were well underway. There was so much of *everything*. The manor was a land of plenty, thought Giles, and at first light, he'd take the next step towards bringing the girls here, to build it with them.

As the fire dimmed to embers, the party settled down, nestling between sofa pillows, folds of fur rugs, the creases of blankets spilling from a wooden chest. When the room was soft and still with sleep, Giles made his way to an armchair and climbed the wooden leg. He tugged at a lace cloth draped across the back of the chair, hoping it might serve as a blanket, then noticed a figure tucked beside the armrest.

Giles mumbled an apology and made to leave, but the woman raised a hand.

'It's OK,' said Isabel through a yawn, 'there's plenty of room.' Giles settled into his corner and pulled the slip over his shoulders.

'All in all, it's been a good day,' he whispered, lying back and letting his focus drift over the vast ceiling.

'Sure,' she agreed and turned to look at him from across the cushion. 'Nice tuxedo.' Then she pressed her feet against the armrest and pushed away, sliding across the cushion until her shoulders came to rest beside Giles's own. 'It's been an absolute fairy tale.' A moment before someone clicked a switch on a plug socket across the room and all the lights went out, Giles caught a glimpse of her intense green eyes, ever so, ever so close.

A crash in the dark. Giles sat bolt upright. Another crash, followed by harsh scratching, the flick of a switch and a fan whirring to life.

'What's going on?' asked Isabel. Giles was already feeling his way down from the chair when light filled the room to reveal a toppled lampshade, kebab meat strewn along the hearth, and several excited bodies gathered around the wood burner. Evelyn and Jayden were pushing up on the handle, trying to keep the door shut as something within pushed against the glass.

Evelyn turned excitedly to Giles, 'She must have crawled down the flume when the embers died. Was fiddling with the latch when we caught her.'

'Turning the chimney fan back on was my idea,' said Jayden, 'she can't go up the way she came.'

Richard beamed at the teenagers as he scrambled towards them, clapping his hands. 'You did it!'

Giles flinched as hair smeared the soot-stained glass, and then a hand slammed against the panel, rattling it violently before receding into shadow.

'You did it,' repeated Richard, 'You trapped the devil.'

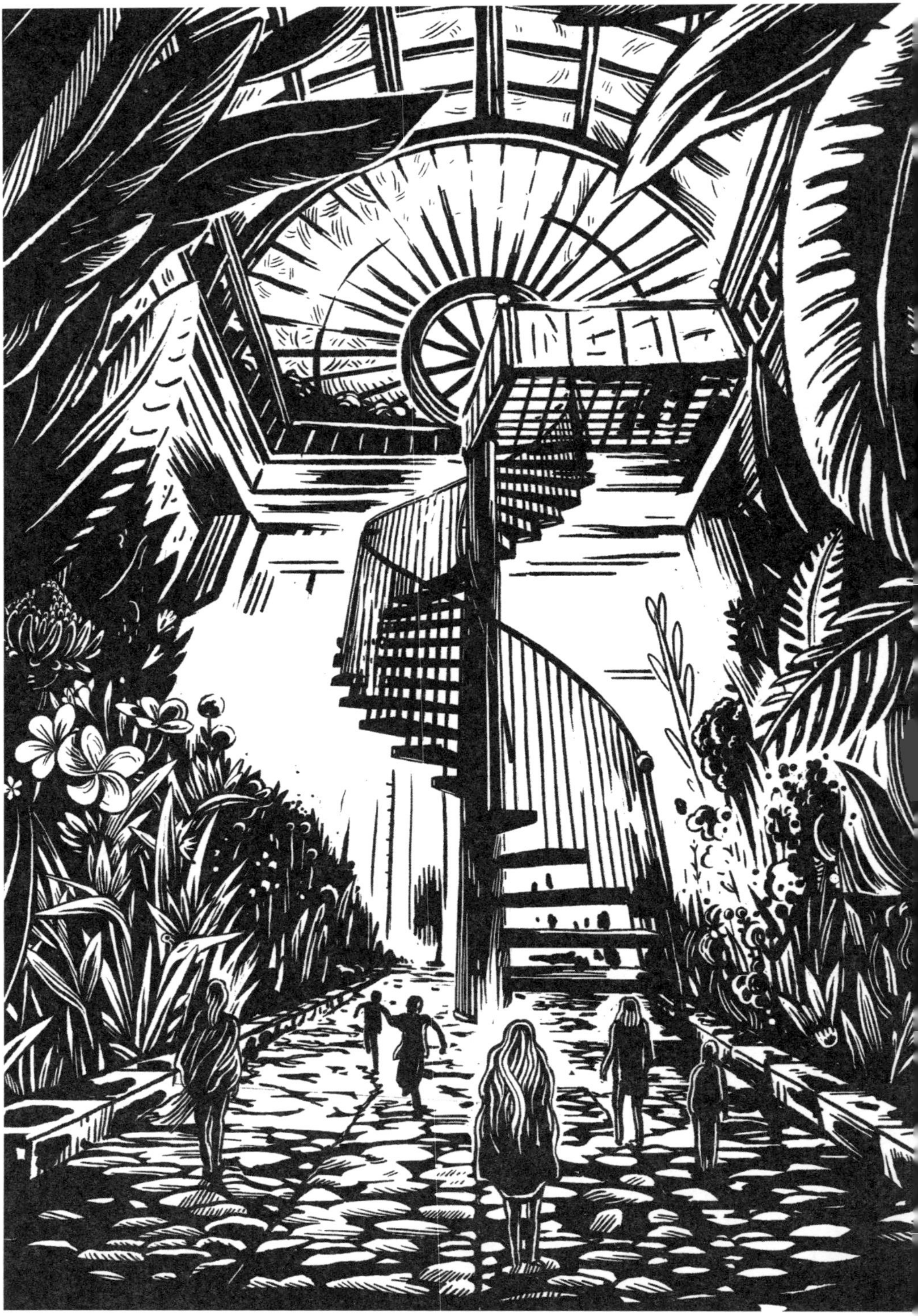

CHAPTER 25

ELSEWHERE,

A QUESTION OF SLEEP

Many have argued that it was not sleep but unconsciousness that swept the globe that fateful day in July. In general, supporters of this argument are the more clinically minded and, as a rule, all have had the good fortune to be born *after* the event in question. Still, their argument is compelling. The sudden rush of blood from our heads and the pure physical shock of having fluids violently shaken from our bodies would easily merit a loss of consciousness in ordinary circumstances. It is perfectly reasonable to suggest that the psychological terror of watching one's own hands wither from plump plum to raisin in a matter of moments might cause our mind to clock out, the way people falling from aeroplanes without parachutes are said to do before hitting the ground, as if their consciousness were sensibly stating, '*Here is a sequence of events I'd rather not see the end of.*' However, those physically there on July Second would all quietly agree that it was undoubtedly sleep and not unconsciousness that took them. It was sleep, they are certain, because of the Dream.

In the days, months and years following July Second, survivors proved reluctant to talk about the Dream. When they did speak of it, they were surprised to find that though the plots were many and varied, the stories were strikingly similar. One would be forgiven for presuming the Dream was feverish in nature, packed with claustrophobia, knotted limbs, infinite deserts and smothering skies. Instead, the opposite was true. The Dream told stories of expansion and freedom. Doors opened, seeds germinated, sponges hydrated, ice melted, flowers bloomed.

Inevitably, the idea that these dreams were not just similar but physically shared gained great popularity. That the sleepers somehow connected in their moment of suffering was a tempting solace in the hard times that followed. Cults and entire cultures were formed on the integrity of this shared Dream concept, though few lasted or indeed ended well.

For one brief moment, or stretch of several hours, depending on the tiredness of the individual, humanity was united by the singular act of sleep. There, a collective narcolepsy brought about a wave of secondary problems. Those scuba divers, free climbers, bungee jumpers, passenger airline pilots and the millions of Sunday drivers could not have chosen a less convenient time for a snooze. For the majority, the idea of sharing a dream was hard to accept. It implied a telepathic link, or access to an astral world.

So it was that the most widely accepted explanation of the shared Dream was the phenomenon known as *Meshing*, one well documented in the years preceding the Descent. Dream Meshing had little to do with fantastical powers of alternative universes, instead it implied that a common dream is born from a common experience – in humanity's case that was the song, the pressure, the sleep.

Still, there are those who believe something else altogether – that sleep was an act of kindness, an anaesthetic administered to smother the horrors of the Descent. The Dream was a sweetening of the pill. Immobile, passive and helpless, sleepers adopt an air of innocence. Even the wicked appear less so when sleeping. By contrast, the unsleeping – the night walkers, the grandparents whose lids do not entirely drop while napping on the sofa – make us nervous. Those neither alive nor dead.

Fewer still were the outliers, those who did *not* sleep at all through July Second. For them, the door stayed open while the world outside reset. There was no shield of sleep, no hopeful distraction of the Dream. They were the ones who saw behind the scenes. For those outliers, the question of sleep or unconsciousness seemed petty. Instead they saw it all, and wondered why they had been doubly cursed.

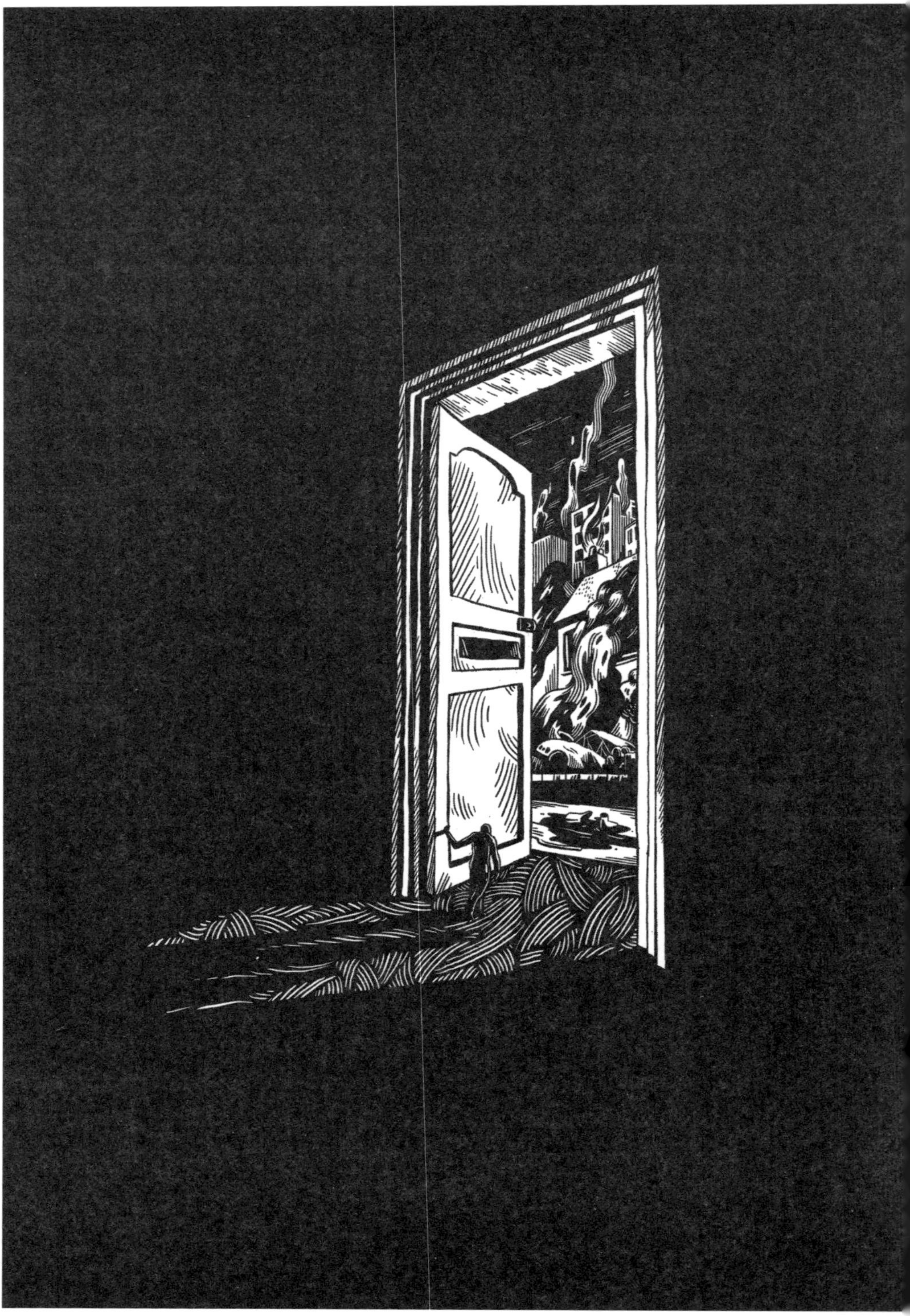

PART VI

CHAPTER 26

THE PATIENT

Her name was Elizabeth Goodwin, or so she'd said, and Matilda and Bob watched transfixed as she hobbled towards the glass booth with her biro, dragging an IV sac across the wet tiles like a sledge. Her head snapped back to look at them.

'Well, come on then. We haven't got all day. In fact, we've less than half a day left. I calculate those idiots will complete their transcription within the next twelve hours.' Goodwin beckoned the giants towards her.

'How is she even talking?' whispered Bob as they took cautious steps about the pool. Matilda unzipped her medical bag and withdrew a stethoscope, though it was far too big to use on the woman. She would have been better off with a veterinary kit, equipment for treating hamsters. She put away the apparatus, deciding instead to make a more holistic appraisal.

'How are you feeling?' she asked, midway across the pool.

'I have a headache above my left eye that feels as though someone's nailed it there, and a spear lodged in my forearm.' She showed the giants the cannula attached to the IV tube. 'But other than that, I feel stronger than I have done in years. Though I suspect it's nothing to do with muscle aptitude and simply the proportional strength of gravity, playing tricks with my ego.' She smiled up at them and continued hobbling into the booth. Her pitch was as it should be, though her voice was small, faint, as if she were talking from across the room, though they were now very close. Unlike the others they'd seen, Goodwin's skin was opaque, free from the translucent outer layer. The most striking thing, aside from her size, were the creases that ran in criss-crossing tracks over her body, all of them on full view to Matilda, since Goodwin clearly had no qualms about being naked.

'Mrs Goodwin, I'm—'

'*Professor* Goodwin,' the woman corrected.

'Right. I'm going to try and take your pulse. H-hold still, OK?'

Matilda crouched beside her and rested a trembling finger against her neck, counting out the faint heartbeats against her watch. They were quick but not outside of normal limits. Goodwin reflected the inspection back at Matilda, craning her head to read the insignia on her breast pocket.

'What are you – Special Forces? MI5?'

Bob leaned in to answer, talking as if to a child.

'I'm a junior officer with the Hampshire Constabulary, and Matilda is a paramedic from Southampton Central Hospital.'

'You *what*?' Goodwin stepped back, incredulous. 'I explained the nature of the emergency to the operator at great length, and they send a couple of grunts?' She rubbed at her tired eyes. 'Oh. Unbelievable.'

This reaction was strangely comforting to Matilda. It was something she was used to, the irritation of a patient when a brain surgeon had not been sent to deal with their migraine.

'Please, stay still, Professor.' She took the bundle of tubes from Goodwin and gently lifted her arm with a finger, turning her around, inspecting for other anomalies on her body. Aside from the obvious, all seemed in place.

'Remarkable,' whispered Bob, photographing Goodwin and the pool chamber with his phone.

'What's the IV for?' asked Matilda.

'Please, no need to shout,' winced Goodwin.

'Sorry, is *this* OK?' she whispered.

'Better. It's for my health. I have long-term degradation of the liver.'

'And what is it that do you do here, Dr Goodwin? Is there anyone else in the facility?' asked Bob, taking in the spectacle of the room and lifting a cluster of tubes beside the pool.

'Don't touch those. I am the CEO of Iplan Hawkes, not that that means anything. And no, I'm quite alone.'

'And this pool? What's its purpose?'

She gave Bob a wry smile. 'Well, officer. This here – this is where I've been chasing dreams. Though I never dreamt *this* would happen ...'

'What would happen, exactly?' said Matilda, glancing back at Bob.

'*This*, of course.' Goodwin waved her arms down the length of her naked body. 'Tinification.'

'*You* did this?' Matilda was back on her feet now, taking a half-step back.

'Well, not on purpose, no. A combination of elements that re-sulted in an unexpected reaction. But you could say, yes. I did the combining. I stirred the pot. I kicked the nest. I explained it all to the man on the phone. That's why you're here, isn't it?'

Matilda and Bob looked at each other, and Matilda turned away, taking in the room for the first time. It was a bizarre set-up, the capillaries lining the walls of the pool, the banks of conical jars simmering with white liquid. The steel vats and convolutes of copper running between consoles. It looked crude, a little cheap, but perhaps something else was hidden here, capable of these phantasmagorical transformations. She turned back to confront the tiny woman.

'Professor Goodwin, we have a multi-car crash site less than half a mile from here, several dead bodies—' she gulped. 'A friend of mine included. All suffering from the same . . . *condition* as you. And you're responsible?' As Matilda raised her voice, Goodwin's hands pressed over her ears. For a horrible moment, Matilda thought she might have sent the woman into shock. Goodwin steadied herself and looked back up at the paramedic, eyes blurry.

'I cannot deny responsibility. Now, I am sorry about your friend and the others. That is . . . truly terrible. As I say, this reaction was not expected.' She turned away from Matilda, holding her chin. 'So, there were people on the road? Transformed? Within half a mile?' She sat down and started drawing circles on the tiles with her finger, counting off numbers with her other hand. She looked back at Matilda. 'Half a mile and no further?'

Dismayed, Matilda nodded and motioned to Bob to join her out of Goodwin's earshot. 'This is no good,' she whispered. 'We're not going to get a straight answer out of her. What do you think happened here?'

'I think they were developing biological weapons,' said Bob, gasping at the shock of his own revelation. His eyes darted about the room. 'Maybe we *should* be quarantined.'

'Everyone in those cars was affected instantly. No tyre marks on the road. It's not contagious. If it was, we were exposed hours ago,' said Matilda, reassuring herself as much as Bob.

Bob pushed his hands up into his cheeks, squeezing his face into a knot. 'Radiation then? Does the ambulance have a Geiger counter?'

'No.' Matilda furrowed her brow, looking from Goodwin and back to Bob. 'But, yeah. Good thinking. We have dosimeter badges. They'll turn black if there's anything nefarious in here. Better get them. They're in the haz-kit.'

Bob nodded eagerly and darted off, skidding on the tiles and nearly slipping into the milk-white pool. Matilda watched as he disappeared up the corridor, and then turned back to Goodwin, who was still muttering on the floor.

'Half a mile, that's not good. If this small volume covers that much ground, then contact with the ocean will be – hey!'

Matilda's heart raced. She had gripped Goodwin's torso with one hand, the IV in the other, and hoisted her up into the air.

'What is the meaning of this? Put me down! There's no time for fooling about. We need to head to the coast. If his connectome makes contact with – oh!' Goodwin spluttered. Matilda held her at arm's length over the pool and began unclamping her fingers one by one.

'I'd like you to tell me *exactly* what you did here,' she said in a quiet, steady voice, only the slightest tremble revealing the rush of adrenaline she felt.

'Put me back! I – I told the operator already. I have made contact with – with another mind, an entity far greater than you or I could fathom. I wasn't expecting a reply, but good God, I got one.'

Matilda squinted at the tiny woman flailing in her grasp.

Goodwin's hand gripped tightly about Matilda's thumb while her dangling legs tried to latch themselves over her wrist.

'How did you do it? As simple as possible, please.' Another finger unfurled. Goodwin gulped.

'Good grief, woman! The pool! There was a reaction in the pool. A combination of elements.'

'So, a chemical reaction?'

'No, but if it helps to think of it in those terms, why not. A *chemical* reaction. Fine.'

'Why do we need to go to the coast. Why the rush?'

'There's another group involved – my old assistant, William Laslett, and his clandestine benefactor, Leonard Leaf. They stole something from me. They mean to recreate what I've done here, but on a much larger scale. They don't know what they're doing. Idiots, really. If we don't stop them, then— please, many more may perish, and your friend would have died for nothing.'

Matilda loosened the third finger about Goodwin's waist and her gaze drifted to the pool below. Perhaps this was the end the professor deserved for causing such suffering. To drop the woman would be easy, and excuses as to why she had drowned rose unbridled in Matilda's mind. Her last finger unlatched, and Matilda felt her heart rate flutter at her own menace. It was as though she was watching herself do it. Goodwin gasped, clawed at the paramedic's knuckles and managed to hook her left leg beneath her watch strap.

'Don't! You need me. Yes, my work has clearly had some awful consequence. But believe me it is nothing compared to what *they* could do – Laslett and Leaf. You have to understand, I can help you stop them. I want to stop them. But only I can do it.' Hearing Bob's footsteps approach from the corridor, Matilda snapped back to reality, returning to her body. Quickly, she lowered Goodwin onto the tiles. Bob entered on the other side of the pool, inspecting a square plastic badge.

'Are we OK?' called Matilda, her heart still hammering, unsure what had come over her.

'No radiation,' replied Bob, oblivious to Goodwin untangling herself from Matilda's watch strap. He beckoned her over. Goodwin brushed herself down and scowled at the two of them as they spoke in low, hurried whispers beside the double doors. Matilda strode back and squatted beside Goodwin, rubbing her neck, looking at Bob with uncertainty.

'OK. Bob spoke to the station, and we're going to leave now.'

'So, your superiors told you what's what, ay? Finally. Get me that glove from the desk – I think it'll make quite a fetching leotard – and we can be on our way.'

With a nod from Matilda, Bob obliged. Then, taking scissors from her med-kit, he removed the little finger from the glove, snipped holes in the ring finger and thumb, and handed it down to Goodwin, who unhooked her IV and pulled the black woollen glove over her waist. 'I mustn't be separated from the bag. Understand? It's a complex cocktail of my own devising. Scarce nutrients. Essential for my wellbeing.' She screwed the tube back on to the needle in her arm and stretched out, filling the glove. It fitted well. The fabric's vertical stripes somehow streamlined the body, lending the scientist a regal, gothic air. Matilda went to lift Goodwin, but she batted her hand away, insulted.

'I don't think so, young lady. I shall not be bandied about again like some child's toy. There, that box, I'll be carried in that.' Emptying the small plastic crate of cables, Matilda tipped it on its side for Goodwin to step into.

'Now, I suggest we set up patrols along the Straits of Dover. The white chalk cliffs are almost entirely comprised of coccolithophore shells. I know how the likes of Laslett and Leaf think. If ever there were a spot to conduct their ridiculous ceremonials, it would be there.'

Matilda, the box under one arm, was already halfway up the dark corridor. She looked down at the tiny woman, small and fragile, holding herself steady by the sides of the box against the shake of Matilda's footsteps. Though she hadn't understood the details of what had transpired inside this pool, the reactions, the transformations, Matilda was convinced of one thing – that Goodwin's warnings were real, and a larger threat was looming. But Matilda had her instructions; she would relay the information and trust the chain of command.

'We're not going to the coast, Professor Goodwin. I'm taking you back to Southampton Central.'

The woman looked up, confused.

'What are you talking about?' Goodwin was bewildered, the wind taken out of her. For a moment, Matilda thought she looked like a child who'd just been told there was no such thing as magic. Matilda spoke to the air ahead of her, not daring to look down at the shrunken woman.

'The thing is, they've gone over the transcript of the call you made, and the chief doesn't—' she corrected herself '—*we* don't think you're being entirely truthful with us.'

Goodwin struck her fists at the sides of a box, then her energy evaporated, and her tiny form sagged to the bottom of the crate.

'The chief thinks you'll say anything to save your own skin,' added Bob.

'My dear boy,' said Goodwin, looking up at the officer with great sadness, 'my skin is far beyond saving.'

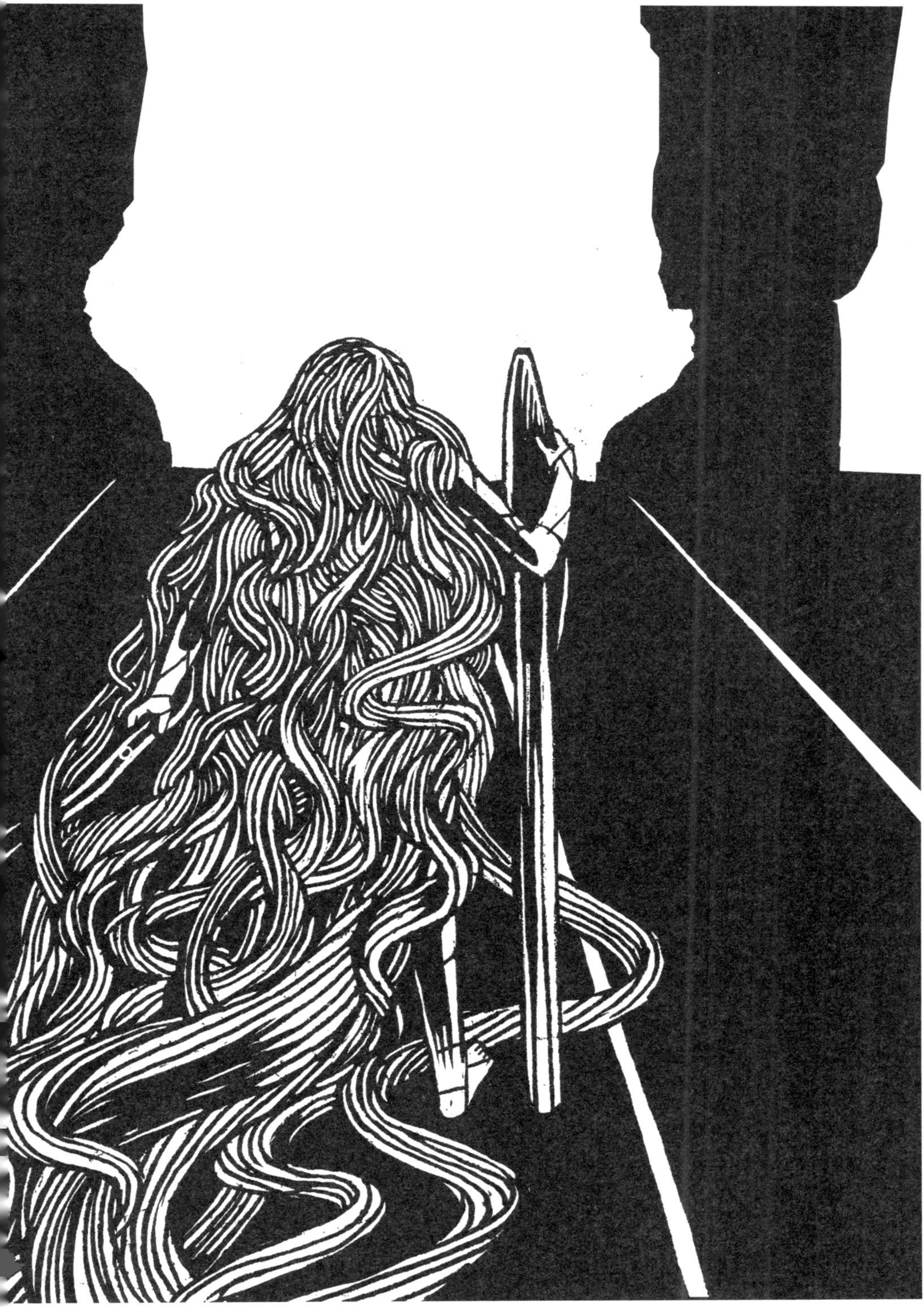

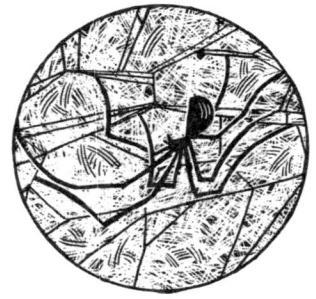

CHAPTER 27

THE MESSAGE

His eyelids blinked at the light like window wipers batting rain. It was morning. Nearby on the armchair cushion, Isabel lay curled asleep, her wild black hair stark against the white lace slip. Giles took in the room. The remnants of last night's meal had turned to charcoal in the grill and in the far corners, several children sat quietly tailoring their soft toy skins, turning them into fur-lined jumpsuits. Beside the wood burner, Ashraf, Richard, Evelyn and Maya were deep in hushed conversation, their babble underscored by the buzz of the chimney fan.

'So then, what do we do with the old terror? Mary, was it?' asked Ashraf.

'Well, as a priest, I am of the view that *all* human life is sacred. But one must ask, after what she's done ...' Richard winced dramatically, touching the plaster still wrapped about his chest, 'after what she's *become*, is she really still human?'

Ashraf raised his arms in astonishment, 'Aw, come on, don't be absurd.'

Evelyn rolled her eyes. 'We're not going to *off* her, Richard. But we can't exactly just let her out.'

'Can't keep her here either,' Ashraf added.

'Have we tried talking to her?' asked Maya, gently rapping her knuckles on the pane, 'Hello?' No response. She leaned closer to the dark glass, now bound fast with twine and sticky tape, and knocked again. 'Mary?' A sudden rattle kicked against the inside of the door, and Maya jumped away, her scream stirring several more sleepers awake.

Giles pushed his thumbs into the corners of his eyes and rubbed. How late had he slept? He had meant to be off at first light, to quietly step out, retrieve the message from Sadie, find out where his daughters were and begin the next phase of his journey. Hastily, he pulled on his makeshift backpack, the remote control bulging from the top, and slipped off the edge of the chair. He was nearly at the door when Ashraf called after him.

'Giles, hold up! Nice suit, by the way. Very fancy.' Giles stopped, placed down his pack and turned. 'What is it, Ash?'

'Mary over there – Richard's convinced she's out to get him, thinks we should keep her locked up, but what d'*you* reckon we should do?'

'Well. I agree she's dangerous. We've seen her kill. But I don't think she means us harm. I think . . .' Giles searched for the words, 'I think she needs help acclimatising, or something.' He thought back to the moments over the past few days when he'd felt himself slipping, the cloud of savagery swelling inside. Part of Giles wanted to stay, to try and talk to the woman and to understand how thin the line between them truly was. The rest of him needed to leave, and urgently. He hoisted the pack back onto his shoulder and continued towards the door. 'I think we should let her go, try to help her adjust.'

'Out of the question,' called Richard, who had shuffled closer to listen in, and looked to the others for support.

'Yeah, don't see how that'd work,' agreed Ashraf. 'We let her loose in here, and there's every chance she'll go ape again.'

'Precisely,' Richard chimed in.

'Well, we can't keep her locked up,' Giles called back, fighting the urge to argue it out. Evelyn stepped forward, sticking out her chin in a gesture of defiance and rocking on the balls of her toes.

'I reckon, since it was me and Maya that caught her, seems only right that we sort this out. We'll take her away from the house, into the woods, and tell her not to come back.'

'Exile,' agreed Maya. Again, Giles rubbed at his eyes, feeling more tired than ever. Though, of all the options, this one probably made most sense.

'OK, how about this? I'll take her. Not to the woods, but to somewhere else, to another group. I'm setting out to find Sadie and Ava, and if I can persuade Mary, I'll take her too.'

Giles winced, feeling the weight of yet another responsibility, but the words were out and there was no taking them back. Something in the way he said it had settled the matter without pause or question. Released from their moral dilemma, Ashraf busied himself tidying the hearth while Maya and Evelyn returned to the radio they had been tampering with, both excited to have picked up a crackling transmission.

'But it just says – *We are the ants* – over and over. Like *that's* not obvious,' huffed Evelyn, 'we're *all* ants, now.' Giles made for the door, catching Richard's eye. For a moment, Richard looked put-out, annoyed at being overruled, but his face quickly softened, and he walked over, smiling.

'You'll be leaving soon then? On foot?'

'Actually, I've a quicker method in mind.'

'Oh. Requisitioning a donkey?'

'Something like that.'

'And once you've found Sadie and Ava, and a place for Mary, you'll return?'

'I promise.'

'A *promise*? Well,' Richard let out a deep sigh, 'you must eat before you go. I'm rustling up a feast for lunch. One of my famous harvest stews. You'll need some fuel for the journey.' Richard affectionately patted Giles's belly, who conceded with a nod. 'Excellent,' the priest clapped and scuttled off towards the orangery. Giles moved on and, this time, made it all the way to the sitting room door before a sleepy voice croaked from behind him.

'Hold up,' said Isabel. 'I'm coming with you.'

'Trying to sneak out without saying goodbye. Unbelievable.' The sunlight, dappled through the leaves above, covered them in leopard-print shadows as they descended stone slabs that led into the garden. 'So, what's in this shed?'

'Tools. Plant seed. Diabolical devices. Usual stuff.' Giles grinned down at Isabel, but she turned away to inspect an umbrella of flowers, walking her fingers along the edge of a drooping stem. As they wandered past weeds sprouting from between the walls of the flowerbeds, Isabel tugged a nuisance sprig of nutsedge out by the roots.

'You missed a spot, groundskeeper.'

'You don't need to worry. I'll be back.'

'I'm not worried.'

'And we'll carry on with the plan, to take people home, if that's what they want.' Giles winced again. The statement felt untrue. It had been an unintentional lie. How could they possibly fulfil that promise? Isabel seemed not to notice.

'Like I said, not worried.'

They walked through boulders of pinecones that were so firmly wedged into the ground they might have been fossilised dragon eggs. A gargoyle covered in moss and lichen stuck out of tall grass beside a pond, its bat wings, bulldog's brow, and ram's horns all scrunched together into a grotesque medley of features. Stepping into the monster's shadow, Isabel craned her neck, tapped her chin with an index finger, and looked back and forth between the sculpture and Giles.

'Reminds me of – hmm. I just can't think.'

'Shh. Get down,' hissed Giles, pushing reeds to one side, revealing a vast green clearing beyond. Across the lawn, several plump, grey rabbits were chewing at some low-hanging rose heads.

'It's a herd of hairy hippos!' chirped Isabel. Giles scowled.

'I've plugged every brick in that wall, but no matter what I do, I just can't keep the buggers out. Look what they're doing to my Gertrude Jekylls!'

'So sweet. Wait. Should we be scared?'

'*They* should be scared.'

'Though something tells me they won't be,' Isabel smirked, taking in Giles and his baggy Ken-doll tuxedo, fastened about the waist with a ribbon.

Giving the rabbits a wide berth, the two of them crossed the lawn to where a small wooden shed appeared beneath a mop of willow.

The shed felt like a derelict factory or an old props warehouse, the lawnmowers and coils of hosepipe theatrical and unreal. Then again, Giles had felt that way about almost everything since the transformation. For the first couple of days, he had been sure that if he could just hit the ground hard enough, its papier mâché facade would crack.

Dust motes dangled daintily in shafts of light, lending a hushed, delicate air to the room as the two of them cut a path through a precarious maze of outsized objects.

'You going to tell me what we're looking for?'

'You'll know when you see it. Back here.'

Giles shifted a plank of wood and grunted an apology as it slipped and crunched into a crate of apples wrapped in newspaper, sending them rolling past Isabel like boulders.

'Watch it!' Isabel reproached as she stepped aside, knocking into a stack of tools resting upright against the wall. To her alarm, a spade dislodged, and she stumbled back as it accelerated into a downwards slice towards her like a guillotine. She scrambled up and over a sack of soil, and the spade's edge cut into the bag's belly with a wet thud, erupting a cloud of dirt.

Coughing and rubbing his eyes, Giles pulled her free, apologising again. Cursing, Isabel pushed past him, and waded straight into a mesh of cobwebs hanging between two rusting oil cans. She swore again as a spindly spider, like the skeleton of an old umbrella, lazily lumbered away. Pushing through the silkwork spool, Giles saw their prize at the back of the shed, amid a cascade of boxes – a wall of twisted black metal tubes sprouting four thick rubber tyres. He ran forward, gripped a convolute of pipe and pulled the vehicle down towards them.

The shed door creaked open to the *put-put-put* of an engine and the vehicle edged into daylight. The model dune buggy's bodywork and figurine drivers had been pulled off, replaced with a wooden box, held fast by cable ties and duct tape – a howdah carriage on the back of an elephant. In it sat Giles and Isabel, nervous excitement evident on both their faces. The remote control Giles had found in the bedroom made for a dashboard at the front of the box, its aerial sticking ahead of the car like a lance. Isabel gave the acceleration lever a tentative nudge, the engine growled, and the buggy lurched over the front step. Though the suspension absorbed most of the drop, the crunch of their landing sent them both tumbling forward. Dust settled. The box rocked back into place, and Giles opened his mouth to speak. Isabel held up a finger.

'No smart comments. I'd like to see you do better.'

'I was going to say, veer left. Next stop's that way, across the lawn.' Giles grinned. 'Give it some welly.'

Isabel grinned back and leaned into the lever. Though it bounced and kicked like a bucking bronco, the buggy had an astonishing pace. It tore across the grass, scattering the rabbits, sending green clods flicking high into the air behind them and, as if they could stop themselves, the two of them whooped with the sheer joy of it.

A few minutes later, panting and laughing with the thrill of the drive, Isabel reached the end of a thin, winding, overgrown path where ahead lay a small wooden dwelling. It was ornately carved and constructed, and clearly the result of much love and labour, though several tarpaulins covering one corner revealed it to be only partially finished.

'Nice hut,' Isabel remarked.

'It's a *cabin*. I prefer to call it a cabin.'

Along the balcony balustrades sat dozens of plants, herbs in colourful terracotta pots, saplings in severed plastic bottles. Above the entrance hung the carved head of the Green Man, his features a tangle of leaves. Together, they shuffled a deckchair to butt against the door, then Giles scrambled up the armrest to twist the handle. The door creaked open with a tinkle of tin chimes. Giles froze, stumbled backwards and cried out in alarm.

'Oh, Christ – the cat!' He caught Isabel, and she let out a cry.

'I'm kidding,' he laughed. 'I'd love a cat. Can't have one though, because of the birds, see?' nodding to the feeders above. 'Oh, Christ – the birds!'

'You arsehole,' said Isabel and shoved him forward. He chuckled, then stopped at the threshold, his laughter quickly abating. Giles felt a twist in the pit of his stomach. What if the message wasn't there? What if he was too late, or the girls were so far away he'd be powerless to help, yet again.

'I just need to . . . check the machine.'

'Want me to wait outside?' asked Isabel, sensing the shift in mood.

'No. No, it's OK. Power's still on. So that's good. Come in. Make yourself at home. Won't be a minute.'

Everything inside appeared to be made of wood and had the impression of being carved from a single colossal tree. Framed folk art, botanical illustrations and loosely painted blocks of colour covered one wall. A folded futon doubled as sofa and bed. Tarp fluttered at a corner window where a section of wall had been cut through, some of the joinery still exposed.

'I'm making a room for the girls,' said Giles as he shouldered a stubby milking stool across the room. Isabel ran her hands over bunk-bed bedposts intricately carved with animals.

'They must love this,' she said, marvelling at a ceiling mounted swing.

'Oh, I'd hoped so. Though, I've not actually shown them yet. Took a little longer to get ready than expected. Wanted it to be perfect.'

'I see,' said Isabel, surveying the work in progress, smiling sadly.

'Working on this, well it felt like spending time with them, you know?' Before Isabel could reply, Giles turned away and began climbing a chest of drawers by its handles, heading towards the box beside the phone, upon which, to Giles's great relief, a green light blinked back at him.

Giles kneeled beside the answerphone and hit the play button.

'*Message left on – Sunday, July second – at – eight forty-nine – p.m.*'

'*Hey Giles, it's Sadie.*' Relief surged through him. As before, her voice was small, miles away. Still, Giles felt elation at the sound of his daughter's voice and pressed his ear into the grill of the speaker. '*Just tried your phone but … We're at Silverbell. We're OK. Kind of. As OK as we can be, considering. If you can, get here, to the farm. Well, try. I love you.*' There was a long pause, then a click.

'*End of message.*'

All the weight pressing down on Giles lifted in a moment and he near threw himself over the edge of the drawers and beamed down at Isabel.

'They're at the farm!'

'That's good?'

'Yes! It's close. Towards Stockbridge. My father-in-law's place. But it's not too far. I can't believe that worked, I—' the electronic voice interrupted.

'*Next new message.*' There was more. Giles hurried back to the machine.

'*Monday July third – at – seven thirty-one – a.m.*'

'—*dy? Daddy?*' Giles froze. Sadie's message had said Ava was alive, and he'd held on to that, but the sound of her actual voice, the concrete confirmation, raised a lump in his throat as her presence brought home how close he had come to losing her.

'*I don't know what they've done ...*' She was trembling. '*But it's ... it's terrible.*' There were angry voices in the background. Commotion. Shouting. A loud bang. A gunshot? Ava continued in a whisper, '*Dad, I'm scared. He's ... he's a monster, I—*' A scream distorted the audio, and the message cut out with an electronic beep.

'*End of messages.*'

Giles stared wide-eyed at the answerphone, the elation of moments before stripped, gone. He pressed a shaking hand against the speaker and it felt as though a barrier inside him might burst. The wall of a dam. The swelling black blister. He was too late. He had been distracted. He had failed. The seal cracked and he wanted to break something.

'Giles?' Isabel's voice. He took a shuddering breath. 'Giles?' No. It was not over. He would leave, go now. He *knew* where they were. He had found them. Yes, if he left now, he could still make amends.

The sound of stones skittering on the gravel outside and the *put-put-put* of an engine snapped Giles out of his thoughts. Someone was starting the buggy. He pressed his face to the cabin window expecting to see Isabel readying the transport. Instead, it was Richard – naked and stained red as first he'd seen him, and he was frantically clambering onto the vehicle.

'Hey!' Giles banged the glass, and the priest looked up, his eyes two white specs of fear amid the red. A rustle in the bushes nearby startled the older man and he glanced back, then pressed on the accelerator. The buggy shot forwards, Richard clinging for dear life as it disappeared from view. Then, with the grace of a stone tumbling downhill, Mary crashed through the foliage and onto the path. She looked to Giles, her face a fist of anger, then bounded forwards, falling on all fours, pursuing the priest like a greyhound to a rabbit.

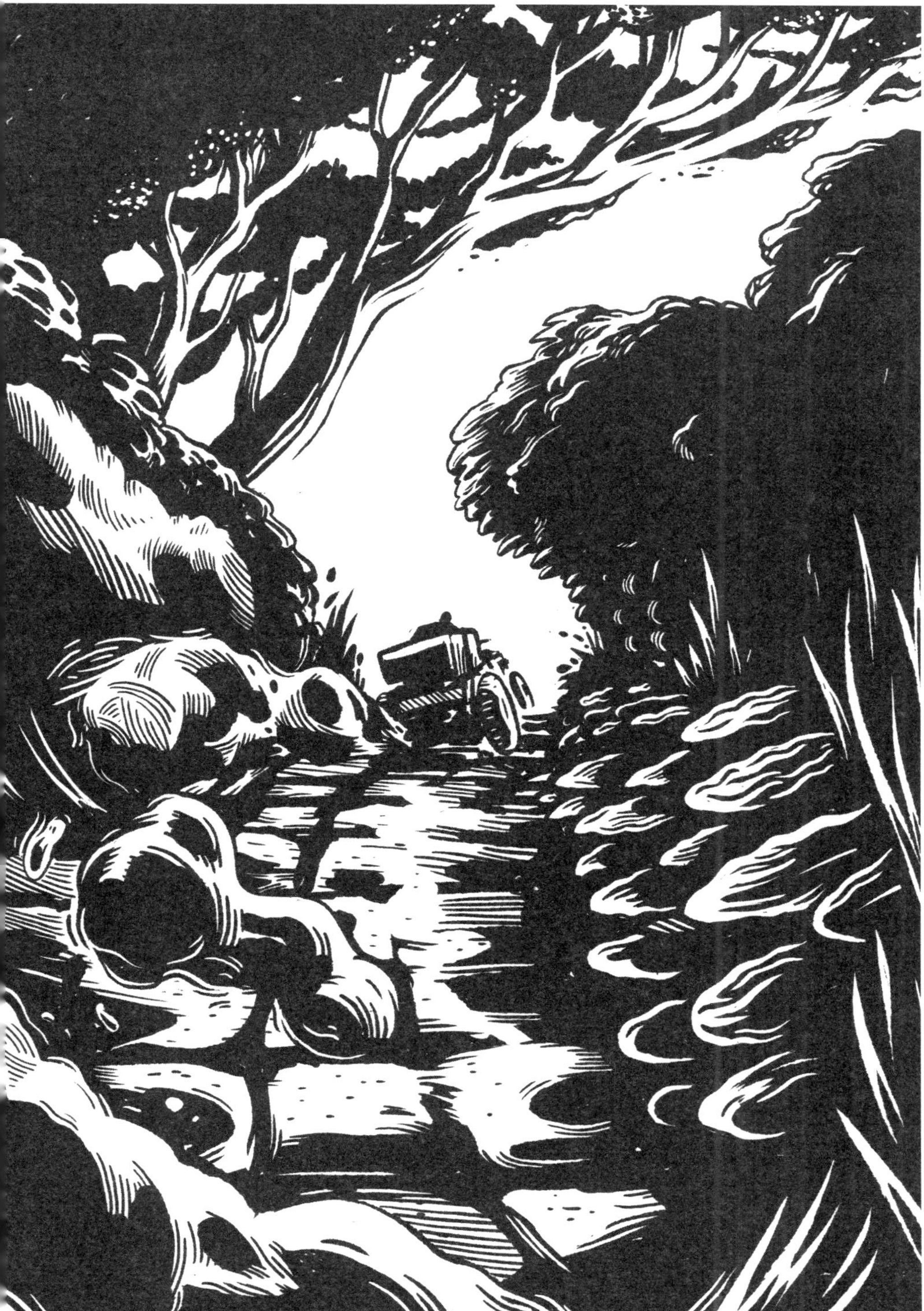

CHAPTER 28

DANGERS OF DEFERENCE

Matilda let the police cars pass, watching them crawl up the hill. Then she pulled out of the lay-by, nudging the ambulance down the country track and onto a narrow stone bridge. Headlights stripped the night away from the wilderness like a pressure hose peeling off layers of dirt, revealing bronze and viridian-green leaves beneath the black. A river rumbled below them, audible over the engine, louder for the lack of conversation. Occasional chatter from the radio broke the cab's silence as Matilda navigated her way out of the New Forest.

'*This is Willis,*' came a voice from the speaker. '*That is confirmed. The pool contains a live, organic agent. Over.*'

Bob sat on the passenger seat, with Goodwin beside him in a plastic box lined with a crumpled nest of blue cloth.

'Tell them not to touch it. Like I've told you a million times, the coccolithophores are sentient and highly dangerous. Not to mention, a subject of unparalleled scientific interest,' said Goodwin, prodding Bob with her pen. 'Go on, tell them.' Bob spoke into the handset.

'The detainee requests we leave the pool alone. Over.'

'*Copy.*' came the reply. '*Please clear the channel. Over. Bring in the bleac—*'

'What are they doing?' demanded Goodwin.

'Try to calm down, Professor. It's being taken care of,' said Bob.

'But they don't know what they're doing! They'll mess it all up. Decades of research mopped away! Call them back. Let me speak to them.'

'We've been instructed to hand you over at the hospital. As you keep on telling us, this is a little above our pay grade,' said Matilda.

'Bollocks. They're going to chop me up, aren't they?'

'No one's going to chop you up, Professor Goodwin. I think there are just a lot of questions,' she said, and Goodwin slid down into the blue nest, burying herself deep beneath cloth. She looked miserable, and Matilda had a sudden memory of a hamster, scared and nestling into sawdust. Her daughter's pet, which had to be returned to the shop after it had bitten Ava's tiny hand four days in a row. *You just need to get used to holding him*, she had said. No. Ava had replied. *This is a bad hamster.*

'Do you need anything? Food, water?' Matilda asked Goodwin.

'What I need is for the two of you to stop being a pair of plums and drive me to the coast. Set up teams along the waterfront. Help me prevent a global catastrophe.'

The words hit Matilda. Despite her abrasive manner, Goodwin's warnings rang true. There was a larger threat unfolding, just beyond the reach of her vision, in the hands of this Laslett and Leaf. Still, she was only a paramedic, and something of this scale was best left to the professionals.

'That's for someone else to decide, once we get to the hospital,' said Matilda.

'And *they'll* take me seriously, will they? I doubt it.'

'If you explain yourself to them, I'm sure they'll listen.'

'Fine,' said Goodwin bitterly, 'in that case, I could toy fitfully with a little chocolate, if you have any. I'm starving.' She pulled the blue cloth up over her legs and folded her arms. They stopped at a junction, and Matilda dug into the glove compartment, fishing out half a bar of Dairy Milk.

'You're in luck,' she smiled, offering a square to Bob, then Goodwin.

'Am I?' replied Goodwin sarcastically, snatching the square from Matilda's fingers. 'Doesn't feel like it.'

The three of them chewed quietly, and Bob picked up the box to allow Goodwin a view from the side window. Somewhat pacified, she gnawed at the corner of the brown brick and commented, 'I'd never noticed how architectural the canopy arrangements can be, must be my new perspective.' She pressed a hand against the glass, leaving a smear of tiny brown finger marks.

'You seem fairly comfortable with what's happened to you,' observed Matilda. Goodwin thought on this a moment, then answered.

'Oh, I'm as baffled as anyone. Though perhaps years spent gazing down microscopes have prepared me a little for this new magnified point of view.'

Bob craned his head to look up at the underside of the passing trees, hoping to glean some of what Goodwin was seeing. But the trees became pylons and warehouses became suburbs, and the world remained ordinary to him as they drew ever closer to the hospital.

From the window, Goodwin watched Saturday night crowds evaporate from bars and recondense around kebab shops. Mobs of matching T-shirts and foreheads strewn with wet hair undulated as one. Stag parties and hen dos collided – Roman warriors battled with furry pink devils against lampposts and toppled bins. Goodwin sighed.

'We are but swine, peddling at the gears of our own grinder.'

Behind her, Bob's radio flicked to life with Chief Deverill's voice: *'This is a call across all units. In response to the B3055 incident, we are issuing a radiation hazard alert. An MO has gone out to all emergency vehicles within the New Forest area. Residents in these catchments should report immediately to the nearest hospital for exposure assessment. All units are then to report to dispatch for updated shift information. A public announcement will be made within the hour. Over.'*

'It's not radiation, though,' said Bob, retrieving the dosimeter badge from his pocket.

'I'm sure she knows what she's doing. It's better to act than to do nothing,' said Matilda as they stopped at traffic lights.

'Radiation. Radiation. So dramatic. Good grief,' mumbled Goodwin, tapping her fingers along the window ledge, watching red brake lights flicker ahead. All of a sudden, she clapped her hands and looked up at Bob.

'Your name's Robert, correct?' Bob nodded, 'Are you in *love*, Robert?'

'Pardon?'

'Love, Robert. Are you in it?'

Bob was taken aback. He glanced sideways at Matilda, who had flipped on the sirens and delicately manoeuvred between two buses. Bob leaned in and whispered, 'Constantly, Dr Goodwin. In and out of it again.'

'Very good!' smiled Goodwin. 'It is the duty of the young to fall in and out of love as frequently as possible.'

'Duty of everyone, I should think,' replied Bob, and Goodwin pressed a hand against her chest, beaming.

'Robert, stop it. I'm far too old and – and too little for you. But when I was your age, yes ... Let me see, at your age, I suppose I was studying. Ha. I remember coming home one Christmas to find my mother terribly worked up. A rival pharma company had used the air-resistant properties of meningitis to engineer a mutant variant of the Marburg virus.'

Bob, unsure as to what this had to do with love, leaned closer to listen, as Goodwin began to pace the box, gesticulating with her hands as she spoke.

'An airborne killer, if you can believe it. The type of apocalyptic pathogen Hollywood makes films about. It was all under lock and key, of course. Nevertheless, there was a risk it might accidentally slip out of the lab. I was appalled and remembered an old saying that evil triumphed when good women did nothing. So, I broke into my mother's office, rooted through her Filofax, found the rival CEO's address, and then – my wild act of rebellion? – I wrote the CEO a *letter*!' Cars parted to make room, and the ambulance rolled on, Goodwin's anecdote in full swing.

'In that letter, I suggested that the person on the front line of virus containment, the body stood beside the innermost seal, should be someone the CEO loved – his twelve-year-old son, Oscar, for example. The idea being that before we risk the lives of strangers, we should risk the people we *love*. Every stranger is beloved to someone, and with Oscar at the gates, whenever the minions were dealing with the deadly substance, the CEO would be forced to see exactly what was at stake. The same principle should be applied to nuclear warheads. But there you go.'

'Did he reply, the CEO?' asked Bob as the hospital came into view. Goodwin saw it too and spoke faster, hurrying over her words.

'No. The papers got wind, and the company liquidated. Following that, there was a spree of public paranoia, select committee hearings. The usual stuff, forgotten about by the next news cycle. But these things strike terror deep into hearts. So do meteorites, nuclear war and what have you. But in cases like those, there is a chance you can hold your breath, seal yourself inside a bunker, outrun the shockwave.' They were at the hospital gates now, the bright doors of A & E filling the windscreen. Goodwin gripped Bob's finger with both hands and fixed him with her bright, beady eyes. 'But there's no hiding from this one, Bob. There'll be no warning signs. No news bulletins. The radius of the affected area, the sudden drop-off. Should Laslett make contact with the ocean, as I did with the pool – this wave will be all-encompassing. Complete global permeation. Everyone, tiny. Handing me over to your superiors is as good as you sealing the deal yourself. Imagine your loved ones, Bob. Picture their faces.'

Matilda shuddered. Again, that image of Ava and the sawdust and the hamster. The pet shop owner taking the box. Ava's tears.

'Bob,' said Matilda quietly, 'close the lid.'

'Don't! Don't hand me in to the hospital. Take me to the coast,' insisted Goodwin, desperate, 'we don't need the authorities. We three can stop this! We can find Laslett and Leaf! *Us!*'

'Bob, close it,' Matilda repeated, louder this time.

'Don't listen to her, Robert. She's mad. She was going to drown me in the pool, she wants rid of me.'

'Bob, I said shut that lid!' Matilda reached over, tears pricking at her eyes, 'I don't want to hear it.'

'Arresting me is inviting Armageddon!' Goodwin cried out as the lid closed above her, folding away the light.

Two plainclothes officers were waiting to meet them at the entrance to A & E, looking awkward and uncertain, shifting weight from foot to foot. Matilda handed the box to the shorter of the two, who eyed it with suspicion and held it at arm's length.

'Some advice,' said Matilda, not looking at them, 'I'd be sitting down when you open that. Oh, and she can't be detached from her IV bag. It's essential for her health, OK?' The men nodded.

'What'll happen to her now?' asked Bob.

The shorter man looked to the other for approval, then said, 'Some specialists are coming down from London to ... interview her. They won't be here until the morning, so we'll suggest she get some sleep.'

There was a light thump on the inside of the box lid and a faint flurry of curses. The taller man handed Matilda and Bob two thick wads of paper.

'It's standard non-disclosure stuff. Everyone from clean-up has to sign them.' Matilda thumbed through the pages, whistling softly.

'This is a serious stack of paper,' she said.

'Biological weaponry is serious stuff,' replied the man.

They watched the officers pass through the reception doors and out of sight.

'I – I have to head back to the station,' said Bob. 'There's a debrief about coordinating this radiation alert.' He turned, stumbled on the kerb, and Matilda caught his shoulder.

'Don't worry,' she said, helping Bob steady himself. 'She'll be fine. We'll check back in the morning, make sure of it.'

'But what if she was telling the truth about the others, Laslett and Leaf, heading for the coast?'

'The chief knows what she said. She has our full report. And there's probably a hundred police and MI5 down there, considering every possibility. Besides—' Matilda laughed nervously. 'She's not all there, that little lady. She can't be.'

'You're right.' Bob nodded. 'For a minute, I let her get to me.'

'She *was* right about one thing – we're not getting paid enough for this.' Matilda tapped him affectionately on the head with the stack of papers. 'Let's be happy to leave them to it. Ay?'

She checked her watch. It was midnight, and according to dispatch, she had another shift in five hours. She closed her locker. There was no point going home, plus the office was empty, so she stretched out along four chairs beside the window and threw her duffel coat over her legs. Perhaps she would call Ava, make sure she had taken her pills – make sure she was sleeping OK. Matilda laughed. Wake Ava up to tell her to sleep. Now there was some sound logic.

She could have sworn her eyes were only closed for a moment, but when she squinted at her watch, it was past two in the morning. Bob was kneeling by her shoulder and speaking in an urgent whisper.

'Mathilda, wake up, I have thomething to thow you.' Was she still dreaming, or in the last hour had Bob developed a lisp? As her eyes adjusted to the light, she saw that he was bleeding from the mouth, twists of red-soaked tissue stuck between his swollen lips. His face too was drained of colour, making the dark circles under his eyes more pronounced than usual.

'We werenth meanth to thow it to anyone but—' Bob pulled out his phone and scurried to close the office door, making sure they were alone.

'You filmed something you shouldn't have on your phone?' Matilda smiled at Bob, who grinned back sheepishly. 'What happened to your teeth, Bob?' She frowned, seeing that the tissues went right up to his gums.

'Dothenth matter. Wath thith. Ith the CCTV from Goodwinth lab.' Bob shuffled Matilda sideways on the seats and squeezed in beside her. He dragged his finger across the screen, scrolling back through the video.

'Thath Goodwin,' said Bob. 'At leasth it wath. Look.' A woman she didn't recognise stood beside the pool, pouring what appeared to be milk into the water.

'... *the dirty milk trick*,' they heard her say. Then the screen went white and the phone emitted a high-pitched screech. Bob clicked off the audio and cycled forward, frame by frame. Matilda watched in horror as Goodwin pressed her hands to her temples, her face contorted in agony. Sweat patches swelled from beneath her arms, joining moments later with a bloom at her chest. With a sharp convulsion, a fountain of fluid erupted from her mouth and splattered into the pool. Then, her crinkling hands squeezed at the sides of her head, juicing it like a piece of rotten fruit, as more fluid poured out from between her dwindling fingers and sprayed from her mouth. Clothes concertinaed as her head, withering like an old balloon, slipped into her collar. Then she sank from view,

286

disappearing into the crumpled pile of cloth beside the pool, and all was still.

'OK, then look at thith.' Bob scrolled the video back a few hours. Several people scurried about the room in time-lapse, pulling consoles and tanks from the pool side and carrying them away.

'Goodwinth locked in that booth at the back. Now look,' Bob paused the video and pointed to the two men taking a small glass bottle and filling it with white liquid from one of the steel tanks.

'Ith juth like Goodwin thaid. Whatever she poured into the pool, they took thome of it too. I think they're going to pour it into the othean. What happened to Goodwin ith going to happen to everyone.' Matilda took a shuddering breath and clamped her hand over her mouth.

'Hey, ith OK,' cooed Bob, stroking her back. He smiled, letting the blood-soaked loo roll fall from his mouth, revealing a black hole where his two front teeth had been. Matilda startled.

'Oh, don't worry about thith, ith juth in cathe. You thaid it wasn't the thrinking that killed you, it wath other thuff getting in the way? The ambulanth driver wath killed by hith fake tooth. Yeth? Well, I had two of them. Acthident on a pedalo.' This made Matilda double over in horror, cover her face with both hands and rock back and forth.

'Whoa! Ith OK. Polith are on it. They'll thind them. You goth some fillingth or thomething? We can geth those taken outh. Goodwin thaid we have another eight hourth. Better to be thafe right?'

'That's just it.' Matilda steadied her breath and wiped her sleeve across her nose. 'It's not me. It's my youngest. She has something inside her that can't—' Matilda sat upright and gripped Bob's arm. 'The chief was wrong, and – and we can't just leave them to sort this out. If we do nothing, those people—' she tapped Bob's phone, a nail clicking on Leonard Leaf's face, 'those people are going to kill my little girl.' She stood, steadied herself on Bob's shoulder, and then led him to the door.

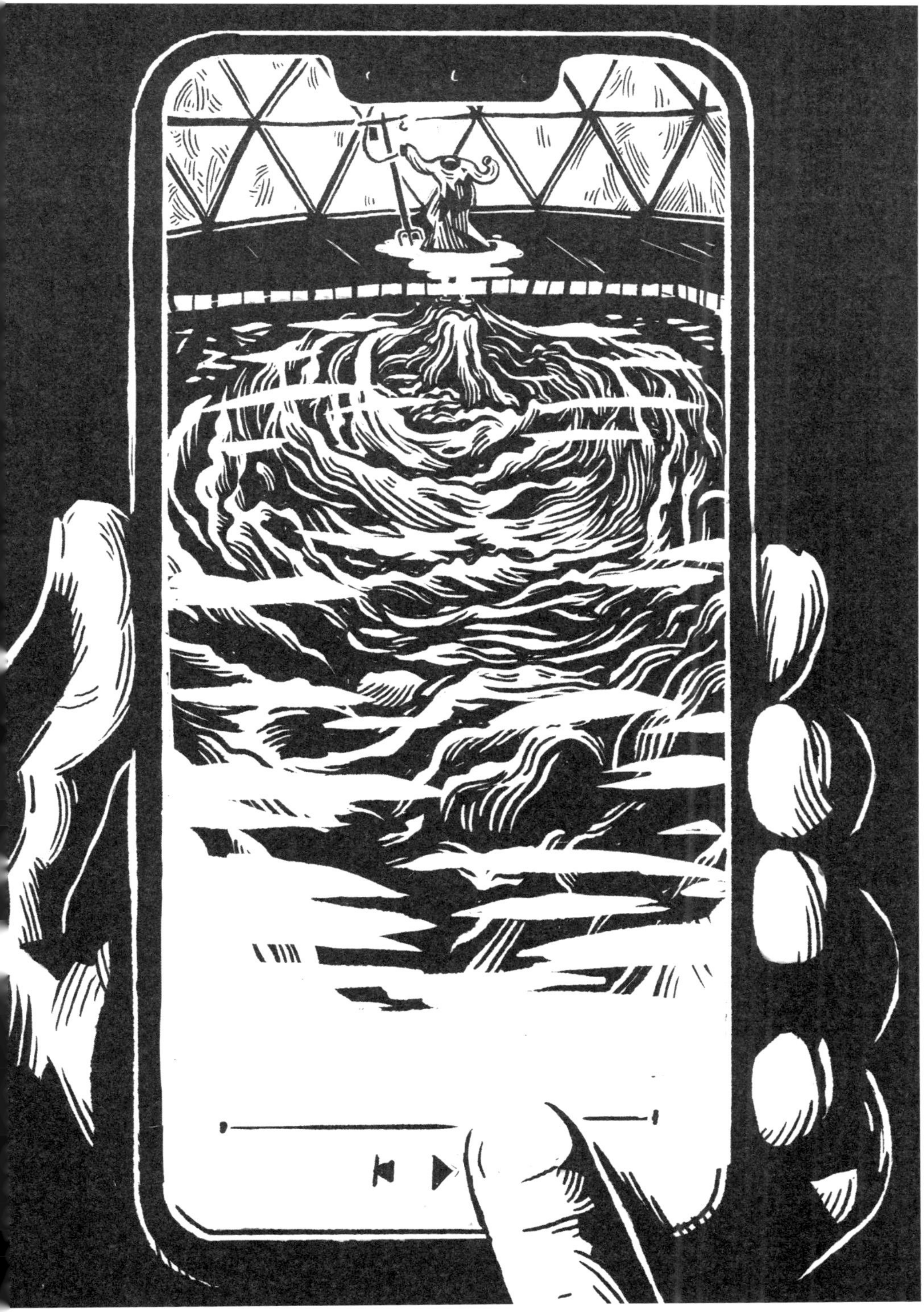

CHAPTER 29

GARGOYLE

Isabel ran back towards the manor and Giles set off in the oppo-site direction, following the sound of the engine, the breaking of foliage and the fresh tyre tracks that cut stripes through the otherwise well-kept garden. Richard had stolen his dune buggy! His only means of reaching Silverbell Farm. All to escape from an elderly woman the priest was convinced was out to get him, and for what? Running away from her giant dog? Being a spokes-person for God, the apparent architect of their suffering? It was completely unreasonable. Any concern he'd felt for either of the parties quickly gave way to irritation. Whatever the feud between these two, it had encroached upon his affairs for the last time.

A splash, and the distant *put-put-put* of the engine cut suddenly short. Giles rounded a copse of hydrangeas to see the buggy rest-ing on its side, two wheels spinning slowly above a wall of grass.

Aside from the sway of the willow canopy, all was still; only the birdsong and the soft thumping of the rabbits nearby broke the silence. Giles ran forward as Richard shot up from behind the upturned vehicle and staggered towards the gargoyle statue. A moment later, a bedraggled Mary emerged from the pond, and waded towards the priest. As she passed the diminutive car, she paused and stooped. To Giles's horror, not for the first time, she straightened holding his snap-blade, which had been stowed in his pack, and extended the scalpel's length with a ratcheting click.

'Hey!' called Giles, bounding through the grass, 'Mary!' At this, she turned. Something in the act of naming her robbed her of power, and the animal fury that had been etched on her face during the chase melted into utter vacancy.

Giles grabbed the snap-blade by the handle and, without objection, she relinquished her grip.

'You stay back,' he warned. Mary offered no resistance and simply stood. Richard must have taken the moment to slip away as, when Giles turned to face the gargoyle, he was gone. He scanned the scene for signs of the older man – the statue, the pond, the buggy protruding above the shoulder-high meadow. Nothing. Movement stirred in the grass behind Mary, coming from the direction of the water. Giles called for the priest, then sighed and grumbled, 'Just a rabbit,' as a distinct form, large and furry, edged closer. Without taking her eyes from Giles, Mary dropped suddenly into the grass, covered herself with her matt of hair, just as she had done back at the campsite, and merged into the roots.

'Go on, shoo, you bugger,' called Giles, stepping forwards, waving the animal away. He stopped dead in his tracks. There was something off about the creature. The rabbit's usual mousey grey colouring was streaked with black, its ears were too short, its flank too long. The striped fur body rippled through the grass and headed straight for him. Then its head raised above the grass, revealing the distinctly rodent-like face of a polecat.

Giles ran, fumbling the blade's clasp, glancing back over his shoulder. With one foot up on the gargoyle's talon, he tried to climb, clawing at moss that fell away in his hands. Too late. The polecat's claws were on his back, and the snap-blade slipped from his fingers. He felt himself dragged back into the grass and pinned to the ground with a paw. Air was forced from his lungs and Giles became aware of fur smothering his body: warm, wet, smelling of earth and something less pleasant. And then the jaws stretched wide open above his head. With a trembling hand, he searched the ground for the blade handle but instead found a rock, and as the animal bore down, Giles thrust upwards.

There was a sound like two marbles clenched inside a fist, and the pressure on his chest relaxed. Not wasting a second, Giles reached out and again gripped moss that fell away in his hand. Then someone else was in there with him, struggling against the fur. There was a flash of silver, a squeal and Mary emerged from the tangle, swinging the snap-blade, pulling Giles back by his bloodied shirt. Giles breathed deep, feeling his ribs realign, and found his balance as the polecat bared its teeth, one of them markedly chipped. Mary slumped to one side, her left hand pressed to her stomach as the snap-blade fell to the ground. Giles reached again and this time found a firm hold of moss and pulled himself up onto the gargoyle's knees. As the polecat repositioned, Giles reached down, grabbed Mary beneath her arm and pulled.

She weighed almost nothing. Giles hoisted her up beside him, and the polecat's claw caught in the woman's lengthy hair, tugging her back down. For a moment, he thought he might drop her, but a dislodged fragment of stone bounced and landed on the polecat's flank, a final straw, and the animal skulked back into the long grass.

They lay there, panting. Giles between the gargoyle's horns and Mary at the nape of its neck. In the gathering dark, there was no sign of Richard or the polecat. Reaching up to the canopy of willow above, Giles tore a leaf and licked the condensation – bitter but refreshing – then tore another and passed it to Mary, who drank greedily and gestured for more.

'So, you're Mary?' asked Giles. She seemed to think on this for a long time, before curiously examining her skeletal hand, and extending it. 'Giles. Nice to meet you.' He took the hand, dwarfed by his own, and shook. 'Right,' said Giles, taking in the wound to Mary's side, 'we need to get you back to the house.' He mimed lifting her onto his shoulders, then gestured back down the gargoyle's tail. Suddenly, Mary spoke.

'Nope.'

Her voice was low and gruff, a croak, a bubble bursting in a swamp. She raised a shaking finger and pointed towards the pond. Following its trajectory, Giles saw a black, shining dot pushing through the grass. The polecat circling the statue like a shark around an island.

'How's – how's your wound?' Careful not to startle her, Giles pushed back a curtain of matted hair covering Mary's belly. The gash across her torso was deep, but the woman didn't flinch. Instead, she croaked, 'Will live.'

It was strange, hearing her speak after all this time. It took great physical effort, as if her whole body was searching, digging for the thoughts. She scrunched her eyes and mouth tight, making her face appear almost concave. Giles imagined her casting a hook into some interior lake, fishing for words. Eventually, when the words bit, her features sprang back into place, flinging them forward, well lubricated.

'Must wait. Cat will get bored.' She was right. Though the buggy lay a short distance away, there was no way he was willing to risk a second encounter with the mustelid.

'Why were you chasing Richard?' asked Giles, and when he got no response he added, 'the priest.'

At this, her face crunched inwards, and she spat, 'He's no priest!'

'Who is he then?'

'*Murderer.*' Her eyes shimmered with anger.

'Did – did you know him from before? From before this happened to us?' She looked confused for a moment, then as if in answer to a different question, she said,

'No priest. But they let him hold ... the collection basket. I told them they shouldn't. But felt sorry for him, they did. He woke up first. Thought he was special. I saw him going row by row ... all their Sunday bests ruined. He ruined them. He wanted to be the only one. He wanted to get me too. Couldn't though. Couldn't get me. They were good boys, they were. Never bit no one ... Liked chasing rabbits. You confused them, is all ... still, they knew me. Good boys.' She looked to Giles, almost shy, and added, 'Even afterwards ...' Then she brushed some hair away from her face and again Giles caught a glimpse of who this woman had once been – well-mannered, serious, and hardy. Finally, she said, 'They never let him close, though he tried.' She sat up a little against the stone wing, spluttered a word that might have been *murderer*, then fell silent – as if those were the last drops of thought squeezed from a dry sponge.

'I'm sure it's a – a misunderstanding. It's been an unusual week. Richard's a good man.' At this, she laughed – short, sharp intakes of breath, like a chair leg scraping on stone.

'No. I've been watching. Determined, he is, but weak too. He likes to wait until you sleep. Until you're wounded or trapped.'

As if on cue, Mary groaned.

'We have to get you help.' Giles scanned the sea of black between their perch and the capsized buggy, their four-wheeled lifeboat. The wind was back, making it hard to discern any creatures moving in the grass. Branches swayed above them. Giles looked up. 'If we could make it into the tree, grab hold of those leaves, we can climb across, avoid the ground altogether.' Giles surveyed the drop; it was a long one. Mary gave another little snort. Compared to him she was frail, yet she manoeuvred this new world with a confidence that made him feel like a child learning to walk.

'Can I ask you another question?' Mary gave a slow and serious nod. 'The way you move, it's – well, it's unusual. I don't know how to explain.'

'Old body,' she answered. Giles looked confused, and she continued, irritated. 'You. You're stuck in the old body. A mouse is not afraid of falling from a tree. I forgot. You need to forget too. Your old body remembers.' And Giles knew it was true. He had spent a lifetime learning not to step off high ledges, and now he felt like a bungee jumper about to leap without rope. Though his mind screamed caution, something in his gut promised he would survive the fall.

Giles leaned forward, peering over the edge, and reached for the dangling branch. Mary placed a reassuring hand on his shoulder and then shoved him hard in the back. He fell. His stomach lurched into his ribs as time seemed to slow. Then he tumbled through moss and rocks and landed with a wet thump in the grass. He sprung to his feet. Looking back up to marvel at what he'd just done, he saw Mary, laughing full-heartedly. Clutching her side, she slid down the gargoyle's tail to join him.

'Cat's gone . . .'

Giles relaxed. He might have been annoyed at being pushed from such a height, but in her own way, he knew she had been trying to help. It was the sort of thing Morris, his father, would have done, and he liked her more for it. She swayed on the spot, and Giles stepped forwards, scooping her into his arms, a tiny curl of person, and began to walk in the direction of the buggy.

'No way! Is it fast? Are there more?' asked Alex, running over to Giles who was hauling the dune buggy into the orangery. 'Can we take it for a spin?'

'No,' said Giles flatly, answering all the questions at once.

A gabble of children had gathered about the remote-control car, muttering excitedly. They fell to a hush as Giles lifted Mary from the box. Maya ran forward and helped place her on a crumpled tea towel in the corner of the greenhouse. Mary had passed out the moment the buggy had rumbled into life, the same way his children, long ago, had fallen to sleep in the back seat of his van. Giles's stomach clenched. He was in the wrong place. He knew it, and yet once again he couldn't bring himself to leave.

Evelyn, in a newly tailored makeshift grey jumpsuit – thick orange fur sprouting about her collar and cuffs – wrapped Mary in a corner of the towel as several children appeared at the far door, dragging a first aid kit. Giles looked again at Mary's face. Though still an alarming shade of red, the strain and tension were gone. It was strange that they had feared and run from this woman. He remembered Richard's words beside the funeral pyre – *death is only terror at a distance, when unmasked it shows a friendly face.* Ashraf stepped beside Giles and gave him an inquiring look. 'Richard?'

'He's still out there. What happened?'

'Not too sure. I was about to sample Richard's stew, when *she*,' Ash gestured to the sleeping Mary, 'came out of nowhere and smacked my spoon away. Rude! She must have got out when the generator died. I guess the chimney fan stopped.'

'So, she didn't care for Richard's cooking. Seems she had a real vendetta against him.'

'Too right,' said Ashraf, frowning at the memory, 'while Richard was legging it, she went to work on the whole pan, tipped it over and then, well, I don't know how to say it. She – she peed in the stew, Giles. No one was very hungry after that.'

'Why would she? Even for her, that seems very . . . crude.'

'Scent marking?'

Giles shook his head, confused. Then, a thought struck, and he strode the orangery path to a small green box, the trap he'd used to cull the mice, remembering how he'd pointed it out in front of the whole group. The box was empty. The poison he'd seen on their arrival, gone.

'Did anyone eat the stew?'

'You kidding? Just finished clearing it up. You don't think he did something to it?' Giles shrugged. Ash peered through the darkened window, out into the garden. 'I should go and look for him.'

'It's too dangerous. There's a polecat. We only just got away.' Ashraf tensed, then checked the door behind them was closed.

'Reckon they got him?'

'I don't think so. He was covered in red stuff again, like Mary. And it moved past *her* like she was invisible. Came right at me, though.'

Across the tiles, Evelyn, who seemed to have taken charge, dabbed at the wound on Mary's belly with a wet cloth, cleaning the rusty hue, revealing skin.

'Go and get Isabel,' said Giles, hoisting his pack onto his shoulders, 'tell her I'll be back tomorrow, or at least as soon as possible. I'll look for Richard on the way to the—' Ashraf held Giles's arm. For a moment, Giles thought he was going to ask him to stay, and he felt a flare of annoyance.

'Isabel? She's not with you?'

Giles blinked. 'She's not here? She said she was coming back. I saw her go.'

'She left again, to find you. I thought . . .'

Giles felt his stomach drop. He let the pack slide from his shoulders, and walked towards the door, reaching for the snap-blade. It wasn't there. With a pang of irritation, he remembered Mary had dropped it beside the gargoyle. As he passed Evelyn and Alex, stretching a plaster across the older woman's side, he lifted the cloth the teenagers had used to clean her red skin, and caught a pungent aroma of spice.

'Where exactly did Richard cook up this stew?'

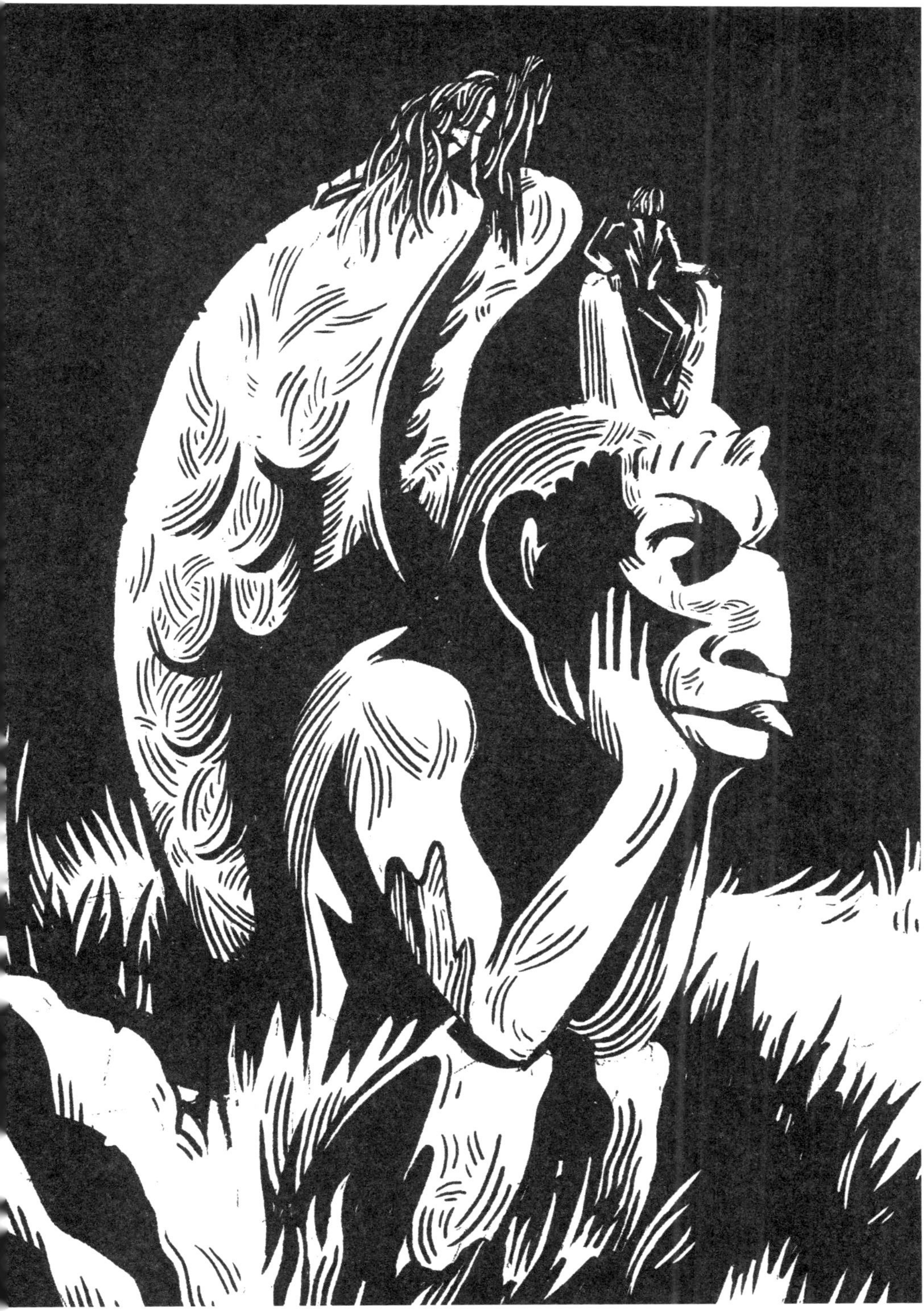

CHAPTER 30

ELSEWHERE,

PASHU DWEEPA

Pashu Dweepa was not a name you would find in any atlas. *The Animal Island*, as it translates, was a local moniker – a taunt and for some, an apology. The generation who remembered the place before the tower block, turrets and razor-wire walls had long since passed. Forgotten too was the mangrove forest – made way for barracks, the wetland – flattened into three exercise yards, and the reef – filled to form the foundation of a jetty. Though the old quarry remained, it had become a hole to throw things into, rather than pull things out of. The new name had first arisen as a joke, chosen for the repurposed island's conspicuous *lack* of nature, and the presence of a new native species – the inmates. The non-people. The animals. It's easy to understand, considering the attitudes at the time, how the new name had stuck.

Legislation prohibited the practice of labelling inmates as *non-people*, but to shed an idea when its message is woven into the very stonework is not an easy task. Every aspect of the institute's architecture had been carefully chosen to emphasise the line between those who were human, and those who were not. From the administrator's gilded office overlooking the square-box windowless cells, to the flowerless yard buttressed against the superintendent's rose garden. The blanketless bed mats, the pig-trough latrines, the beatings, the flavourless dal chawal, the numbers assigned in lieu of names. Every detail perfectly tailored to remind the prisoners that, when they stepped off the boat from Suryakoti, they had descended, they had been dethroned, stripped of their divine essence, their *atman*, knocked from their elevation as people, cast down to become animals – *the Pashu*.

It was exactly this kind of attitude that made Pashu Dweepa one of the more favourable prisons in which to wake up on July Second. For the wave of change that suggested humans should not be kept in literal cages had yet to reach these shores.

On the first morning of their new, physically reformed lives, the resized inmates stepped freely out through the bars of their cells. The iron grill that so many had pressed their faces against the night before, hoping for a breath of clean air, became as passable as any other open doorway. There, in the corridors, the surviving prisoners met the surviving guards.

Relations between the jailed and the jailers are at best built upon conspiratorial cooperation and at worst fraught with hostility, injustice and abuse. The dynamic of Pavan and Amit sadly fell into the latter category. Only one week earlier, Pavan had awoken Amit by upending a bucket of greywater, after the guard had discovered graffiti, rendered in Amit's signature hand, depicting him in the passionate embrace of a pig. Though the victories were small compared to Pavan's punishments, Amit relished the opportunity to remind the guard that there was still fight in him. That he had not been broken completely. Both men had been scarcely more than boys when they took up residence on either side of the bars. Now, in their middling years, the roles were so deeply entrenched, the spark of their rivalry so long forgotten, that wagers were made upon not *if* but *when* the conflict would end in fatal blows. No other outcome seemed possible.

When Amit, draped in a torn strip of once white mundu cloth, stepped over the threshold of his cell to be faced with Pavan, crawling from his crumpled uniform, having suffered a transformation, a *punishment*, that mirrored his own, one can only imagine his thrill at seeing his superior so humbled. As Amit padded the board towards the fallen guard, three fellow inmates fell in beside him. Officers of Pashu Dweepa were well used to being outnumbered. Since the island operated at twice its capacity, there had been many instances of unrest, and minor riots. All had been quickly quelled with the display of firearms. Faced with the advancing group, Pavan stumbled on his unsteady feet, tangled in his trailing hair and fell upon the butt of his sidearm, an IOF revolver, loaded with six rounds each as thick as his arm. With great effort, he slid it from the crushed mess of uniform, and spun the barrel to face to the party. Pavan had fired the weapon many times in training, but he'd never shot a person. But was Amit a *person*? Certainly, he looked less like one than ever before. Yes, undoubtedly, these were animals, *Pashu*, who had crawled from

302

the cells. Though the blast would surely deafen him, and the recoil break some ribs, the alternative of letting these creatures come closer would expose Pavan to a fate far worse. He hugged the handle, both hands wrapped about the trigger, and felt the spring of the hammer pinch his shoulder.

Amit and the others stopped but did not dive for cover. Instead, the inmate looked above and behind Pavan, then whispered something to his companion, who thought for a moment, then burst out laughing. Pavan, confused as to why he was not being taken seriously, followed their line of sight.

Behind him stood a door. Just a door. Pavan failed to see the joke. He turned, taking in the cells, the corridor walls, the drop to the yard, then looked back to the door – the only exit, re-enforced with heavy interlocking bolts. Its handle, several times his own height, out of reach. At last, he understood what the inmates had found so amusing – Pavan was as much a prisoner as the rest of them. In his diminished state, escape from this island would need more than passcodes and keys. If he was to leave, to see his parents again, he and the inmates would need to cooperate. As they stood there, facing each other on the corridor planks, the laughter subsided. Amit and Pavan took each other in and in the context of this expanded world, the old dynamics, their bitter past, suddenly seemed petty.

Pavan relaxed his grip and shoved the weapon across the floor, so that it spun beneath the balcony barrier and broke on the yard below. He returned to the folds of his uniform and emerged a moment later pulling a set of keys.

It took the group three days to break through the several layers of security that kept them from their freedom – The corridor blast doors, the warden's stairwell, the courtyard ramparts coated in anti-climb paint. At last, they arrived, with the hundred surviving inmates and employees they had gathered along the way, at the final layer of security – the ocean.

Pashu Dweepa was visited twice daily by a ferry carrying inmates, visitors, employees and supplies back and forth to Suryakoti, an hour's sail to the west. The fire from the eighty-foot vessel had been spotted two days earlier. But it was not until they reached the start of the jetty that they saw the reserve boat, the one meant for emergencies, their last hope of escape, a smouldering twist of wood and metal, half absorbed into the larger craft's hull. Despair had gripped them then – a realisation that for jailer and jailed alike, there was no escape from the island.

Though at the time it felt like further punishment, their confinement was in fact a blessing, as over the coming years war ravaged the nearby resort town of Suryakoti. While on the island, doors reopened and piece by piece, the land transformed. At first necessity forced cooperation between the not so long ago divided parties. When the stores depleted the following spring, a group of once farmers organised a system of agriculture, reclaiming plots from the rose garden, seeded from the canteen scraps. Several prisoners, adept cattle rustlers, utilising their mastery for coaxing large animals, learned to farm the bird and rodent population to great effect. Guards and inmates worked the pools along the rocky shore, harvesting a bounty of mussels, cockles, periwinkles and crab. As the years passed, who had been what became the least interesting aspect of their new relationships. Attempts to build rafts and convert vessels came and went and plans of escaping on the back of a migrating great hornbill were hastily abandoned under the snap of its frightening beak. Throughout the facility, ground gave way to nature. Though the mangrove forest would never return, a smaller jungle of pioneer plants – ferns, grasses, moss and succulents split the concrete, lending the grey a welcome wash of green.

Pavan and Amit were never truly friends, but instead kept a respectful distance, only working together when the task deemed it necessary. On one occasion, Amit saved Pavan from a falling roof tile, calling to warn him in the moment before it hit. They both understood that this kingdom was their rebirth, a second chance. When, at last, relatives of these long-lost residents arrived on a small boat and weighed anchor on the crumbling jetty, they found an ageing community, with no desire to leave. The cages and uniforms that had made animals of them all had long since been repurposed.

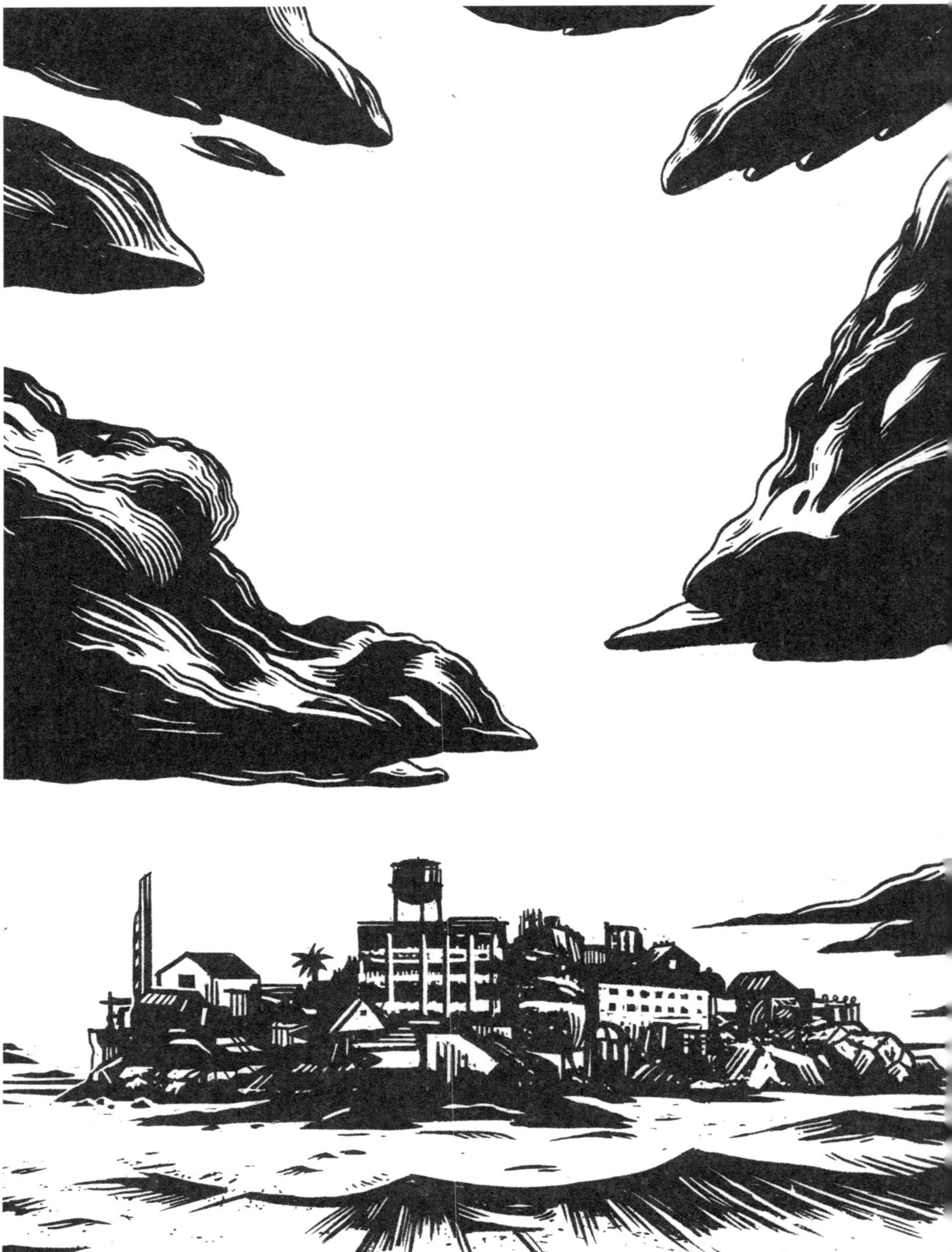

PART VII

CHAPTER 31

A COUNTER MEASURE

The lift smelled like a cocktail of cologne, whisky and TCP. Matilda held her breath and watched the floor numbers climb the dial. Doctors, nurses, a couple of gurneys and two guys in floral shirts supporting a third half-naked peer all vied for space inside the crowded steel box. On a typical night, patients in custody were taken to the coronary care unit on the second floor, and Bob was there now, scouting for Goodwin. But on the Friday late shift, the hospital took on the air of a chaotic nightclub, and the usual rules did not apply. Hence, Matilda wasn't taking any chances, she was looking everywhere else. The two men burst into song as they passed the third floor and announcements barked through the Tannoy, summoning staff this way and that. Through the compound of distractions, Matilda heard two words that made her ears prick up.

'Advanced acromicria?' The voice was hushed and squeaky. Matilda knew the condition caused abnormally small and under-developed extremities.

'Perhaps. However, it might be one of a hundred causes. Or a combination of things. A tumour on the pituitary gland. Extreme hypoplasia or synostosis? Or it might be none of those. We won't know until we examine her properly. And even then ...'

Hurriedly, Matilda looked over to see who was talking. Two men, one tall, grey and scribbling notes onto a clipboard, the other a foot shorter with a crown of black hair haloing his bald spot.

'Jesus,' said the shorter man.

'Tell me about it. Let's start with the endocrine glands, thyroid. Check basal metabolism, catabolism. Can we do iodide tests here?'

'I – I don't see why not.'

'Good. Add those to the list. What do you make of this, Lander? Any theories?' The lift announced their arrival at floor five, and the men followed several others out into the corridor. Matilda followed after them, straining to keep within earshot.

'I have one theory, sir. Have we considered a negative nitrogen balance? She could be throwing off more nitrogen than she's retaining. It serves to reason that since nitrogen is one of the major building blocks of the body, she – she would consequently have shrinkage.' The taller of the two stopped in the corridor, and Matilda busied herself with a hanging rack of charts. He raised an eyebrow. The other cracked a nervous smile. 'I'm just kidding, sir. That's the plot of the Incredible Shrinking Man. I looked it up on the way in.' The taller man relaxed his shoulders and pinched the bridge of his nose.

'Christ, Lander, I was about to strip you of your licence. That's the most ridiculous thing I've ever heard. We've no time for jokes. In less than an hour, the HPA and God knows who else is going to come marching in. If we don't have an explanation that doesn't sound like we've copied it from a bathroom wall, it's going to get very embarrassing, very quickly.'

The pair turned a corner, and Matilda peered around its edge. At the end of the long white hallway, she saw an officer sitting slumped in a plastic chair outside a room, flicking through a newspaper. The officer startled at the approaching footsteps then relaxed and greeted the two doctors with a nod.

'Absolutely, Dr Pearson,' said Lander, holding open the double doors beside the officer.

'And find out what's in that damn IV drip. She was being a total arse about it.'

'I'll – I'll send a sample down to the lab right away.'

'Good. Now, once we're done with the glands, we'll administer ACTH to monitor for catabolic breakdown of tissue. Think you can get me what I need for all that?' Pearson pressed the clipboard into Lander's chest.

'Right away, sir.'

Matilda leaned back and messaged Bob – *Goodwin on fifth. Maternity. Get here now.*

Double doors slammed, and the sound of footsteps hurried back up the corridor towards her. Matilda strode forward as if she'd only just left the elevator, collided with Lander and sent his clipboard skidding across the tiles.

'Goodness! I'm such a klutz,' Matilda blushed, embarrassed less by her deliberate clumsiness, more by her poor attempt at theatrics. She kneeled to retrieve the clipboard, sure he had seen through the obvious ploy. Looking back up, she saw Lander was as flustered as she was. She glanced at the chart and then handed it back to him.

'The patient, she's in a stable condition?'

'Patient?' asked Lander, his voice hushed, glancing over his shoulder towards the officer.

'Professor Goodwin,' said Matilda, as if this was obvious.

'Goodwin? I – I'm sorry – I'm under strict instruction not to discuss—' He made to move past, but Matilda stepped back with him, insisting.

'It's just – I'm the paramedic who brought her in. I still can't quite believe . . . Well, I was hoping you might be able to tell—'

'Really, there's nothing I can say. We – we all signed the paperwork.' Lander continued towards the lift doors. Matilda followed and waited with him. With the lift only seconds away, she abandoned caution.

'Did she say where they were going? The people who took the equipment from her lab?' Lander furrowed his brow.

'What? No. That's—. She hasn't said a word since we got her. She kicked up such a fuss. The chief had her sedated on the way up.' The lift arrived. 'Now, please, if you'll excuse me.'

'Sedated?' said Matilda, to herself as much as Lander. Her heart thudded louder in her chest. The silver doors opened, and Matilda was pleased to see Bob emerge. Taking him by the hand, she led him to the end of the corridor.

'They've sedated Goodwin, the one person who could have told us where her colleagues were headed.'

'Lathleth, she thaid their names were Lathleth and Leath.'

'The chief doesn't know what she's doing. She's going to get us all . . .' Matilda trailed off, clasping one hand in the other to steady her nerves.

'She'th down there ith she? Profethor Goodwin?' Matilda nodded.

'Yes, but there's an officer on the door.'

'Gimme one minuth.'

312

Before she could stop him, Bob had slid around the corner. A few moments later, the guard hurried past Matilda towards the elevator.

'Everyoneth on double shiftth. She couldn't wait to leave,' whispered Bob from the plastic chair, the newspaper open on his lap. 'Now get in there and get thome antherth.'

Matilda peered in through a porthole window at the tall, grey-haired man pushing X-ray transparencies along a lightbox. 'The other doctor, he's still examining. I – I can't . . .' She looked down at Bob. He'd most likely be suspended for this, she thought, relieving another officer of their post without permission, abandoning his duties on her behalf. He grinned, a black hole for front teeth, and nodded reassuringly. Matilda took a breath and pushed aside the double doors.

The room was cast blue by a sterile ceiling bulb that buzzed and flickered. Pearson was still hunched over a green glow in the far corner, his back to Matilda.

'Dr Pearson?'

He turned. She had been expecting a stern, commanding face to match his voice and stature. Instead, she found a squat lower jaw and bulbous forehead split through the middle by a bushy mono-brow. His head was pink and wrinkled as a peach, the caterpillar eyebrow nibbling about the crease.

'Yes, what is it?'

'You're . . .' She was no good at this. Never had been. Lying was foreign to her. What was it she had been told once – the best lies are grown from a kernel of truth? He stared at her, the caterpillar twitching with irritation.

'Yes?'

'You're required in reception.' Pearson groaned and threw back his head.

'And why on earth would that be?'

'Visitors, in need of debriefing. In regards to the patient. From the HPA.'

'Already? Christ. They didn't waste any time. They get here by jet? Hmm. Wouldn't surprise me. Fine.' Pearson began replacing the X-rays into a folder, then raised one half of his eyebrow.

'Why'd they send you? Tannoy not working?'

'Thought the message best relayed in person, what with the sensitive nature of all this.'

'Suppose they want their hands held as well, a grand tour, made to feel special.'

'You know how it is,' agreed Matilda, rolling her eyes. She bit her lip as she watched Pearson grab his jacket and leave without another word.

The green glow he had been hunched over was an incubator, the kind used for premature infants. Matilda knew who she would find inside, strung with electrodes and monitoring pads, from which wires fanned out like ribbons from a maypole. In lieu of handcuffs, one arm had been bound to a rail with a cable tie. She looked foetal, the saddest, smallest, oldest child Matilda had ever seen. Here, in the maternity ward, the instruments were well fitted to the shrunken woman, as her field kit had not been. Matilda was still taking in the peculiar sight when she heard the door.

'What are *you* doing in here?'

Matilda turned and froze. There stood Chief Deverill.

In an instant, her mouth dried. Then, she sought out a kernel of truth and grew from it a new lie, easier this time.

'Dr Pearson was called to the front desk, and he asked me to keep an eye on the patient.'

'*Detainee*,' corrected the chief. 'How is she?' Matilda relaxed and scanned the monitors. That had been too easy.

'We don't have a lot to compare with. From her size, I'd assume she'd have a newborn's heart rate and blood pressure. The heart rate's right, the blood pressure's over. But who knows, that might be normal. She appears stable. No smaller or larger than when we found her, at least.' The chief stared into the black bulge of a heart monitor and straightened the line of her fringe in its reflection.

'Yes, well. I look forward to your report.'

'Oh, paramedics don't do rep—'

'You can go now. I'll wait for Pearson and the others.' Matilda took a step towards the door.

'Was it – was it necessary to knock her out, Chief?' The woman straightened but kept her back turned.

'Excuse me? If I deem it necessary, then it is necessary. Thank you.'

'Right. Absolutely.' The chief pinched her nails and ran them along the seam of her collar. Matilda stared at the back of her head. 'It's just that she might have helped in the search for the missing equipment, the hazardous material taken from her facility.'

'Our detainee is a liar. We simply cannot trust a thing she says. She would do anything to weasel out of what's coming to her. She is guilty as sin.'

'But the CCTV footage looked pretty convincing,' said Matilda.

'That footage is classified. Who showed you?' The chief shot a glance towards the door. 'I'd hazard one guess. There'll be reper-cussions.' At Matilda's evident distress, the chief sighed, placed a conciliatory hand on her shoulder and edged Matilda towards the door. 'Listen, it's fine. We've got our best people on the case. The whole facility is wrapped up tighter than a tick's tushy. We've put a call out for the individuals, even got their vehicle's number plate.

The county services are on standby in case anything else crops up. We're following protocol to the letter. No one's arse is on the line for this. We caught our culprit. I'm not sure what a step-up looks like for paramedics but whatever it is, you're in line for one. Good work.'

The chief attempted a smile, though her face did not suit the expression. Matilda fumbled with the buttons on her uniform, struggling to find her voice.

'We need to get this on the news, warn the public. They could help with the search.' The chief gripped both of Matilda's arms and gave her a little shake.

'Young lady, I'll let you in on a secret. You don't get to a position like mine by sticking your neck out. It'll only end up on someone's chopping block.'

'So, you're just passing this up the chain?' Matilda shook her arms free and moved to block the door. She was tall, taller than the chief by a good foot and a half.

'Get out. Now,' commanded the chief, her face blossoming rouge. 'No one speaks to me like that.'

'Deferring responsibility.' Matilda's voice grew stronger, her shoulders straightened. 'You don't care what happens, if more people die, so long as it's not your fault. So long as—' Matilda didn't see the hand coming, but felt the thud and the sting of the door handle biting into her lower back. The chief had shoved her. The paramedic's heart raced, the way it did outside a burning building or a car crash, filled with a familiar sense of emergency. The chief gritted her teeth and planted her feet.

'You're a coward,' said Matilda.

Again, the chief went to shove her through the door, but this time Matilda deflected the hand, letting the woman follow through into a stack of plastic boxes. She moved to regain her balance but before Matilda could catch her, the chief caught a foot on a stretched cable

316

and careered into a trolley. Her head hit the side of a monitor with a soft thump, and Matilda watched in horror as the chief tumbled onto the floor.

Bob burst through the doors. Matilda felt dizzy, a cold tingle prickling under her skin. She inspected the spot where the chief's head had struck the monitor. There was no blood, but a large lump was beginning to swell on one side.

'I thaw it all. The chief hit you. Thith,' Bob pointed to the prone officer, 'wath an accident.'

'Help me get her up.' As they hoisted her under the shoulders, the chief let out a small groan.

'Onto the gurney? We thould get her to A & E,' suggested Bob.

'No. In here.' Matilda stripped the internal shelves from a steel cabinet with one swift downwards swipe, spilling medical supplies across the hospital floor. Then with a coolness that Bob found alarming, Matilda bound medical tape around the chief's mouth and wrists and bundled the small lady into the cabinet's base. Bob stared, mouth agape as Matilda slammed the steel doors shut. She stood for a moment, eyes downcast.

'I don't care. I don't care if I lose my job or go to prison or whatever. It doesn't matter. Only, I'd better tie you up too, Bob. Can't have you getting in trouble, they have to believe I'm doing this alone.'

Bob rubbed his eyes, so tired it looked as though he could have slept right there, standing up. The officer shook his head, his face filled with resolve.

'We're in thith together,' said Bob, and Matilda smiled weakly. They turned to the incubator. The green glowing plastic plumbed with wires and tubes drew the room's focus like a campfire in a forest. Impossible as it was, the tiny figure within was alive. Her ribs pushed up through cracked and folded skin, protecting a beating peanut heart. The paramedic moved forwards and rested a hand on the clear plastic chamber.

'And this woman is going to help us.'

They were on their way to the ambulance, parked at the end of the hospital's underground garage, when Matilda heard her name. 'Keep going,' she hissed, upping her pace. The person called again, behind her, twenty, thirty yards perhaps.

'Matilda!' It was a man's voice. One she didn't recognise. Pearson? Lander? The first of an armed unit sent to bring her in? She pressed the first aid box into Bob's chest, mindful that his grip didn't block the crude air holes puncturing the lid.

'No matter what, keep going. Find those people. Stop them.' Bob shook his head and went to turn on the pursuer, but Matilda stopped him, hand gripping his shoulder hard and pushing him towards the ambulance. 'Go,' she hissed again and turned to face the figure jogging towards her.

The white light of the exit behind him obscured his features. Matilda felt her fingers knot themselves into fists, readying herself, standing her ground. This was not like her at all. The man stopped, stooped, hand on knee and caught his breath.

'Ha. You – you rushed right past me,' said the nurse between deep inhales, his white and blue overalls billowing behind him. Matilda's fists unfurled and her heart rate slowed. 'The lady you brought in, Anthea, you said you wanted to know when she woke up.' Matilda, too shaken to speak, nodded dumbly. 'Well, she's awake and stable.'

'That's good,' murmured Matilda, amused by her own skittishness. 'Thanks. I was worried about her.'

'No need. Whatever happened out there in Lyndhurst, she seems fine.' The nurse smiled and gave Matilda a conspiratorial look. 'Say, what *did* happen? We've heard all sorts of—'

But Matilda was no longer returning his stare. Instead, she saw past him into an undefined point in space. Then, as if someone had flicked an invisible switch, she turned and called across the car park. 'Bob, get ready to go. There's one more thing I need to do.' Bob nodded, confused, but climbed up into the ambulance.

'Hey,' Matilda said to the nurse, 'sorry, I didn't get your name.'

'Oh. It's Owen.' He gave her a coy, crooked smile and stood up straight. Matilda craned her neck to one side, tucking a strand of loose blonde hair behind one ear. She returned the half-smile.

'Hey, Owen. Is that her chart? Mind if I take a peek?'

'Well, I ...' and before he could object, Matilda was leafing through the stack of papers, running her finger down each page as she went. Then, finding what she was looking for, she tore a small strip from the bottom of a sheet.

'Hey!' called Owen as Matilda sped past him back towards the hospital. The nurse followed a few steps, then stopped again, clutching the stitch in his ribs. When he looked up, the car park was empty, the exit door swung back and forth, and Matilda was gone.

Minutes later, Bob jumped at the sound of the back doors opening and slamming shut. He had been staring at Goodwin's tiny form nestled up against her IV bag, cradled inside the first aid kit box.

Bob twisted in his seat to peer through to the rear cabin. A crate had appeared, piled with syringes, IV bags, tourniquets and topped with a large white plastic bottle. Matilda appeared at his side window. He shot her a quizzical look.

'We're going to go public, and we're going to find Laslett. But now, just in case, we have a plan B.'

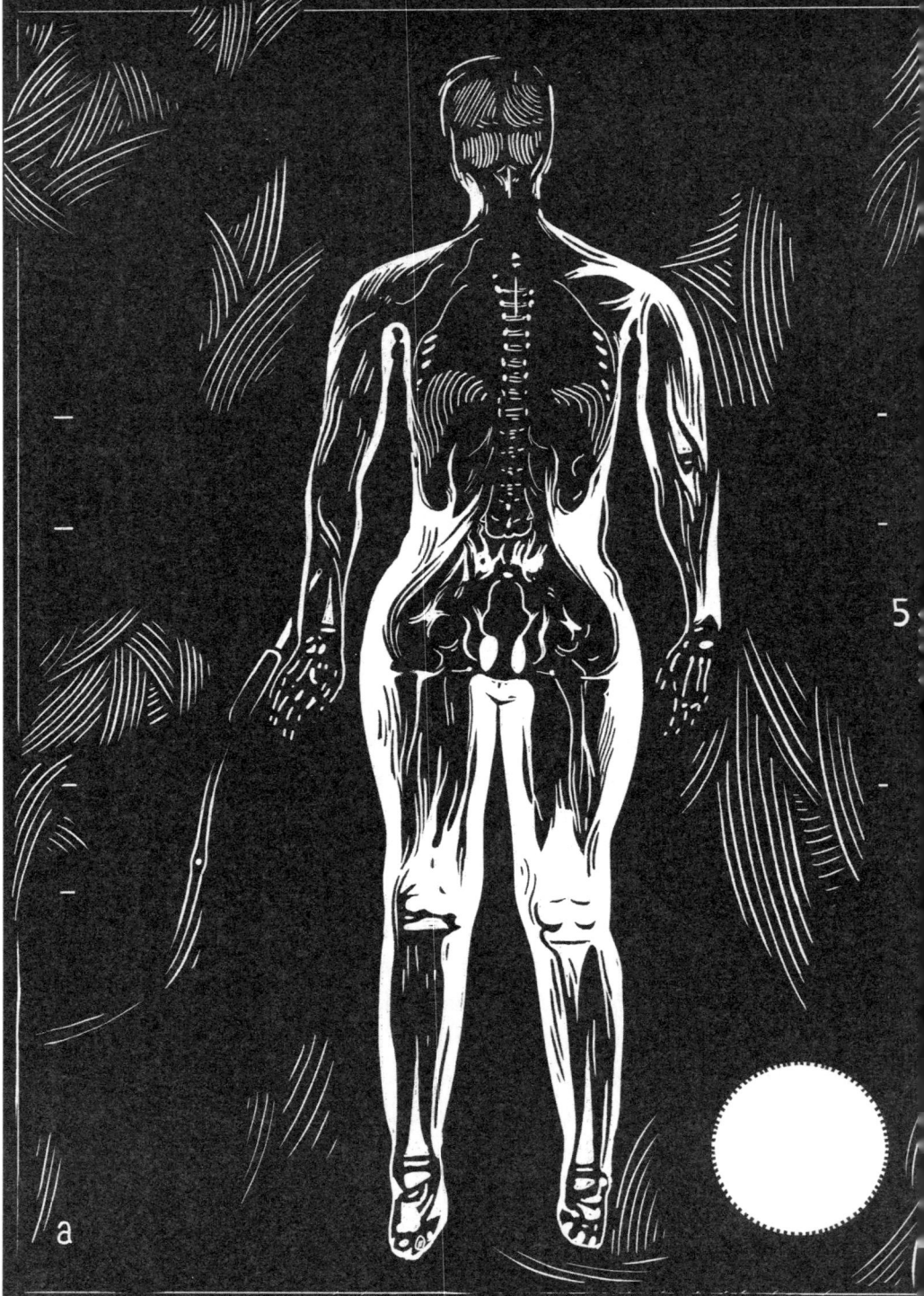

a

CHAPTER 32

THE BURROW

The two diminished figures descended the stone steps, their once clean clothes caked in what might have been red clay.

'Good grief. Couldn't we have used lavender, or baby oil or something?' Ashraf winced as he tenderly trod through the darkened garden. 'It's got right into all my cracks and crevices.'

'The spices worked for Richard and Mary. The polecats didn't touch them. Nor the dogs. We'll experiment later,' replied Giles.

The cloud-covered moon did little to illuminate their path. Night driving had proved impractical, and after a near-miss with a gnome, Giles had insisted they abandon the buggy and continue on foot. To Ashraf's great annoyance, he had even left the thumb lantern behind. Recalling his adventures in the bramble woods a few days earlier – swiping at monsters that turned out to be moths – Giles decided they would be better off letting their eyes adjust naturally. They called through the dark for Isabel, for Richard, keen to find their missing companions, but wary of the unwanted animal attention too much noise would bring.

'*You see that?*' hissed Ashraf, pointing suddenly across the pond. '*A light.*' On the far side of the lawn, a small flickering flame moved quickly through the thorned stalks of the rose garden, its carrier obscured by underbrush. As quick as it had appeared, the light went out. Giles and Ash ran the length of the lawn half crouched, calling quietly for Isabel, until they arrived at the bed abutting the dry-stone wall. Beneath the parasols of leaves, the ground opened up to reveal the mouth of a burrow – a broad, dark circle, inviting and repellent in equal measure.

'So *that's* how they've been getting in,' Giles muttered to himself, tutting.

'Who?'

'The rabbits. Been plugging this wall, but of course it—' A glow, faint and flickering, bloomed deep inside the hole, interrupting Giles. The pair leaned further into the void and Giles reached for the comfort of his weapon, the snap-blade, only to remember that it wasn't there.

'You still got your tin-opener?' he asked.

'Oh, this little fella?' Ashraf pulled the Swiss Army knife from the sling on his back – one of the few useful relics retrieved from the boy's bedroom. 'Tin-opening is but one of its many talents.' He chuckled and folded out a thick serrated blade with a click. Ashraf glanced back over his shoulder, perhaps checking the sling hadn't caught in his robes or perhaps, Giles thought now, as if he were expecting company. As if they were not alone. The hair on his forearms bristled. He searched Ashraf's face, but darkness obscured it, two pin-prick highlights the only indication of eyes.

'After you,' said Ashraf, absently fiddling with the tie about his waist and wafting a free arm towards the hole in the ground.

Giles held fast, then nodded towards the burrow. 'Youth before beauty, eh?'

They stood quietly for a moment, neither budging.

Then, with a wink, Ashraf said, 'Not wrong there, mate,' and stepped into the tunnel, the jagged blade pointed forward.

The passage was wide, carved from the spongy flesh of the earth. Though it was not tall enough to stand up in, neither did it necessitate they crawl. Instead, Giles and Ashraf hunched and shuffled, like workers in an ancient mine, backs pressed against the soft mud walls and eyes stretched impossibly wide, searching the darkness ahead. The path curved downward into a steep incline and only the small roots beneath their feet saved them from sliding its length in one go. The glow ahead grew steadily brighter, and Giles thought again of the dog's open mouth, and the funnel ride into hell it had presented. As they shuffled forward, a smell, more odious here than the dog's breath, grew stronger by the step. Then, the yip of a small animal broke the silence, and the light went out.

'*Isabel?*' hissed Giles, doubling his pace, feeling his way along the wall as the tunnel opened out. There was no answer. Slowly, their eyes adjusted, and Giles took in the room – a circular chamber, perhaps ten times as wide and twice Giles's height. Rocks and the gnawed stumps of roots punctured the walls and ceiling, hanging in a mishmash array of gothic chandeliers. A dense and nauseating smell washed over them and the warm air, wet and thick enough to bite, halted their progress. Ashraf stifled a gag in the crease of his elbow, and Giles bit a knuckle to muffle his gasp. On the floor ahead, stretching from their end of the tunnel and disappearing back into the gloom, were half a dozen soft furry mounds, rising and falling with the slow movements of breath.

Something twitched at his feet – the long, elegant oval of a rabbit's ear. Giles relaxed just a little. He squinted, making out two more rabbits. A tight family unit, perhaps, sleeping in a pile. Yet the image was at odds with the smell.

'Rabbits,' said Ashraf. 'The heck is she doing in a rabbit warren?' Ash pushed forward, and an odd shape drew Giles's attention. He signalled Ashraf to stop, then pointed. Jutting out from between two mounds of fur was a small turquoise wing. Giles edged away. As his eyes grew accustomed to the darker depths of the chamber, the picture became ever stranger. Here, the tail of a rat. There, the white underbelly of a toad. And more – voles, birds, amphibians.

'It's a larder,' whispered Giles. He kneeled beside the rabbit's head and gently lifted the ear with both hands. 'They're not asleep. And they're not dead.' Beneath the ear, above a half-open twitching eye, was a small circular wound. 'They'll all be like this. The polecats, they puncture the skull to keep them alive. Keep them fresh. Like an induced coma.'

A look of understanding passed between them, and then Ashraf called louder, 'Isabel!' There was no answer. They crept ahead, deep into the chamber, gingerly navigating the undulating bodies. Soft unseen objects gave and snapped underfoot. 'Twigs,' Giles assured with false courage, then forced himself to look down. Under the breathing fur and feathers lay a wet abstract layer of half-decomposed bodies and the source of the strong odour.

'You think Isabel's ...?' said Ashraf, glancing down. Giles shook his head.

'Whatever that is, it's long gone, weeks maybe.' They tiptoed further into the burrow, continuing to whisper Isabel's name. In answer came the same muffled animal yip. The cry of the polecat's wounded prey, Giles wondered, or something else. At the far end of the chamber, an exit appeared, a steep slope leading upwards to the faintest trace of light.

'A back door,' whispered Ashraf with relief. The claustrophobia of the space urged Giles towards the dim opening when, to his left, he spotted a second, smaller hole in the wall. 'Another larder?' asked Ashraf. Giles shook his head and leaned through the circular doorway. A new smell. Clean, damp moss, earth, and the source of the quiet animal cries. Several juvenile polecat kits, their fur a dark cinnamon red, returned Giles's stare.

He was startled by the thud of footfall descending the tunnel at the opposite end of the chamber. A small avalanche of mud tumbled into the larder ahead of it. 'Mother's home,' hissed Giles. He stumbled away from the kits, knocking into Ashraf and the two of them fell, landing between unconscious fur mounds. Pain shot down Giles's arm and he looked to see the serrated knife biting into his shoulder. An accident, surely, yet the teeth of the blade tearing at his skin and Ashraf's face, caught again in shadow, looming above him sent a jolt through Giles. He felt as though he was back in the cocoon of his former life, trapped in the wet folds of fabric, sinking, smothered, and choking on fumes. He had to get out. Claustrophobia, the burn of spice mixing with blood and the sudden fear of his companion, conspired to create panic. As the polecat slipped into the chamber, his elbow jerked out and struck Ashraf in the side, who stifled a cry. The serrated knife fell away, and without looking back, Giles gripped fistfuls of fur, pulled himself out from the animal bodies and scrambled through the tunnel towards fresh air.

The way was wet and muddy, and several times he slid backwards. Ashraf hurried behind him. The light grew stronger, the tunnel levelled out and the exit came into view. It was partially covered in wet leaves and torn lengths of moss, and something about the arrangement struck Giles as unnatural, as if the foliage had been placed there to deliberately conceal the opening. Pushing through it, a sodden rug of fern fell on top of him, soaking his hair and shoulders. He shoved it aside and collapsed onto the grass, taking long breaths and clutching his shoulder, letting the night sky wash over him – vast, calming and unaltered in scale. Ashraf tumbled out and sprawled on the ground beside him.

'What was that about? Made me drop the knife.'

'Sorry, I panicked. It ... it caught me on the shoulder.' In the relative light of outside, Ashraf seemed himself again, absolved of the sinister air the burrow had lent him. His friend peered back through the curtain of leaves.

'It's not following. Sounds like it's tending to the cubs. Where are we?'

Giles shook away the nausea of the larder and rolled over to take in his surroundings. The burrow had passed directly beneath the dry-stone wall, putting them outside the garden, into a clearing on the edge of the woodland surrounding the manor. Ahead of them stood a line of trees. Behind, the wall loomed like a tower block built by some Neolithic civilisation. Jaunty slabs of rock balanced at impossible angles, held together by weeds, dirt and gravity. Perhaps future generations would speculate on the wall's construction. His great-grandchildren might look up at it the way people marvelled at Stonehenge and the pyramids. Clouds parted, and moonlight flooded the woodland, unmasking its true colour, setting the greens of the grass in stark contrast to the redness of his clothes and skin.

A tree stump sat prominently in the clearing. Sulphur caps – small yellow mushrooms – covered one half of its bark, and the moon's blue backlight made their gills glow purple. Something moved at the base. Tucked into the fork of two long roots, a small creature took a shuddering breath then shuffled deeper into the shadow. As Giles stood, he saw the blades of grass where he had fallen were smeared with blood. So too were those leading towards the stump, like a row of trees marked for felling. Giles turned on his heels and saw the trail led back into the burrow as well. The wet tunnel and attempt to block the exit suddenly made sense. Whatever was hiding by the tree stump was wounded. It had crawled there from inside the burrow.

'Isabel?' Giles ran forwards, reached for the slumped figure, and his hand sank into fur. Though the elongated form and foetal position had been passably human, it was not Isabel, but a polecat kit. As Giles rolled it towards him, the animal let out a long and anguished cry, the same cry they had heard when the light went out.

He stepped away, tumbling over a clump of mushrooms that disintegrated beneath him like rotten wood. The kit shuffled back between the roots, and Giles caught a glimpse of a long clean cut, a gash running down its side. He stood, leaving a red handprint on a yellow mushroom and saw that, where he had fallen, again, an almost perfect garnet imprint of his body remained. Tentatively Giles extended his tongue to taste his lips. There was the sweet bitterness of paprika, but another flavour mingled with it, sickeningly rich and metallic. Giles looked back to the burrow mouth, the wet sheets of moss he had crawled through, and understood two things – the kit had not crawled to safety, it had been dragged, placed here as bait, and both he and Ash were covered in its blood.

Brambles, shrubbery and a log pile overgrown with vines fringed the clearing. Through the cracks and dark hollow spaces, Giles saw tiny eyes watching him, assessing him coolly. Two eyes, small and red – a rabbit or a mouse – and there, just for a moment, two piercing dots of green. Two distinctly human eyes staring right back at him. Richard? Or Isabel? A moment later, they were gone.

This clearing was a trap. Giles felt his throat tighten and his muscles tense.

'Honestly, I think you might have cracked a rib, and—' Ashraf, rubbing at his side, was halted by Giles's look of alarm.

'Down!' he cried. Obediently, Ash fell to his chest, the way Richard and Mary had fallen earlier that day. The branches and moss tumbled aside, and the parent polecat emerged from the burrow. It stretched to its full height, easily twice that of Giles, its head raised, a shiny nose twitching in the middle of a black mask of fur. It paused, taking in the scene. Then with one swift downwards swipe of a paw, it pinned Ashraf to the ground.

He looked up, confused, panicked and desperate. He had just enough time to whisper, 'Giles?' Then, above him, the polecat opened its mouth.

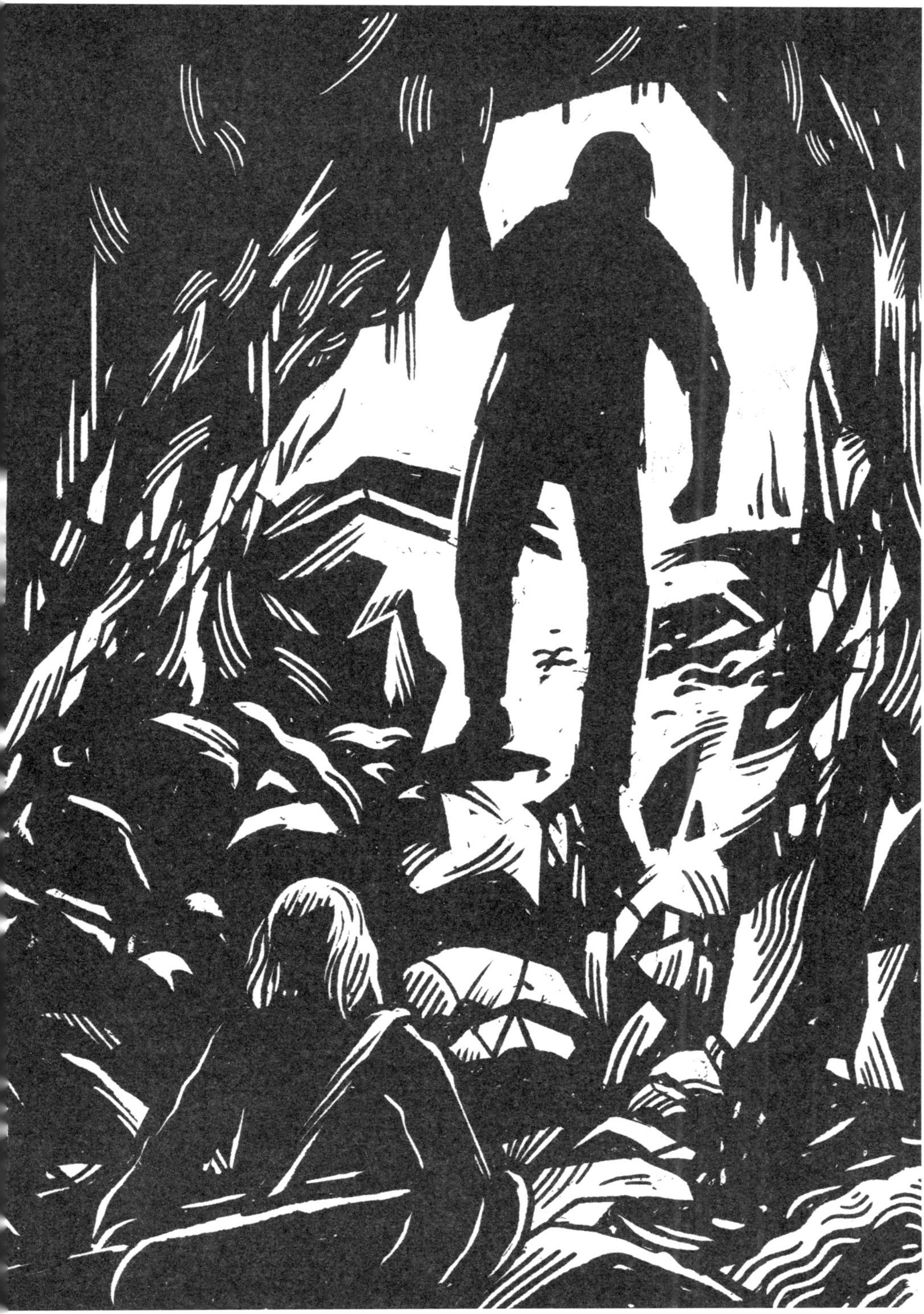

CHAPTER 33

TO SILVERBELL

'*SC Thirteen, we have a house call on Bassett Avenue. Are you free to attend? The system reads you as green. Over.*'

'Are you not going to answer thath?'

'We're on the run, Bob. We don't answer call-outs.' Matilda pulled the ambulance into a sleepy side road, scattering a pair of foxes mid-meal beside a toppled bin. She killed the engine. 'There's an OBD port under the bonnet. Best we throw the tracker away.' Obediently, Bob hopped out. Matilda pulled the medi-kit onto her lap, and with the tip of her thumb, she nudged Goodwin, asleep inside Bob's beanie hat.

'Professor Goodwin?' the woman's eyes crept open. Matilda couldn't help but be disarmed by the shrunken figure. Her proportions were impossible, yet her gestures were those of any other person. Hours earlier, the still body of Simian in the back of the ambulance had been easier to dismiss. A hoax. A prop. Here though, in front of her, were the mannerisms and movements of a fully grown adult.

Goodwin, too, was struggling to adjust. As the colossal head above her came into focus, she shuffled back into the folds of the hat and covered her face with her hands. Memories realigned, and slowly she stared up at Matilda with a suspicious frown.

'Buggeration. It's *you*.'

'I'd just like to ask you some questions.'

'And why on earth would I answer them?' said Goodwin, sitting back and crossing her arms in a manner of sulk befitting a toddler. Matilda thought on this a moment, then lifted Goodwin's IV to eye level. 'Because if you don't, I'll pour whatever's in here out the window.' Goodwin leaped and tugged at the connecting tube as if trying to retrieve an ascending balloon.

'No! I need it. I'll die.'

'Very well. Then play nice.' Matilda returned the bag to the medi-kit as Bob climbed back into to the cab.

'Done. Thould we chuck our phonth too?' On cue, the device in Bob's hand lit up. 'The radiation warningth out. Looth like they've closed off the New Foretht.'

Goodwin turned, taking in her surroundings for the first time. A smile creased the corners of her mouth.

'Have I been kidnapped?' she clapped in delight. 'My goodness. This is the *third* most exciting thing to happen to me all week.'

'We're on the run.' Bob nodded. Goodwin beamed, and Matilda tapped the box for her attention.

'This is important. There was a lady, a survivor from the crash site near your lab in Lyndhurst. She was dosed up on barbiturates when it happened, and unaffected by whatever shrunk the others.'

Goodwin reeled in her IV bag, hugged it beneath one arm, and asked, 'What were they for then, these *barbiturates*?'

'To induce a coma. I'm not sure why they did it, exactly. A prolonged seizure possibly, or brain swelling. A head injury perhaps? Either way, she was put into an unconscious state to rest the hemispheres, mitigate any harm until she could reach the hospital.'

'And you think this induced coma intercepted the transformation?'

Matilda nodded. Goodwin hoisted herself up by the side of the box. Reflexively she reached for something that wasn't there and looked suddenly lost.

'Oh. Here. You'll want this.' Bob handed her back the ballpoint pen. With a nod of thanks, Goodwin wrapped an arm about its length as if it were a staff and proceeded to pace the box.

'Perhaps. It's curious that of all the animals, only humans were affected. If indeed it is some signature of the human brain that singles us out, it stands to reason that a lack of activity, or a disruption like a seizure, or indeed unconsciousness might throw off the mechanics. Neural camouflage, so to speak.'

Matilda massaged her temples, then passed Bob the medi-kit box and pulled the ambulance back onto the road. Goodwin steadied herself, then continued to pace her enclosure.

'Now, exactly *how* the transformation was broadcast, via a frequency, seismic, quantum field or some other band of delivery, that's another question. It's not chemical. The clean radius around the lab showed a defined impact area with no fall-off. If we could return to the scene, perhaps—'

'As long as we can block the transformation, that's all that matters for now,' interrupted Matilda.

'Block it? We must *stop* it all together!' Goodwin snapped, gripping the sides of the box, scanning through the windscreen for road signs. 'Why are we heading north? We need to head to the coast. Locate Laslett and Leaf.'

'We're going to find them. You were right,' assured Matilda, and at that, Goodwin seemed somewhat pacified. Leaning against the side of the box, she examined a forearm, running her fingers over the cracks and folds of her skin.

'The barbiturates, inducing sleep, that's a *good* idea. I'm pleased you've made that connection. But Matilda, we must tell people. Secrecy, it's all wrong. It's reckless.'

'We will. We're going to do all of that. Very soon. First though – first, there are a couple of people we need to pick up.'

Bob cranked the window an inch lower, letting a stream of cool night air run through the cab. Behind them loomed the hospital and the mess they had left there. Members of some unnamed government agency would be arriving shortly, expecting to meet the sole survivor of the Lyndhurst incident, the shrunken Professor Goodwin. Instead, they would find Chief Deverill bound and furious inside a medicine cabinet. Bob imagined assets being deployed, a troop of uniforms, hovering spyware and metal-studded tyres tearing up the road behind them.

Ahead was uncertainty. They now lived with a terrible knowledge, a threat that at any moment, a ringing in their ears would force the excess water from their bodies, contract tissues, flush bacteria and by-products through pores, ducts, via any available exit. Or perhaps they would collapse at an atomic level. The empty space between their atoms squeezed impossibly tighter and tighter as each piece cascaded downwards, shuffling closer into a suffocating knot. Picturing his body being juiced like a fruit, Bob pressed his lips to the rush of air coming through the crack of window and pulled deep, nursing the nauseous churn in his stomach as they joined the main road. To his right was the thin line of dawn, and their best-case scenario was worsening by the minute.

'She moves with the sun, you know,' said Goodwin, looking up at Bob with some concern. 'The coccolithophores. The White Algae. Emiliania. She follows it around the globe, rising from the depths to embrace the light, sucking up carbon, and building new shells. Sinking again. Of course, no one knew what the shells were for until *I* found out.'

'Yes. We read your theory in the transcripts. So, we have until sunrise?' asked Matilda. Goodwin scoffed.

'Nothing so romantic. Laslett must transcribe Leaf's connectome into the bio-binary. It takes time.'

'Conecthome?' asked Bob.

'Connectome – whatever happened to your teeth? The connectome is a map of neural pathways in ones and zeros. We streamlined the process, but it's still slow. You know it took twelve years for researchers to map the three hundred neurons of a worm. A worm! And we humans have sixty-five billion of the buggers. Though I wouldn't be surprised if a halfwit like Leaf had significantly fewer.'

'So, how long do we have?' Matilda pressed.

'Yes, yes. Fewer by half, the cretin.' Goodwin chuckled, caught Matilda's eye, and then continued seriously. 'Once the map's complete, we transcribe it into plankton binary. We use an alphabet disk inscribed to recognise reoccurring patterns and arrange the shells in open or closed positions. Ones or zeros. Terribly complex stuff. But after years of painstaking research, patience and personal sacrifice, I can say with great humility that—'

'How long, Goodwin? How long until Laslett can trigger a second incident?'

'Fifteen hours. No less. All being well. Impressive, isn't it? Now, they left Catalant at nine p.m. last night, so, let me see, they could be ready anytime from midday onwards. They won't hang about once its transcribed. What's the time now?'

'Half four. Sun'll be up in an hour or so.'

'Well then. We'd better get a wriggle on.'

The school was dark, shaded from the dawn by hills that flanked it on either side. She hadn't liked the idea of sending the girls to Buckridge. But with Matilda's hours, their father's increasingly patchy involvement and the round the clock supervision Ava needed, this seemed the best place for her, the chance of a normal life. When the news about the means-tested bursary came through, it seemed foolish to turn it down.

Bob left the ambulance parked in the driveway, settled Goodwin into the glove compartment and killed the engine while Matilda made the phone call. Moments later, a yellow light flicked on in a window above the rampart, and a small face pressed itself against the glass, waving.

'Come on down now, Ava darling, and wake your sister too. No need to pack. We won't be gone long.'

'But Mum,' the small voice pleaded, 'I'm fine.'

'I know. Just hurry. And quiet, we don't want to wake anyone.' But before Matilda's phone was back in her pocket, several faces joined Ava's at the window.

Minutes later, a half-oval oak door heaved open and a statuesque man trudged towards the ambulance, pulling his chequered dressing gown tight over his barrel chest, plastering his combover into place and smoothing the length of his ample beard. Behind him, several teenage girls crowded in the doorway. Ava was among them, a foot shorter than the rest, her smile beaming out at Matilda.

'Whoth that?' whispered Bob, nodding to the man.

'Her housemaster. Back in the van, Bob, I'll handle this. Dr Baggstrott, how are you this morning?'

'Morning, is it? Congratulations, Ms Hellstrom, you've managed to wake the entire dorm. I can assure you the only thing young Ava is suffering from now is acute embarrassment. For the last time, I do wish you'd call before turning up.'

She had been expecting this. Too often, she'd shown up on a whim and been turned away, only to sit at the end of the drive, waiting in the dark until the day pupils arrived, content just to be near Ava and Sadie. Now she had a plan. She had experience in deception. She reached for a kernel of truth and let it grow into a lie.

'Do you mind if speak to you, privately?' Matilda took Baggstrott by the shoulder, spoke a few hushed words, then pressed her lit up phone into his hands. A moment later, he shook himself free, scanning the screen with alarm.

'Radiation?' The housemaster ran anxious fingers through the bristles of his beard, eyes darting to the sky. 'I've, um, well . . .' His bravado had fallen away. Matilda placed a hand on his back and ushered him towards the school.

'As you can see, this is just a precaution, of course. We're well outside the contamination zone, but this alert *is* countywide. Everyone's to check-in at their nearest medical centre as soon as possible. Again, it's precautionary. But if you don't mind, considering Ava's condition, I'd like to take the girls myself. You understand.'

'Yes, well, quite. Considering Ava's condition, I suppose ...'

Behind them, Bob leaned out of the cab window, wafted the dosimeter badge above his head and gave it a pantomime inspection.

'Yup. All clear here, but orderth are orderth.' He shrugged, and Matilda glared at him.

'Well,' said the housemaster, visibly flustered. 'I'll – I'll let the head know you're taking the girls.'

'Please do.' While the housemaster dug in his robes for his phone, Matilda beckoned Sadie and Ava from across the lawn. They shuffled reluctantly, hands buried in pyjama pockets. 'Hello, my loves,' cooed Matilda, running her hands over the backs of their heads and pulling them in. Ava wrapped her arms around her mother's waist while Sadie untangled from the embrace.

'What are you doing here? Like we don't get enough attention as it is,' scowled the elder sister.

'No, you don't. Never enough. It's nice to see you both. There's no time to explain, but you have to come with me. Into the cab, quick, before Baggstrott changes his mind.' Matilda watched as Ava climbed gently into the cabin of the ambulance. Something about the image sent a jolt through her chest. Across the green, Baggstrott, phone clamped between ear and shoulder, grinned nervously up at Matilda, and beckoned her to wait. His rosy complexion had become somewhat more pallid. He spoke in hurried whispers, dramatically gesturing with his arms as he did so. As Matilda fastened the belts on the benches and closed the doors to the back cabin, Baggstrott bounded over. 'So, you're treating for radiation poisoning?'

'In a sense. We're – we're administering premeditative doses of potassium iodide. It blocks radioiodide, in case of—'

'Yes, thank you. I know what potassium iodide does. I *am* a biology professor.'

'Of course, sorry.' Baggstrott craned his neck to peer back into the cabin, glancing at the bag of tourniquets, the large white tub, and Matilda thanked her foresight for having torn the label from the bottle.

'And you have clearance, do you?' Matilda met his eye. The thing about a lie grown from a kernel of truth is that it soon becomes a sprawling plant with full ears of corn, dropping its own kernels of half-truths.

'Yes. Another team will be coming by later today to see to the rest of the students and staff, but for now I'll just take my girls.' Back in the driver's seat, Matilda leaned to close the door, only to find it caught in Baggstrott's firm grip.

'This *preferential treatment*, well, it doesn't quite seem right. Plenty of room back there. Anyway, I'd just as soon we get it over and done with, and since the entire dorm is up already.' His nervous smile became a serious frown. 'And – and I should go with them too. An escort. A familiar face. Terribly traumatic for the young ladies, all this.'

'Well, I—'

'It's OK. I've cleared it with the head, and he'll inform the parents. An emergency scenario. The news was clear on that. It's all taken care of.' Baggstrott waved an arm behind him, not relinquishing his hold on the door. 'Come on, girls. We're all going on a trip with Miss Stromhell.'

Matilda glanced at the small group fidgeting in the doorway, laughing and talking among themselves. There was no radiation, but the threat and her hope at avoiding it were real. Why shouldn't they also be given a chance?

'Of course,' Matilda conceded, 'Of course. We'll take as many as we can fit.'

*

338

The cheese-wire barbed fence sliced the morning light into thin strips that lay neatly across the fields. Small against the open green, the ambulance trundled down the concrete drive towards the main gates. Security had been tight since activists liberated a third of the herd two years earlier. Now the farm was a fortress, little left to resemble Silverbell Meadow, the name by which it once went. Dawn softened the buildings, but it wasn't enough to hide their brute architecture. Matilda drummed digits into a keypad, fished an old card from her purse and pressed it against a box beside the gate. Inside, nominal efforts had been made to reclaim some of its former wholesomeness. There was a clearing with a hand-crank well, a hastily planted sapling forest, too young to mask the thick steel fence that skirted a hamlet of worker cottages. Rustic wooden signposts directed the flow of traffic along newly tarmacked driveways.

'What are we doing *here*?' asked Sadie, pressing against the cabin window. Behind her, on the crowded bench, the eight other passengers jostled for space.

'Yes. I thought we were going to Southampton Central?' asked Baggstrott.

'The medical centres are over-run,' said Matilda, 'We'd be waiting for hours. The potassium has to be administered via IV drip, and the farm has a small veterinary clinic at the back. It'll serve our needs just fine.'

'Sadie's mum's going to milk us,' whispered a girl with black hair, loud enough to send the others into a renewed fit of giggling. Sadie's scowl deepened.

'*Officer Prewett. Come in, officer Prew—*'

'I told you to switch that off,' Matilda hissed at Bob.

'Shouldn't you be listening out for radiation updates?' sneered Sadie through the glass. 'This a load of bull.'

Matilda grimaced. Sadie knew her too well. Of course, she could tell there was something amiss. It didn't matter, so long as the girls took the barbiturates. So long as they were unconscious before midday. So long as they stayed under until Laslett was caught, or if he wasn't – at least they'd be under when it happened. God forbid it came to that. Matilda dug deep, pulled her most innocent smile and flashed it in the mirror.

'That's enough, Sadie. If nothing else, it's a good excuse for you to come and see your grandfather.'

Roland was in the office when they arrived, the same place he was most mornings at this time, preparing the rota for the barn, field and production line workers. On any other farm, a Sunday might have meant reduced personnel. However, as he'd always said, the animals didn't take a day off from eating, shitting and dying, so why should they.

'Matilda. What an unexpected treat. Ava! Sadie! Come give your grandfather's back a good cracking. That's right, really get in there.' He beamed down at the girls encircling him in a bear-like hug.

He was nearly as tall as Matilda, though hunched and sinewy with a mouth wide and thin, peppered with well-spaced teeth, like a zip purse on its side. Roland's water-blue eyes raised to meet his daughter's as his smile faded. 'And what brings you to us, darling . . . with so many guests.'

'Have you seen the news?'

'Yes, and I heard something on the radio. Absolute rubbish. Honestly, Matilda, whoever heard of—'

'Dad, how many people are on the farm?'

'Now, come on.'

'I'm serious.'

'Workers and families? Forty. Forty-two, depending on whether the Taylors managed to stumble home from the pub or not. Darling, what's going on?'

From an elevated steel walkway, Matilda looked down at the disgruntled faces of Roland's workforce, assembled in the veterinary yard – swaying and unshaven, clutching gowns about their waists, nursing coffees and hangovers. At the back of the yard, Ava's dorm mates joked and played with the suction cups of a milking unit. Matilda coughed for attention.

'Morning, everybody. I'm sorry to have got you here so early. I know some of you were already on shift, and one or two might – who knows – have even had the Sunday off.' Matilda waited for a chuckle that never came. She cleared her throat and continued.

'Well, I'm very sorry about that. But rest assured, you'll be back in bed soon. Those who are on shift, Roland's agreed that after the treatment, you'll get the rest of the day off.' This piqued the group's interest, and with a swelling sense of authority, Matilda found her voice again.

'As some of you may have seen, the New Forest wider area has been issued a potential radiation alert. There's nothing to worry about. It's just precautionary.' The lies came easy now. She told of the mandatory potassium supplement, of how it would cause some drowsiness. Hence camp beds and hay bales had been laid out along the veterinary clinic walls and corridors all the way up to the Rotolactor milking station. They'd need to be reclining to be administered the treatment and might want to sleep it off. They might not have believed her if it hadn't been for Bob, who stood at her side, nodding, pretending to check his radio and talk into his earpiece.

She caught her eldest daughter's eyes and for a horrible moment, feared that Sadie would call her out in front of everyone. The lie was so fragile. It would just take one person to say, 'I don't believe you,' and this precariously assembled structure would be blown away. But Sadie's scorn remained stolid and silent.

'Here you go, Matilda,' said Baggstrott, putting down the crate of medical supplies, and handing her the white bottle of barbiturates, 'potassium iodide!' Around them, people took to the camp beds. 'Thought I'd save you the trouble and fetch it from the ambulance.'

'That's – that's very kind.' Matilda eyed Baggstrott suspiciously as he rolled up his sleeve and reclined onto the nearest camp bed. He was just keen, that was all. Her story about the radiation had hit home a little too hard.

'How about I pave the way. Show them there's nothing to worry about.'

As he watched the white fluid bloom into the saline solution of his IV, Dr Baggstrott felt a moment's alarm. Perhaps combining potassium iodide with water would have an adverse reaction. He should just own up to it. Confess. Tell Matilda. There was nothing to be embarrassed about. He hadn't meant to spill half the bottle. Then again, he *had* removed the cap. He just wanted to make sure he got a good dose. There might not be enough to go around with all these extra people.

Hell, why make a fuss. It would be fine, just like diluting Dad's gin bottle from the cabinet. No harm done. Besides, he was a biology teacher. He knew what he was doing. This was all precautionary anyway. Local authorities overacting. So what if all the doses were half strength. Half of nothing is nothing. Besides, this potassium iodide was undoubtedly having an effect. He was so drowsy. If he didn't know better, he'd say he was feeling positively comatose.

It was eight a.m. by the time Matilda made it up the long line of makeshift beds to where Ava and Sadie sat, cross-legged, playing Rummy with a deck of dog-eared playing cards. Their bags of saline solution hung from a coat hanger attached to the curtain rail. Matilda laid tourniquets on the thick woollen blankets that covered their beds and asked, 'So, who'd like to go first?' Without looking up, Sadie spoke, her voice low and accusatory.

'Are you going to tell us what's really going on? I know you're hiding something.' Matilda's stomach turned. She knew Sadie revelled in defying her will. In most cases, Matilda's will concerned summer activities or an inappropriate boy. This was different. Sadie's obedience was critical. Her mind flitted to lifting Goodwin over the pool, an act of force. Instead, she sat beside her eldest and cupped her face in one hand, turning it, so their eyes met.

'My love, you must trust me. I know this is frightening, but—' Sadie sat back.

'I'm not scared. That's not it. I just know when you're lying. You're terrible at it.' Sadie held her mother's gaze, staring her down, daring Matilda to flinch. Then Ava shuffled between them, rolling up her sleeve.

'This stuff, it's good for us?' asked Ava. Her almond face formed a barrier between them, benign and vulnerable, breaking the tension between her mother and sister. Matilda smiled.

'That's right, darling. Thank you. It's just a little pinch.' Sadie shrugged, sighed, blew away some loose strands of hair, and rolled up her sleeve.

'Well, if Ava's OK with it, I suppose . . .' Sadie lay back on the blanket-lined Rotolactor, tightened her own tourniquet and presented her forearm. Matilda connected the drips, gave each bag a full dose from the white bottle then sat with the girls as their eyelids fell and the drugs took effect. She stroked their hair and kissed their heads before continuing around the circular cage.

Beneath the blanket, Sadie's fingers gripped the tube running up to her IV in a vice-like pinch. She had not stopped the fluid completely but slowed it enough to stay conscious as she listened to her mother's footsteps disappearing up the corridor. Keeping the rest of her body perfectly still, she found the plaster in her left forearm beneath the blanket and slid the needle out. With narrow eyes, she examined the row of bodies. So many people were asleep, yet no one was snoring. Of all the dorms she'd ever slept in, this would be the first silent one. Still, she was tired and, pulling the blanket underneath her chin, Sadie drifted off into a restless sleep.

Matilda inspected the rows of family, friends and strangers. Her father, her children – safe for the time being in a state of neural hibernation.

'What now? We're running out of time to find Lathleth. Shouldn't we get back on the road?' Matilda sat against a wall, her body relaxing for the first time in hours.

'I know. I've been thinking. They're already out there, looking for Laslett and Leaf, doing far more than we can. We're just two people, Bob. Even with Goodwin's help, we'll never find them on our own. Stopping Laslett, I think that's out of our hands now.' Bob looked confused.

'So, we're giving up?'

'No. We're going to do something they couldn't, something they *wouldn't* do. We're going to tell everyone. Tell them what's happened and how to protect themselves.'

'Ecthellent. I'll go and get Goodwin.'

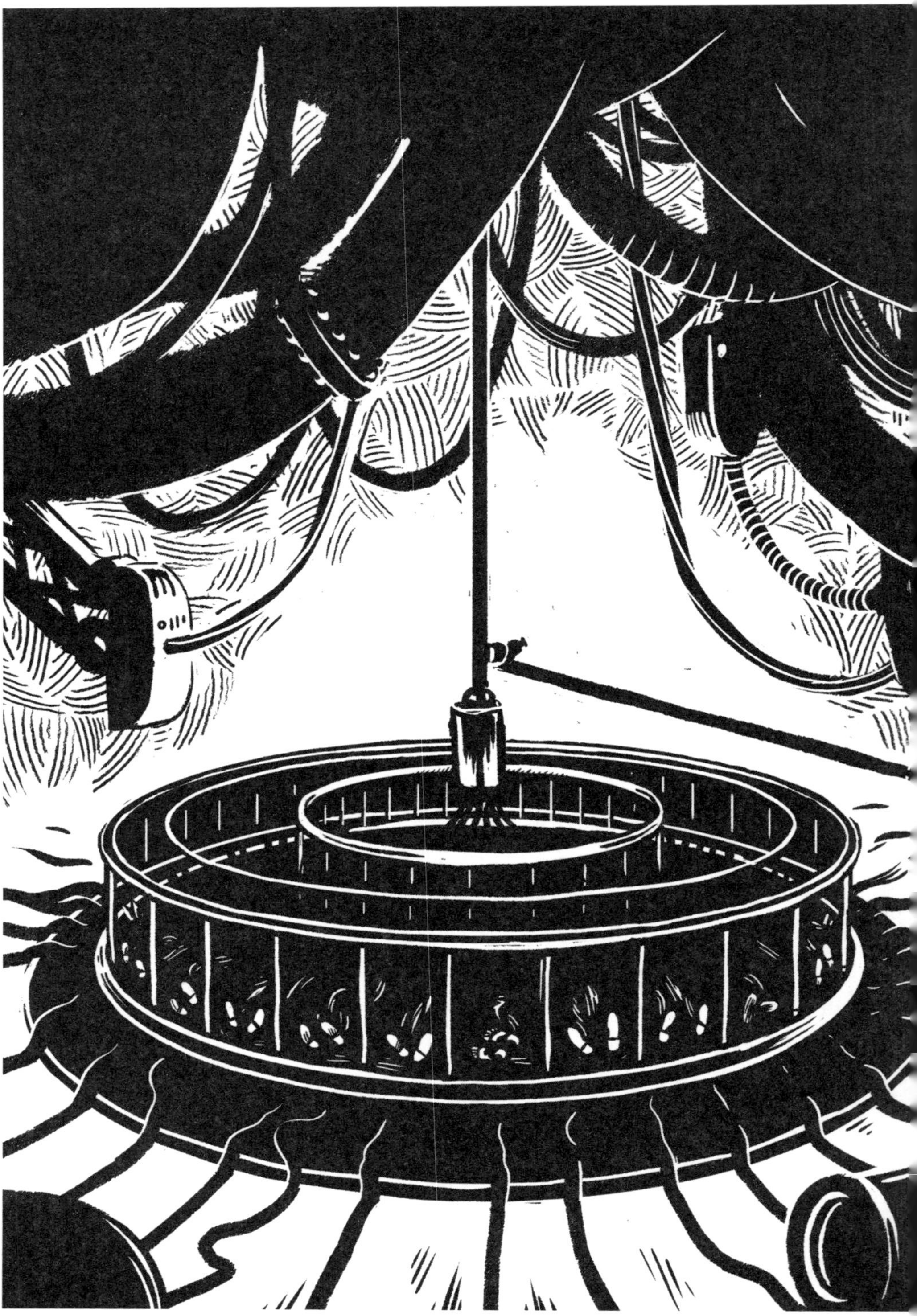

CHAPTER 34

MOUSE TRAP

The chipped fang sank into Ashraf's cheek. Thunk. Giles clutched his sides, fighting the urge to scream or empty his stomach into the grass. Time warbled and the world seemed to tilt as the polecat raised onto its hind legs, dangling Ashraf by his jaw, his tiny body hooked over a row of blunt incisors. As Ashraf was lifted higher and higher still, the upper canine sank deeper with a slow, cruel smoothness. Yet Ash had not gone limp. Instead, he writhed in slow motion. Hands clawed at empty air. Feet struggled to find purchase on ground now far out of reach. Then, with a final wrench, the animal pulled Ashraf between the curtains of moss and disappeared into the burrow.

Before Giles had a chance to stand, the polecat re-emerged, tumbled out into the clearing, arched its back, and gave a low, sorrowful bark. Kicking at the dirt, Giles slid away from it into the cover of the tree stump, where his hand pressed into wet, red soil and an elbow landed in the wounded kit's side. It mewed feebly. The parent's head snapped towards its offspring. The creature slunk forwards, then, to Giles's surprise, it halted and edged away.

Giles twisted around and looked up. Behind him, a fox reared its head. It towered over the stump, breath silvering in the moonlight, its ears two black triangles silhouetted against cloud. An amber paw slid forwards, gently toppling a clump of sulphur cap mushrooms that tumbled down the wooden cliff face. Then, like a wave, the creature cascaded towards him, crashing its paw down onto the kit. Stalactite teeth pulled apart, revealing a dark, cavernous mouth. The cave would have collapsed over Giles had it not been for the polecat, with a sudden blur of black and white fur, wrapping itself about the fox's snout.

Claws and paws and tails thrashed the ground. Sensing his moment, Giles scrambled around the stump, caught foot on bark, pitched into soil and landed hard on his mauled shoulder. He bounced back up. Everything he'd touched was now stained red with the kit's blood – a perfect scent-trail marking out every step. Clutching his shoulder, Giles stumbled away through grass. The burrow's entrance was blocked by the writhing, squealing, snarling knot of hopelessly mismatched animals. Any hope of going back underground for Ash was lost.

Earlier, the ring of shrubbery haloing the clearing had been dotted with prying eyes, a single human pair among them. Again, Giles wondered if they had belonged to Richard or Isabel. And now Ashraf was gone too. It was entirely plausible that all three of them had been eaten. *Eaten.* The horror that such a thing could happen raised bile to his throat. He steadied himself, knocked by a pang of grief, guilt and sheer repulsion. Ash's final look of accusation played over in his mind. A new horror dawned – the strong likelihood that Giles was the last surviving adult of their party, and that the burden of responsibility now rested solely with him. The idea of setting out to find Ava and Sadie became as intangible as a dream. They were further away than ever.

Nearing the edge of the clearing, he rubbed his body against a lichen-covered rock in the futile hope of wiping off the blood. Behind him, the growls and whinnies grew fainter until, with a snap, they stopped altogether. He crouched low as the fox stepped around the stump, sniffing the grass and creeping forward, so close, the animal might have bridged the distance in two strides. With no other choice, Giles fled, throwing himself into the tightly knotted undergrowth, hoping his diminished size would serve, for once, as an advantage. Yet the fox yipped and pounced with apparent delight, its head ploughing through brambles with an agility Giles could only dream of – its body contorting to weave through the maze like a lace pulled through the eyelets of a shoe. Giles beared left, running the edge of the circular clearing, leaping roots that rose from the mud like a Kraken's tentacles. In another second, the fox would have been on him, but to his relief, the dry-stone wall appeared through the thorny shrub. Giles ran a small incline, leaped at a cave-like opening and clawed forward, fingers sinking into mulch, burying himself between the cold stone slabs, and came to rest beyond the fox's reach.

Panting at the back of his cave, Giles hugged his knees, expecting to see the snarling gnash and snap of yellow teeth darken the entrance. Instead, the fox sniffed quietly at the opening and appeared content to have been bested, though its whiskers quivered like quills on a porcupine's back. Giles collapsed, cushioned by a mound of moss. Sprouting from it were flowers that were, for the first time in days, the correct scale, the way flowers used to be.

He plucked one, turning it between a shaking, bloodied finger and thumb, trying to enjoy the oddly tranquil moment, the way the stem and stamen— The fox's paw burst into the cave! Giles lurched, smearing the petals against rock, kicking at the ivory talons – each a handspan in length – diverting them away from his shins and into stone. As the paw retracted, readying for a second swipe, a rock behind Giles shifted, and he found himself sliding on a mudslick and falling backwards into darkness.

The dry-stone wall was a network of crannies and chasms, small hollows and narrow passageways – a warren of rock, verdure and insects cutting through a lost and crumbling temple. Giles bounced, slid between wet walls and landed with a thump at the bottom of a short, conical chamber. He patted the stone, dislodging three limpid-like nodules – woodlice – and was struck by their resemblance to trilobites, the hard-shelled arthropods that teemed the oceans millions of years ago. Again, Giles felt the pull of deep time, and an affinity with his ancestors, cowering in darkness. Ahead, a narrow passage opened into moonlight. He shuffled forward and had one hand on the wall's outer edge when a wrinkly human foot darted between a crack above his head.

'Richard!'

There was a crunch, bone hitting rock, and then the foot was gone. Giles pushed himself up, breathed in and shimmied between two vertical slabs. Immediately, he regretted it. The walls seemed to press down against his chest and claustrophobia stirred in his gut. He punched at the dirt above him, feeling the soft velvet ceiling crumble, and a moment later, he emerged, relieved and gasping for breath.

He was in an enclave midway up the wall. Below and to his left, the fox, or at least the magnificent swish of its tail, could be glimpsed through the cracks, close enough that Giles might have jumped and caught hold of it. He looked further down the jagged stone cliff face and had a flash memory of the games he'd played with Morris as a child, on a beach not far from here, toppling jittery piles of stacked stones. There was a sound like crushing shells above him, and Giles wriggled back into the wall.

Slabs rattled and slid as he climbed, and twice Giles thought he might collapse the whole structure on top of him. With a grunt of effort, he shifted a loose stone to one side, like a trapdoor to an attic, and there was Richard – red and naked as he'd first seen him. He was pushing his way down a passage that led back to the garden. Beneath one arm was the silver flick-lid lighter and somehow, impossibly, slung across his back hung Giles's snap-blade scalpel.

'That's my scalpel,' said Giles. Richard turned, his face startled, nervous and then, to Giles's surprise, the older man relaxed and smiled.

'Oh, thank goodness it's you, Giles. Thank the lord. I thought it was that *demon* woman. My! Your *skin*. Are you bleeding?'

Giles touched his shoulder.

'A little. It's mostly paprika though, and the cub's blood. Do I have you to thank for that?' At this Richard looked genuinely hurt and confused.

'For what, Giles?' He cowered further against the stones.

'The trap you set, from the burrow, the clearing.'

'I – I'm afraid I don't understand.' Richard looked anguished, and shuffled away. Giles was resolute. He remembered Mary's warnings. He would not fall for this act. He edged forward and decided upon a direct approach.

'Alwyn was murdered. The stew was poisoned. The cub's blood at the burrow was a trap, and now Ashraf's gone, and I – I think

351

it was all *you*. You're not who you say you are. Why would you lead us here if you wanted us gone?' Richard's confused expression crumpled into offence. He scowled back at Giles.

'How dare you. *You* brought us here, Giles, not me. Be rid of you? My goodness, why on earth would I want that? How could you think I – I . . .' His words stammered into unintelligible mumbles. Richard fumbled with the grip of the snap-blade and ran his fingers up through tufts of dark brown hair. Then he started to cry, little sobs that rocked his chest, intercut with short, sharp, shuddering breaths.

'Why did you run?' asked Giles, trying to steady his voice.

'She was going to kill me,' whimpered Richard. Faced with the snivelling figure, it was hard to hold his nerve. His impulse was to comfort Richard. Perhaps it was, in part, the reminder of his father. Richard and Morris could well be the same age. He shook away the thoughts.

'Give me the scalpel, Richard.' The priest wiped a bony hand under his nose and looked at the knife as if, in this moment, it had suddenly appeared in his lap.

'Oh, this? Yes, I saw it, by the pond. I thought I might need it, you see, in case I ran into the devil.'

'She's not a devil,' sighed Giles. 'She's an old lady who's – she's not adjusted well.'

'Old lady?' Richard raised his head, perplexed, tears streaming down his cheeks. 'No. No. Not her. *Isabel*. The devil. Isabel – *she* killed Alwyn. Wicked, wicked. She . . .'

Giles felt as though the wind had been knocked out of him. It couldn't be. It was a lie.

'I saw her, you see, with Alwyn,' Richard began. 'Before you did. When I confronted her, she told me it was an accident. A slip. I wanted to tell you, but the seal of confession forbade it. But then, there were *signs*. Suspicions! And then the stew, ah! I knew. I knew she was *wicked*. And a trap, you say? Oh, she means to get us *all*. Giles, she's hunting us.'

Giles's mind raced. Where was Isabel? Indeed, she had been there in the tent. He'd caught her red-handed. He realised he knew very little about the woman he'd grown to feel such affection for. Where she had come from, and what she was doing, alone at the campsite? Richard was shaking now. Giles stretched out a hand and spoke softly. 'The scalpel.' The older man turned the orange handle, studying the blade, lost in thought. Then he blinked himself back to the present.

'Sorry. I'm just – I'm just so *tired*. Confused.' He smiled, sniffed and slid the scalpel down the passage. Midway between them, it stopped, lodged in sediment.

And there it was. The rouse. The trick. The trap, like the kit in the clearing, like the bloodied burrow-mouth. Squinting through the darkness, a thin chord caught the light, the fishing wire strap that had kept the scalpel slung across his back. One end was attached to the scalpel's handle, the other now slyly coiled about Richards's bony fingers. He had no intension of giving it back. But Giles would be quick.

'It's OK, I've got it,'

As Giles sprang, Richard yanked at the string, and the scalpel jerked to life. Skittering towards his outstretched hand, it jammed against a crack in the wall. Richard looked genuinely panicked, and Giles saw his chance. He pushed forward into the passage, but his wounded shoulder buckled and his face crashed into the rock. Until now, he had forgotten the tear in his shoulder, and the sudden pain was overwhelming. At the same moment, Richard let go of the string, wedged his feet against an upturned slab and pushed, hard. There was that sound again, like crushing shells. A

353

coffin-sized rock toppled towards Giles. He saw it just in time to shuffle back, pulling his head down as the opening between them closed with a muffled crunch.

Giles felt numb. Something was wrong. Dirt settled and his eyes readjusted to the light. He explored the length of his arm. There, pinned between the wall and fallen slab, were his little and ring finger. He cried out, bit his lip then searched the crevice for something to lever them free, but the wall's stones had contracted inwards and settled into new positions, cutting off the path by which he had entered. Giles rested his back against the rock and pulled at his trapped fingers. A further wave of pain radiated up his arm, burning all the way to the elbow. A familiar sound came from above – the ratcheting *click* of the snap-blade extending. Then silence. Giles startled as, to his left, the fox's tail brushed against gaps in the rock, creating a thrum, like the beating of wings or the patter of rain.

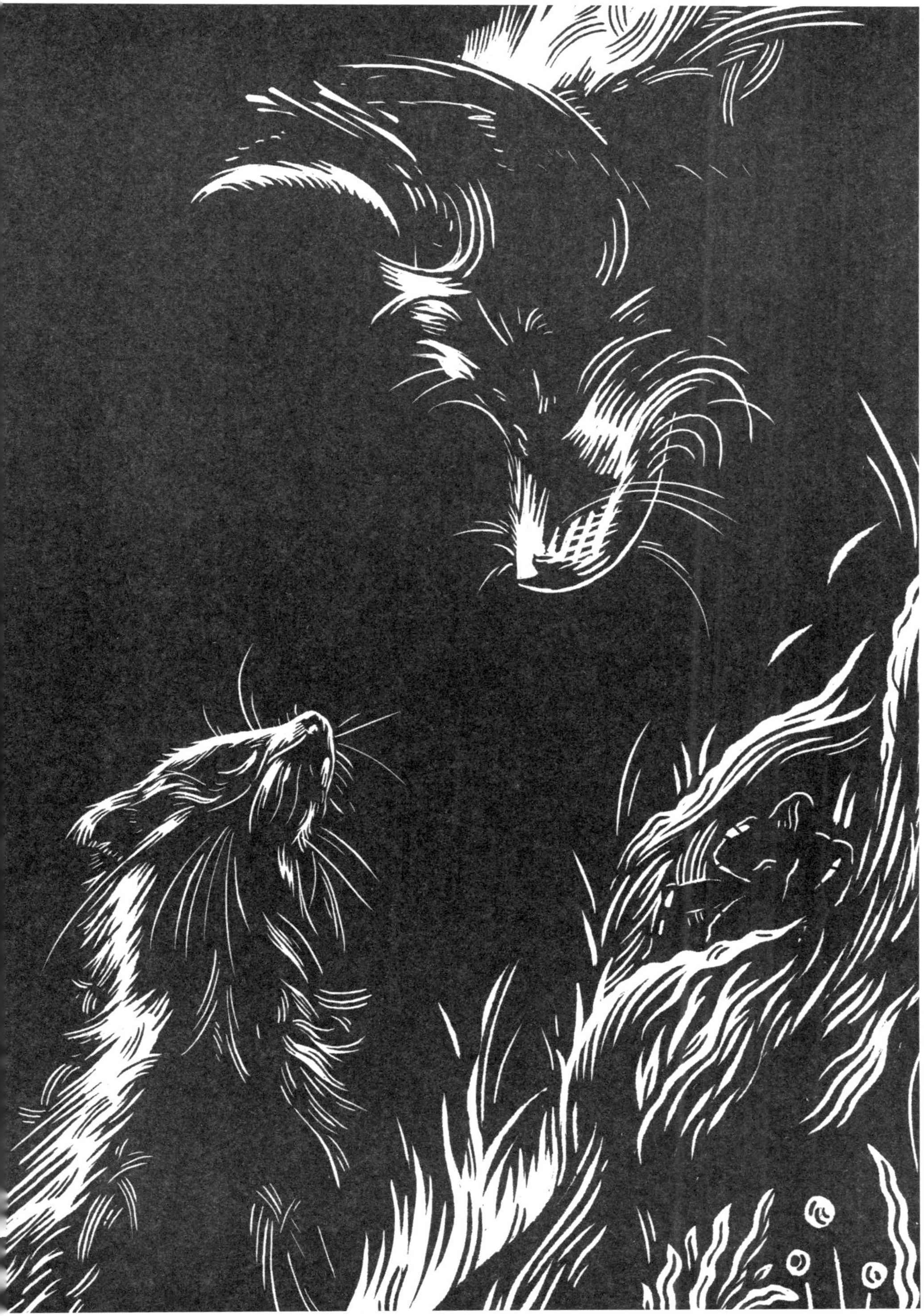

CHAPTER 35

ELSEWHERE, UCHO BOGA

To look at it, one might not have thought much of the small seafront lay-by, a meagre stretch of coarse concrete split by clovers and ringed with rusted bars, unremarkable for its view of the formless road and sea. There was no beach – instead, a long drop below the railing, waves crashed against cement bricks buttressed by black, jagged rocks. Visitors stopped here only to break the journey on their way to somewhere else, somewhere better. Yet in the years following July Second, it became the most hotly contested two-hundred-square-metre stretch in all the British Isles. Many heroes were born on this battlefield, spilling blood as they fought for their claim over what they believed to be *The Point of Origin*.

*

356

The lay-by became known as the very spot from which human-kind made contact with the Ocean god and awoke her to our presence. And like many other sacred sites, ownership of this land shifted from party to party, through force, diplomacy and insidious takeover, each group asserting themselves as champions of the one, true and righteous cause.

Despite these conflicts of opinion, the years of turmoil would one day calm, and the desolate war-zone that was once a forgettable car park would become something else. From a collection of tents and vehicle husks, a cooperative settlement grew. In time, what might be called an institute or even a temple pieced itself together – a repurposed bus shell, grown over with intricate architecture. Pilgrims and the scientifically curious would make the long and dangerous journey to this place, through ruined cities and deadly wilderness. They'd come in droves for their chance to stand on the spot where the line in our history was drawn, to look at the point of contact and wonder what, exactly, was said. The lay-by went by many names, but none stuck as well as Ucho Boga, a Polish name that roughly translates as *God's Ear*.

Whether or not the once lay-by was indeed the *actual* point of origin was debated long after the temple's construction. Some claimed the song sprung from a river three miles to the west, and others had heard stories of a silver headwater in a glass-covered lake. That was until a film, passed from device to antique device and carried by a set of pilgrims from the other side of the globe, confirmed the truth. The footage settled the matter. The sequence of blurry images had been salvaged from a long-buried thumb drive that, legend told, fell from space. It was hard to believe, but upon watching the film, there was no other explanation. The scholars, scientists and priests huddled together about the hazy screen and watched with awe as the bloom spread from the south coast of Britain, from the unmistakable spot of the lay-by, and wrapped its tentacles around the earth.

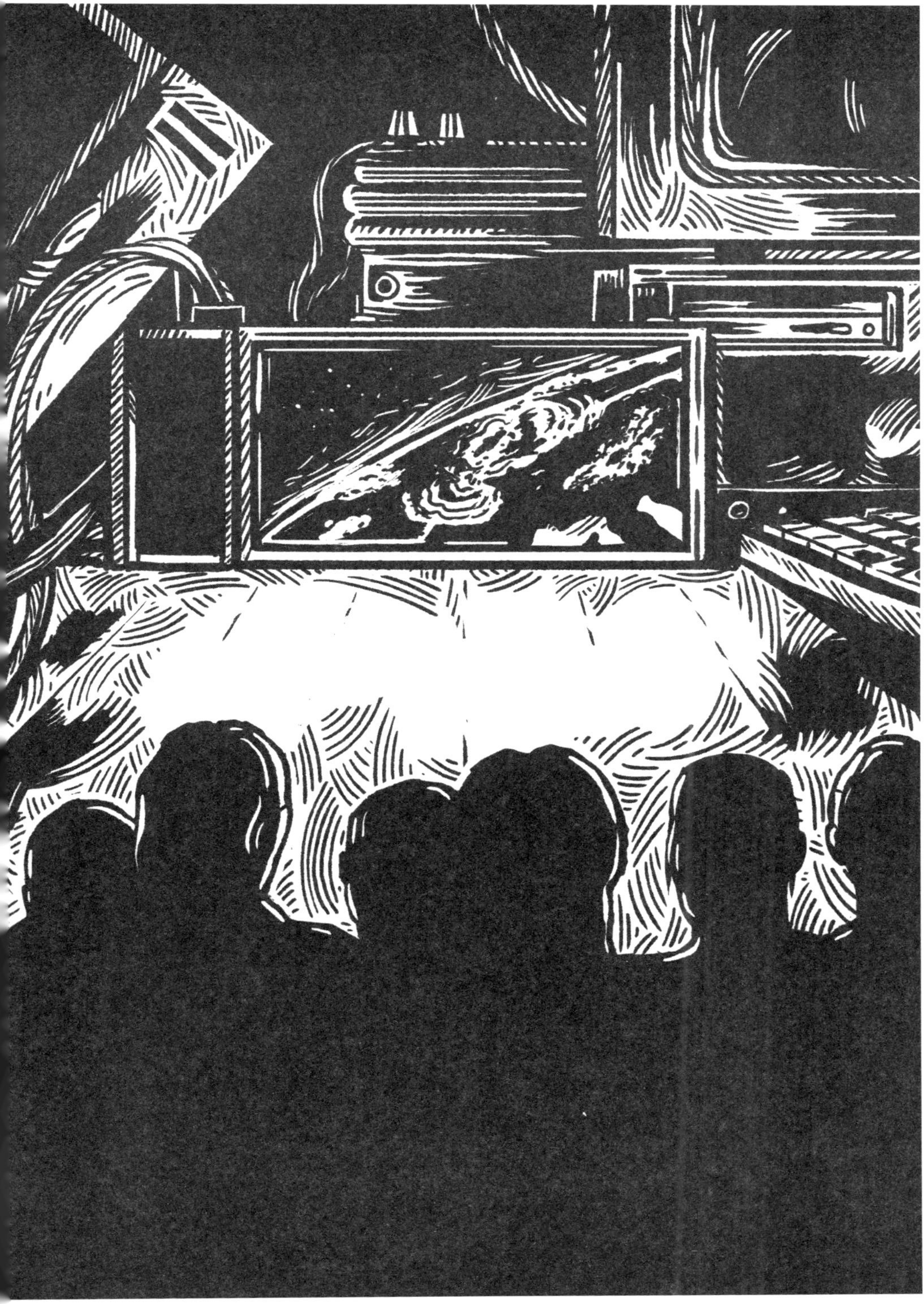

PART VIII

CHAPTER 36

THE WOMAN IN STRIPES

Bob nudged the chair forward, his phone bound to the backrest with sticky tape, and inspected the camera's framing.

'OK. A little to the left. Yeah, thath good. Remember, interact with ath many thingth ath you can, it'll prove you're not a thpecial effect.'

'A special *what*? Gosh, you're impossible to understand. Here, pass me those notes. Are all these things necessary?' The table was strewn with household objects – fruit, matchboxes, a steaming cup of tea. All of which Bob insisted would help establish a sense of scale.

'It's not enough,' said Matilda, taking in the scene. 'They won't believe it's real. I think Bob should sit behind you.'

'Really?' sighed Goodwin.

'Yes, the two of you together. It looks more credible with a copper backing you up.'

Bob grinned.

'Fine,' conceded Goodwin, 'just don't say anything. I'll do the talking.' They looked good, Matilda thought, composed like that. The officer with his palms flat on the table on either side of Goodwin, his dark, deep-set eyes staring down the lens, his face in almost complete shadow. Between the amphitheatre of his arms Goodwin stood, clad in a black and white striped glove jumpsuit, leaning jauntily on a ballpoint pen, her face deadly serious. Little could they imagine how iconic that image would become in the years that followed, re-rendered and retold, painted, carved, dramatised and speculated upon for generations to come.

'My name is Elizabeth Goodwin. If that name means anything to you, it is perhaps associated with the words fruitcake, nutcase, crackpot. With that in mind, I hope my physical state, my diminished scale of less than ten per cent of my previous height, will help to validate the claims I am about to make. At the least, I hope it will hold your attention until you have heard, in full, my words of warning, and my message of hope.'

Goodwin paced the table, engrossed in her speech. This time, she'd do it right. Behind her, silent and composed, Bob shifted objects to let the small figure move unobstructed.

'I come to you at a brilliant and terrifying time. A dawn of sublime discovery and yet, with it, the greatest peril humankind has ever been called to witness. I shall put it plainly – we are not alone. In our quiet arrogance, we have assumed humanity occupied the highest rung on the ladder of earth's intelligence – er – ladder. This was untrue! Abounding in our seven seas is a network of interconnected microbial life – an innocuous breed of plankton called the coccolithophore. Though we long believed them to be comprised of trillions of individuals, I tell you today that they are, in fact, a single conscious mind. We have no means to measure the scale of this mind's intelligence or influence, but from a single interaction which left me in the altered state you see before you, we can assume her capabilities outstrip our understanding.

'This is the advent of a new age and perhaps a cause for celebration were it not for the immediate threat we are now faced with. It was my own meddling, my own attempts to communicate with a small fraction of this *mind* in an isolated pool, that wrought my body to be transformed in the way you can plainly see.

'I am here with a stark warning. There are people at work who intend to communicate with the coccolithophores *in their entirety* – to make contact with the singular mind in her full expanse, throughout the oceans. These people want, for reasons of ego and self-elevation, to be the first to connect with this supermind, unaware that in doing so they will trigger a reaction so violent it will leave every man, woman and child on the face of this earth as diminished and disfigured as I. Laslett, Leaf, I beg you, if you're watching, please, cease this mad pursuit. Look at me now and see where your actions will lead.'

And just like that, the names Laslett and Leaf became lore.

'If these people succeed, and there is every possibility that they will, then no structure will shelter you from the oncoming wrath of the ocean. Once she is made aware of our presence, she will lash out. I fear that it was the very knowledge of our existence, who we are and what we have done, that brought about this violent attack. She is nature, and nature does not recognise good or evil, only balance and imbalance. It is my belief that in her own way she is trying to reset that balance, restore harmony to a world she can feel sliding off-centre.'

*

365

Goodwin's head drooped and Matilda worried she had fallen asleep. Suddenly, Goodwin clapped her hands, startling the room, and brought her attention back to the camera.

'But there is hope. A controlled dose of barbiturates, an induced coma, will shield you from the effects of this rebalancing. She knows the shape of our mind, and so we must camouflage it with unconsciousness. *That* is my urgent message. Do not waste any time. Run to your hospitals. Do it now. Do it before midday GMT. Be under for as long as you possibly can.' Goodwin stepped back, sat down between a pepper grinder and a porcelain frog, and mumbled, 'I'm sorry. Good luck.' Then, remembering something, she leaned forward and punched a box of peanuts, scattering them across the table.

Matilda stopped the recording.

'Well, you got there eventually. Crackpot. What's wrong with peanuts?'

'Interaction,' said Bob. 'My idea. Prove sheth not a thpecial effect.' He beamed down at Goodwin. 'I thought that wath very good, I'll get it uploaded. Thith and the footage from the lab. Thend it to newthroomth, blogth, everywhere I can think of.'

As Bob hurried to Roland's office, Matilda took a syringe full of the remaining barbiturates from the white bottle.

'OK, Elizabeth Goodwin, you've done quite enough for one day. Let's put you under with the rest.' Goodwin scrunched her nose in distaste.

'I beg your pardon.'

'You want to shrink twice?'

'I'm not sure that's possible but … suppose it's best not to take any further risks.'

'Good. Now.' Matilda lifted Goodwin's IV and inspected it. 'If I were to add the barbiturates directly in here …'

'No!' Goodwin caught the clear tube connecting to the needle in her arm and pulled. Matilda relinquished and placed the bag back down beside her.

'Really, Elizabeth, there's no need to.' She stopped as something in the tube caught her eye. Goodwin yanked at the IV.

'Give that back. Use a different IV. This one is not to be tampered with.'

'What's that in the tube?' Matilda squinted, lifting it closer.

'Nothing. It's nothing.' The paramedic threaded the tube through her fingers. Sure enough, wedged deep inside, just visible where medical tape had peeled away, was a small silver ball.

'Looks like a pinhead, blocking the intravenous tubing. Why have you blocked the tube, Goodwin?'

'It's better that way, it's . . .' Matilda swiped the bag off the table, unclipping the IV from the cannula in Goodwin's arm.

'This isn't medicine. What is it?'

'Please, I need it. It's very important.' Matilda, her eyes cold, lifted the little woman into the air.

'I'm not afraid of you! Put me—'

'The chief was right. You're a little liar.'

'Takes one to know—'

'Oh, stop it.' Matilda stepped back and, with her other hand, held the bag over the sink, massaging the silver ball down the length of the tube, white liquid butting up against one side. 'Tell me what this is now, or it's going down the drain.'

'It's nothing. A rare compound.'

'Now, Goodwin.' Matilda's fingers tightened around Goodwin's waist, and the small woman gasped, collapsing over the index, arms outstretched towards the bag.

'Stop! It's – it's my connectome. My mind. Please. I couldn't let them. My life's work washed away with their stupid bleach.' Matilda held the bag up to the light.

'You have any idea how dangerous this is? After everything we've done?' She nudged the ball further towards the end of the tube. White metallic swirls coiled about themselves inside the bag like a storm seen from space.

'No! Matilda, please, you'll kill us all. If those cells find their way to the ocean, and connect with Emiliania, even in part, there's every chance *we'll* trigger a second event. I was going to tell you, I ...' Matilda put Goodwin back on the table and leaned against the sink, arms crossed.

'How do we get rid of it?'

'You ... you *can* pour it away.' Goodwin sighed. 'You just have to boil it first.'

As Matilda dug through a low cupboard for a suitable saucepan, Bob re-emerged from Roland's office.

'Well, ith uploading. You know, this meanth they'll be able to track uth here. The polith, to that computer.'

Matilda nodded, then smiled weakly.

'It's ten-thirty. There's not long now. At least you're sounding better, Bob.'

'Yeah. I think the thwellinth gone down.'

'Everyone OK out there? The girls?'

'All good. That teacher, Baggthtrott, he was making some noises, but I gave him a shove, and he quietened down. Worried he might wake the—'

Matilda, thumb on the ignition spark of the cooker, looked up in alarm. 'Baggstrott?' She dropped the pan and set off at a jog, rounding the corner towards the nearest Rotolactor. Bob followed.

The row of patients lay in a blissful chemical slumber as Bob and Matilda hurried down the corridor.

368

'Those weren't sleeping drugs, Bob. If he's mumbling, he's not unconscious. He's dreaming.'

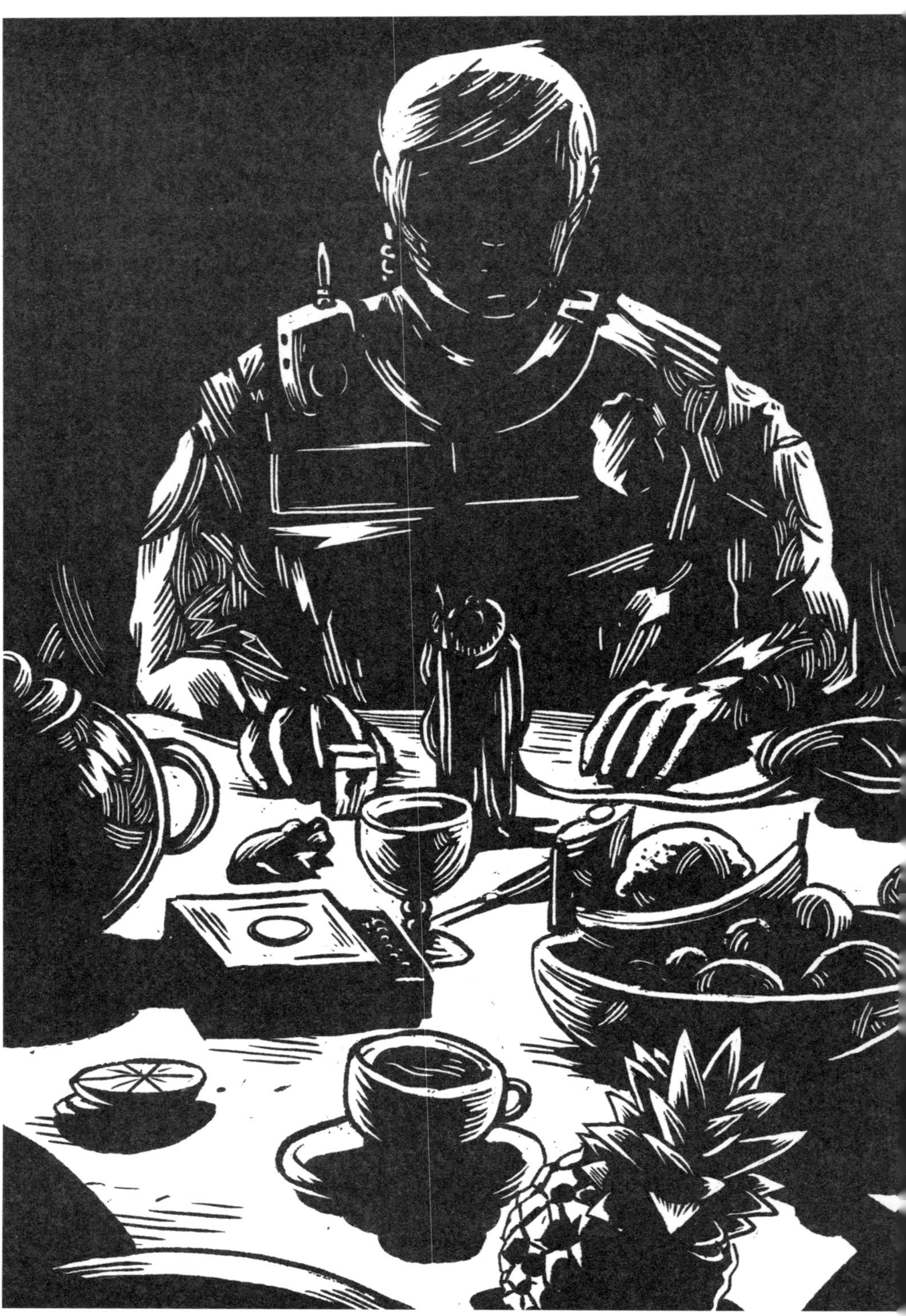

CHAPTER 37

ALL THINGS
BRIGHT AND BEAUTIFUL

Giles was no stranger to constricting spaces. In the old world, cars were forever too small. A door he didn't have to stoop for was a rarity, and his knees were invariably crunched into his chest on buses and planes. Part of the attraction of gardening was the ability to stretch out. In this new world, that abundance of space had been impossibly multiplied. For most of the past week, Giles had been free to move wherever he pleased. Conversely, it seemed that in his new shrunken state he could finally be his full self. Moving through this swollen landscape had been a guilty kind of bliss, but it was a pleasure that required his vision and thoughts to be blinkered to the horrors that made it possible. So perhaps this was his punishment, being buried alive in a dry-stone wall. It was the world's way of pushing back, claiming some rec-ompense for his insensitive revelry.

Desperate pain spread across his back, and he turned in the narrow crevice to see Richard retract the snap-blade through a thin slit in the rocks. The older man thrust a second time, sliding the blade through a different fissure, this time aiming for Giles's chest. Giles pivoted and, with his free hand, caught the blade on its side, shoved it against the rock, and snapped the serrated knife midway. Richard huffed in frustration and pulled the now trun-cated sword up and out of the coffin-like cave. 'I really am sorry about this, Giles.'

'What did you—' Giles gasped, struggling to form words. '*Isabel?*'

'Is-a-bell?' Richard repeated, contemplating the question. 'I'm not sure what you mean.' His concerned face flashed through the crack, and then it was gone. A moment later, Richard's muffled voice sounded somewhere behind him. 'Let's try something else, shall we?'

Giles pulled again at his fingers. A knuckle clicked, and the pain edged further up his arm. He scanned the narrow chamber. On a small ledge beside his shin were several fragments of rock, among them a flint the length of his arm. Richard was humming now, digging through a pile of tightly packed rubble wedged between two larger slabs, presumably to lessen the gap between Giles and the now shorter, but equally deadly blade.

'I'm curious,' he said from behind the wall, all the snivelling gone from his voice, 'how much thought have you given to the *cause* of all this?'

Giles edged the flint onto his foot and shuffled it up the wall. He had tried his best to avoid such conversations over the past week.

With so many pressing practical matters, there seemed to be little point in grandiose speculation. Now, without pause, he answered.

'I don't know exactly, but there's no *great plan*. It was thoughtless. Random. Like the changing of the wind. Just something that happened.' Richard stopped digging and angrily threw aside a rock that skittered and ricocheted through the warren below.

'*Wrong*. It was a divine and conscious act. It had to be. Do you not remember His voice in your ear? Did you not hear the *word* when He called?'

Despite himself, Giles thought back. There *had* been a noise, a rumble both distant and close. It had grown louder, unbearable in those final moments on the coastal path before sleep took him. The image of the white ocean conjured in his mind. Richard, who had been watching Giles through the gap, smiled and continued.

'Yes, we all heard it. Ask anyone. They'll remember if you press them. Now, myself, I never had children. But as a father, how do you discipline yours? I believe parents should use the stick. When those to whom we have given life abuse it, are they not to be set straight? Is that not our responsibility?'

Giles ignored him and continued to struggle with the flint. Richard, too, carried on digging, occasionally testing the length of the blade through the gap.

'You agree, I take it. Good. How then can we expect our own Father to behave when we have abused his gifts so abhorrently? Are we to be blessed or cursed?'

The flint, clamped against Giles's knee, scraped further up the wall. Richard continued in a firm monotone. 'I heard His voice, and I could see in their faces that they heard it too. But it was too much for the congregation, so they pressed their hands to their ears to keep Him out. Me? I opened my arms and let Him in. And so, while he gave the others sleep, he kept my eyes *open*! Yes, I did not sleep, because I *knew* it was coming. I had prayed and He answered. This is what we deserved, and it was my job to bear witness.' Richard stopped his impassioned sermon, shuddered, then carried on in a whisper. 'I remember every ugly moment of it. The looks on the faces of my friends. Absurd!' A nervous little laugh. 'Dentures peeling away from jaws. Arthur's face giving birth to a glass eye. False teeth and plastic hips sprouting around me like saplings in spring.' Richard clapped, vigorous again, 'And then I realised! Oh! It's so *good* to talk to you like this, Giles. I've been so pent-up, you know?'

Richard lunged with the blade, and again it fell short. At last Giles gripped the flint – long and fat at one end, like a caveman's club. He wedged the thin point beside his trapped fingers and leaned into it, attempting to lever the rocks apart. Richard dug faster.

'Oh, it was ghastly. An actual glimpse into hell. And you know what I thought? I thought, *yes*, this seems about right. We really fit in here. We *deserve* this. We don't belong in the garden, not anymore. I won't bore you with talk of floods, et cetera. But did you notice, the rain that first sunny morning? There was no rainbow. *No rainbow*! And so too, there'll be no ark. You understand now, that we're not *meant* to be here. This is our last generation, Giles. Our farewell. Humanity's swan song.' Giles stopped struggling with the club and listened to the rant. He was beginning to understand the man – the gaps in Mary's words, filled with Richard's own.

'But come now, it's not all doom and gloom. We are not the ones the rapture left behind. We are the raptured. And by His grace, we've been given hope. This is our chance to say sorry. We can repent, escape the hell the others were called to. All that's needed is the right kind of guidance.' He closed his eyes in a way that implied a deep inner calm. Giles interrupted.

'The church, the one you and Mary were in,' Richard startled and fixed him with a green, beady eye. 'Did you want to lead that flock too? But they didn't let you, is that it? So, when you came through unscathed—'

'Not unscathed,' Richard cut in, 'stronger, younger.'

'—you thought you were special. *Chosen*. Except others survived too. How many was it, Richard? How many others woke up?' Richard didn't answer. Instead, he squeezed his face through the widening gap in the wall, the skin pulling tight across his cheeks.

'*I* will steer us to the end. *Me*. Only I was allowed to see. See it all.' His skin stretched tighter, revealing red beneath his eyes. 'I know the course. Not you. Not Isabel or Ashraf. You saw what happens to sheep with a bad shepherd. That tinfoil boy. Pah! You? You think *you* can do it? You can't look after your *own* children. You left them, Giles, and you should have left us.' Hit with that uncomfortable truth, the fight left Giles.

'You murdered those people,' Giles countered, though somehow it felt like a weak retort.

'Murder was a *human* act. We are no longer human.' Richard carried on scratching through the rubble. 'The house, your idea of building a settlement, it's all wrong. Every step you made to reclaim the old way was undoing the good work I'm here to complete. We were never meant to survive, Giles. We buggered it up! You know that. This is the last page. The end. *That* is His plan. All I can do now is help *them*, the innocents, prepare.'

Richard's words, the sentiment, the thinly veiled threat to the children, disgusted Giles. He turned, and with one last effort, he shifted his weight against the makeshift club, trying to free his trapped hand. The flint buckled and with a loud crack, split in two, leaving him panting for breath, gripping a stone the shape and size of a skull. Richard laughed and carried on clearing away the rocks, testing the blade's length with another lunge.

'No,' said Giles, breathing in. He caught a glimpse of his mangled fingers between the two slabs and felt light-headed. The blade swung perilously close to his neck, and Giles pressed into the rocks to avoid the swipe. 'You're not pious. It's not *grand* work. You're guilty too, guilty of something, and you're trying to make up for it, same as me.'

Richard blinked, taken aback.

'Well now, there you have a point. I am not guiltless. But mine is not quite so ... *domestic* as yours. Good grief. In answer to my own question, why did this happen? Well, it was *me*. I caused this. I prayed for our punishment, and for once, He answered. I never imagined His wrath would take such a strange form, but so it goes.'

Giles stared, dumbfounded, delirious. He laughed. This was a joke. A twisted, hideous joke. Richard continued to dig, and near Giles's feet, something glinted in the dark.

'I'm not a cruel man. We all got on so well – you, me, Ash, Isabel. I wanted to let you go quietly, with my famous harvest stew, no less! But *Mary* ruined it, once again. Now I have to do this, one by one. Unpleasant. Regrettable. I am sorry, Giles. I do wish you hadn't promised to come back.'

The glint came from the broken segment of the snap-blade. Carefully, Giles began to shuffle it with his feet, manoeuvring it within reach. Richard's face appeared between a chink in the rocks, resting his chin on one side, looking terribly sad.

'You called me Morris once. Do you remember? Quite by accident, I'm sure.' Then, suddenly struck by an idea, he brightened. 'I know! Remember when I asked you what you would have said to your father, given a chance? Well, go ahead. Pretend I'm him.'

He did resemble Morris. There was no denying it. Giles remembered that coastal path. The last conversation they'd had. How annoyed he'd been. He looked at Richard – serene and patient.

'I would have said – I would have told you that you're *wrong*. I can do this alone.' Richard smiled, delighted the younger man had played along.

'That's very nice, Giles. Nothing too soppy. You're right, too. You would have had to do this on your own, as I have. Like me, your friends are all gone. Ashraf, Isabel ...' Giles flinched.

'Where's Isabel?'

'Now *there's* a properly phrased question. Hand on heart, I have not seen her.' Richard smiled, and Giles, drunk with pain, smiled back. Then Richard's eyes narrowed, and a slyness wormed into his voice. 'However, I *heard* her. I believe she was being chased through the garden. Crying for help. Terribly sad. She was looking for you, was she not? But take comfort. She'll go a long way between all those little mouths.'

Richard came closer, out of reach from Giles, but near enough for the scalpel to find its mark.

'Well now, Giles. Here we are.' He leaned back, preparing to strike. Giles didn't pause to think. If he hesitated, it'd be over. He shoved the broken blade across the knuckles of his trapped hand, raised the skull-shaped rock and with as much force as he could muster, brought it down hard on the blade's edge. There was a sound like breaking wood. A spray of blood.

At that moment the scalpel came slicing through the wall but Giles, free now, rolled to the side. He fell with a backswing, catching Richard across the chin with the rock. With a look of indignant fury, his jaw set at an odd angle, Richard stumbled backwards through a curtain of lichen that crumbled under his weight. He tumbled from sight, away from the high wall, and a moment later Giles heard the thud of a body hitting rock.

Faint and trembling, he forced himself to look at his mangled hand – two white button-like stumps where his ring and little finger had been, blooming with blood. He cradled the wound against his chest, wrapped it in what remained of his shirt, crawled through the gap in the wall, and peered past the lichen. Ahead lay the clearing, the tree stump, surrounded by a moonlit woodland. Beneath him, the entrance to the burrow. Richard's body writhed upon an altar-like slab as the fox approached. The animal lowered its head, its magnificent mane a canopy of golden spines. Then it took Richard between its teeth and padded calmly into the woods.

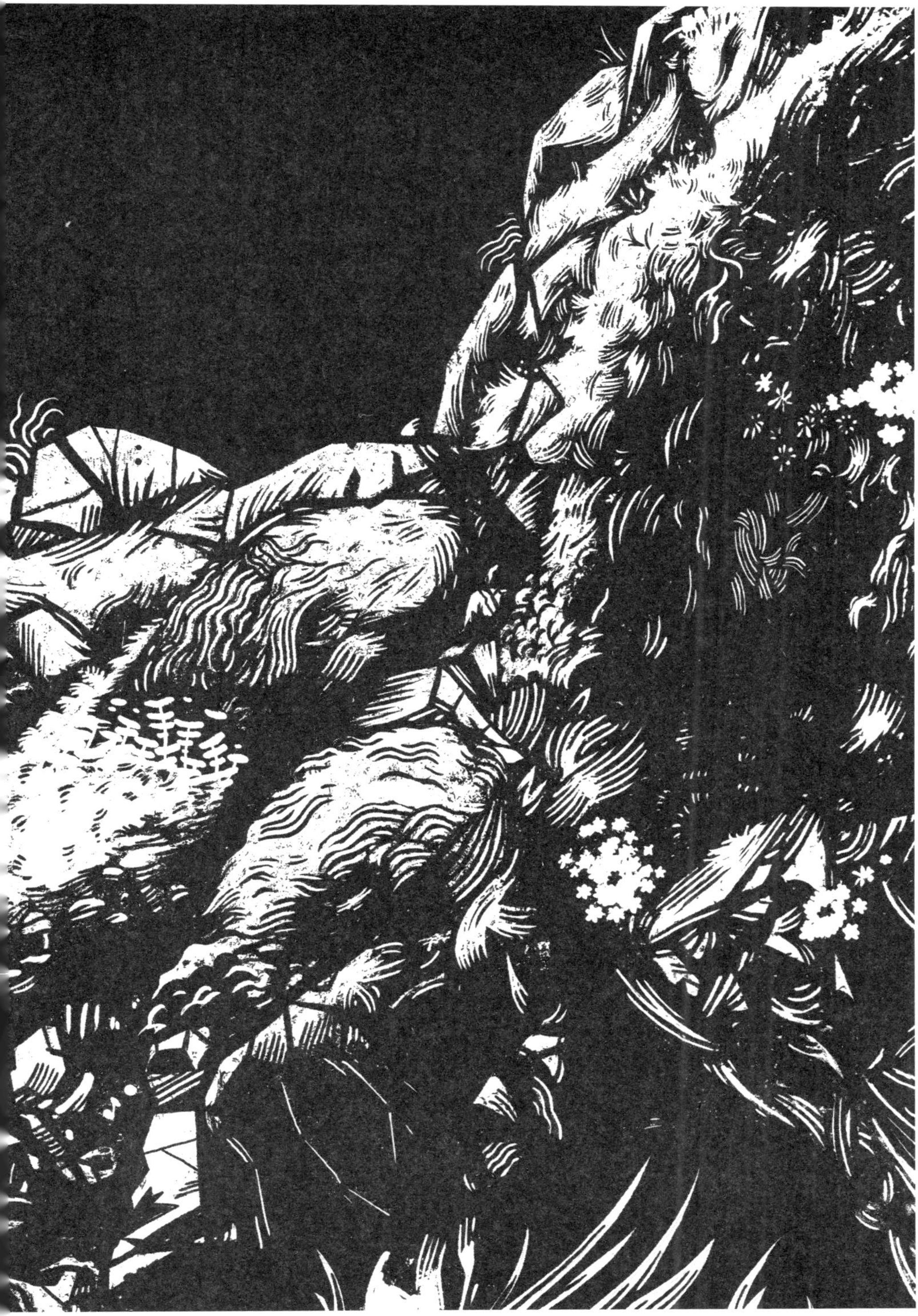

CHAPTER 38

INTERESTING
THIRD SHIFT

Dark spots speckled the concrete floor. Pools had formed. Limp hands, half-turned heads and the underside of the Rotolactor reflected in the liquid. The carousel, designed to hold dozens of cows at a time, was one of four such outdated machines at Silverbell, each of them now populated by comatose farm workers, their families, Matilda's father, her daughters and a handful of their schoolmates. Nearly fifty in all. Above them, curling cables and thick fluted tubes hung from the ceiling, looping down to the chipped, paint-peeling olive green machinery.

The bays had been laid with blankets, in some cases padded underneath with hay. Elsewhere on the farm were several small cottages, each containing sofas, camp beds and soft benches – comfortable, human places to rest – and many had argued that any of these would make for better places to administer the potassium iodide. But Matilda needed everyone in one place, and eventually, with the threat of the radiation warning now playing over the radio, they had relented. She was not an anaesthesiologist, but she felt confident she knew enough. Each patient had been weighed upon entering their stall, and their information inputted into an online dosage calculator. At the end of each makeshift cot was a hand-scrawled note containing the patient's name, dosage and time stamps for when they went under and when they should awake.

For the fifth time in the last hour, Matilda read Baggstrott's note, scanned the back of the barbiturate bottle and checked the time on her watch.

'This should have worked.' Baggstrott lay slumped to one side, dribbling unintelligible words into his beard as Bob struggled to sit him up straight.

'Ask him again,' demanded Matilda, putting down the bottle and wringing her hands, casting anxious glances back at the other patients.

'He's not making sense,' said Bob. Matilda kneeled, clasped Baggstrott's face in her palms, rolled it gently from side to side, eased up an eyelid and flooded it with light from her pen torch.

'He's doped but coming round. How the hell? He was the first to go under. Due to be up before the others, but this soon? Christ, it's barely eleven o'clock. He should have been out until six, if not the rest of the day.'

Baggstrott gurgled. Matilda let his head droop and Bob leaned in, putting one arm under his shoulder in the practised manner of comforting a drunk. A red light flashed on Bob's hip. His radio had been back on since they uploaded the video, the anonymity of their whereabouts sacrificed for updates on the police search for Laslett.

Matilda watched it dumbly flick on and off. Her heart raced. The mass anaesthetic had been the right thing to do. She was sure of it. But the illegality, the grey moral ground of what she'd done made her stomach curdle. Who was she kidding, it wasn't grey, it was jet black. But she trusted Goodwin's science, and the professor couldn't have been clearer – in less than an hour, humankind would be wrought down to her level, rendered as small and deformed as Simian in the footwell, as the victims at the crash site. If not for her actions, many, if not all the people under her care would have died. But now an idea consumed her – she'd made a mistake, somehow screwed up the dosage. They would all wake too soon. Scenarios circled in her head. As these sleepers slowly came around, she would likely have to answer to them for her actions, without any proof of the pending threat. If it came to that, she would reveal Goodwin, that would convince them. But then what?

Baggstrott let out another gurgle.

Matilda looked down to see the schoolmaster nudging the bottle on the floor with his foot.

'Terribly sorry about the bottle,' blurted Baggstrott in a sudden burst of coherence, swaying and bobbing like a bouncy castle in the wind. He fell to one side, reaching for Bob and muttering at him.

'What's he saying?' pressed Matilda, and Bob translated.

'He thayth he didn't mean to thpill it. I think he diluted the iodide.'

'He *what*?' Matilda pulled at the collar of Baggstrott's dressing gown, lifting him forward with surprising strength. 'By how much?' Bob put his arm between them, and Matilda let go.

Baggstrott, a momentary wild look in his eye, managed to squeak 'half', before slumping onto his back, and emitting a tremendous grunt that signalled his return to sleep. Matilda went to kneel beside a tall, thin woman on the adjacent stall, pulled back an eyelid and shone the torch into her pupil. The contraction was feeble, but it was there.

'Feels like this one's on the way as well.'

'Give them another dose?' suggested Bob.

Holding the bottle up to the light, Matilda ran her finger down the embossed measuring notches, then jotted some numbers on a scrap of paper. She looked at her father, the teenagers, then sighed deeply.

'We could do a small top-up. It'd give them another hour at most. But if the police don't find Laslett and these people are awake when he does whatever Goodwin did to that pool, all this is for nothing.'

They were down to administering the top-up to the last five patients when Bob startled. 'You hear that?' He turned and pressed his hands against the window, his expression one of alarm.

'What is it?' But then she heard it too – the distant wail of sirens. Moments later, blue lights cast patterns across the fields from beyond the high wire fences. Bob and Matilda pressed their backs against the wall below the window.

'How many are out there?' asked Matilda. Bob peered over the sill and attempted a count. He shrugged and drummed his fingers in a gesture she understood to mean many.

'Unith from everywhere. Andover, Basingthtoke . . .'

His radio flashed and Bob pressed a finger to his earpiece.

'What are they saying? Have they found Laslett?'

'They found their coach.'

Matilda's gasp of relief was cut short by Bob's shaking head. He winced.

'It's empty. Sounds like all their resources are now focused on finding us. Think you pissed off the chief.'

Vans gathered at the gate, and among the uniforms, Matilda made out Chief Deverill. One of the officers took an angle saw to the lock and a stream of sparks erupted like a roman candle. Matilda massaged her scalp, circulating the blood in the hope it might help her think.

'It won't be long until they get in here.' She pulled a shaky lungful of air. 'The way I understand it, Laslett will trigger this event at some point today. We just don't know when. These people could wake up before he does it. We can't stop him, and the police won't stop him either.' An eerie calm came over her. 'A lot of people are going to die. A lot of people are going to end up like Goodwin. We've warned them, but we can't save them all. But these people here . . .'

Several minutes later, Matilda watched the angle grinder cut through and the white gate swung inwards.

'You're sure about this?' said Bob.

'It'll take me forty minutes to get there. Just make sure you're under by midday, latest. It's a very small window.'

'I'll make sure.' Bob nodded, tapping the syringe on the desk beside him, then parted the curtains to check how far the police had advanced. The light cast his profile into sharp relief. She looked at him, thin and gaunt but handsome. Better than that, he was kind. She wondered if he was doing this for them or her. He was a little young for her, but not by much. She squeezed his arm and kissed him on the cheek.

'You didn't need to do that,' said Bob as she pulled away.

'Keep them safe, OK?' She glanced down to the rifle in his lap, no less menacing for its age.

'Interesting third shift,' he said, then continued picking through a box beside him, discarding the bullet shells that had tinted green. Outside the window, a convoy of vehicles made its way down the arc of the driveway. Two black vans splintered off from the main group, cutting across the fields and ploughing through the young forest, laying the saplings flat beneath their wheels.

'Hold them off as long as you can, then hide and put yourself under, OK?'

Again, he nodded. She gave his hand one last squeeze, slung a leather bag across her shoulder, crouched and ran down the corridor into the yard.

At the end of a row of cattle pens, a large circular manhole cover was embedded in the ground. Levering it with the edge of a spade, she shifted the grill to one side, threw a wave back to Bob and descended a rung of rusted hoops set into the wall. The latrine dropped into darkness and then connected to a long trench, a sanitation system that led to a distant spot of light. She sank shin-deep into the thick, dark sludge, clamped a sleeve across her mouth and strode forward.

Though the sounds were muffled, Matilda sensed the conflict above. The vibration of running feet and heavy vehicles carried through the ground, and was she imagining it, or was that the hum of a helicopter? She turned and shone the torch into the stretch of the tunnel behind her. It made no dent in the darkness. A noise startled her and she spun about again to face the exit, a distant spot of light. The tunnel was still empty. Perhaps it had been a gunshot. It had come from above, she was certain. She lowered her head, heaved her legs and waded towards the light.

It was eleven twenty-two a.m., on July Second. Forty-nine minutes before the Descent.

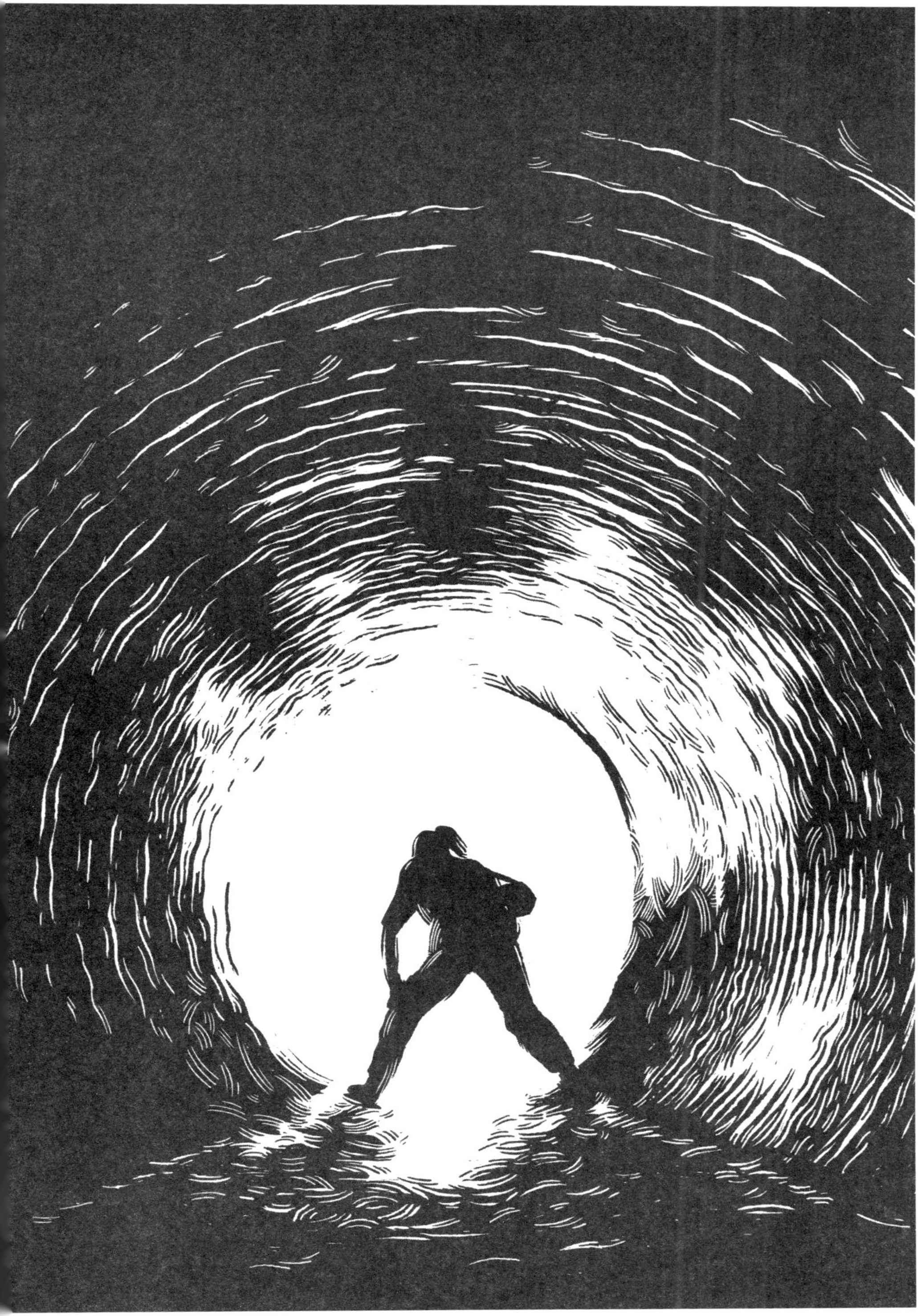

CHAPTER 39

ALL CREATURES
GREAT AND SMALL

Giles positioned the scalpel across his back, nudged the lighter so that it tumbled ahead of him, then crawled, slipped and stumbled down the wall and into the clearing. The bodies of the polecat and her kit were gone, presumably removed to the fox's warren and soon to be joined by Richard's. He stood swaying gently for a minute, facing the black hole of the burrow mouth, bloodied hand curled tight into his chest. Then he flicked the lid of the lighter, kicked the flint into life and cupped its silver case beneath one arm. The warm, dancing flame made the entrance glisten red. Fearing further hesitation might make his nerve falter, he stepped quickly, with all the confidence he could muster, down into the tunnel.

Immediately he slipped, half-rolled and half flew down the muddy slope. Gathering himself at the bottom and reigniting the lighter, Giles surveyed the chamber. Though the catatonic animals breathed and twitched unnervingly, and the air felt thick with death's scent, the flame's light diminished much of the larder's previously ominous atmosphere. Just a muddy hole in the ground, Giles told himself, the likes of which he had dug a thousand times.

He called for Ashraf, and to his surprise, an answer came back from the antechamber to his right. *Isabel*. Her voice was faint, but she was alive. Giles fell against the waist-high root separating the two rooms and thrust the flame across the divide. At the back of the auxiliary chamber stood his friend, caught in a semicircle of polecat kits, her new leather jumpsuit torn and muddy. Behind her, slumped and unmoving against the wall, lay Ash, half his face a mess of injury. The kits turned to look at Giles, drawn by the light, and he counted six, maybe seven black-eyed, unblinking faces. Whereas their parent had moved with a deft, agile certainty, these juvenile polecats were clumsy, lopsided and skittering. Still, their teeth, claws and strength meant that together, as a pack, the kits were no less dangerous. Sensing Giles was not an imminent threat, they returned their attention to Ash and Isabel, apparently undecided whether they were playthings or prey.

'Hold on!' called Giles, as Isabel swung Ash's serrated penknife in an arc, doing her best to keep the critters at bay. It looked heavy in her arms, and a slow backswing allowed a kit to creep forward and nip at her elbow. Isabel yelped, the animal jumped away and the knife almost slipped from her grip. Falling over the divide, Giles waded through the smaller chamber, waving the flame wildly, shouting, pushing the curious animals back as they hissed and clambered over each other. Reaching the others against the wall, he was able to see the extent of their wounds. Across Isabel's neck and shoulder were three deep cuts, concurrent with the swipe of a claw, and another running down her leg. She had suffered a mauling, but she was likely to survive. Of Ash, Giles was less certain, though his spirits lifted to see Ash's chest shudder a rasping breath. Two deep puncture wounds, like the one he'd seen on the rabbit, sat high on Ash's cheek and under his jaw, from where the polecat had lifted him in its teeth. The way his face swelled on one side suggested that even if Ash were to survive the night, he would be scarred for life.

Giles swept the lighter behind him, holding the creatures at the edge of the flame's protective halo. Isabel slung Ash's arm over her shoulder and heaved.

'Here, help me get him up,' she urged. Giles pinned the lighter between his elbow and hip, and wrapped his uninjured hand around Ash's waist. Moving as quickly as their injuries allowed, the two of them dragged Ash about the circumference of the room, backs against the wall.

'How are you here?' Giles asked, pausing to swing the torch.

'Came to look for you,' hissed Isabel. 'Got trapped by the polecat. Then it ran off, back to her kids, I guess. On my way back to the house, I heard Ash calling. He was awake when I got here, fending these guys off with this.' Isabel gave another swipe of the penknife. Still, the kits edged in and twice Giles had to push back their snouts with his heel. Underfoot, the floor of the chamber crackled, a nest of dry twigs, leaves and grass. A tinderbox, Giles noted, that might catch at the smallest spark.

They were halfway out of the enclosure when the bright yellow flame spluttered blue. The fire would die, conserving its fuel as it was designed to do, before they reached the exit. A thought struck Giles, that if he dropped the lighter, the nest would catch alight. The threat to the community would be eliminated, but what horror there would be in that act. What unforgivable cruelty. Worse though than the three of them being eaten? He loosened his grip on the lighter. The flame dimmed and kits edged closer, truly now, in the fading light, they appeared to be a ring of full-grown bears. Giles clenched his teeth, ready to torch the nest when, as one, to Giles's utter bewilderment, the kits recoiled.

Wincing from an unseen force, they cowered their heads. Stupidly, Giles's first thought was that they were hearing that unbearable song, the one he had tried to close his ears to, the one Richard had embraced. Again, in unison, the animals flinched, shuddering, lowering their heads in a gesture that was hard to read as anything other than subservience. The flame flickered and died. Giles braced, readying for teeth to sink in from all sides. Still, unexplainably, the creatures kept their distance, squirming and uncomfortable. Giles became suddenly aware of voices coming from the larger chamber and the hurrying of feet. Three figures ran through the mounds.

Evelyn was the first to appear, pushing her way past a hillock of fur, playing what, at a glance, appeared to be a large flute. It took Giles a moment longer to recognise the short sliver tube as the dog whistle. She paused for breath and, seeing the kits relax, quickly resumed blowing into the seemingly silent instrument. Alex and Maya followed behind, simultaneously impacting the root wall. Maya reached into a pouch slung across Alex's shoulder and threw fistfuls of ground meat over the animal's heads. The kits turned, chasing the morsels, remnants of the meal Ash had made the previous night. While they ate eagerly, the three newcomers pulled the wounded up and over the divide.

Safely out of the nest, Isabel and Giles fell back exhausted against the flank of a rabbit. The younger boy upended the rest of the meat over the roots and the animals fell upon the pile. Evelyn lowered the whistle and peered over the ridge. Keeping a wary distance from the carnivores on the other side, her mannerisms reminded Giles of a visitor testing their limits at a zoo or safari. The mortal threat had abated, and the survivors had been replaced by thrill-seeking spectators. Maya, seemingly unable to stop herself, reached over and rested a hand on the hide of the nearest kit. It turned, regarded her passively, then resumed its meal. Giles did a double take.

'Did . . . Did Maya just *coo*?'

Evelyn sparked the lighter back to life and, ushered by Isabel, the party moved slowly towards the garden end of the burrow. Giles and Isabel followed from behind, propping up Ash between them, while Evelyn lit the way, and the others cleared a path.

'Are there any more adults about?' asked Alex, casting furtive looks through the subtly swaying furred bodies. Giles shook his head.

'The fox got their mother, just now, and . . . and Richard too.' Maya clamped a hand to her mouth. Giles held his tongue, aware that this was not the right moment to share the truth about Richard – what he'd said and what he'd done. To Isabel though, he shared a look that implied there was more to say.

'What about the dad weasel?' asked Alex.

'It's a polecat. We've not seen the male. Males don't have much to do with their young.'

'So, who's going to look after those cubs?' asked Evelyn, glancing back at the opening to the enclosure.

'It'd be crazy to try to train them. Wouldn't it?' asked Maya.

'Crazy,' agreed Isabel. And yet something about the way Maya, Evelyn and Alex exchanged glances made Giles think that they were not all in complete agreement. Reflecting on the horror of their ordeal, the nightmare of this larder, the idea of finding a way to live with the predators somehow felt hopeful to Giles. The image of the three children riding on the backs of saddled mustelids raised a weak smile. Isabel stepped over a crumpled wing and, as if reading his mind, shook her head then muttered,

'Some bloody safe haven.'

Clouds blushed orange with dawn as the party approached the manor. While the younger residents had slept through the night's drama, Jayden and Rosalie, a teenager from Claybourne, had kept watch and their pent-up nervousness spilled over as tears as they prised open the front door and helped the wounded inside. Speaking little and acting quickly, the five teenagers spread a plastic bag over the sitting room rug and lowered the injured adults onto it.

They went to work on Ashraf first, ferrying capfuls of water back and forth from the dripping conservatory tap, moving methodically from the head down, washing away the dirt and blood. From across the hallway, Maya rolled a bottle of pills that rattled like a raffle tombola.

'I'm – I'm pretty sure these are antibiotics.'

She cracked the lid open and extracted an oval capsule. Giles eyed the label. 'Ampicillin. Well, it *sounds* like penicillin.'

Maya tugged at the capsule, which suddenly split, scattering its granules. She swore and in trying to pick them up, Giles saw her hands were shaking, the trauma of the burrow still bubbling to the surface. Ash would have known what to do. He looked to the younger man, his face wrapped in reddening cloth, but his breathing now steady. A hum rose to fill the quiet room, and to the occupant's surprise, it came from Giles. It was the kind of song he'd heard his friend sing over the past week, a wordless melody, a lullaby of sorts. One that you'd recognise but had forgotten until now. No one acknowledged it, but invisibly steadied, Maya scraped the granules back into the cup and continued her work. The others relaxed as well, calm and serious, as they built the bed around Ash and splinted Isabel's leg. A sense of pride, a deep affection for this pack of survivors filled the gardener, as the song came round again.

Giles found Ashraf's keychain keepsake, tucked it beside his bed, then watched, contented, as one by one the last of the children drifted into exhausted sleep. With his cuts washed, dressed and bound, his arm hooked in a sling, he stepped through the slumbering bodies, past Mary curled in a nest of clothes beside the hearth, plasters covering her chest and stomach. Easing open the sitting room door, Isabel called to him.

'Giles,' she rasped and beckoned him over. He had thought she was asleep. *Hoped* she had been asleep. 'Don't go. Not yet. *Rest.* Go tomorrow. I'll – I'll come too.' He saw she wouldn't be going anywhere for a long time – weeks, maybe.

'I have to. I might be too late already. You understand. You're *safe* here now.'

She shook her head. 'What happened to Richard?'

Giles did his best to convey the confrontation. When he was done, Isabel looked out over the sleeping passengers of the sedan, stirring in the early morning light and said, 'I'm glad he's gone.' Giles nodded.

'I think he would have hurt them, eventually.'

He surveyed the room. They were no longer the band of displaced refugees he'd stumbled upon in the tent. They had become a group of explorers, well-kitted settlers, wrapped in tailored furs. Many of the packs beside their beds were bursting with repurposed equipment – fishing hook grappling lines, matchstick torches, makeshift water carriers from sushi box soy bottles. The sleepers felt ready, prepared for the start of something new, an unknown frontier.

'I think you'll be OK without me, for a while.'

Isabel shook her head, holding him by the wrist. 'You being here, it matters. Them knowing you're near, being present. That's important.' Isabel raised her head, indicating that Giles should look behind him. He turned and saw the toy troll, with its crazed purple hair, resting against the glass window, looking out into the garden, as if it had been put there to keep watch. 'Stay,' she repeated, but the request lacked conviction. Giles smiled and rested his hand on hers. She let it drop.

'Before all this, what did you do?'

Isabel laughed. 'So *now* you want to know. Why the sudden interest?'

'No reason.'

'Well, if it'll make you feel better about leaving then I'm *definitely* not going to tell you. I want this to be hard. Besides,' she let the faintest ghost of a smile crease her lips, 'I wouldn't want Maya to hear.' Isabel leaned forward and whispered, '*I worked at an equestrian centre. I trained horses.*'

'Oh,' said Giles, and then '*Oh!*' understanding the need for discretion.

'Now go on, I can see I'm getting nowhere. Get lost. But come back soon.'

Giles stepped away, smiled and said, 'I'll bring back some saddles.'

The sun was fully up as he leaned his good shoulder into the back of the buggy and pushed. Alex and Evelyn, groggy from sleep, prised open the door, and Giles edged the wheels over the step and out into the garden.

'I'll see you soon,' he said, nodding thanks to the pair, 'look after the place.'

The two children waved him off, then stood in the doorway for some minutes, watching Giles start the buggy, trundle up the gravel path, and disappear through the wooden gate. As the pair turned to head back inside, Maya ran to greet them. She hunched over, panting and excited, and held up a hand, instructing them to halt.

'The radio,' she said, gripping Evelyn by the back of her head, 'We misheard, got it wrong. They're not saying – *We are the ants.* It's *Be-ware. Beware the giants.*'

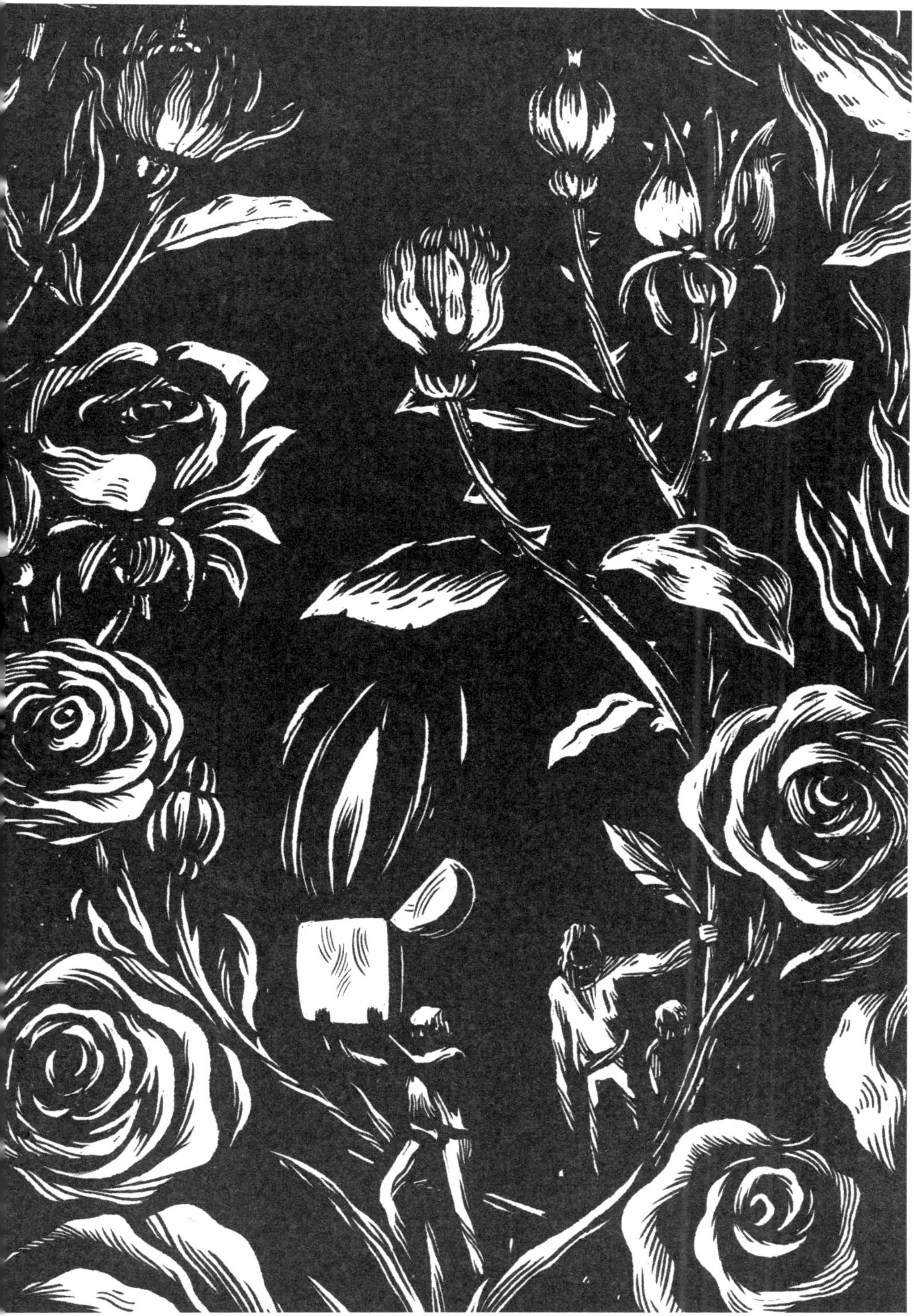

CHAPTER 40

ELSEWHERE,
THE GREEN GIANT

An ocean-spanning super-organism had risen from their long, dark sleep. A god now swept physically among humankind, wielding the very power of creation. As you might well imagine, this provoked a myriad of reactions. From love to repulsion, devotion to indifference, and simply running for the hills or, to be more accurate, running *away* from the coast. Wherever groups gathered and settlements formed, one could be sure that tenets would follow. People talked. Terms were coined. Texts were scribed. Ideas were bitterly defended. Though these new ways of thinking fell beneath countless banners, all could fit into one of three distinct ideologies.

First were those who revered the interconnected microscopic

water-dwelling creatures for being God themself – a benevolent force, a protector, a creator, a shepherd of life who had *saved* humankind from a spiral of self-destruction by unseating us from our place at the top of the food chain. In these orders, chalk and salt water were often used as sacramental substances, conduits of the White Algae's divine power. Festivals and rituals, though largely reappropriated from earlier traditions, took on an air of animism and vitalism, honouring nature in a way unseen since the Pagan rule of Britain.

The second group consisted of those who perceived the plankton network as a new classification of animal, a collective organism, an extraordinary and dangerous one at that. The kind that researchers should study, but at a distance and, above all else, never again communicate with. For once bitten, no rational person would be foolish enough to put their hand back through the bars of the cage. These scholars devoted their lives to understanding the plankton, the forgotten trunk in the tree of evolution, and the physical device by which the hive mind enacted its control. Cymatics – the manipulation of matter via sound, and Neurophysics – the study of the electromagnetic field of consciousness, became twin disciplines, the cornerstone subjects for these academically inclined.

Then there was the third way of thinking – those who believed that the white swirls in the water *were* indeed a deity, an immortal architect of life, but not a benevolent one. The many followers of this doctrine considered the entity to be a hunter, a destroyer, a vengeful spirit out to blanch us from their skin. She was not the Gaia, the nurturing Earthmother, but the Gaia Medea – a filicidal force of nature. If we were to raise our heads once more, they would finish what they started and crush us beneath their thumb.

The largest of these collectives might have been the Order of

Arboreal, a monastic forest-dwelling society who hid themselves in hollow trunks, ate only the fallen fruit and swept away their footprints with reed tails tied to the backs of their tunics. In the early days of the sect, devotees would show their holiness by rounding their shoulders, adopting a hunch to help hide from the Medea's watchful eye. But as the years progressed and in efforts to outstrip each other, the Arboreal gave up their humanity piece by piece, eventually descending to all fours, their tails swishing behind them.

Indeed, the generations that followed the Descent had many contrasting ways of understanding the world, but one common consensus between them – that in the time before July Second, all the ways in which we thought the world worked were wrong. And in the twilight of these ancient creeds, as they dwindled and died, came the genesis of new doctrines as varied and bright and sinister as the human imagination.

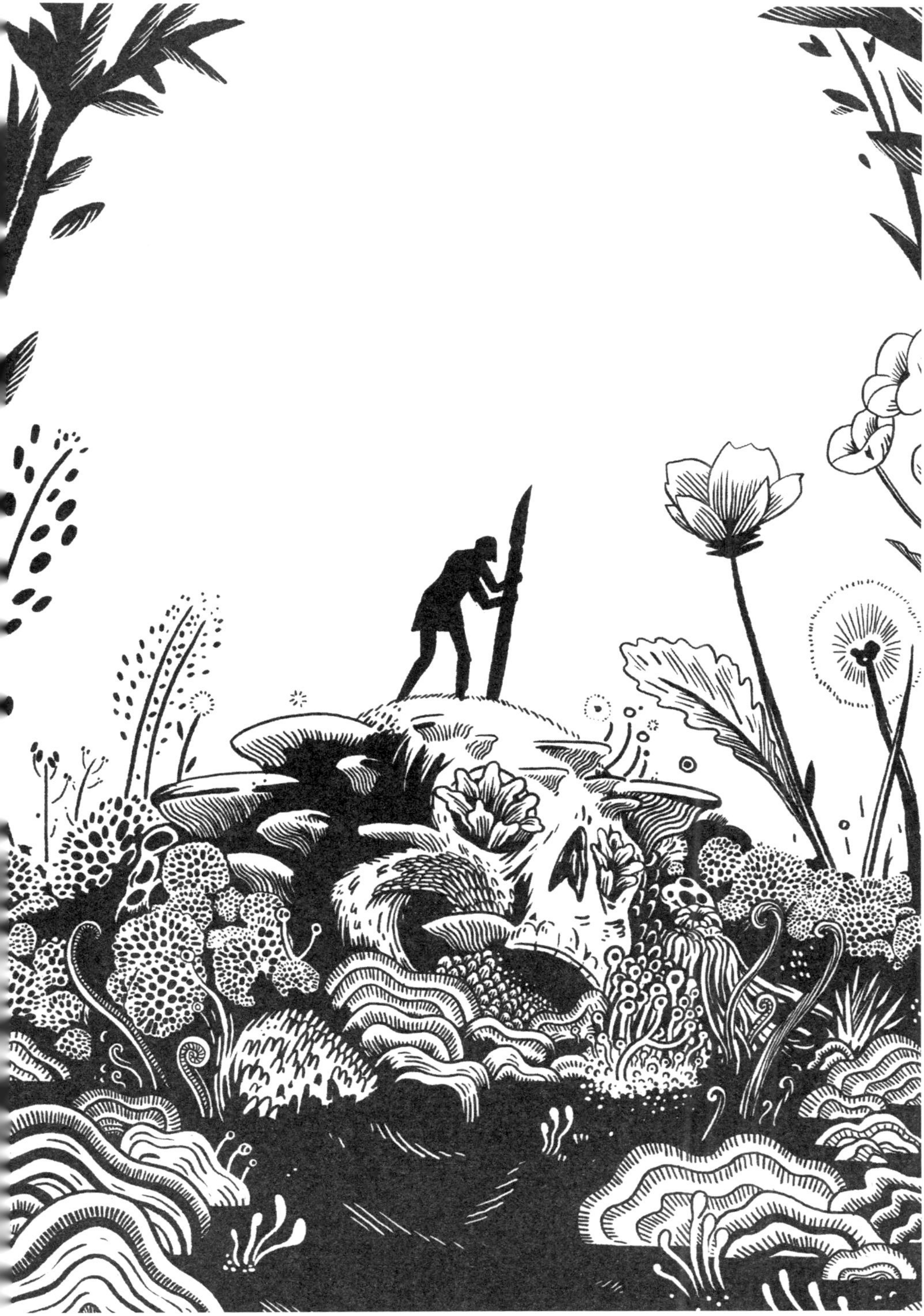

PART IX

CHAPTER 41

MEANWHILE

SADIE

11.32 a.m. – Thirty-nine minutes before the Descent

Sadie sits bolt awake. To her left, beneath a window, a hay bale burns. Flames lick their way up the tangle of cables hanging from the ceiling, filling the room with smoke. Her sister, Ava, lies beside her, still covered in a blanket, an IV drip strung from the rail above her head. Sadie pulls the needle and tube out from Ava's arm and tries to shake her awake, but her sister does not stir.

Thin red lines cut through the haze. They are beams of light, tracing delicate paths over walls and doors, exploring the contours of the smoke-filled space. Sadie realises the red lines are searching, feeling their way, looking for something. She coughs. Her face is numb. She can't explain it, but the world feels only half there. It is then that she sees a man's face, smeared with ash, crying out in pain and crawling towards her.

She shakes her sister again, but the man is too close, and there is something in his hand – a weapon – and she must get away. She falls backwards and comes to rest against the inner Rotolactor wall, her bed of blanket and straw spilling beside her. The man tumbles after her, and she kicks desperately to stop his advance. She lands blows to his face, but he won't stop. He drags himself over the Rotolactor rail, and now she notices his wound, the hay around him staining red.

Sadie realises that what she took for a weapon is a syringe. He smiles at her, revealing a dark space where his two front teeth should be. He mouths something that ends with the word, 'OK,' and his face softens. Sadie recognises him now, and she stops kicking.

There is a flash. Bob shudders, his eyes roll back, and his body collapses across her legs. Blood seeps through his shirt and onto her nightdress as Sadie finally finds the air in her lungs to cry out.

A gas-masked figure steps out of the smoke, tall, dressed in dark blues and browns and carrying a pistol. Sadie coughs again. The figure removes its mask and places it on Sadie. She does not recognise this person. She sees him speaking through the smeared plastic visor, but her ears are ringing, and she cannot understand.

A second figure joins the man, a woman, shorter, with a perfect red helmet of hair. She kneels and puts her fingers to Bob's neck. Her face is sharp and angry and dangerous. Sadie is glad that the woman does not look at her. A third figure hurries through the smoke, coming to an abrupt halt beside the red-headed woman. Cradled in his arms is a baby.

Sadie wants to lean forward and see if the baby is OK, but she doesn't want to touch Bob's body, still laid across her legs, any more than she has to. The woman with auburn hair takes the baby in her arms. She seems pleased, and Sadie is relieved too. The baby must be all right. Then, to Sadie's horror, the woman lifts the infant carelessly into the air with one hand and shakes. It is then that Sadie sees something is wrong. The woman is not holding a baby at all. She is holding a toy. A doll. It must be a toy, yet it looks so real, and so old. It looks so ... She feels Bob's limp body move, then the prick of a needle at her thigh.

The smoke fills her mask, and everything around Sadie fades to black.

RICHARD

11.45 a.m. – Twenty-six minutes before the Descent

Richard picks at flecks of lint gathered in the crease of his elbow. His top button is too tight, but he bears it, knowing how smart and respectable it makes him look. He's aware of what they think of him, that he's too old, that his past is a stain that cannot be cleansed. He's not good enough. Not *holy* enough. The hypocrites. Besides, he's changed. He's better now. Perhaps his friends were changing too. After all, today, they'd let him hold the collection basket.

An older lady comes to sit beside him, followed by two large greyhounds who bury their heads into the folds of her thick denim dress. On the ground by Richard's feet are his shopping bags, bursting with spices and root vegetables. He eyes the dogs – disgusting animals – and shuffles the bags away from them.

'What are you cooking?' asks Mary, scratching one of the dogs beneath the chin.

'Stew. Harvest stew.' He wants to add how he's famous for it, that everyone loves it, but stops himself.

'Sounds lovely. Though a bit *hot* for stew, if you ask me,' she says, with a smile. 'I'll have an ice cream and a G and T, thank you.' She winks. He wants to tell her to piss off. He wants to pray for her hastened death. But he's not like that anymore. He's changed. He'll show them. So, instead, he smiles and chimes, 'Soberness is next to godliness.' The old lady screws up her face and returns her attention to her dogs, now curling beneath their feet.

Father Erall loves stew. Everyone knows it. Richard's not trying to curry favour. Curry favour with curry *flavour*? That's good. He'll drop that into polite conversation later. All he's after is a chance of being this year's parish representative at the Elect Conference. It would be the keystone in his seminary application. Look at them, his friends. There are so few of them now. Once the pews had been packed. Oh, how this flock has dwindled. Richard would make this place great again. His leadership would be strong, stronger than old Erall. A silence falls over the murmuring parishioners who seat themselves as Father Erall takes to the pulpit. Then Richard's heart nearly stops. He pulls at his collar, allowing a hot prickle of sweat to bloom. He has seen Jonathan Wicks on the front row with a steaming pot in his lap. *Stew!* The bastard! Jonathan smiles back at Richard, who feels a renewed rage building from his chest. He knots his shaking hands together into a single fist and bows his head to pray.

GILES

11.49 a.m. – Twenty-two minutes before the Descent

Morris stoops to pick a yellow flower from prickly green gorse and crushes it between his thumb and index finger.

'Smell that,' he says and thrusts the crushed petals abruptly beneath Giles's nose. 'Like desiccated coconut. Makes a nice wine if you get enough of it.'

He knows his dad has never made wine from flowers and doubts he's ever even tasted it. Still, he smiles and nods. The insight is nourishing in itself – a delicious titbit.

Little white stones crunch beneath their feet on the high coastal path. Tall wild grasses sway on either side of them. The sea is to their right. Gulls in the sky. White cliffs ahead. He turns to look at his father, shielding his eyes from the high noon sun. This is how he always pictures Morris, dawdling behind, rummaging through the underbrush. All of a sudden, Morris stands bolt upright and looks over Giles's shoulder.

'Sublime, isn't it. The wonderful and frightening force of nature. Look at that. Those cliffs. Waves. Phwar.' He sniffs at the air. 'Where are all the bloody birds of prey when you want them. I'd love to see a red kite.' They carry on a few steps, and Morris stops again, staring now into the grass.

Giles wonders if perhaps he's seen a grass snake, and Morris says, 'You should patch things up with Matilda.' Giles is taken aback, scrunches his nose and stoops, pretending to be interested in the underside of a rock. Morris continues. 'Never too late. How will you know if you don't try? No shame in it. We can't do this alone. Not meant to. We're too small, Giles, even you, you great oaf.' Giles is annoyed by the set of assumptions. It's not that simple. He's about to say so when Morris turns and wedges his hawk head walking stick into the side of a bush.

'Right. I need a pee. Catch you up in a minute.'

LASLETT AND LEAF

12.02 p.m. – Nine minutes before the Descent

The little wooden boat is inconspicuous against the vast expanse of water. From afar, the green, blue and white stripes painted on the side of the vessel look like light refracting on the waves. Land has been reduced to a thin slither on the horizon. It is swelteringly hot. The engine is off. The boat bobs quietly with the ebb and flow of currents beneath it.

There are eight of them aboard – William Laslett, the six choir members and Leonard Leaf – all sitting about the boat's circumference on shallow benches, heads bowed. It is cramped. Despite the heat, the whole party is dressed in dark suits, a silver circle sewn above each breast pocket, the only sign that the suits are, in fact, a uniform. A patch of sunburn blooms on a balding choir member's head. Leaf is in possession of the sole umbrella and life jacket.

No one has spoken for ten minutes, and now, with sudden cheer, Leaf says, 'Well, I, for one, am rather excited!' The others stir. There are polite chuckles and nods of agreement.

Laslett, taking this as an instruction to commence, slides

412

something out from beneath his seat. It is no bigger than a lunch-box, wrapped in red cloth embroidered with gold thread.

All eight sets of eyes are drawn towards it. The ceremony is unnecessary, Laslett thinks to himself, but being the benefactor affords certain eccentricities. Still, he wishes they hadn't left Goodwin the way they had. He would make it up to her later.

With a pale, slender hand, Leaf reaches into the inner pocket of his suede jacket and, from it, produces a silver conductor's baton. As Laslett folds back the first corner of cloth, Leaf flicks a wrist. The bald man, the largest of the group, begins to sing a low, singular drone. Laslett hears Leaf mutter something like a grunt of concentration.

His wrist flicks, and one by one, the choir members join in with ascending tones until the whole boat resonates. As each chorister joins the song, Leaf mutters beneath his breath.

'Ree. Mi. Fa. Sol. La'

Laslett recognises the solfeggio scale, a tenth-century Benedictine hymn, six levels of assent culminating perfectly on a frequency of five hundred and twenty-eight hertz. Leaf believes it to be the frequency of transformation. He had spoken about the ancient song on the journey here. He peels back the final fold of red fabric, revealing a copper vase embedded with small red stones which he offers to Leaf. With a pinch of his fingers, Leaf instructs his choir to hold their note.

He takes the vase, raises it above his head and says, 'In these hands, I hold a whisper for the ear of God. A prayer, hand delivered.'

Leaf leans over the edge and gently lowers the vase into the sea. As water pours in, silver-white liquid blooms from the vase's mouth. Leaf's eyes widen. The liquid disperses, disappears, and the vase sinks from view. The choir struggle to hold the note, but Leaf waves back at them to continue, his fingers still pinched.

Laslett wasn't sure what to expect, but he had hoped for a sign, some sort of reaction. After another minute, Leaf slumps back and with a casual wave, he signals the choir to stop, though most have already gone quiet. Shoulders sagging in defeat, he turns to Laslett.

'Well, I'm not sure what *you* were expecting, but I have to admit, *I'm* a little underwhelmed.'

CHAPTER 42

A HOMECOMING

On the ninth morning, Giles drove the buggy from Waterlow Manor to Silverbell Farm. Once he had mastered the controls and accommodated his sling and two-finger deficit, the drive was pleasant. He weaved easily between the stationary cars and pile-ups that would have halted a larger vehicle. The sky was clear, and the July sun had not yet come out in force. He felt both optimism and sadness. He thought of his children ahead. He thought of the manor growing distant behind him, the scores of people he'd brought there, settling in now, making it their home. He thought of Alwyn, of Ashraf, of the Southampton children, of Richard even. The countless masses. Everyone had been a victim, in their own way, of the strange fate that had befallen them a little over a week ago.

Aside from his conversation with Richard, Giles had not spared much thought for the cause of the transformation itself. He knew that to understand a storm, you looked at thermal currents and weather patterns. Easy to analyse from satellites, but when caught in the head of the wind, you run for shelter and to hell with analysis. It occurred to him now, on this early morning drive, that in a sense Richard had been right – what had happened to them was so specific, so precise and perfect that it could not have been an act of nature. But neither was it an act of God. Their change had not been the random accumulation of a storm, but the deliberate targeting of surgery or a well-aimed bomb. Nature, Giles knew, did not make exceptions. It was not sparing, and yet they had been spared. Slowly, over the course of several hours, Giles changed his mind. What had happened to them had been a *human* act. Somehow, impossibly, they had done this to themselves.

He kept to the motorway, stopping every hour or so to syphon petrol by unscrewing drainage valves under chassis, and refilling the small tank via a network of tubes. Leaving the buggy made him anxious, certain that the moment he exposed himself, a threat would strike. A mob. A dog. A polecat. Yet no one came, and each time he moved on in peace.

Though it was rare to see other survivors, evidence of them was everywhere. A car door left ajar. A charred patch of broken twigs. A spot where a camp had been. Twice he passed small groups walking by the side of the road, refugees clad in plastic bag ponchos, cotton sock skirts. Once he saw a solitary young man pulling a food-stuffed rollerskate by the laces, like a horse drawing a cart. As he approached, all had kept their distance. All were heading in the same direction, towards London, and Giles wondered if they were being drawn inland or pushed away from the sea.

Past Winchester, he left the motorway and found the country roads. Forced to navigate through hedgerows, he weaved past a tractor turned on its side, scattering the road with hay bales, and skirted around a herd of sheep, woollen dinosaurs that wandered aimlessly en masse. Passing through a silent village, Giles saw a dog sleeping outside a shop. He stopped the buggy at a safe distance, crept and cut through the rope attaching its collar to the lamppost. He hoped the dog was sleeping, though it had not rained in several days.

Nearing his destination, Giles noticed a change. No cars were blocking the roads. Instead, they were slumped in gullies and hedgerows. The road had been *cleared*. Giles rounded another corner, and the gates of Silverbell came into view. He was in the process of formulating a joke, how many shrunken people does it take to push a car into a ditch, when he heard a rumble behind him.

With a sharp jerk of the joystick, Giles steered the buggy beneath a van straddling the embankment. He climbed out of the box and crouched behind the van's front wheel, peering back up the road through waves of heat shimmering off the tarmac.

Giles gasped. A green Volvo was rumbling up the road towards him. The sedan can't have been the only converted car. Still, Giles felt a great unease. The vehicle passed, and reflections obscured its interior as it halted outside the gates. A window rolled down, and a hand that could have gripped Giles about the torso reached out and swiped a key card against the plastic box.

Then he heard a voice, female, loud and familiar.

'Ah, bugger.' Then another voice, younger, lighter.

'I'll do it.'

Ava stepped out of the car. Aside from some scrapes and a bruise on her left leg, she was unhurt. She was unchanged. She had not shrunk. Casually, she leaned back into the car, speaking to someone out of sight.

'Sadie, come on. Don't be like that. Pass me the screwdriver. Fine. I'll get it.'

So, Sadie was there too. They were both safe. Then there was Matilda, getting out the other side, leaning her hands across the car's roof, resting her chin on her wrists. She stared, smiling as Ava bickered with her sister. Matilda seemed to glow in that strong light, staring at her daughter, drinking her in. Giles couldn't begin to guess how, but he saw Matilda's pride and knew then that somehow, *she* had saved their daughters.

Giles staggered back into the shadows, dumbfounded. His daughters and the woman he'd once loved. They fitted the world. Not just their clothes, the car and the architecture, but their skin, hair, and every detail down to the last eyelash. All hung in perfect balance.

Giles looked at his own hands – bandaged, cracked, wrinkled, red and two fingers down. His face, too, lined with creases that shattered his features like a broken mirror. Even without his wounds, he was monstrous by comparison. He was inhuman. He thought about the photograph in his wallet, the dogs, the tents in the field and realised that the opposite was also true – the same thing but smaller was not the same thing.

Worse still, they clearly did not need his help. For a moment, he forgot the absurdity of the past nine days. He was simply too late. His children had grown up. He and they were worlds apart, and now there was nothing he could do for them. The precious window had been missed. One by one, his fantasies of heroism evaporated. Giles could not defend them from wild beasts or carry them from a burning house. Provide them with food or shelter. Once, he could not pay for Ava's operation. Now he could not even bring her a glass of water. As he had failed her then, so too would he fail them now. His journey had been for nothing.

Ava reattached the panel onto the box beside the gate and brushed the key card against it. With a clunk and scratching of metal on concrete, the gate into Silverbell slid open. Feeling unable to support his own weight, Giles leaned against the buggy. He took a shuddering breath. He should head back to the manor, to the people he *could* help. Being there, being present was important, Isabel had said. He closed his eyes and Sadie, six years old, crouched beside him, drumming sandals on his belly. Ava drew a face in ketchup. His face. The girls screamed *faster* as he spun them on a workshop chair. He felt his daughter's cool toes nestling between his knees for warmth. Heard a dirty gurgle of laughter. Felt their breath on his ear. Held their weight in his arms. He saw a hundred moments and kept his eyes closed for as long as he could bear.

Giles stumbled out from behind the tyre and into the middle of the road, shaking off the backpack, and spilling its contents. He ran. His shoelace sandals unravelled, and the hot concrete burned the soles of his feet. He shouted and waved and ran. Giles sprinted with all the fury his body could bear, towards the giants, towards Ava and Sadie and Matilda. Shouting, calling up, calling towards his children, desperate for them to see him, tears blurring his vision until he could hardly see a thing.

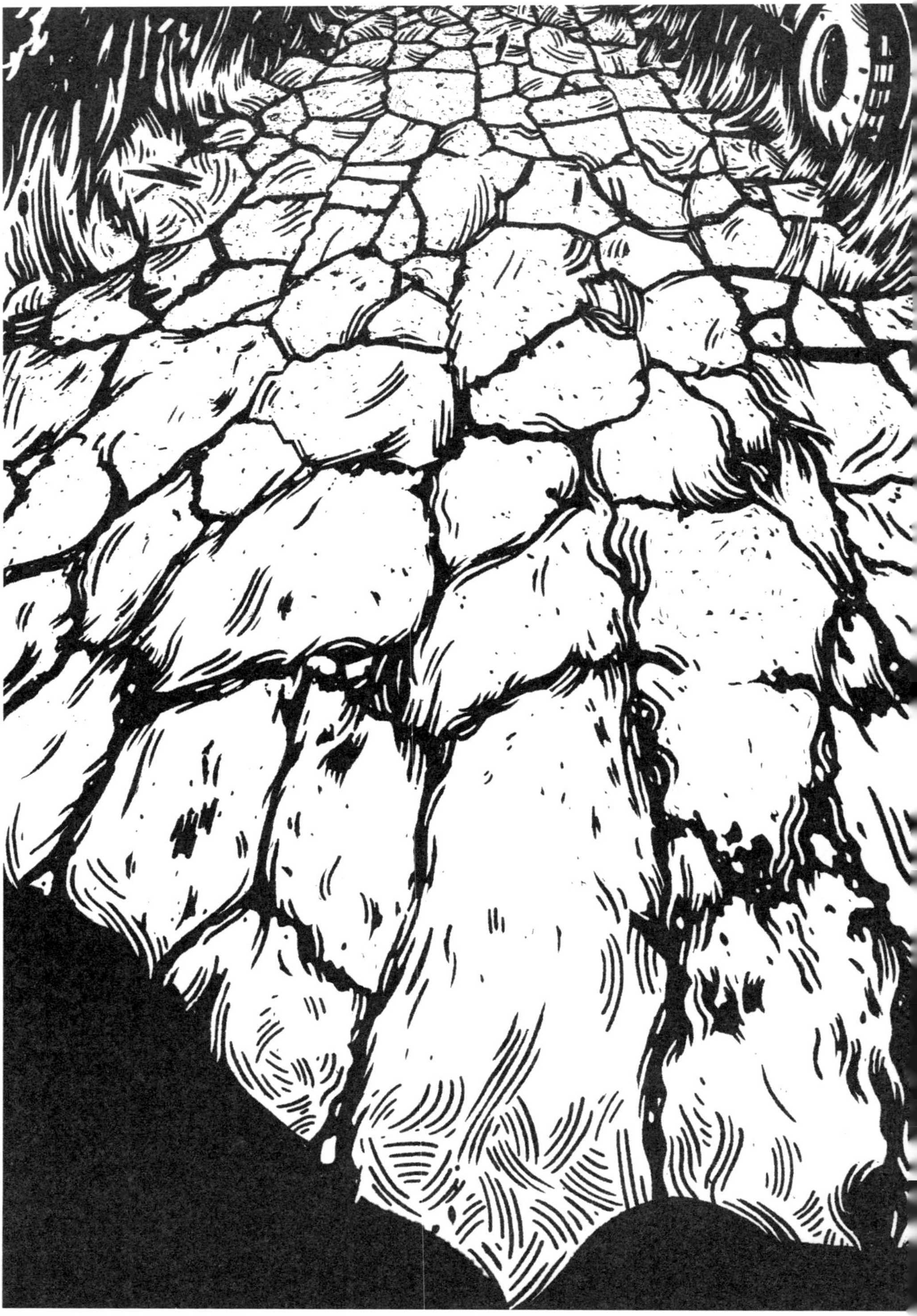

CHAPTER 43

ELSEWHERE, MATILDA

12.07 p.m. – Four minutes before the Descent

Arnold buttoned his jacket tight about his neck and got out of the car. He shoved his hands into his pockets, thrust his hips towards the sea, took a deep breath of salty air then forced it out through his nostrils. So peaceful out here. Just the sound of the wind and waves.

Begrudgingly, his wife Amelia and their fourteen-year-old son Bertie joined him in the empty car park.

'There we go. Not so bad, is it?'

'Smells like fish,' mumbled Bertie.

'That's the sea, silly. That's a *good* smell. There! You see that? A seal!' Arnold pointed to a distant spot of whiteness in the dark green ocean.

'That was a wave,' said Bertie.

'No, it was a—' Just then, the sound of an engine cut above the waves, and behind them, a lorry adorned with the words Silverbell Meadow pulled violently into the car park and screeched to a stop, the tanker on the back rocking precariously.

'My goodness!' said Amelia, clutching Arnold's arm and pushing Bertie behind her. A moment later, the cab door swung open. The figure inside, drenched below the waist in thick, dark sludge, slid down the steps and staggered into the car park, oblivious to the nearby family. Huddled beside their car, they watched in frozen horror as the lady, presumably fresh from the swamp, sprinted towards the sea wall.

'She's going to throw herself over the edge! Stop her, Arnold!' Amelia cried, shoving him forward. Arnold managed a meagre '*Hey*', though the woman appeared not to hear. Stopping sharply at the edge, she peered over at the waves crashing below.

'No, no. I think it's all right,' Arnold stammered, laughing nervously. The lady kneeled, reached into her satchel, and withdrew a parcel, around the size of a small loaf of bread. Then, searching through her pockets, she found what appeared to be an oversized pen.

'What's she doing?' whispered Amelia.

'I can't see.'

'Well, get over there and find out. Go on,' she insisted.

'Come now. She's not doing anything wrong, just having her sandwiches, like us. Reminds me – why can't you get hungry in the desert?' Arnold smiled, 'Because of all the *sand-which-is* there ... Eh?'

'Well, she might wash her hands first,' said Amelia, ignoring her husband.

'She looks disgusting,' agreed Bertie.

As they watched, the lady unwrapped the loaf-size parcel,

revealing a bag of silver-white liquid attached to a long clear tube. She squeezed a tiny ball from the end of the tube and leaned over the wall, arm coiled, preparing to throw. She faltered, letting the bag dangle over the water, then pulled it back and clutched it to her chest. She shuffled away from the wall, turned on the spot and ran a blackened hand through her hair. They saw her face was contorted with anguish, a feral line of lower teeth glinting through the filth.

'Mental,' said Bertie as, again, the woman made to throw the bag over the wall and again stopped herself. She shook her head violently and then became very still. Arnold must have blinked because without him noticing, he saw the woman was staring straight at Amelia, Bertie and him from across the car park. Something in her sad, mournful expression made them draw closer together, and Amelia's arms instinctively wrapped around Bertie's shoulders. The family looked on, transfixed, as the woman's head slumped forwards. She clamped a hand across her mouth to muffle a sob. Then, in one fluid movement, the swamp woman darted forwards, hurled the bag over the wall and stabbed the pen into her neck.

The spell broke and Arnold strode forwards, shouting, 'Hey, you there, stop! That's littering!' The woman's knees gave way, collapsing her backwards, hitting her head hard on the ground.

'Good God!' cried Arnold, and a moment later, he was at her side, lifting the woman's head onto his hat and checking for blood.

'Bert, into the car. I'll – I'll call an ambulance,' said Amelia, ushering the boy inside.

'Oh! She smells like a sewer!' said Arnold, wrist against nose as he edged her hand away from her neck. He called back to his wife. 'Looks like she stuck herself with a needle. Addict, I expect. She's alive though.'

'Careful, Arnold, don't get too close.'

'It's fine. She's out for the count.' Behind Amelia, Bertie kicked his legs over the door's rim, filming the incident on his phone.

'Stop that, darling. It's distasteful.'

Arnold walked to the sea wall and leaned over. Fifty or so feet below, he saw the IV bag of silver-white liquid, snagged and un-broken against a rock. 'Goodness, what a litterbug,' he grumbled and shook his head, adding, 'unbelievable.' In the same moment, a wave impaled the sac upon a black jagged rock. Its contents melted into the water, and a startling, bright halo of white radiated from the cliff wall.

Arnold had just enough time to be reminded of a timelapse film he'd seen in his youth. A lake freezing overnight. Then he heard a ringing in his ears and felt a pressure all over his body as if he had been suddenly plunged deep, too deep, underwater. There was a low, singular note – a song heard from a great distance. Then his hands clamped on either side of his head and squeezed.

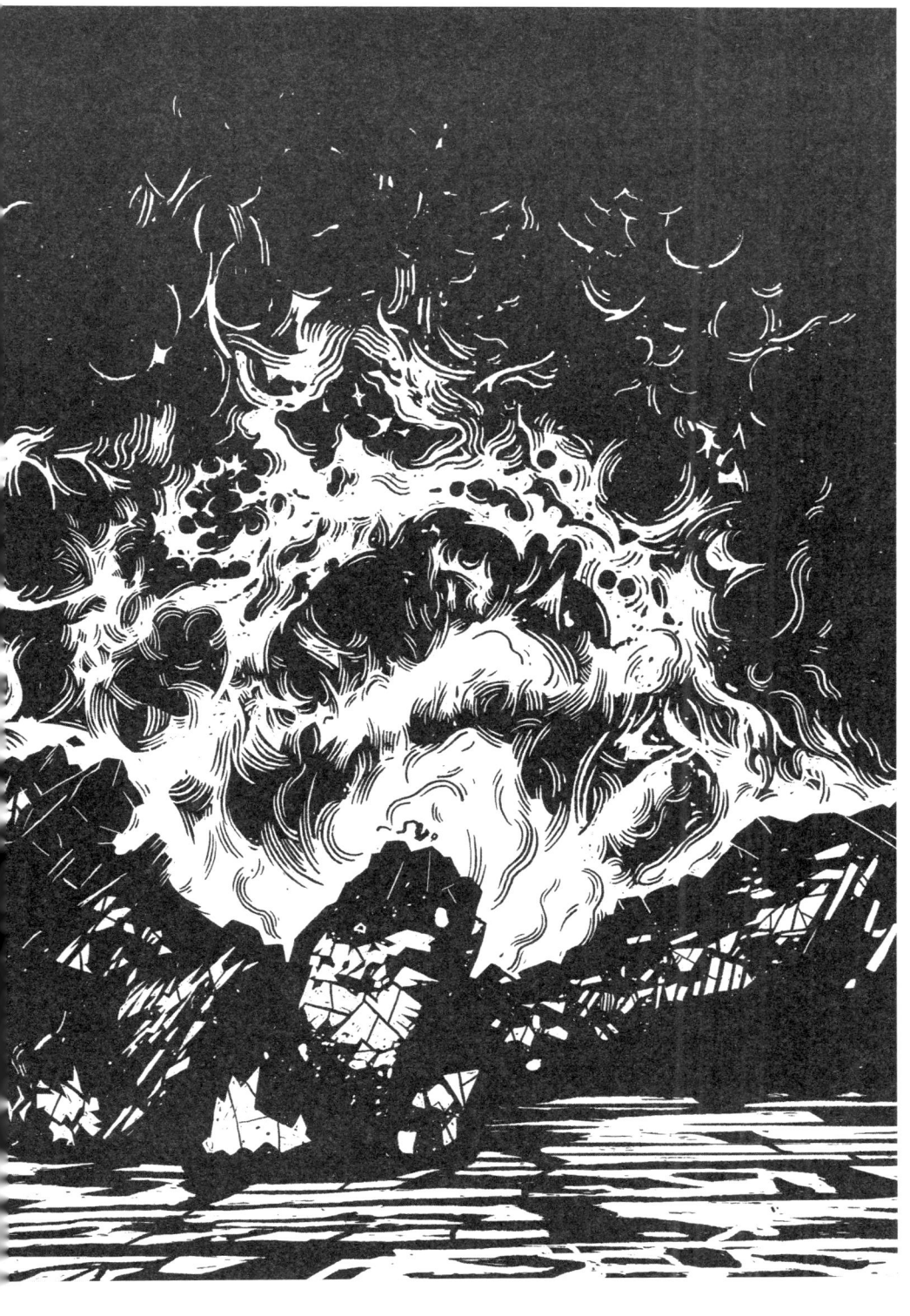

Here ends

THE EXPANDED EARTH

Book 1

ACKNOWLEDGEMENTS

I write this sat in the garden of my childhood home, delighted / relieved / utterly spent from having stayed up rather late to deliver this final (can it really be true?) manuscript. The rumble of the city nearby mingles with the sound of my two young children playing inside with their grandmother, all just out of sight. Hidden too, behind a high wall at the front of the house, is a graveyard, and here at the back, on full view, lies a second cemetery. A steeple pokes out above a canopy of pine, and below, tombstones speckle the grassy hillside. I won't be the first to make the comparison, but they've always reminded me of rows of wonky teeth. The garden, ten or so metres long and as wide as the terraced house, is beautifully wild and overgrown, richly flowered, landscaped and peppered with my mother's sculptures – rusted steel dancers and weathered sandstone eagles. This story was born on the two-metre-square patch of lawn at the end, from long idle summers, thirty plus years ago, pushing action figures through the grass, into bushes, under rocks. These days, whenever my mind wanders into the Expanded Earth, I invariably start here.

So, it's with my first and my greatest thanks that I must acknowledge my parents – Peter Please, who built this garden and from whom my love of nature and stories has been inherited. And

Caroline Waterlow, who tended to the garden, and from whom my love of pictures and people grew.

Most of my professional life has been spent directing stop-motion animation and it occurred to me rather late in the day that the urge for me to write this story is probably the same desire that fuelled this tradition of lording over miniature figurines. Was it the megalomaniacal desire to create and control small worlds, or the longing to be back beside this shed? I honestly can't say.

Either way, I raise my cup of tea to the independent animation community who, like me, have spent much of their adult lives chasing the dragon of childhood. To everyone who made a film that placed me back here, nose deep in the grass. Ainsley Henderson, Pat McHale, Nina Gantz and Marc and Emma De Swaef spring quickly to mind, but there are many others.

Chief among these is my long-time collaborator Daniel Ojari, whose lent ear has helped to focus the sprawling threads of this novel. Thanks also to my film agent Kelly Knatchbull and to my friends at Aardman for your support and encouragement in this final leg of the run.

What a run.

In late 2021, proudly sending out my latest draft, I arrogantly thought I'd conquered the mountain, only for the fog to clear and reveal that I was still a donkey ride and six-month hike from base camp. Thankfully, an elite team of professionals soon swooped in to help me take this manuscript up to the actual summit.

Thank you, firstly, to Luke Ingram, my fearless agent, who somehow, through the mist of that early draft, saw *The Expanded Earth*'s potential, extended his hand from the world of books and pulled (carried?) me over the chasm. I realise how easy it would have been to have never had the luck to meet someone as gracious, passionate and talented as Luke. I don't take that for granted.

428

Recognising a shared suffering from Alice in Wonderland syndrome, I knew, from our first meeting, that I'd met a fellow traveller in my editor extraordinaire, my champion at Corsair, Sarah Castleton. Thank you for taking a chance and glugging the entire bottle labelled 'DRINK ME' and joining me down on this altered plane of existence. Thank you for your steadfast guidance, for humanising and bringing such joy to what might have been an otherwise dauting task. Hold on tight, there are two more to go!

To David Bamford, Hannah Wood, Alice Watkin, James Gurbutt and the team at Little, Brown, who raised this project to a standard I didn't think was possible, I'm hugely grateful.

My gratitude also to my early readers – Ben Please, Jamie Lewis, Karleung Wai, Bertie van der Beek, Rob Hunter, Tom Cole, Elliott Dear, Matthew Marsh, Adam Morley, Sean Hogan, Amer Chadha Patel, Dan Chester, Daniel Kwan, James Stevenson Bretton and Theodora van der Beek. Also, my apologies to all these people. Having reread the draft I sent you, I hope you won't be too traumatised to give this final, slightly less bloody, version a try. An extra special thanks to Jaz Clarke for your encouragement and eagle eye on the last stretch. And to Suki Ferguson for your meticulous early proofread and encouraging more fancy flourishes like 'buttery translucence'.

I'm grateful to Daniel Scheinert who, in my mid-twenties, looked at me, mouth agape and muttered, 'You've never read *The Sirens of Titan*?!' A week later a beaten-up copy arrived through my post box and my mind was forever tilted to the idea that a different kind of science fiction story was possible.

Thank you to all the people who bring complicated scientific ideas down to my moronic level. In particular, the producers of the NPR show *Radiolab*, who introduced me to the inexplicable altruistic behaviour of coccolithophores (yes, that bit is all true!

The interconnected hive-mind bit, not so much). And the actual scientists, like neuroscientist Dr Robbie Drake, for schooling me on the complexities of connectomics and the meaning of the word 'winkie' (which, it turns out, is not a bottom. Farewell, my innocence).

To Gina Glover for her boundless enthusiasm, spirit and lending me a quiet space to write that all-important outline. And to Geoffrey Rayner, for combing through the final manuscript, for providing the philosophical, historical and ecological context of it all, and opening my mind to just how deeply one could think about deep thinking. I love our conversations / your sermons.

Lastly, and mostly, thank you to my wife Jessica Rayner, for your unwavering support. This project has spanned the birth of our two children, the house moves, city moves, the replacement of all the atoms in our bodies. Thank you for your patient listening on the long car journeys, your frank and thoughtful feedback. For blowing raspberries at bad ideas when words are not enough. In all, thank you for helping me, small as I am, to live the big life.

Mikey Please

July 2024

Book 1
of

THE
EXPANDED
EARTH

Trilogy

For my parents,
Caroline & Peter

CORSAIR

First published in the United Kingdom in 2025 by Corsair

1 3 5 7 9 10 8 6 4 2

A CIP catalogue record for this book is available from the British Library.

HB ISBN: 978-1-4721-5834-5
TPB ISBN: 978-1-4721-5833-8

Typeset in Sabon by M Rules
Printed and bound in Great Britain by Clays Ltd, Elcograf S.p.A.

Papers used by Corsair are from well-managed forests
and other responsible sources.

Corsair
An imprint of
Little, Brown Book Group
Carmelite House
50 Victoria Embankment
London EC4Y 0DZ

The authorised representative
in the EEA is
Hachette Ireland
8 Castlecourt Centre
Dublin 15, D15 XTP3, Ireland
(email: info@hbgi.ie)

An Hachette UK Company
www.hachette.co.uk

www.littlebrown.co.uk

THE
EXPANDED EARTH

MIKEY PLEASE

*with illustrations
by the author*

corsair

Also by Mikey Please

The Café at the Edge of the Woods

Sept 2.25

THE

EXPANDED EARTH

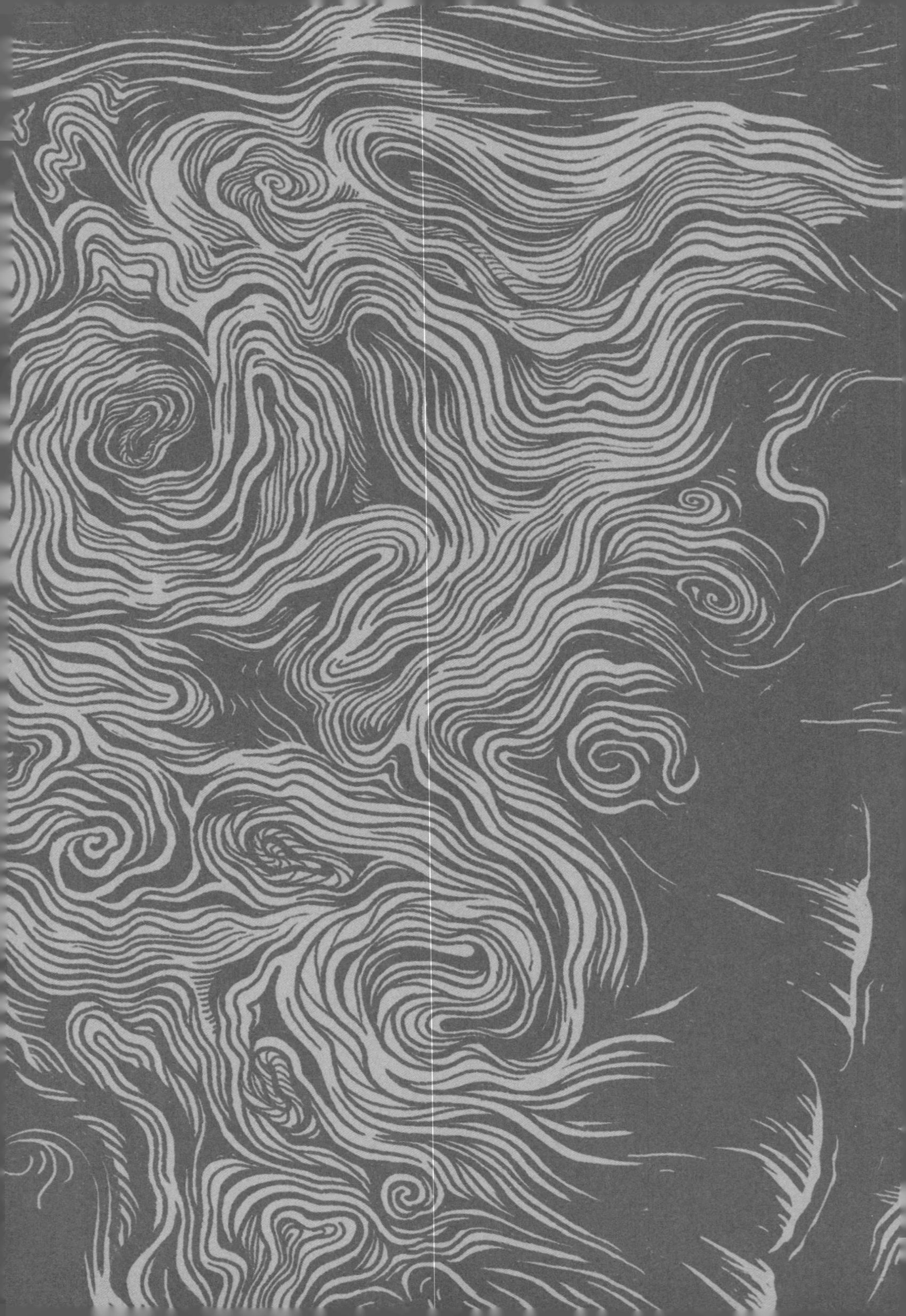

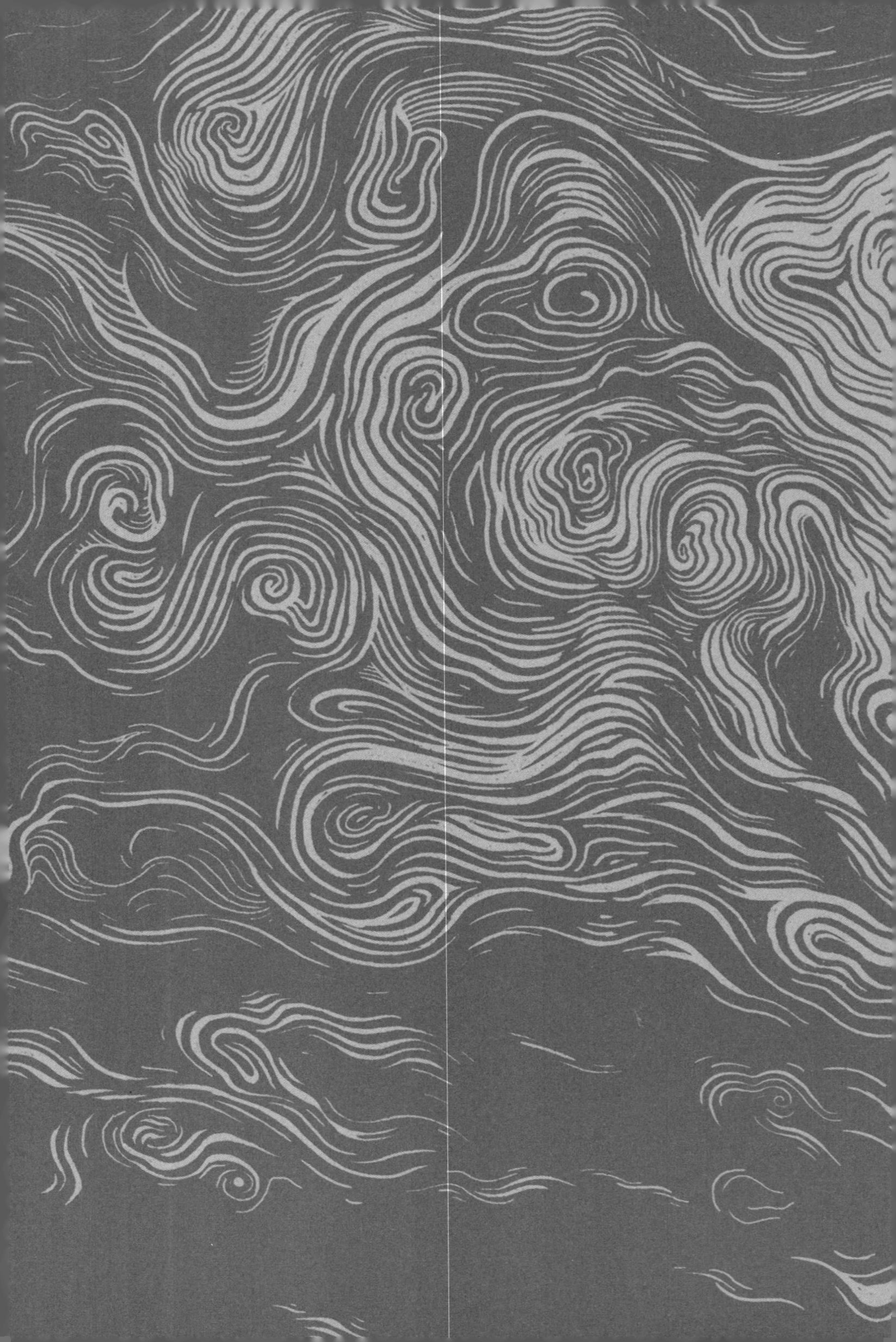